THE HORSES AT THE GATE

Also by Mary Mackey

Immersion
McCarthy's List
The Last Warrior Queen
A Grand Passion
The Kindness of Strangers
Season of Shadows
The Year the Horses Came
The Dear Dance of Eros

The Horses at the Gate

A NOVEL

THE EARTHSONG TRILOGY

Mary Mackey

HarperSanFrancisco

An Imprint of HarperCollinsPublishers

For A.W.

THE HORSES AT THE GATE: *A Novel.* Copyright © 1995 by Mary Mackey. All rights reserved. Printed in the United States of America. No part of this book may be used or reproduced in any manner whatsoever without written permission except in the case of brief quotations embodied in critical articles and reviews. For information address HarperCollins Publishers, 10 East 53rd Street, New York, NY 10022.

HarperCollins Web Site: http://www.harpercollins.com

HarperCollins®, ♨®, and HarperSanFrancisco™ are trademarks of HarperCollins Publishers Inc.

FIRST EDITION

Library of Congress Cataloging-in-Publication Data
Mackey, Mary.
The horses at the gate : a novel / Mary Mackey. — 1st ed.
ISBN 0–06–251069–X (pbk.)
I. Title.
PS3563.A3165H67   1996
813.'54—dc20   95–39502

95 96 97 98 99 ❖ HAD 10 9 8 7 6 5 4 3 2 1

An Historical Note

Although there is no conclusive evidence that the people of Old Europe had a written language, some archaeologists have theorized that the untranslated hieroglyphic script of ancient Crete known as Linear A was based on a much older script developed by ancestral non-Indo-European speakers. If such a script existed in Marrah's time, it was probably used primarily for religious and ceremonial purposes (such as the inscription over the gates of the city of Kataka). Kataka is a fictional place, but circular cities containing thousands of inhabitants existed in northeastern Rumania and western Ukraine at the time this story takes place and for hundreds of years thereafter.

Sea of Grass

Shambah

Kataka

Mahclah

Shara

Sweetwater Sea

Blue Sea

PROLOGUE

Stavan and the Witch: A HANSI FOLK TALE

Vlahan the Bastard almost killed the witch from the west on the day Zuhan, Great Chief of the Hansi, was buried, but through foul magic the witch wove a spell that snatched out the eyes of his warriors, leaving them blind and helpless. Throwing their eyes into a leather bag, she tied it at her waist, stole five horses, and rode west, taking Arang, heir to the Twenty Tribes, with her.

Great was the lamentation of the warriors when they regained their sight. Some gnashed their teeth, and some cut their own arms, and some offered to kill themselves to wipe out the shame, but Vlahan ordered them to go on living. Seizing his longest spear and sharpest arrows, he slid the sacred gold cup over the end of his penis and stood potent and fearless before them.

"Revenge is sweet," he cried. "I will take her scalp to line my cape. Ten head of cattle to the man who sees her tracks! A hundred to the man who brings Arang back!"

And so, trusting in Lord Han, God of the Shining Sky, the warriors rode forth to hunt down the witch.

EASTERN UKRAINE
FIFTH MILLENNIUM B.C.

And the snow touched her
and the snow kissed her
and the snow lay on
her lips and eyes

Dark-haired Marrah,
priestess of Shara,
slept in the snow
like a winter flower
next to Stavan
her nomad lover,
next to Arang, Hiknak, Dalish.

She slept while the nomads
sharpened their spears;
slept while their dogs
sniffed for her scent;
slept while scouts
hunted the steppes
with ice on their beards
and hate in their hearts.

Praise to the Goddess
who spread Her white cape
over the blessed, innocent sleepers!
Praise to the Great Owl
whose cloak of cold feathers
concealed Marrah,
priestess of Shara!

FROM "THE GODDESS SENDS SNOW"
A MEMORY SONG OF THE SHARATANI PEOPLE
BLACK SEA COAST
FIFTH MILLENNIUM B.C.

BOOK ONE

The Butterfly Goddess

CHAPTER ONE

The Ukrainian Steppes, 4368 B.C.

ll night the snow fell, heavy and wet, forcing the long-stemmed feathered grasses of the steppes to the earth and weighing them down. The flat land seemed to flatten even more under the assault of the storm, until it seemed as if the Goddess Earth Herself had shaken out the world like a great linen sheet and spread it for winter. By midnight there was hardly a track—animal or human—to be seen. The mice and voles crouched in their burrows, sheltering against the wind; the hawks and owls took refuge in their nests. Even the wolves nestled down with their cubs and resigned themselves to empty bellies. Only one thing on the steppes hunted, and it was human.

As the snow fell, a band of Hansi warriors rode northeast, pushing their weary horses into the wind. They were a strange-looking group, bundled in wool trousers and hooded wolf-fur capes; beards frozen; hands muffled in great, pawlike mittens. They came well armed with stone axes heavy enough to split a man's head open and long spears that could be used without dismounting. The feathered ends of sharp, flint-tipped arrows protruded from the quivers they wore at their waists, and their bows were supple, bent in the center, and deadly accurate. In the unlikely event that he was forced off his horse and had to fight hand to hand, each warrior also carried a dagger so sharp he could gut a man as easily as a rabbit.

The men rode forward silently as the snow drifted into their beards and icicles formed below their nostrils. Out in front, almost lost in the white mist, their half-wild dogs ranged in a pack, sniffing the ground, pausing at places where the wind had blown back the snow, exposing bare earth. The Hansi dogs were great burly beasts with thick fur and sharp, intelligent eyes, and if a stranger had appeared at that moment, they would have torn him apart before the warriors could have stopped them, but there were no strangers in sight, so the dogs moved forward briskly, finding nothing of interest. Only once did the lead dog stop short, throw back her head, and give a long howl. When she broke into a run, the warriors kicked their horses into a trot and followed, but soon she stopped again and began to sniff at the ground.

The warriors exchanged glances, but no one spoke. Their eyes were red with fatigue, but they held the luster of excitement. There was no need for words: they were hunting five people—a boy, a man, and three women. The boy was their dead chief's adopted heir, and one of the women was his sister. This sister was a powerful witch who could blind the bravest warrior, but her magic was not proving to be as strong as they had feared. She and her companions had ridden for almost an entire night before it started snowing, leaving a line of tracks any boy could have followed. Now their trail was harder to see, but the warriors never rode far without coming on something that told them they were moving in the right direction: a turned stone; a faint, half-filled indentation; a bit of grass bent the wrong way. On several occasions the dogs had picked up the scent. True, they always lost it again, thanks to this cursed snowstorm, but the snow would not fall forever.

At present the men knew for certain that the fugitives were headed northeast instead of southwest toward the Motherlands. No doubt they were trying to sow confusion and escape pursuit, but Hansi warriors were the best trackers on the steppes. As long as the snow fell, they did not dare to move too fast for fear of overlooking something, but tomorrow or the next day, the snow would stop, the hoofprints would form a wide track, and the dogs would be able to pick up a continuous trail. When that happened, the warriors would fall on the fugitives and round them up like stray cattle.

In their minds, the men were already dividing the spoils: silently they totaled up the cattle that Vlahan, their chief, would give them when they brought the witch to him; they imagined fingering the fine bits of gold they would receive from Vlahan for returning the boy unharmed, and the skins of fermented *kersek* they would drink to celebrate the death of Stavan the traitor. Yesterday afternoon when they stopped to rest their horses, they had drawn lots for the honor of killing Stavan, and as usual Mukhan, their leader, had won. Mukhan was the second-best tracker in the tribe, a big man, with a shock of hair the color of dried blood and a wolf tattooed on his left cheek. Everyone suspected him of cheating, but no one was inclined to speak of this, since it was well known that he had killed his own cousin over a lesser insult. Besides, Mukhan had generously agreed to leave the women for the others.

As they rode on with their heads bent against the north wind, they considered the possibilities. There would be the witch, Marrah, but perhaps no man would want her, because a witch, it was said, could shrivel a man's penis like a dried goat pizzle and curse him impotent. Also, she had once been the chief's wife—just a second wife, a slut who had cuckolded Vlahan and deserved to die for it, but you never knew how Vlahan might take it if you forced her. Fortunately the two other women were both concubines, sentenced to die for their betrayals. The warriors had agreed that there was no point in killing the concubines too quickly.

Yet although the nine warriors moved with the deadly precision of a wolf pack, they were nine separate men with nine separate ways of seeing the world. Only six of the scouts were really loyal to Vlahan, and while they warmed themselves with thoughts of rape and plunder, three of their companions were thinking other thoughts, dangerous thoughts, thoughts that would have gotten them killed if Mukhan had suspected. Tonight as they rode across the great frozen of the steppes, doubts rode with them, and the wind, which only howled in the ears of the others, whispered to them like the voice of a beautiful woman begging a man to come into her bed. *Honor*, the wind whispered, *rebellion*. There was something wild and sweet in the voice of the wind, something seductive enough to drive a man half crazy, but no matter how hard they tried, the three warriors could not stop hearing it.

The speaking wind had begun to blow and whisper on the morning their old chief Zuhan died so mysteriously and his bastard son, Vlahan, suddenly rose to power. For several days now it had gone on blowing, so relentless that they heard it even in their sleep. It was the kind of wind that made a man long to kick his horse into a gallop and try to escape, but only a fool would attempt to outrun the wind, so the three warriors let their horses plod slowly along beside the others and stared into the storm with expressionless faces.

When Mukhan glanced back at them, he saw nothing to rouse his suspicions. They looked as obedient and loyal as the rest: just as cold, just as tired, just as eager to find their quarry. But inside, in the dark places of their minds that Mukhan could not penetrate, all three had started to make plans. Dakhan, a large, burly man with a nose like a piece of raw beef, was trying to figure out a way to destroy the tracks of the fugitives before the others saw them. Karthan, who was in charge of the dogs, was wondering if he might somehow be able to arrange for the lead dog to develop a limp before morning. The third, a young warrior named Werthan who had hardly grown his beard, was entertaining rash fantasies of galloping on ahead to shout a warning, even though this would almost certainly end with him lying dead in the snow with an arrow in his back.

Werthan had no idea that the wind was also whispering to two of his companions, but he knew, as they did, that Stavan, the legitimate son of Zuhan, was the only rightful heir to the chiefdom and that Vlahan was a usurper who had probably poisoned his own father. Honor thus demanded that Stavan, not Vlahan, rule over the Hansi.

For the two older men, honor was reason enough to try to see that Stavan was not captured, but Werthan had an additional reason for wanting the fugitives to get away: he loved Stavan like an older brother. Werthan was not an important person, only the youngest son of a captured concubine, and when he was less important still—when he was only a boy herding sheep—Stavan had often stopped to talk to him and tell him funny stories. Stavan had never yelled at him or threatened him with a beating the way the other warriors did. He had always treated Werthan with kindness, and once he had even sat down beside Werthan and showed him how to make a whistle out of a blade of grass.

Werthan loved Marrah too. It was an innocent love, of course, because he had never so much as spoken to her, but he had admired her beauty from a distance many times. You could tell just by looking at her that she had not been raised like a Hansi woman. She never averted her eyes in the presence of men, and she had taken a lover right under her husband's nose. Whenever Werthan thought of Marrah and Stavan together, he wanted to laugh out loud. He liked the idea of Marrah cuckolding old Vlahan, who was a pompous ass. He had always pitied her for being married against her will to such a brutal lout. Marrah was definitely the kind of woman who knew how to get even, a trait Werthan could not help but admire.

As for the other two women they were hunting, Werthan knew next to nothing about them, but he hated to think what the warriors were going to do to them when they finally caught up with them. Werthan had always found it disgusting to see men fall like a pack of wild dogs on the women they had captured. Although he was young, he knew that sex was no good unless both partners enjoyed it. Sometimes he thought that perhaps the gods had made women physically weaker than men so that men would learn compassion and self-control. This was a radical thought for a Hansi warrior, and not one he was willing to tell anyone, since it would have made him the laughingstock of the entire camp, but he went on thinking it just the same.

Near dawn, the wind began to die. Soon the disembodied voice that whispered incessantly of honor and rebellion was so faint that it was no louder than two blades of grass rubbing together or a rabbit settling down in its burrow, but as they rode through soft drifts that cushioned the clop of their horses' hooves, the three warriors still heard it, and Werthan heard it most clearly.

Up ahead, Marrah lay asleep, sheltered from the wind and cold under a pile of snow. As dawn approached, the darkness around her started to thin, and a pale, flat light began to fill the snow cave. The light was blue and winter-washed; it gave her dark skin an icy tone and touched her full lips with frost. Her long, black hair glistened in it, and every tuft of fur on the border of her wolf-skin cape looked as sharp as the tooth of a comb. It was warm under the cape, and lulled by that warmth, Marrah was dreaming of her mother. In her dream, Marrah was not a woman running for her life, but a girl of thirteen. The snow and the steppes and the warriors who pursued her were gone; and she was back in the little village of Xori, where she had spent her childhood, sitting on a straw mat in her great-grandmother Ama's longhouse, wearing the feathered cape she had worn on her coming-of-age day. It was a fine spring morning, the birds were singing, and she was drinking a bowl of warm goat's milk and eating strawberries.

"Have more, my darling," her mother kept saying, and as she spoke, she fed Marrah ripe berries, dipping them in winter honey, so thick and dark that the sweetness lay on the back of Marrah's tongue like a kiss.

Marrah laughed. "Give me another, Mama," she begged. Marrah's mother laughed too, and held out an especially large berry, twirling it by the stem. Marrah opened her mouth, tilted back her head, and closed her eyes, but when she swallowed there was nothing: only darkness and a strange humming sound.

She started and fought her way up from the depths of sleep. Her eyelids fluttered, and she clenched her fists and moaned. Opening her eyes, she found herself, not in her great-grandmother's longhouse, but in a small space filled with bluish light. To her left, Stavan lay in a warm huddle, snoring softly. To her right, her brother Arang was curled around Hiknak, who had curled around Dalish. For a moment she felt a sharp sense of dislocation. Why were the five of them sleeping in a heap like this? Where were they? Why was the roof over her head so low and white? Then she remembered, and the fear came back, striking her in the pit of the stomach like a clenched fist.

They were in the snow cave Stavan had built last night. The cave was an ingenious creation, something she would never have had the wit or experience to make: just a large pile of snow about one and a half times the length of a man, left for a while to harden, and then hollowed out, with an air hole punched in the ceiling, and a small entry hole, built a little lower than the level of the floor to keep out the cold. It was not much of a space for five people, but wrapped in their fur-lined cloaks, with their heads pillowed on their saddlebags, they had generated so much warmth that her hair was plastered to the back of her neck with her own sweat. Still, warm as it was, the snow cave would not offer any protection if the nomads caught up with them. She lay still for a moment, trying to convince herself that the storm had covered their tracks so thoroughly that not even the best Hansi scout could find them, but in the dim light of early morning that seemed even more unlikely than it had last night.

She listened anxiously for some sound that would indicate they had been discovered, but all she could hear was the gentle hum of Stavan's snoring. Relieved, she relaxed, turned over onto her side, and tried to go back to sleep, but tired as she was, sleep wouldn't come.

They had been on the run for almost five days now, ever since Zuhan's funeral, when she and Stavan and Dalish had come within a breath of being strangled and thrown into his grave as a sacrifice to the nomad sky god. The marks of the leather thongs that had tied her to the stake still had not faded from her wrists, and as she listened to Stavan snore, she thought again that if Hiknak hadn't put the powder of invisibility in the nomads' *kersek*, she would not have had the luxury of sleeping next to the man she loved. She would have gone back to the Goddess with mud in her mouth and a bowstring around her neck like Akoah, the little sailor, and those poor slaves Changar had so brutally murdered. At the thought of Changar, the Hansi diviner, her anxiety was replaced by a feeling of grim satisfaction. Never again would Changar slaughter helpless women and children in the name of his cursed god. Changar was dead. She had seen him slip and fall into Zuhan's grave. No doubt he had broken his neck on the stone floor. Good riddance, she thought, and then she was ashamed.

Closing her eyes, she breathed a quick prayer to the Goddess to make her more forgiving. It was wrong to hate another human being with such intensity, even one who had done so much evil, but if the Goddess was softening hearts that morning, hers wasn't one of them. When she opened her eyes, she was still glad that Changar was dead, and she sincerely hoped that even the Goddess Earth in all Her infinite mercy would wait a long, long time before She called him back in a new body. Let him return as a maggot, she thought, or a louse. On second thought, even maggots and lice were children of the Goddess, which made their bodies much too good for Changar.

She was just making a second attempt to go back to sleep, when all at once she heard a sound that made her stiffen. Somewhere in the distance a dog barked and then fell silent. The bark came quickly like ice shattering in the frigid morning air, but Stavan must have heard it also. Waking instantly, he sat bolt upright and clutched at his dagger. She sat up too, and they stared at each other in alarm as the sound was repeated.

"Maybe it's a wolf," she whispered, but it was the wrong time of day for a wolf to be out hunting, and they both knew it.

"That's not a wolf," Stavan cried. "It a dog!" He grabbed the cloaks that covered Hiknak, Dalish, and Arang and yanked them off. "Quick!" he yelled. "Get up! Marrah and I can hear the Hansi dogs. They must have picked up our scent!"

There was no need for him to say anything more. The five of them simply fled, scrambling out of the cave so fast they knocked part of it down in the process. The world outside was a white blur of falling snow, dung in dark steaming piles, ice like crystal dust in the manes of the horses. Stavan undid the hobbles, and Marrah and the others leapt onto their mounts, kicked them into a gallop, and made a dash for safety. But where did you ride to in a land where there were no trees to shelter behind, no forests to lose yourself in, not even a real cave where the horses could be hidden?

Marrah rode until the breath burned in her body, until every bone ached, until she felt as if she were being pounded to death. She had never been on a horse until she was a grown woman—had never even seen one—but when the nomads had kidnapped her and taken her east, she had learned to enjoy the sensation of riding, and had come to love the horse that carried her even though it was carrying her away from her own people. Horses, in her experience, were better than most people, certainly better than the nomads who had tamed them. They were generous beasts, patient and uncomplaining and certainly not responsible for the uses the nomads put them to, but this morning the wild flight across the steppes brought back all the fear she had felt the first time she had climbed onto a horse. She was the least experienced rider in the group, not always able to cling to her mare's back, tossed from side to side, sometimes nearly thrown. Often she lagged a little behind, and when this happened, the others slowed down and waited for her. She wanted to call out to them to ride on and leave her behind and save themselves, but she knew they would never do it. If she fell off and broke her leg, they would pick her up and carry her, and she would be the death of all of them, so she clung to her mare with grim determination, thinking that at least it was still snowing. If the snow stopped, they wouldn't have a chance. On the steppes in fair weather you could see from horizon to horizon.

"Don't let the warriors catch us," she prayed. "Don't let the weather clear." But her prayer was chopped up and thrown to the wind, drowned in the beat of the horses' hooves as they broke through the snow to strike the frozen earth.

She never knew how long that first frantic ride lasted. It seemed to take most of the day, but it couldn't have, because the horses would have died under them if they had kept it up that long. At last Stavan reined in his stallion, and the rest of them followed suit. For an instant they waited in absolute silence, hardly daring to breathe. Marrah looked from face to face, feeling the moment freeze forever in her memory like images fired on the side of a clay pot. Hiknak had lost her hat, and her dirty blond hair was spread wildly on her shoulders. Arang's face was so pelted with snow that he looked as if he had a beard, although at thirteen he was too young to grow one. Dalish's lips were cracked and chapped from the cold, and she was so pale that the blue tattoo marks on her cheeks looked like fissures in ice. As for Stavan, he was as motionless as a temple statue. His blond hair lay flat against his skull, his eyes were hard; his beard seemed to have been carved out of stone. Nothing on him moved, not even an eyelash.

"I don't hear the dogs anymore," Dalish whispered. But even as she said the words, the baying of the pack rose up in the distance.

"This way!" Stavan commanded. And they were off again, galloping frantically due east, then north, then east again. This time, they rode twice as long as before, and when they stopped at last to listen, they heard nothing except the wind moaning across the drifts.

"We've lost them!" Arang cried, but they all knew the reprieve was only temporary. At any moment the bark of a dog might send them into flight again, and when Marrah got her breath back and calmed down enough to look around, she realized that the snow had stopped falling. The hoofprints of their horses were deep and clear and wide as a path. A blind man could have followed them.

Dalish looked up at the sky and then at the great, flat, white sheet that spread out around them in all directions. "What do we do now?" she asked Stavan, who was the only one of them trained in the art of attack and escape. Stavan had once been a Hansi warrior, and although he had given up war for the love of Marrah and the Goddess Earth, he knew all the tricks of the Hansi.

"Keep going," he said, "and hope they don't pick up our trail again."

"I bet we've outrun them," Arang said, wiping his nose on the back of his mitten. Marrah looked at the hope in her brother's eyes, the delicate lift of his cheekbones, the graceful way he sat on the big, broad-rumped roan, and felt a pang of sorrow. Arang had the body of a dancer. When Zuhan, the great chief, adopted him and named him heir to all the Twenty Tribes, the Hansi scarred his cheeks with clan marks—which was their way of honoring him—and then beat him half senseless trying to turn him into a warrior, but they never managed to break his spirit or drive the music out of his soul. For a moment she wished she were as young as he was, because when you were that young, you thought anything was possible.

For the rest of the day, they rode more slowly, trying to spare their horses. At dusk the sun set in a fiery display of reds and pinks that turned the snow the color of rose petals. It was beautiful but terrifying. Marrah couldn't help thinking how easily they could be seen, moving across all that redness like ants on a piece of dyed linen. The last of the red was hardly out of the sky before the moon rose, so full it seemed about to split in half. As they rode along, it shone down on them like a second sun. Marrah had always loved the full moon. Every month she felt moon energy streaming into her. The moon excited her, and making love in moonlight was one of the things she liked best, as Stavan well knew, but tonight the moon made her feel naked and cold as a plucked sparrow. When she looked up and saw the sacred Moon Rabbit, she didn't greet Her with joy the way she usually did. Instead she hunched down, tried to make herself as small as possible, and prayed for clouds and more snow.

But no clouds appeared. It was a calm windless night, so cold that frost flowers blossomed on the sleeves of her tunic. If it had not been for the warmth of the animal between her legs, she would have frozen, but the two of them kept each other warm, and slowly she fell into a hypnotic state where everything was reduced to the rocking motion of her mare. When they finally stopped, she felt startled as if a long dream had ended. She sat for a long time listening before she dismounted, but the air was still, and all she could hear was the breathing of the horses and the beating of her own heart.

Stavan poked through the snow, gathered up armfuls of dry grass, and spread it on the ground. Piling their cloaks over the grass, he had them sit down in a circle with their feet in the center, and blankets draped over their heads like a tent. He called it a "heat trap," and it was stuffy but warm enough to keep off the worst of the cold. They slept fitfully, taking turns staying awake to listen for the nomads' dogs. Sometime in the small hours of the night, Arang woke them, and they heard a distant barking. Rising to their feet, they looked at one another in despair.

"Don't they ever sleep?" Dalish moaned as she began to stuff the blankets back into the saddlebags.

"Hush." Stavan stood for a moment, poised and listening, and they all stopped packing and stood with him. The barking came again and then died away, and a great silence filled the steppes.

"Those dogs aren't moving forward," he said. He turned to Marrah, and she expected to see hope in his face but it wasn't there. "The warriors have to rest their horses too, you know. They must have stopped about the same time we did."

"Then let's get out of here while we still can." Marrah grabbed one of the saddlebags from Dalish and started stuffing it as fast as she could. She felt the weight of Stavan's hand on her shoulder and turned to see him looking at her in a way that made her heart freeze.

"It's no use, Marrah. Forget the packing. We can't possibly out-ride them, and we can't throw those dogs off our trail. Without any snow to cover our scent, the whole pack can track us down like rabbits, and the warriors know it, which is why they've decided there's no hurry."

"What are we going to do then? Just sit here and let them catch up with us?"

"We'll have to make a stand."

Marrah looked at their pitiful collection of weapons and tried to imagine what kind of chance they'd have against trained warriors. She'd seen the nomads attack only once, but it had been a nightmare. They had ridden out of the forest screaming their awful war cries and killed without mercy. For a moment she saw the city of Shambah again, burning in the afternoon sun, its men impaled on stakes, its children slaughtered, its women enslaved. Shambah had been sacred to the Butterfly Goddess, but after the nomads were through with it, there had been nothing left but corpses and ashes.

"Fine," she said. "We'll fight." Her voice was level, but she could feel the fear rising into her throat. Along with the fear came a kind of wild defiance. She had never killed anything larger than a bird in her entire life, but she knew how to shoot a bow, and when the Hansi warriors attacked, she planned to do as much damage as she could. The memory of Shambah had been burned into her soul. She had seen how the nomads treated their captives. Better to go down fighting than live to be raped and tortured. Her fingers tightened around the drawstring of the saddlebag, drawing it taut, and she gave Stavan a level glance that said: Even though we don't have a chance, I'm with you.

They stood by their horses, ready to mount up at the first sign of an attack. Stavan and Arang unsheathed their bows, and Dalish and Marrah did the same. Only Hiknak seemed calm. She stood with her arms at her sides, staring in the direction of the barking.

"I think I know those dogs," she muttered.

Stavan turned to her. "What did you say?"

"I said I think I know those dogs. I recognize their barks. They belong to Mukhan." There was a moment of silence as they all absorbed this information. Mukhan was one of the best trackers in the tribe. If he was on their trail, they didn't have a chance.

"I used to feed them," Hiknak continued softly, almost as if she were talking to herself. "They're nice enough beasts when they aren't out for your blood. Friendly and loyal too. The lead dog is named Frostwalker. From the sound of those barks, I'd say she has her two daughters with her: Dusk and Birdbringer, and maybe her year-old son, Feathergrass." She turned to Stavan, who was looking at her with a peculiar expression. "Beautiful names, aren't they? Odd how the warriors name their dogs as if they had poetry on their tongues when they called them. My mother always used to say our men loved their dogs and horses more than they loved their wives and children, and from what I've seen, she was right."

Stavan looked thoughtful. "You say you used to feed them?"

"Yes, it was my job. I fed scraps and bones to all the tracking dogs and slept out in the cold with them at night like one of the herdboys. Vlahan made me do it after he stole me from my people. He thought it would break my spirit because it's supposed to be shameful to be sent to live with the dogs, and it was midwinter and cold as a demon's breath outside. But the dogs were warm, and I'd rather sleep with them any night than share the bed of the man who killed my mother and father and my sweet lover, Iriknak."

Stavan walked over to Hiknak and put his hands on her shoulders. "Do you realize what you've just said?"

Hiknak started and took a step back, and Marrah saw that she was used to being hit when a man touched her. "No." She shook her head and then took a step forward again, as if apologizing for her fear, because she knew Stavan would never hurt her.

Stavan turned to Marrah with a smile on his face—not a small, tentative smile, but a wide smile of triumph. His eyes glowed, and his beard seemed to bristle with energy. "We may escape after all," he said. There was so much conviction in his voice that Marrah knew he must have thought of a very good plan indeed.

In less time than it took the moon to move half a finger's length across the sky, they found themselves on horseback again, following their own trail back over the steppes. As the horses walked silently through the drifts, Marrah stroked the neck of her poor, tired mare with one hand and rehearsed Stavan's plan in her mind, examining it from all angles as if it were a piece of fine ceremonial jewelry crafted from thin copper wires.

His plan did have a certain thinness and wirelike quality. It was lean and straight, and hinged on one simple idea: instead of running away from the nomads, they were going to attack them. Not attack them openly, of course. No one with even a shred of sanity would pit two men and three women against a band of trained warriors. The attack was to be soft and sly: not the attack of the lion that leaps out of the tree raging and clawing or the attack of the wild boar that runs at you snorting loudly, Stavan had said, but the attack of the snake, sinuous and quiet; the attack of the moth that eats a hole in your tunic before you know it's there.

Put less poetically, they were going to sneak up, steal the nomads' horses, and leave them stranded. Stealing horses was an old Hansi game, and Stavan was good at it, but there were two complicating factors. Normally when you wanted to steal horses, you simply rode in yelling and stampeded them, herding off as many as you could. But in this case, Stavan emphasized, they couldn't afford to leave even one horse behind, so they were going to have to come in silently on foot and lead the animals away one by one, which would have been dangerous, but doable if there had not been any dogs. Sneaking up on a Hansi camp guarded by dogs was virtually impossible. Let so much as a snow hare hop by, and they could be counted on to raise an alarm that would wake everyone.

Stavan had explained that the Hansi dogs were so reliable that warriors who were not in enemy territory often did not bother to post a guard if they had dogs with them. Why depend on a man who might fail to hear the dry grass rustling, when you could sleep in peace knowing the dogs were on watch? Hansi dogs could not be poisoned because they would not take food from anyone they didn't know, and no scout, however silent, had ever gotten close enough to slit a dog's throat before it raised the alarm.

So to steal the horses, they would have to get past the dogs, and that was where Hiknak came in. The dogs knew Hiknak, and they wouldn't so much as lift their heads if she walked into the camp.

"I can't kill them," Hiknak had insisted stubbornly. "Don't even ask. Those dogs were my only friends for a whole winter, and I love them. They can't help it that Mukhan has set them on our trail. What I can do is coax them around to the other side of the camp, away from the horses, and do my best to keep them quiet. That way, if they bark, the warriors will come in my direction and the rest of you will have plenty of time to get away." She didn't bother to add that she herself would have no time to escape. She just pressed her lips together and stood there with her thin arms folded across her chest, and they saw that there was no reasoning with her, so they agreed. Marrah was secretly glad the dogs would not have to be killed, but it frightened her to think of the risk Hiknak was taking. She saw Arang staring at Hiknak admiringly, and it dawned on her that her little brother was closer to becoming a man than she had realized, but that was a thought for another season.

Quietly they had turned and followed their own tracks back toward the southwest. It had turned colder and the snow had hardened slightly. It made a small, crunching sound when the horses' hooves broke through the crust, but to Marrah the noise sounded like boulders crashing down a hillside. When she looked ahead, she could see nothing but the steppes, rolling slightly, covered with bluish gray snow. The moon was getting lower in the sky, and when it set, the sun would rise. If they didn't come across the warriors' camp soon, daylight would catch them out in the open, too close to run away. Her doubts grew with every step the horses took. They were staking everything on Stavan's plan, but what if Hiknak had been mistaken? What if the dogs following them weren't Mukhan's but strange dogs who would raise an alarm?

If Hiknak was having similar doubts, she didn't show it. She rode on steadily just ahead of Marrah, guiding her mare around the larger drifts and never looking back. The moon was low in the sky by the time Stavan reined in his stallion and motioned for them all to dismount.

"We leave the horses here," he whispered. Silently they dismounted. Dalish, who was staying behind, took the reins of Marrah's mare and looped them together loosely. The moon was still bright enough for Marrah to see the red tassels on Dalish's hood, relics of the time when Dalish had been old Zuhan's concubine. The tassels blew softly in the wind. Their gaiety seemed out of place, like dancers in a sickroom.

"Good luck," Dalish whispered, kissing Marrah lightly on the cheek. Her kiss burned in the cold like a warning, and Marrah shuddered slightly. Joining Hiknak, Stavan, and Arang, she began to walk along the trail their horses had made when they rode east, stepping in the hoofprints in order to move as quietly as possible. The snow crumbled silently under her boots, and the air was so still that she could hear her heart beating. She presumed they were getting closer to the camp, but how Stavan and Hiknak knew where it lay was beyond her. Still, they must have had some sixth sense, or maybe their steppe gods gave them some kind of second sight, because suddenly they both stopped.

Stavan looked at Hiknak, and Hiknak nodded. Walking over to Marrah, she gave her a quick hug that smelled of wet wool, and sweat, and horses. The hug surprised Marrah, but she hugged Hiknak back, afraid to let go. Goodbye, Hiknak, she thought, and the sweet Goddess Earth go with you. But she said nothing, only released Hiknak and watched as she turned and walked away as silently as a shadow. For a while she could see her, a black form moving against a gray background. Then she must have stepped over a small rise in the land because she suddenly disappeared.

Arang walked up to Marrah and took her hand in his. He stared at the direction Hiknak had gone as if he might cry, but he didn't make a sound. They waited for a while, expecting at any minute to hear the barking of the dogs, but to Marrah's immense relief, the silence of the night remained unbroken.

After a while, Stavan touched Marrah lightly on the arm and nodded to Arang, and without a word the three of them set off together toward the camp. Soon Stavan stopped again and sniffed the air. Marrah sniffed too, but she smelled nothing but the cold. Then she noticed a faint smoky odor. Fire, she thought. They walked a little farther, and soon she could smell the unmistakable scent of horses. They walked up a small rise in the land, not a hill really because there were no hills anywhere on the steppes, but just a bit of earth less level than the rest, and all at once she saw the silhouettes of horses etched against the moonlit sky.

Stavan crouched and began to crawl through the snow, and Marrah and Arang followed. It was cold going, but even though the snow got into her mittens and numbed her hands, she felt less vulnerable close to the earth. Finally they stopped. The horses were directly in front of them now, loosely bunched together in two small herds. Some had pushed aside the snow and were grazing on the dry grass; others appeared to be sleeping. Marrah could not see their legs distinctly, but she knew they must be hobbled, otherwise they would have spread out more.

Her heart sank. There were nine altogether, which meant they were going to have to make three trips because there was no way they could lead off more than one horse at a time without making any noise. And that wasn't the worst of it: nine horses meant nine armed warriors, and when she looked a little beyond the farthest herd, she saw them. They were only a dark pile, heaped in a rough circle, but by now she knew a heat trap when she saw one. The warriors' blankets glittered in the moonlight, covered with frost and bits of snow. From this distance she couldn't make out the clan signs, but she imagined she could hear the men snoring. How soundly they were sleeping was anyone's guess. As for Hiknak and the dogs, there was no sign of them, and there was no guard either. She supposed she should feel lucky, but the idea of creeping up and stealing the horses when the nomads were practically sleeping on top of them made her throat go dry with fear.

Stavan crept forward, and the horses looked at him curiously. They must have found it odd to see a man crawling, but they were used to the human scent and his presence didn't seem to bother them. Slowly he moved toward a large black animal marked with white spots that shone blue in the moonlight. Marrah couldn't see exactly what he did next, but the horse took a small step backward, so she assumed Stavan had undone its hobble. Immediately he was on his feet, sliding a rope around the animal's neck, making soft, whispering noises to it as if calming a child. Carefully, he guided the horse away from the rest, who looked after it with mild curiosity. Marrah supposed that in their experience horses were always being led off.

When Stavan reached Marrah, he motioned for her to get to her feet. Handing her the end of the rope, he indicated that she was to lead the horse back to where Dalish was waiting. Obediently, Marrah turned and began following her own tracks. The gelding came willingly, nudging her once in the back with its warm nose as if protesting that she walked too slowly.

When she reached Dalish, she handed her the rope without a word. Their horses seemed to accept the new horse without question. They had all come from the same herd, and no doubt this was not the first time they had spent the night together waiting for humans to accomplish some inscrutable purpose. Marrah had no sooner delivered her horse up to Dalish than Arang appeared with a large white mare. Stavan came soon after, leading a gray gelding.

Once again they returned to the camp, and once again Stavan crept up and undid the hobbles, and they silently led three horses back to Dalish. There were only three left now: two mares and a large, spirited stallion that probably belonged to Mukhan. Marrah didn't like the look of that horse. As the others were taken off, he had become increasingly uneasy. By the time they returned for the third time, he was making snuffling noises, moving restlessly as if disturbed that his comrades were missing. Stavan brought one of the mares to Arang and another to Marrah. So far everything was going well. The stallion still seemed restless, but he was looking after the mares as if he wanted to join them, and for a moment Marrah thought that he might come of his own accord. Instead he simply stood there, twitching his ears and tail, so Stavan started in for the last time, not bothering to crawl since speed was essential, and it was obvious by now that no one in the camp was awake.

Marrah knew she should take the mare he had just handed her and go back to Dalish, but she had a feeling that there was going to be trouble, so instead of turning around and following her tracks back through the moonlight, she did precisely what Stavan had told her not to do: she waited to see if he got away safely.

Her intuition was right. When he threw the rope over the stallion's neck, the beast reared and let out a loud whinny. Then, as if that were not bad enough, he did something far worse: wheeling around so fast that Stavan couldn't stop him, he galloped straight toward the pile of sleeping nomads.

Stavan managed to jerk the stallion sideways, but not far enough. The horse's front hooves struck the edge of the heat trap, and the blankets exploded, scattering in all directions as the warriors leapt to their feet, cursing and kicking one another awake. It took only an instant for them to see what was happening, and then three of them were on Stavan, surrounding him and trying to pull him away from the stallion. Somehow he got up onto the beast's back, but Marrah saw that he wasn't going to stay there. Already the remaining warriors were going for their weapons. She could see the long spears in their hands, the axes, the bows being strung with arrows, even the whites of their teeth and eyes as they yelled to one another.

She never knew what possessed her to do what she did next. Perhaps it was the realization that Stavan was going to be killed, or

The Horses at the Gate

19

perhaps the Goddess gave her a moment of crazy courage, but the next thing she knew, she had mounted the mare. Screaming at the top of her lungs, she rode straight toward the nomad warriors, knocking them aside. She had no reins or bit to guide with, only her knees, but the horse was beautifully trained, and as Marrah pushed against her sides, the mare wheeled and Marrah came back again.

Something whizzed by her ear—an arrow or a spear—she never knew which; and then she was in the middle of the nomad warriors again, and they were running to keep from being trampled. Later she thought that the very sight of a woman riding down on them must have startled them, because none of the things they hurled at her hit their mark. One of the warriors tried to catch her horse by the neck, but the short mane slipped through his fingers. She got one quick look at his face, contorted with rage. He must have been Mukhan because he had a wolf tattooed on his cheek, and his teeth had been broken and filed to points.

Mukhan screamed a terrible curse, but Marrah was past fear. In less time than it took to take a breath, she had left him behind, but another warrior stood directly in her path, armed with an ax. She tried desperately to turn her horse, but it was too late. As the mare galloped straight for the warrior, Marrah crouched over her neck and held on, waiting for the blow that would split her skull. But to her astonishment, the young warrior jumped aside at the last moment. She rode so close to him that she could see his face. He was young and almost beardless. He looked vaguely familiar, and if she had not known that it was impossible, she would have sworn he gave her a smile as she passed.

Then she was out of the camp, and she and Stavan were riding side by side. The snow flew up like dust as their horses' hooves thudded across the frozen ground. Out of the corner of her eye, Marrah saw Hiknak running for safety. Before she could go to her, Arang was at her side, sweeping Hiknak up onto his horse and riding off with her. Marrah could hear the dogs barking furiously, but the sound no longer terrified her. She felt elated and powerful. Kicking the mare to urge her forward, she gave a yell that echoed across the steppes.

"Batal!" she cried. It was the name of the Goddess, a name that had always been associated with peace, but the world had changed. "Batal!" Marrah cried again. Later, "Batal" became the battle cry of all who fought the nomad invaders, and even the fiercest came to fear it.

CHAPTER TWO

F ree from the fear of being followed, they now turned and rode southwest, driving the nomads' horses toward the Motherlands. Marrah had a lot of time to think as they pushed on through the snow. From childhood she had been trained to respect all living things as children of the Goddess Earth, and although she would fight when attacked, even fight to defend others if there was no alternative, she had never been a willing warrior, or even—if the truth be told—a very good one. She had experienced a moment of ecstasy when she screamed out Batal's name, but for several days after she felt a vague sense of shame.

Still, she was not the sort of person who wasted time worrying about things that could not be helped, and comforted by the certainty that she had saved Stavan's life, she gradually made peace with her misgivings. Mostly, as she rode, she thought about the city of Shara and how she longed to return to her old way of life. The rocking of her mare put her into a dreamy state, and she would pass most of the day imagining her favorite places. Sometimes, if she squinted her eyes behind the slits of the bark eye coverings Stavan had made to ward off snow blindness, the white flatness of the steppes would seem to rise in front of her like the wall of a cave, and the faces of all the people she loved would float there for a few moments like colored shadows. When this happened, she would always feel a sharp pang of homesickness, and she would shake herself awake briskly, telling herself that if she went on dreaming this way she was likely to fall off her horse.

Still, it was hard not to dream. Now that they were not running from nomad trackers, they moved at a measured pace so as not to tire their horses or excite them into a stampede. Stavan's and Mukhan's stallions had taken a dislike to each other, and Mukhan's always seemed on the verge of escaping and taking several of the mares with him. Marrah could hardly blame the stallion. She would have tried to escape too if she had been in his place; but Stavan insisted they keep all nine of the extra horses, even though taking care of them slowed them down considerably.

"We may need them," he warned, and his warning proved as good as a prophecy, because not more than three days later the roan Arang had been riding began to stumble. By evening when they pitched camp, it was clear that the poor thing was sick, and by morning it was dead. Arang cried over the horse, which he had come to love, but Stavan was more practical.

"We'll eat it," he announced.

Marrah and Arang were horrified. The horse had served Arang so faithfully it seemed almost a member of the family, and besides, everyone knew it was risky to eat sick animals, but Hiknak and Dalish agreed with Stavan.

"There's a lot of meat on him," Dalish said, and she got out her knife and began to gut the horse in a matter-of-fact way that reminded Marrah of how long she had lived among the nomads. Soon the butchering was complete, and they rode off with fresh horsemeat in their saddlebags, leaving the bones and scraps behind for the wolves. The horsemeat soon froze solid, and in the days to come both Marrah and Arang were glad to eat it.

They had delayed too long and moved too far north trying to throw the nomads off their trail. Now the first of the great storms moved in, with winds so high Marrah felt as if she were riding into the center of a cyclone. The first storm was followed by another and then another. Soon the snow was half as deep as a man was tall, and as the wind lifted it back into the air, it began to form impassable drifts. Riding became hard and dangerous. Sometimes the horses floundered almost up to their bellies as their sharp hooves broke through the crust, and there were days so white and blustery that not even Stavan could tell which direction they were riding.

"It's too late in the season," he said grimly one evening as they huddled in their snow cave listening to the wind moan across the great emptiness outside. "We'll have to find some place to winter over until spring. The horses are having trouble getting through to the grass, and if they don't eat, more of them will die."

"Won't the warriors catch up with us if we stop?" Arang asked. He looked over his shoulder as if he expected to hear the dogs barking, but Stavan shook his head.

"Not in this weather. Not even the Hansi are foolish enough to send out war parties when Aitnok the Storm God drives his white herds across the steppes."

Marrah was disappointed. She wanted to get back to Shara as quickly as possible, but she knew Stavan was right. These storms were like no storms she had ever seen, and the cold was frightening. The north wind numbed her fingers and toes the moment she crawled out of the snow cave every morning, and it was easy to imagine all of them—horses and people—wandering through that blowing, trackless whiteness until they starved or froze to death.

So for the next few days, Stavan rode off every morning by himself, scouting for some place they could take shelter. Luck was with him, and by the time the next storm blew down from the north they were safely camped in a small ravine. In this inhospitable land, a good ravine was as comfortable a place as you were likely to find to wait out the winter, and despite her impatience, Marrah was relieved. There was a good stream, frozen but not frozen solid, which was important when you had to keep thirteen thirsty horses supplied with fresh water. The dry grass was luxuriant, stored under the snow as neatly as if it had been tossed into a shed for safekeeping, and close enough to the surface for the horses to get to during the first few weeks (although later they were forced to dig it out). There was even a grove of stunted oaks, which provided firewood and a few acorns for bread and porridge, and half a dozen bare-twigged willows that had a way of arching so gracefully across the sky that on clear days Marrah could pretend she was camped along the River of Smoke.

The best thing about the ravine was its overhanging mud banks. They were thick and sturdy, frozen to the consistency of house-clay.

For the most part they looked solid, but in several places the stream had washed out small caves that only needed a fourth wall of snow to make them perfectly snug.

Snow was the one thing they had plenty of, so they all set to work, scooping and hauling, then piling up snow and throwing water on it to freeze it solid. That night when the wind began to howl down from the north, they had a stable for the horses, two medium-sized rooms, and one small one. Stavan and Marrah took one of the rooms; Dalish and Hiknak took the other; and Arang spread his blanket on the floor of the third, which was just big enough for him to comfortably stretch out in. They were fortunate to have such warm holes to retreat to, because this time when the snow fell, it went on falling for days, burying them in soft, white heaps.

Luckily most of the snow blew across the top of the ravine, otherwise they would soon have been up to their necks, but still, almost every morning when Marrah woke up, she found herself lying in partial darkness. She and Stavan would dig their way out, to find Arang, Dalish, and Hiknak just emerging from their caves like sleepy rabbits popping out of their burrows. First they would make sure the horses had water and grass; then they would set about cooking breakfast, which like every other meal consisted of horsemeat, acorn mush, or—if the snow had cleared enough for Stavan and Hiknak to go hunting—a few birds or (during one particularly lucky month) venison.

After that, there was nothing to do but sleep, talk, and poke around under the snow for grass and firewood. At first the wait seemed boring, but bit by bit Marrah became accustomed to the rhythms of winter. They were so far north that the days seemed half as long as they did in Shara, and as one long night followed another, she felt herself slowing down like tree sap, turning thick and going to sleep at the roots.

Of course life wasn't all sleep. Almost every night, she and Stavan made love—not spring love, but winter love, long and slow and sweet. Holding each other in the darkness, they would kiss as the snow slowly drifted outside their cave, every kiss building to the next, like small strings vibrating into music. Sometimes, she would feel the blood rush into her ears, and she would rise and straddle him; and sometimes he would come to her, quick and eager, wanting more but always waiting until she gave her consent.

There were times when they cried out passionately in the privacy of that little cave, and times when they rolled together and laughed like children, and times when they simply reached out for each other in the night for comfort, like two old people who had been partners for longer than either could remember. But no matter how they made love, there was never a touch of the violence that had made Marrah's life with Vlahan so unendurable. She and Stavan treated each other as equals, and by the time that long winter ended, they knew they would be friends forever, even if someday they stopped being lovers.

But there was more to their love than lovemaking. Marrah had been through terrible things. Now as she lay beside Stavan in the safety of the cave, she was free to feel the pain of them for the first time. She had witnessed a massacre, been taken captive, raped, and almost killed, but the Goddess had given her a merciful numbness and the courage to survive. Now that the numbness was no longer needed, it peeled away, layer by layer, unwinding like a long strip of linen. As it dropped away, she talked, and Stavan held her and listened.

Five years ago, when she was thirteen and newly a woman, she and Stavan and Arang had made a long trip from the western lands to the city of Shara to warn the people of the east that an invasion of "beastmen" was coming. That was how Marrah had thought of the nomads in the days before she had ever seen a man mounted on a horse: as strange half-human beasts with six legs and two heads and a tail. The beastmen had appeared to her in a prophetic vision too terrifying to be ignored. So she and the others had set off on a journey that had taken them the better part of two years, crossing all the Motherlands and following the trade routes to the shores of the Sweetwater Sea.

On their way east, they had stopped for two days at the Caves of Nar, one of the oldest temples on earth. There the priestesses had given Marrah three gifts: the powder of invisibility that she had later used to blind the nomads and escape death; some clay balls that they had called "dried thunder," which made a terrible noise when you threw them into a fire; and a piece of yellow amber the size of the end of her thumb with a butterfly frozen at the center. The priestesses had called the amber the Tear of Compassion, and she still wore it on a leather thong tied around her neck, but for weeks there was no compassion in her.

Sometimes she raged against Vlahan and Changar, and sometimes she mourned for the little sailor Akoah and the other women Changar had strangled on the brink of Zuhan's grave. Often she wept for the people of the city of Shambah, massacred and enslaved, their beautiful butterfly gardens destroyed, their motherhouses reduced to ashes. And sometimes she wept for herself, for the trust she had lost and would never quite regain, for the old world of the Goddess Earth that was passing away, where rape was unknown, and men and women met each other without fear.

Stavan did not do much except listen and comfort her, but that was all she needed. At first she was afraid her mourning would have no end, but slowly, like the snowstorms outside, it subsided. At last, fear and humiliation no longer slept beside her or haunted her dreams. The memories became only memories; unpleasant certainly, but bearable. By the time the last of the storms blew across the steppes, scattering a thin dust of spring snow, she felt that she had talked herself back to life.

By spring, something else had happened too: something she suspected at first, then welcomed with growing certainty. A child was growing inside her, conceived not in the ravine but back in the nomad camp. Putting their heads together, she and Stavan counted up the weeks, and arrived at the conclusion that they had started this new life on the very night he first came to her in Vlahan's tent. The idea that she had conceived a child with Stavan right under Vlahan's nose gave Marrah particular satisfaction. As for the child being Vlahan's, she knew in her heart it wasn't—a fact Stavan confirmed.

"Vlahan's women never conceive," he said simply. "That's part of what makes him so crazy to get his hands on Arang. Vlahan is a bastard with no legitimate claim to being Great Chief. The warriors laugh behind his back because he can't get his women to breed."

Marrah wrinkled up her nose at the word *breed*, which reminded her all too much of horses. "Then Vlahan is barren?"

Stavan chuckled. "The Hansi never say a man is barren. When a woman doesn't have children, it's always supposed to be her fault. But Vlahan has had plenty of women, and not one of them has ever produced a child." He touched her belly, caressing it softly, and smiled at her. "I love this baby already," he said. He paused. "And I have a favor to ask."

"What's that?"

He cleared his throat. "I know your people believe children belong to the mother. As I recall you don't even have a word for *father*, but . . ." He paused again and looked at Marrah and saw she was smiling.

"But what?" she said.

Encouraged, he continued. "I have a favor to ask." He picked up both her hands and kissed them. "I would like very much to be this child's *aita*." Among Marrah's people, when a man became a child's *aita* it was a lifelong, sacred obligation. Stavan, who had been Arang's *aita* for almost four years now, had already proved himself in more ways than Marrah could count, but he asked respectfully, just as a man of the Motherpeople would have.

She said nothing, only went on smiling.

"If it is your will, Lady," he added formally. "I think I would make a good *aita*. I know that this is an honor that is usually given to a brother, but Arang," he was unable to repress a grin, "seems preoccupied."

Marrah broke out laughing, and Stavan joined her. They had both noticed how Arang followed Hiknak's every movement. If Hiknak was aware of Arang's adoring glances, she gave no sign, perhaps because she wasn't interested, or perhaps because she still thought of him as a boy. Marrah wondered if Arang would ever get up enough nerve to ask the little nomad to share his bed. She hoped so, because as far as she was concerned, winter sex was too good to waste, but perhaps Arang would just go on looking. Even though Hiknak was only a year or two older than Arang, she had been Vlahan's concubine, and that must make her seem very grown-up. Of course if the two of them had been raised together in Shara, they would have played sex games from the time they could walk, and Arang wouldn't be so shy. But Arang wasn't becoming a man in the usual way. Life was so much harder for him than it should have been.

She stopped laughing and gave Stavan a quick kiss. "It's been quite a winter for love," she said. "You and me; Hiknak and Arang; even the mares and stallions seem to have been making the most of being snowed in." She brushed Stavan's hair off his forehead and kissed him again, and a great tenderness washed over her. Partly it was tenderness for Stavan, but it was tenderness for other things too: for the new life inside her; for Arang's last winter as a child; for the Goddess Earth decked out in Her white skirts, and the coming year, which seemed so full of promise. She laid her head on Stavan's shoulder and watched the firelight dance on the walls. After a while she spoke again. "Of course you can be my child's *aita*," she said. "I was planning to ask you all along."

They sat in companionable silence, and her mind drifted back to the horses. In the last few weeks the mares seemed to have known spring was coming, even though it was still snowing. Stavan had explained that mares experienced desire only at certain times of the year, and this seemed to be the case, because she had noticed that if the stallions came near when they weren't in the mood, the mares walked away. If the male followed and insisted, the female would lay back her ears, squeal, kick, and even bite. But when the Goddess sent them desire, the mares became flirtatious and encouraging. When the stallions whinnied and pranced, the mares lifted their tails invitingly and allowed themselves to be nibbled, smelled, licked, and mounted. Recently, the horses had been mating, and Stavan said that next year, at about this time, several would probably foal.

She closed her eyes and imagined her baby and the young colts. She thought of trees and mountains looming up on the horizon; but mostly she thought of Shara and how good it would be to go home.

While Marrah laid her head on Stavan's shoulder and dreamed of the Motherlands, Hiknak and Dalish were having a conversation that she would have found particularly interesting. For weeks the two women had sat side by side every evening, keeping each other warm, and tonight, as on so many previous nights as they fed bits of wood and dried dung to their small fire, they had fallen into a confiding mood. Dalish had just complained in a friendly way that Hiknak had not been bringing much dried grass to the horses. At first Hiknak had claimed it was too cold to go out, but although Dalish listened politely, she knew Hiknak was stalling. Hiknak was perfectly capable of wading through breast-high snow to hunt partridges, and she often stubbornly refused to put her hood up even when the wind was blowing hard enough to ice her hair. For a while the two of them sat there, mending mittens, grinding acorns, fanning at the smoke, and talking in circles while Dalish waited for Hiknak to say what was really on her mind.

"I'm afraid to go out by myself, because I can tell the boy wants me, and I'm afraid he'll jump me," Hiknak confessed at last.

Dalish looked up from the mitten she was mending. "Jump you?" She attempted to look surprised, but she had suspected for some time that Arang was the cause of Hiknak's sudden love for staying inside. "What do you mean 'jump you'?"

"Throw me to the ground and force me to have sex with him," Hiknak said bluntly, shaking her hair out of her eyes. "That's why I haven't been hunting or hauling my share of the grass lately. I don't want to go off by myself. That boy has eyes like a sick wolf."

Dalish laughed and threw down the mitten. "In the first place, Arang isn't a boy anymore; he's a man. Old Zuhan himself had Arang circumcised and tattooed, and if Zuhan had lived, he'd probably have ordered Vlahan to give you to Arang as a coming-of-age present."

Hiknak wrinkled her nose and frowned.

"But," Dalish continued, "we aren't living with the Hansi nomads anymore, Arang doesn't want to be the heir, and no one is going to give you to anyone. You own yourself, Hiknak my dear, and I promise you Arang knows that."

"Ha," Hiknak snorted. "When men get that sick-wolf look it doesn't matter what they know. Vlahan used to force me almost every night except when he got too drunk. Then, thank Han, he got tired of me. If he hadn't, I don't know what I would have done. Probably bashed him over the head with his own ax some night when he was asleep." She picked up a bit of acorn shell and cracked it between her thumb and forefinger. "The point is, Arang is Marrah's brother, but if he jumps me, I'll have to bash him." She smiled wanly. "This would cause problems. Also, I like the boy well enough when he's not making wolf eyes at me." She giggled slightly. "Although to tell the truth, he does look more like a puppy waiting for someone to throw him scraps."

"Relax. He's not going to so much as lay a finger on you unless you ask him to." Dalish yawned, and the red tassels on her hood swayed slightly, casting small shadows on the opposite wall.

She was a dark-haired woman, with eyes the color of almonds, and her face was covered with delicate blue tattoos that always made her seem as if she were peering out from behind a veil like a nomad woman, but Dalish was no nomad. She had been born in the Motherlands and served four years in the Temple of the Bird Goddess before the nomads attacked her village, killed her relatives, stole her, and took her into the steppes, but even though she had spent many years as a concubine, the nomads had never managed to subdue her, and when she offered an opinion, people usually listened. Hiknak was one of the few exceptions. Hiknak was good-natured, but she had a stubborn streak.

Hiknak put a few more acorns down on a stone and began to crack them with the handle of her dagger. It was a well-made dagger. It had, in fact, once belonged to Vlahan, her lord and master, and Hiknak had particularly enjoyed stealing it from him. There was a brief silence broken only by the sound of cracking shells. After a while Hiknak spoke again.

"How can you be so sure Arang won't grab me one morning when I go out to feed the horses?"

"Because that's not the way of the Motherpeople." Dalish pushed the strand of sinew through the thumb of the mitten with a bit of sharpened bone, and looked at Hiknak wondering what it would take to make her understand that not all men were like Vlahan. "The men of the Motherpeople always ask first. Or the women ask. It doesn't matter who makes the first move as long as someone asks and someone says 'yes.' For example, when a woman wants a man to enter her, she gives him a little tap on the thigh. If she doesn't tap him, then he stays outside the corral, so to speak." She laughed. "My mother used to tell the story of *The Woman Who Didn't Know How to Tap*. You see, there was this woman living in the village of Shiabu who—"

"You say the women *ask* the men?" Hiknak interrupted. She looked puzzled, as if the very idea of asking was foreign to her—which no doubt it was. "Why in the name of Han would they do that? If the men left the women alone, why would the women ever even *mention* sex?"

Dalish, who had been about to launch into a long, funny story, was mildly annoyed. "Because the women enjoy it, that's why."

Hiknak threw back her head and laughed so hard that Dalish thought she might choke. "Enjoy it! The women *enjoy* being jumped on? They enjoy being rubbed raw? I can understand having sex because you wanted a child, but asking for it? I'd as soon ask a horse to kick me."

Dalish looked offended. "Our men don't do it that way. They pride themselves on giving women pleasure. For your information, what you're describing doesn't even qualify as sex among the Motherpeople."

Hiknak suddenly looked interested. "You don't say." She stopped pounding on the acorns and thought over what Dalish had said. "I've had pleasure with women, but never with a man. My dear friend Iriknak was such a sweet lover, but in the end Vlahan killed her, and I've had no pleasure since." She cleared her throat and looked at Dalish apologetically. "Um, Dalish, just how *do* the men of the Motherpeople make sex feel good? Do they do what women do?"

Dalish looked at her with a perfectly straight face. So the girl was curious, was she? Well who wouldn't be? She paused just long enough to make Hiknak fear that she wasn't going to answer, and then she laughed. "I was only ten when I was taken from my people, so I can't say exactly what they do, since I've never done it, but I think they do everything."

"Everything?"

"Everything." Dalish grinned and went back to mending her mitten. By now Hiknak was looking interested indeed.

"Don't just sit there like a lump!" Hiknak cried. "Out with it! For the love of Han, Dalish, what do they *do*?"

Dalish decided that she had teased Hiknak long enough. "As I said, I don't know firsthand, but the Motherpeople sing teaching songs about how to give pleasure. I heard a lot of those songs at the winter and spring festivals when I was serving the Bird Goddess, and some were very explicit. I remember one in particular that went like this." She let the mitten fall unnoticed in her lap and began to sing. It was a quick tune with slightly uneven rhythms because as she sang, she translated the words into Hansi so Hiknak could understand.

> *Sweet lips*
> *sweet tongue*
> *suck as the bee*
> *sucks the flower*
>
> *let your hands wander*
> *let your fingers play*
> *the waterfall tumbles over the rocks*
> *as your hair tumbles over my belly*

Dalish raised her voice until the small cave echoed. Caught up in the song, Hiknak began to clap her hands.

my desire is like a river
my desire is like a fawn
I am shy in your arms
I am as wild as a bear

If you were a field
I would be your wheat
If you were a lark
I would be your song.

Hiknak begged for another verse, but Dalish couldn't remember one. "As I said, it's been a long time. I was only a girl when I learned it." She picked up the mitten again and went back to her mending, but Hiknak wasn't satisfied.

"That was a very pretty song," she grumbled, "but I still don't know how the men give the women pleasure. What does it mean to 'be your wheat'? And what's all this about fawns, and bears, and larks?" She giggled. "If I let Arang bed me, I don't think I'll enjoy it if he starts flapping around like a bird."

"I take it you need a nonpoetic description?"

Hiknak nodded.

"Well then, let me share a secret with you." Dalish wrapped her arms around her knees and leaned a little closer. "Once, a very long time ago, my first master, Irehan, gave me to a guest. You know how it is: an important visitor comes into camp, and the chief wants to please him, so he gives him a concubine for the night."

Hiknak nodded. She too had been given to visitors.

"The guest was also a chief—not a very important one; not young; and not at all handsome—but a chief nevertheless from some small tribe that lived near the Motherlands." She paused and looked thoughtful. "I don't know if he'd ever visited the Mother-people, but this bald, fat old man was a wonderful lover." She sighed. "I had the best night of my life with him, and when morning came I was sorry to see him go. I used to hope he'd come back and I'd be given to him again, but it never happened."

"What did he do that was so wonderful?"

"Mostly he went slow."

"How slow?"

Dalish laughed and her cheeks colored with pleasure. In the dim light she suddenly looked like a young girl. "More slowly than you can imagine. With Irehan it was always over faster than you could snap your fingers, but my old chief took all night. I always imagined that was the way the men of my own people would have made love to me if I hadn't been taken from them. Irehan would have killed me if he'd known how much I enjoyed that old man."

"Slow, eh?" Hiknak picked up her dagger and went back to smashing acorns with the handle. "Do you think Arang would be slow?"

Dalish grinned. "Who knows, but there's one sure way to find out."

Some two months after this conversation, Stavan announced that spring was not only coming, it had arrived. Hiknak and Dalish, who had lived on the steppes almost as long as he had, agreed, but Marrah and Arang were skeptical. As far as they could tell, it was still winter. True, the days were getting a little longer, they had to dig less snow away from the entrance to their caves each morning, and the wind did not seem quite as relentless; but nothing was melting or blooming, and when they struggled up over the rim of the ravine on the snowshoes Stavan had made for them out of deer gut and bent willow twigs, all they could see was the same unbroken whiteness spreading from horizon to horizon.

"The little whinchats are changing into their spring feathers, the storks are coming back, and the sap is rising," Stavan insisted. Taking his dagger from his belt, he slit the trunk of the nearest willow, and sure enough a spring wetness oozed from the cut. Marrah and Arang would have been more convinced if they could have seen a blade of grass, but Stavan usually knew what he was talking about, so when he said they should start traveling again as soon as possible, they agreed. For several days they all worked furiously, smoking fresh game and baking the last of the acorn meal into travel cakes. By the end of the week, they had packed the saddlebags, sewn up all the holes in the blankets, and were ready to set out.

The morning before they left, Marrah knelt beside the stream for a moment while Hiknak, Arang, Dalish, and Stavan looked on. Picking up a stick, she scraped away the snow. The ground beneath was as black as the night sky, strewn with small pebbles, and small white snail shells—good signs, since the snail was sacred to the spirits who watched over childbirth.

Picking up a small bit of the frozen soil, Marrah placed it on her tongue. "Bless my unborn child, Sweet Mother," she said simply.

Suddenly Hiknak was kneeling beside her, taking earth into her own mouth, and saying the same prayer.

Marrah gasped and Stavan gave a snort of surprise, but Dalish only laughed.

Hiknak laughed too, and pointed to Arang, who had suddenly turned as red as an apple.

"Blame him," she said. And then she turned and took Marrah's hands, and they swallowed the Earth, Mother of all things, as generations of pregnant women had done before them.

"I didn't even know they were sleeping together," Marrah complained to Dalish later that same day. "How could they have kept it secret in such a small place, and why would they bother?"

Dalish sighed. "Hiknak made me swear not to tell you, and I suspect she extracted a similar promise from Arang. It seems she was afraid Stavan would be furious because Arang didn't marry her properly and pay a bride price."

Marrah looked at Dalish blankly. "What in the name of the Goddess are you talking about?"

"Stavan is Vlahan's half brother, and Hiknak was Vlahan's concubine. As Hiknak sees it, that makes Stavan her lord and entitles him to Han knows how many head of cattle before she beds down with anyone."

"But surely Hiknak knows Stavan better than that. I'm sure the idea of owning her never crossed his mind. As for him getting angry about her having sex with Arang, that's the most ridiculous thing I've ever heard. In the first place, he likes both of them and wishes them happiness; and in the second place it's none of his business."

"Hiknak knows that; the problem is, she doesn't quite believe it. She's always waiting for something bad to happen to her, which—when you consider what her life has been like—is perfectly reasonable."

Marrah frowned impatiently. "I hate the thought of her living in fear all the time. How do we make her realize that no one is going to hurt her?"

Dalish shrugged. "We can't. All we can do is love her and take her back to the Motherlands, where the nomads can't ever get their hands on her again. She's making your brother very happy, you know."

Marrah looked back at Arang and Hiknak. They were riding so close to each other that the flanks of their horses almost touched. "Love can heal a lot," she said, and there was a note of hope in her voice. But Dalish, who had lived among the nomads most of her life, was more realistic.

"A lot," she agreed, "but not everything."

He loved her. He loved the way she moved, the way she walked, the sway of her hips, the color of her hair; he envied the horse beneath her legs and the little flies that landed on her arms, and he knew he would never love anyone this much again, because Hiknak was his dear and his darling, and she had been badly used and mistreated, and his love had healed her.

Now she laughed and tossed her hair, and he thought of sunlight. Now she smiled, and he looked at her lips and thought of the climbing roses that had grown on the walls of his great-grandmother's longhouse. Her breath was as sweet as honey; her eyes as blue as the ocean that lapped around the island of Gira. All this was poetry and hardly worth singing because it was simply the poetry of a young man in love, and all young men sang the same songs, but he sang them to her anyway, making a flute from bird bones so he could play to her while she sat warming her feet in front of the fire, and they were such small, wonderful feet that he could have spent the rest of his life admiring them.

Ever since she had come to him that day in the stable and asked him to kiss her, all the hurt of his own past—all the humiliation, and the beatings, and the Hansi warriors taunting him and saying he was a coward and would never make a man—all had melted away like the snow. Hiknak was his spring flower. He imagined her as a child growing out of the warm wet earth of the steppes with her petal-soft lips and her long-stem legs, so strong and fearless. Fierce and a woman now with her dagger at her waist, his darling nomad woman. He would never want another, he knew that, not even if the entire human snake of Gira danced around him and a hundred women tapped and enticed him and begged him to share joy with them. Other women meant nothing to him. He loved only Hiknak, and he hoped she would make him her baby's *aita* the way Marrah had made Stavan the *aita* of her baby, but even if she didn't, he would be content, because he wanted her to do whatever she wanted.

He had always wanted to be a man, and now that it had happened, he felt as if Hiknak was partly responsible, and he intended to be very good to her and respect her and never treat her the way Vlahan had treated her. There was so much passion and love and gentleness in being a man. What did the nomads know about it? They taught that men were made to kill, but he knew that the Goddess had made men to love. Knowing this, possessed of this fine secret, he rode happily, not even really caring anymore if they ever reached the Motherlands because Hiknak was beside him, carrying the child, and as long as they were together, he was content.

At night after they made camp, they would go off from the others and make love under the stars. Afterward she would pillow her head on his shoulder and point out the constellations and tell him the stories of her people, and he would tell her different stories about the same stars, and they would be amazed at how two people could look at the same sky and see such unlike things.

The most amazing thing she told him was that the nomads had thought she was ugly because she was thin, flat hipped, with small breasts, dull blond hair, and a sharp chin. He loved her breasts and her hair and her hips and her chin because they were hers. He would have loved any body she had come to him in: a large body with wide, wonderful hips and great breasts; a lean, horselike body; even a furry goat body. He tried to tell her that his people believed all women were beautiful, but he could never convince her.

"The nomads were fools," he told her, and he hugged her fiercely, but still she went on thinking she was ugly.

Often, despite the cold, he would strip off his tunic and dance bare chested for her in the moonlight, moving as gracefully as a moth. He would turn, and jump, and sometimes take the thin belt of fine wool she wore around her waist, dancing with it so it flowed behind him like smoke. Then his little nomad woman would clap her hands and laugh like the child she had never been.

During the day, they rode close to each other so they could whisper and hold hands. He knew the others were getting annoyed at the way they kept to themselves, but Marrah had spoken up for him. Marrah was the best of all sisters. She had told Stavan and Dalish that there was always a time like this when the Goddess sent two people desire. "A time of madness," she had said, and then she had laughed, and he had felt a little offended because he had never felt saner in his life, but at least she had understood, perhaps because she had felt this way when she first fell in love with Stavan.

"In six weeks they'll start to get a little bored with each other," she predicted, but Arang knew that he and Hiknak would never be bored with each other as long as they lived. "Let them enjoy each other," Marrah said. "They've both had so much pain, let them have a little joy."

Thanks to her, Stavan and Dalish had stopped grumbling, which was only fair. He and Hiknak did their part. They tended the horses, and cooked, and hunted just like everyone else, but during the day they went on riding hand in hand. Around them, the land was beginning to lift up, and the earth was beginning to roll itself into gentle hills, but he and Hiknak weren't as excited as the others. True, life would be safer once they were out of the steppes, and they were both glad for that, but home was wherever they put their blankets at night. Even when they saw the first stunted bushes and trees, they didn't go half crazy like Marrah and Dalish, who cried with joy and even got off their horses and embraced the trees as if they were long-lost relatives.

He and Hiknak were younger but more dignified. They carried their love into the Motherlands, but they could just as easily have carried it anywhere and been content.

CHAPTER THREE

A s they rode south, spring rode with them, growing stronger every day. The frozen rivers of the north had been easy to cross, but now when they came to a stream, they had to move cautiously, letting the horses test every step. The southern sun made the ice rot, and sometimes the surface cracked under them with a sharp sound that reminded Marrah of hot rocks exploding in a fire. The days were mostly fair, but when the sky did cloud over, it rained, and as the rain fell, the snow gradually melted, exposing sheets of soft mud that sloshed under the hooves of the horses with a sucking sound. By the end of the day they were so splattered they could barely recognize one another, but despite the mud, they enjoyed the turn the weather had taken. After the harshness of the steppes, the land seemed gentle and accommodating. The oaks and willows had already turned a fertile reddish brown, and now they began to put out fat, sap-filled buds. Overhead, great flocks of ducks and greylag geese suddenly appeared, flying north to their summer breeding grounds, and at night the frogs sang in a crazy, lovesick chorus that made it hard to sleep.

The birds and frogs were right: spring really had arrived. As they rode still farther south they began to see familiar flowers: pale yellow crocuses, white-petaled narcissus, and sometimes small clumps of blue hyacinths so sweet-smelling that when Marrah dismounted and knelt to take them in, she felt almost dizzy. As she rode through the forest, she had the sensation of waking up from a bad dream. Let the nomads have their treeless wasteland; here everything was sweet and familiar.

The others shared her love for the south. Dalish, who had not seen the flowers of the Motherlands since she was a child, laughed with joy at the sight, and often when they stopped to rest, she would wander around picking the prettiest blossoms. Sorting them by color, she would sit and weave long chains, which she would toss over the necks of the horses with songs of praise to the Goddess who had led her safely out of captivity.

"We always look as if we're decked out for some kind of festival," Marrah joked one afternoon as Dalish crowned her with a circle of white crocuses. Dalish only smiled, but later that evening as they sat around the fire, she talked for a long time about the village where she had been born, describing her mother and other relatives, the beautiful pottery her *aita* had made, and even the dog she had been given when she turned six. Hiknak and Arang were entertained by her stories, but Stavan was worried.

"Dalish sounds as if she thinks she's going home," he said to Marrah the next morning. "But who knows where her home lies?" He waved toward the forest. "The trade routes all stop at Shambah. There are no well-marked trails this far north, and if we turn aside to hunt for her village, we could wander around for months without finding it."

Marrah glanced back at Dalish, who was riding next to Hiknak. The two of them were laughing as if they did not have a care in the world, but she knew better. "Dalish never expects to see her home again. She told me a long time ago that the nomads killed her mother and most of her relatives and burned her village to the ground. She's just dreaming of her childhood, but in her heart she knows she can't go back."

"Good," Stavan said. "Let her dream, then. There's no harm in dreaming." Something in his voice made Marrah look up. He was frowning, and his eyes had narrowed slightly. She knew that expression: it meant he was keeping something from her—something he thought she would be better off not knowing.

"What's going on?" she demanded.

He smiled, but his smile had a troubled quality that was not reassuring. "It's probably nothing you need to worry about, but a few days ago I saw signs that men on horseback had passed this way. Nothing recent: a few hoofprints, a strip of leather that looked like an old bowstring, branches broken off at a certain height."

Her throat suddenly felt dry. She looked at the forest, which only a few moments ago had seemed safe. "Do you think they are hunting us?"

"No; it looks as if they came this way last fall a few weeks before the first snows. There's not much chance the news of our escape made it this far south. Probably the war party—if it was a war party—has already gone back where it came from, but I think we should ride toward the Sweetwater Sea as fast as we can. Once we get beyond Shambah and cross the River of Smoke, I think we'll be out of danger."

"Should we tell the others?"

"Why worry them? Hiknak and Arang are happy together, and Dalish is dreaming she's a child again. Telling them won't make them ride any faster."

Although she believed Stavan when he said the tracks were old, Marrah slept badly for the next few nights. Once many years ago the Snake Goddess, Batal, had sent her a terrible vision. In it, she had seen beastmen riding down from the east to lay waste to the Motherlands. She had traveled for the better part of two years to warn the people of Shara of the coming invasion, but although awful things had indeed happened, they had been far less horrible than the things she had foreseen. All the time she was a prisoner in Zuhan's camp, she had been comforted by the thought that the nomads had only raided Shambah and not gone farther south. Now it looked as if a second raiding party might have crossed into the Motherlands—which meant that the prophecy, like all prophecies, was slowly coming true.

But if there were any nomads around, they were well hidden. For the next week, she saw nothing but forest and more forest. They had gone too far west, and realizing their mistake, they turned east again and made directly for the shore of the Sweetwater Sea. With every step the horses took, the weather grew warmer, and Marrah grew more optimistic. Here the trees stood like a wall against the winds of the steppes, casting scarves of golden pollen into the air. The ground was littered with buds, and the bushes were full of bees. One morning they saw the first butterflies, and by afternoon they had counted five flowers that grew only in the warm lands near water.

Near noon on the next day, they came over a ridge of low hills and saw the sea stretching out before them. It was dark blue, studded with whitecaps, and as Marrah and Arang stood gazing at it, letting the sea wind blow back their hoods, they instinctively looked to the south. Somewhere in that direction lay Shambah—or rather what was left of it; and beyond Shambah, still farther south, lay the city of Shara.

At this time of year the fields of Shara would be fringed with the first green sprouts of wheat, and its walls would be freshly whitewashed for the Snake Festival. Tonight when the full moon rose, perhaps Queen Lalah would lie in the dreaming cave, looking for signs of her two lost grandchildren. Marrah was filled with a wild impatience. In the distance five gulls were flying south. She watched them and was filled with envy.

Arang must have been thinking similar thoughts. "If we had a boat, that wind would drive us home in two weeks."

"What's a boat?" Hiknak picked up a rock and tossed it in the direction of the sea, then adjusted the leather band that held back her hair.

Everyone stared at her in amazement. "You've never seen a boat?"

She shook her head. Stavan tried to explain, but Hiknak couldn't grasp the idea that there was a part of the world where trees were so common that people chopped them down and lashed them together so they could float from one place to another. "I don't see how you'd get your horse onto one of those things," she said. She put her hand up to shelter her eyes and squinted at the sea. "Still, I can see why you'd want to try. That's the biggest river I've ever seen." She turned to Arang. "I suppose we'll have to swim the animals across. How far is it to the opposite bank?"

As they followed the coast south toward Shambah, Marrah began to remember things she would rather have forgotten. Shambah had once been the northernmost city on the shores of the Sweetwater Sea, a pretty place of white-domed motherhouses sacred to the Butterfly Goddess, famous for its fine linen cloth and its gardens and the generosity of its people, but she had only seen it burning and in ruins. By now the birds would have taken the flesh of the dead back to the Mother, and grass would be growing in its shell-paved streets, but no matter how time had softened the ruins, she knew she would never be able to look on them without remembering the day she and Arang had landed their boat just outside the great sandbar that blocked the mouth of the river, waded ashore, and found death and war waiting for them.

They had been captured by the nomads at Shambah; she had seen her first horses there and her first armed Hansi warriors—seen things so terrible that she couldn't even bear to dream about them. For a long time, she had managed to put Shambah out of her mind—not forget it, she could never do that—but set it aside like an empty cup, drained of a bitter draft. But as they drew nearer, her life began to unwind in reverse, and the cup of bitterness filled again. Every tree and rock seemed to hold a bad memory: here was the stream on whose banks they had camped on the third night of their captivity, here the grove of oaks where the first slave had died; and wasn't that the very tree that marked the place where Akoah, the little sailor, had sat and wept inconsolably, begging Marrah to save her?

If Marrah was thinking of the past as they rode toward Shambah, Stavan was thinking of the future. He had seen no more signs of armed men on horseback, but he had been raised in a land where surprises were often fatal and only the wary survived. In all likelihood, when they came to the place where Shambah once stood they would find only ashes and bones, but he was not about to stake his life on that, so when they were half a day's ride away from the city, he called a halt.

"I'm going up ahead to have a look," he said. His voice was casual, and he sat on his horse with an easy air, not even bothering to loosen the top of the leather case that held his bow, but they all knew what he was up to. Marrah—who knew even more than the others—hated to let him out of her sight, but she was growing larger by the day. Already her pregnancy was slowing them down, and if Stavan had to fight or run for his life, she would only be in the way, so she sent him off to scout out Shambah with a smile she didn't feel and settled down to wait.

That afternoon while Arang and Hiknak were off in the woods sharing joy, she and Dalish burned some sweet herbs to the Butterfly Goddess and prayed that Stavan would come back safe bringing good news. When they finished chanting, Dalish caught a butterfly, chasing it along the seashore with whoops of joy. It was a pretty thing, all green and gold, and when she carried it to Marrah, careful not to brush the dust off its wings, they saw it was marked with a black spot shaped like a double-headed ax.

"It's the sign of the Butterfly Goddess Herself!" Dalish exclaimed, "and a wonderful omen." But Marrah wasn't sure. Before the nomads captured her, she had always thought of the double-headed axes as butterflies, but now axes and war were all mixed up in her mind.

Stavan stayed away all afternoon and evening. As they tended to the horses, cooked some rabbits over the fire, and spread their blankets out for the night, they began to worry.

"What's keeping him?" Arang said, and he went down to the sea to look south along the beach, but when he came back he reported that Stavan was nowhere in sight. They waited for Stavan for a long time as the full moon rose and the stars moved east to west in a stately dance over the gray-white water, but it was almost dawn before he returned, and as soon as Marrah saw his face, she knew the news he brought was not good.

"Nomads," he announced. He looked as pale in the moonlight as a man of bone, stiff as the alabaster death goddesses the Girans put in the graves of their relatives, and when he dismounted and came to the fire to warm his hands, his flesh was as cold as copper. They fed him and waited for him to speak, knowing that he was not a person who could be rushed. Sometimes Marrah disliked this part of him, the nomad part that could be so silent when there was so much to say, but tonight she understood. She handed him the roasted rabbit flavored with the wild rosemary that grew along the beach, and after he had eaten, the color came back to his face, and he told them what he had seen. A party of armed warriors had settled on the ruins of Shambah—not Hansi warriors, but warriors from another, smaller tribe.

"By their markings I'd say they were Shubhai, a mean, worthless lot, cowards mostly. Last I heard, the Shubhai were being ruled by a petty chief named Nikhan who's known mostly for his unwillingness to fight his enemies face to face. He and his warriors like to come around after the battle is over and pick through the ruins, take whatever hasn't been taken, kill whoever hasn't been killed. The Hansi call the Shubhai the Garbage People because they always eat the scraps no one else wants. In theory, they owe allegiance to the Great Chief, but the Shubhai aren't one of the Twenty Tribes,

Mary
Mackey

44

and they never join the councils. They live in the west, almost in the Motherlands. As long as anyone can remember they've been looting the northernmost villages of the Motherpeople, but what they got was always so worthless no one ever paid much attention to them."

Dalish turned pale. "Were these the ones who burned my village and killed my family?"

Stavan looked at her, and his eyes softened. "It's hard to be sure. When I was a boy, the Shubhai sometimes came east with a slave girl or two, and offered them to the Great Chief so the Hansi would let them alone, but they really didn't need to bother because no one cared what they did at the end of the world."

Arang leaned forward, elbows on his knees, his face intense in the firelight. For the first time in weeks he seemed fully present, as if the bad news had torn him out of the private world he shared with Hiknak. "You say they're at Shambah?"

Stavan nodded. "They're camped right on the ruins."

"How many of them are there?"

"Too many for us to fight, if that's what you're getting at. I counted ten tents, all looking as if they'd been made out of new hides and green wood by someone who didn't know much about tentmaking. I think they've forced the Shamban women who survived to do some sewing for them, but that's not the strangest part of it." He paused. "They've built something."

"What is it?" Hiknak said impatiently.

"A kind of house." He waved his arms. "A big one all made of wood. It's square and it goes on for a couple of hundred paces in all directions. I think it's a storehouse of some kind, but it could be a temple. It has two stories, and there are strange little windows all around the top, not really big enough to see out of, but big enough to shoot an arrow through if you were so inclined.

"This house—or whatever it is—is surrounded by quite a barricade. Perhaps the barricade is meant to serve as a corral, because the warriors seem to be keeping some of their horses inside; but if that's true, they could have saved themselves a lot of trouble by using brambles. This corral is twice as high as a man; the sides are made of tree trunks stuck into the ground like posts, and there are other tree trunks piled up all around it so no one can walk up to it—much less ride up to it. The Shubhai must have built shelves of some sort on the inside at the top of the walls, because I saw at least two sentries standing on them, and I was lucky they didn't see me first."

He paused again and helped himself to more rabbit. No one spoke. They were all trying to imagine the strange house the nomads had built at Shambah.

"What do you think it's for?" Hiknak pushed her hair out of her eyes and grew thoughtful. "I've never heard of warriors building anything permanent. When I was a child the grown-ups were always telling me: 'If you can't carry it on your back for half a day at a dead run, leave it.' That was an exaggeration, of course. We carried plenty of things on the horses that no one could have lugged around for half a day, but still, everything we had was made to be picked up and *moved,* and when we left a campsite, we even kicked apart the corrals and used some of the brush to cook breakfast."

Stavan ate the last of the rabbit and wiped his fingers on his leggings. "I've been asking myself the same thing: If I were the Shubhai, why would I go to all the trouble to build something permanent? The answer is not immediately obvious because right at the start you're faced with the fact that the Shubhai are about the laziest people on the face of the earth, so first I have to conclude that they must be using Shamban slaves to do the work for them, and probably working them to death, because that's the Shubhai way."

Marrah inhaled sharply but did not interrupt. The idea that some of the people of Shambah might have survived only to be enslaved and worked to death was horrible, but she could see that Stavan must be right.

"Fine, they have slaves—slaves who fear for their lives and will do anything. Then you have to ask why they'd waste all that energy building something they'll ride away from come summer, and the only possible answer is that they have no intention of going back to the steppes. Something's holding them here, something worth more than the wives, and slave girls, and the horses and cattle they left behind. What is it? I have no idea, but I suspect they think that this treasure—whatever it is—is going to bring the other tribes down on them once they hear about it."

He sat for a moment staring at the fire as if he were seeing Shambah. "It's the Shubhai way to loot and disappear. To be honest, that's the way of the Hansi too. The way we fight is based on the idea that you can ride up on a camp, sack it, and ride away and lose yourselves in the steppes. We've always been a people who move constantly and our strength is in the speed of our horses, but this wooden house is built to hold off men on horseback in a way they've never been held off before. If the Hansi attack, Nikhan and his warriors won't have to ride out and fight hand to hand. They can cower behind their walls and shoot from the safety of their little windows, and no one will be able to get at them. No one will be able to sneak up on them; no one will be about to rout them; a dozen—perhaps even half a dozen—warriors might be able to hold off a whole war party. It's a brilliant idea, really. Not to mention that if someday the slaves took it into their heads to rebel, they'd never have a chance. There's only one thing Nikhan seems to have forgotten."

"What's that?" Arang asked.

Stavan lifted his head and smiled. "Wood burns." Brave words, but Stavan was a practical man, and as he went on talking it soon became clear to everyone that he had no intention of leading two pregnant women, a former concubine, and an untried boy against a band of seasoned warriors. After hearing more details, including the fact that there were at least twenty armed men encamped on the ruins of Shambah, the others reluctantly agreed that attacking and burning the Shubhai war temple would be suicidal.

Marrah said very little during this discussion. She was upset at the thought of abandoning the Shamban slaves to their fate, and it frightened her to think of a band of nomads living permanently on the shores of the Sweetwater Sea, but she could see no way to drive them back to the steppes. Using Shambah as a base, this Nikhan could send his warriors south into the heart of the Motherlands. Shara was on the other side of the River of Smoke and would probably be safe from the invaders for a long time, but step by step, Batal's prophecy was being fulfilled, and as she sat by the fire listening to Stavan describe what he had seen, she felt as if an invisible net of terror were being cast over her world.

By the time the eastern sky began to pale, they had come up with a plan that satisfied no one, yet was the only one they could reasonably make: they would circle around Shambah. As Marrah rode back into the forest, she cast one last look over her shoulder, but there was nothing to see but the Sweetwater Sea glowing dully in the early morning light like a plate of beaten copper. *Are we paying too high a price for our own safety?* the hooves of her mare demanded as they clopped over the soft leaf mold. She thought of her unborn child and the future she was giving it by running away. Against all reason she still longed to turn around, ride to Shambah, burn the nomads' war temple, and drive them out of the Motherlands forever; but a small voice spoke inside her head, whispering harsh truths, telling her she was not a warrior—only a pregnant woman, big and awkward, full of more courage than sense. The voice was practical and persuasive, and no doubt she would have listened to it, put Shambah behind her, and let the troubles of the future come in their own good time, had it not been for the villages.

Villages were rare north of Shambah, but there were a number west and south of the city. The first one they came to was small: only a few houses set along paths of crushed seashells beside a small stream that ran through half a dozen fields. The houses had been built in the Shamban style, partly underground so they would be cool in the summer and warm in the winter; they were dome shaped, with a frame of willow twigs and mud plastered over with white clay, and once they must have been painted with flowers and butterflies because you could still see traces of color.

That was about all you could see because where the village had once been, there was no village anymore—only ruins. The houses were not houses in the sense that anyone could still live in them. They were burned and broken, shattered like eggshells: roofs caved in, white walls stained with soot, and other stains too that might have been excrement or blood. Beyond them, the fields stretched—unplanted and covered with nettles, burdock, and the green shoots of new brambles.

They sat for a long time looking at the devastation. Finally Stavan dismounted, went into what was left of one of the houses, and came out grim faced. "The Shubhai walled everyone up inside and burned them alive," he reported. "Children too, from the looks of it."

"May the Mother receive their souls," Dalish whispered.

Marrah said nothing. She put her hand on her belly protectively, as if that thin shield of flesh could protect the child inside her. When she looked over at Hiknak, she saw her clutching Arang's arm.

They rode on in silence, too upset to speak. Soon they turned south, and as they drew nearer to Shambah—although still well to the west of it—villages became more common. Here the land was marshy where most of the settlements had once grown flax. Often as they crossed streams, they could see the wicker weirs where the newly harvested flax had been laid for retting before it was dried, stripped, cleaned, and sent to the temples of Shambah to be woven into the fine linen cloth the city had been famous for. Now the weirs were empty and broken with gaping holes that reminded Marrah of mouths with knocked-out teeth.

By the mercy of the Goddess, the villages here had not been burned and the villagers were still alive, but something terrible must have happened to them that did not show on the surface; because as soon as they caught sight of strangers, people screamed in alarm, threw down their digging sticks, snatched up their children, and fled into the forest, and no matter how loudly Marrah and the others called out that they came in peace, the villagers stayed hidden.

The news of their presence must have traveled fast, because soon they came to villages that contained no people at all. Pots sat cooking on hastily abandoned fires; water jars lay beside the streams; cows and goats had been driven off so fast that often the reed fences that surrounded the corrals had been knocked down and trampled. It was upsetting to inspire so much terror and even more upsetting to realize what must have happened to make the people so afraid of strangers on horseback. "Next time, we should get off and walk in," Marrah declared.

Hiknak and Arang thought that was a good idea and so did Dalish. Even Stavan, who always hated to walk when he could ride, was tired of being mistaken for a raider. So the next time they smelled smoke and heard dogs barking in the distance, they dismounted, and leaving Hiknak and Arang behind to watch the animals, Marrah, Stavan, and Dalish set out on foot.

But they might as well have galloped right into the center of the village: as soon as they appeared, the villagers grabbed their children and ran for the forest. Only one old man stayed behind, and as they drew closer, calling out that they came in peace, he began to curse and throw rocks at them.

"You murdering hunks of goat dung!" he screamed. "You maggots! May the Goddess curse you with cold wombs! May She refuse to take your souls when you die! May the blessed snakes turn on you and bite you! May the holy owls shit on your heads and the sacred crows spit out your flesh!"

Dalish and Stavan, who were used to nomad swearing, were unimpressed, but Marrah stood openmouthed. She had never heard anyone utter so many terrible curses in a single breath. The old man lobbed a good-sized stone in her direction but it fell short, kicking up a little spurt of dust at her feet. She looked at him more closely:

he was gray haired and frail and bent almost double with the sore-joint disease, which was probably why he had not run with the others. There was something else about him—something strange she couldn't quite put her finger on. He didn't look normal: he was hollow cheeked, with a potbelly and arms and legs no thicker than willow twigs. His head was skull-like, almost fleshless, and his eyes were sunken, rimmed with black circles; yet he didn't look ill and he certainly didn't throw rocks like someone with a wasting disease. It took her a moment to realize what was wrong. She had walked from the Sea of Gray Waves to Shara, seen the islands of the south and the treeless steppes of the north, but she had never before seen anyone starving. She was shocked. How could he be dying of hunger in the middle of a forest full of game and some of the most fertile land on the shores of the Sweetwater Sea? He was an old man whose relatives should have presented him with the best of everything. The Fourth Commandment of the Divine Sisters was "respect old people," and she had never before been in a village where it was not obeyed.

"Honored uncle," she cried in Shamban. "Stop, I beg you. We come in friendship."

The old man gave no sign that he had heard her. Throwing his last stone, he sat down stubbornly in the middle of the path and folded his skinny arms across his chest. "Go ahead and kill me, you yellow-bearded pig's pizzle," he called to Stavan. "What does it matter?"

It was clear that he had mistaken them for raiders, which was not unreasonable since Marrah and Dalish were dressed like nomads and Stavan actually was one. We're going to have to get some new clothes, Marrah thought. She hurried forward with words of apology and tried to help the old man to his feet, but he pushed her away with surprising force. The next thing she knew, she was sitting on the ground next to him, and before she could offer more reassurances, he spat in her face.

"Stop that!" she yelled. "Have you lost what little wit the Goddess gave you? Can't you see we mean you no harm?" She very nearly called him an old fool, but years of training made it impossible for her to insult a man of his age, so she just sat there glaring at him and wiping the spittle off her face.

The old man looked surprised. "You speak Shamban?"

"Of course I speak Shamban. I'm Marrah of Shara, grand-daughter of Queen Lalah, on my way back home, and I'll thank you not to spit at me. It's poor hospitality." Stavan and Dalish stood to one side watching. Stavan was doing his best not to smile, but Marrah did not feel in the least amused.

The old man unfolded his arms and looked at her as if trying to decide if she was telling the truth. "Do you worship the Dagger or the Butterfly?" he demanded suspiciously.

"The Butterfly. The Dove. The Snake. The Deer. All the sacred forms of She Who Is Everything. I'm a priestess, and if you'd take a closer look, you'd see that I am carrying a child."

The old man looked at her belly and a flush of shame rose from his neck to his face. "I pushed a pregnant woman," he muttered. "Oh, dear Goddess, what have I done?" Tears came to his eyes and rolled down the creases in his cheeks. "Forgive me, Lady. I thought you were a nomad."

The sight of his tears softened her. "Did the nomads ride through here?" she asked gently.

He nodded.

"What did they do, uncle?"

"Terrible things!" he wailed, and it was a long time before they could get him calmed down enough to tell his story.

In the end it was a simple tale, no worse than dozens of others they would hear in the days to come. The village had been home to about thirty people until last fall, when just after the harvest, men mounted on strange beasts had appeared out of nowhere. Killing the Village Mother and anyone else who offered the slightest resistance, the raiders had demanded that the villagers hand over all their food, the bows they hunted with, all their knives and axes, and their pigs, goats, and cows. Then they had rounded up the young men and women, tied them together by the neck, and marched them into the forest, leaving the rest to starve since they could no longer hunt and it was too late to plant a second crop. No one had seen the captives since, but rumor had it they had been taken down to Shambah, where the nomads were building some kind of strange temple in honor of a god who lived in the sky.

The old man, whose name was Klatif, had had an older sister named Jaloaj. The two of them had sat on the village council together with the other elders as was the custom, but the nomads had killed Jaloaj when they saw the Goddess signs around her neck.

"They took all the older priestesses out to the forest and buried them alive in a big hole," he said, "and then . . . " his voice broke and he hid his face in his hands, "they had their translator tell me that the 'rule of women' was over, and that I was to run the village from now on. I'm supposed to send two-thirds of whatever we grow down to Shambah to feed them, and if I don't, they'll be back, but we can't feed our little children if we give that much away; and how can we plant our fields with all the young people gone and all the seed taken? There are so few of us left: five old men, two women they didn't want, a young girl with a clubfoot, some toddlers, two babies who are living on the milk of a she-goat we managed to hide."

As he spoke, the villagers—who had obviously been watching from the shelter of the forest—began to drift back. By the time he was finished, about a dozen people had gathered, all too young or old or sick to be of much use. Marrah wondered how many had starved to death over the winter and how many others would starve next winter if the nomads really did take two-thirds of the harvest. She looked at Stavan and Dalish and saw her own thoughts reflected in their faces.

They would have to go to Shambah after all. Someone had to drive the nomads back to the steppes. Could they do it? Probably not; but you couldn't look into the eyes of these starving children and old people and ask yourself if you should abandon them to save your own skin.

They walked back, collected Hiknak and Arang, and spent the rest of the afternoon sitting in front of Klatif's hut trying to figure out what they should do next, but—as Marrah had feared—they got nowhere. No matter how they counted, there were always five of them and twenty—perhaps thirty—armed Shubhai warriors. Marrah still had two of the powerful charms the priestess of Nar had given her: the amber Tear of Compassion and the dried thunder; but neither thunder nor compassion seemed appropriate to the occasion. Things looked so hopeless that even Hiknak, who was always spoiling for a fight, admitted that they would all probably be killed if they attacked the fort.

By the time the afternoon drew to a close, they had run out of ideas and were ready to ask for help. Fortunately, in the land of the Butterfly Goddess, help was always close at hand. Just after dusk, the young girl with the clubfoot came to Marrah with cupped hands. She knelt and spread her palms to reveal a fat green caterpillar. The caterpillar was a gorgeous thing, bristling with yellow hairs. Its six red eyespots looked like glowing coals, and it had blue circles all along both sides.

Marrah admired the caterpillar warily. She had heard how the Shambans summoned their Butterfly Goddess, and she had a fairly good idea of what was coming next.

"What am I supposed to do with this?" she asked.

"Swallow it, my lady."

"Alive?" The caterpillar reared up and waved its front feet at her. "Couldn't you dry it and dip it in honey or at least fry it in a tasty sauce?"

"No, my lady." The girl pointed to the caterpillar's quivering legs. "The Messenger must be alive and dancing, or the Goddess won't speak through her."

"That's a pity." She tried to imagine what it would feel like to swallow a live caterpillar. Maybe it would wiggle all the way down her throat. Ugh. "Why am I being given this honor and not the others?"

"Because you are the granddaughter of Queen Lalah of Shara, and a great priestess."

Marrah sighed, accepted the caterpillar, and sat for a moment staring at it. Tilting back her head, she popped it into her mouth and swallowed. It was a furry, squirming, bitter mouthful, and she almost choked before she got it down. She opened her eyes to find the girl staring at her with unconcealed curiosity.

"What did it taste like, my lady?"

She gasped and wiped the tears out of her eyes. "Frankly, it tasted like shit rolled in fur." She was immediately sorry she'd said that, because she had no intention of offending, but the girl seemed relieved.

"Then I brought you the right one."

"You mean you weren't sure!"

"No, my lady. I've never looked for a Messenger before. I'm much too young to be a priestess, but the nomads killed all our village mothers."

"How long does it usually take for the Messenger to speak?"

The girl shrugged. "The Goddess descends in Her own time." Marrah sighed and resigned herself to her fate. Too bad the village mothers weren't alive, but it couldn't be helped. If the girl had accidentally poisoned her, that was that. She felt sorry for the child. She was a thin, sickly little thing with big eyes and a dirty face—nine or ten at most. "You've done your best," she said gently. "Let's hope the Goddess guided you." And then she went off to try to find something to take the taste of raw caterpillar out of her mouth.

By midnight the Messenger still had not spoken. The sky was overcast and dark, and a cool wind blew in from the sea carrying the smell of salt and great distances. Around a small fire in the center of what had once been a prosperous village, strangely painted human figures were dancing to the rhythm of drums, weaving through the smoke like visitors from a world of dreams. The dancers wore no clothing, only the flesh they had been born to, but they seemed to be dressed in robes embroidered in complicated patterns. Every breast and arm and elbow, every knee and thigh and face, was painted with delicate red lines that curved gracefully, following hips, and shoulders, the turns of ankles, and bends of wrists.

Sometimes the firelight made the dancers look as if they were wrapped in webs of red thread; then they would turn, or lift their arms, or throw back their heads to cry out another verse of the Butterfly Prayer, and the threads would break into rainbow-colored bands. Their bodies would appear to grow larger, and the lines would rush inward, filling their navels with whirlpools of holy energy.

"Chilana!" Marrah and Dalish cried as they danced hand in hand, tracing out the sacred patterns on the hard-packed earth.

"Chilana!" the villagers responded as they dipped and weaved, tying up the last loose ends of the invisible chrysalis.

Chilana, the Butterfly Goddess of Shambah, was being invited to come down to earth for a night, to flutter around the fire and enter the hearts of the dancers. The Divine Butterfly, Most Gentle Mother, She Who Overcomes Death, was being asked to show Herself and do what no human could do: tell Marrah and the others how to go to Shambah, drive off the nomads, and come back alive.

"Chilana," Marrah cried. "Give us a plan." She lifted her face to the white spot in the sky where the moon rested beneath gray clouds like a caterpillar wrapped in a cocoon. Her eyes were half closed, her lips parted slightly as if about to offer a kiss to some invisible lover. When the villagers looked at her, they thought that the Messenger must finally be ready to speak, but they were wrong. Except for leaving an incredibly bitter taste in Marrah's mouth and upsetting her stomach, the caterpillar seemed to have vanished into her with no effect. She had danced herself into a trance—which was something any competent priestess could do—but it was a light trance and very fragile.

She danced on, willing herself into the other world. In her right hand she held the Tear of Compassion, and as she danced the little butterfly frozen in the center of the tear danced with her. When the villagers had seen the butterfly, they said she must have been sent by Chilana to save them from the nomads, but Marrah was not convinced. The tear might be a powerful charm, but she had lived with the nomads too long to believe they would run back to the steppes if she waved it in their faces.

"Chilana, help us," she prayed. "Tell us how we can free the slaves without being enslaved. Tell us how to fight the nomads. Chilana, Sacred Butterfly, You Who Never Die, speak to us." Sweat broke out on her forehead, and her mouth grew dry from chanting. Time passed and the ghostly cloud-light of the moon began to move farther west, but still nothing happened. The dancers danced; the fire burned; the drums throbbed; but the Goddess Chilana still refused to descend. For the most part, Marrah was not conscious that the night was waning, but every once in a while she would separate herself from the music and see that the ritual was a failure. She would stumble, break the rhythm, and lurch out of the trance to find herself surrounded by a circle of weary villagers smeared with red ocher; she would see Arang dancing his heart out for nothing; Stavan and Hiknak tramping awkwardly through the unfamiliar steps; she would see old men, sick women, toddlers barely old enough to walk, and realize what a pitiful sight they made.

When this happened, she would close her eyes, dance harder, chant more loudly, and pray with all her heart for the Messenger to speak, but the girl must have brought her the wrong caterpillar after all.

As dawn approached, Marrah's feet began to feel like lumps of mud; the breath burned in her body, and she heard her voice and the voices of the others croaking like frogs. She was about to give up and flop down by the fire, when the caterpillar finally climbed into her brain and spoke.

It started with a buzzing in her left ear. The sound was annoying, like the humming of a gnat. Or . . . like voices—many voices all whispering at once. She stopped dancing, stood absolutely still, and listened. Around her, the other dancers stopped and the drums fell silent, but she was not aware of this. All she could hear was a great murmur, like a distant crowd coming closer.

The murmur grew louder. Suddenly she had a sense of rushing out of her own body. For a moment, she saw herself standing by the fire: a big-bellied, painted woman with sweat-tangled hair and bare feet covered with grayish dust. Then everything went black, and all at once she saw thousands of butterflies. They were blue and gold, green and crimson, beautiful beyond description; and they were all flying together in a great circle that pulsed and turned like a single, living being.

As she watched, the butterflies began to speak in sweet voices, high and clear as the voices of children. *Listen to the life inside you,* they said—only it was more like a song than words. *Your womb is the chrysalis; your child is the butterfly;* and flying toward her, they brushed her naked belly with the tips of their wings.

Marrah knew at once that this was the answer she had been seeking and that she must do exactly what the butterflies ordered. She put the palms of her hands over her belly and listened, and as she did so, she saw something strange: not a face, but *two* faces, one male and one female. The faces melted into each other as she watched, so the woman part and the man part were now one, now two; coming together and coming apart again the way she and Stavan had come together and then separated after they conceived their child.

"Who are you?" she asked.

The face that was two faces smiled. *Rely on the truth,* it said, and then it laughed a laugh that was like a second rush of wings.

"What do you mean?" Marrah said. "Please, explain. I want to do your will, but I don't understand it."

The face laughed again. It was the face of a boy and a girl, the face of a man, and a woman; it was all the faces Marrah had ever seen, and all the faces that had ever existed; and it was the face of *Mary Mackey* something else too: something with bright wings larger than the earth and sky put together.

Ride into Shambah, it said. *Ride in openly and tell no lies. Ride in and rely on the truth. Only the truth can save you.*

56 Marrah felt something invisible flutter against her lips. "I will obey!" she cried, and as she spoke, that same something lifted her and laid her down on the ground. She landed so softly that she felt as if she were sinking into a pile of wool.

After that, time passed or did not pass; it made no difference. When her sight finally returned, she found herself lying on her back under a warm sheepskin. Stavan was kneeling beside her holding her hand, the drumming had stopped, and the villagers were standing around her in a semicircle looking expectant.

"What happened?" old Klatif demanded.

Marrah tried to find her tongue but couldn't.

"Let her dry her wings first," one of the women said.

"She has a caterpillar in her throat," said another. The villagers laughed and grew happy. For the first time in many months they felt hopeful. They only had to look into Marrah's eyes to see that Chilana had spoken.

CHAPTER FOUR

Nikhan, chief of the Shubhai, sat in the main room of his fort, sprawled out on feather-stuffed cushions with his boots resting comfortably on the edge of the fire pit. He was drinking Shamban wine from the gold chalice his warriors had looted from the Temple of Chilana, and every once in a while he would belch a cloud of sweet wine fumes into the smoky air. It was past midday and he was already pleasantly drunk, but not half as drunk as he would be by nightfall.

The chalice was a fine piece of work, delicately fluted around the rim, and decorated with the myth of Chilana's perpetual resurrection. On one side, the Butterfly Goddess appeared in Her caterpillar form, the fringes of Her many legs lightly brushing the palm of a child's hand; turn the chalice slightly, and you could see Her spinning Her chrysalis; wrapping Herself in a soft bundle for Her long sleep; then finally emerging in all Her glory to dry Her wings and take flight.

The story of Chilana's transformation and rebirth was one of the great myths of the people of the north, and in the old days, before Shambah had fallen to the nomads, the children of the city had danced every spring in honor of the newborn butterflies. Dressed in short tunics of yellow and white linen and wings woven of gauze and wicker, they had laughed and tripped over one another and gobbled honey cakes, and for three whole days the city with its white-domed houses and gardens of blue and purple flowers had echoed with the sound of flutes and drums.

Today would have been the first day of the Butterfly Festival, but most of the children who had danced so beautifully only last year were now dead, as were their mothers, grandmothers, cousins, uncles, aunts, and *aitas*. Nikhan's fort was built over their bones, and the chalice itself was dented on one side and a little melted from the heat of the fire that had destroyed the temple. All along the sea coast, the butterflies were emerging on schedule, and even now dozens were fluttering over the heads of the sentries, looking for flowers that had escaped the flames, but none of the invaders had noticed this blessed event. The story depicted on the side of the chalice meant nothing to the nomads or their chief. Everything they worshipped was in the sky, not on earth, and Nikhan valued the cup only because, first, it was made of gold; and second, it contained wine.

Nikhan had come to appreciate wine although he did not have the slightest idea how it was made. Before he conquered and enslaved the survivors of Shambah, he had never had anything to drink but *kersek*, a kind of fermented mare's milk. Wine was a big improvement. He hadn't liked the taste at first, but it was a lot stronger than *kersek*, and if a man drank off a few jars, he felt the way a man should feel: warm and powerful and potent. Sometimes—although he never would have admitted this to anyone—Nikhan even felt taller.

I should always be drunk, he thought foggily as he tilted back the chalice and let the last bit of the slightly sweet liquid run down his throat. Some of the wine missed his mouth and dribbled down his chin, but he didn't notice. He stuck out a purple-stained tongue, flicked it against his teeth, and frowned as he tried to put his thoughts in order, but they kept wandering off in all directions like a herd of stupid cows. He belched and scratched his nose, and his mind cleared for a moment. "To be drunk is to be like . . . " he scratched more vigorously, "like a god! Ha!" He was very pleased with himself. "That's it. Some god brought me here. Some unnamed god, because Lord Han has never favored me in all the days of my life. Some little son-of-a-bitch god without a name has put his spirit into this stuff especially for my benefit, and tomorrow I'm going to order that second-rate son-of-a bitch diviner of mine to find out who this god is so I can sacrifice a horse to him." He knew good and well that one horse was almost an insulting sacrifice, but he hadn't brought very many horses with him, and he had no intention of marooning his warriors among savages. He might be drunk, but he wasn't that drunk. He scratched his nose some more and contemplated the riddle of the unnamed god of wine who obviously loved Nikhan of the Shubhai above all men.

This was a complex and rather philosophical concept for a warrior whose intelligence was of the crafty variety, sharpened by endless minor raids, most of which had taken place in foul weather against enemies who had already been weakened by someone else. It emerged from his brain piece by piece, and even after he had thought it, it took him a long time to grasp all the implications. When at last he did, he smiled, wiped his mouth with the back of his hand, and signaled for the slave girl to refill the chalice.

The girl was about ten years old, a pitiful, ragged, dark-haired thing with a dirty face and sores on her skinny arms. She scurried forward, clutching the delicately made Shamban wine jar as if she were terrified of dropping it, and when she looked at Nikhan her eyes were the eyes of an animal caught in a trap, but he didn't notice her any more than he noticed the individual stones in the fire pit. He was lost in the contemplation of his own genius.

A new unnamed god. Yes. By Han, why shouldn't some new god favor him? After all, he was living in a new land and everything he did was new. He had thought of things no man had ever thought of, done things no man had ever done. It was he who had realized there was more to be gained by keeping some of the savages alive than by killing all of them; he who had conceived the brilliant plan of building the fort; he who had come up with the idea of demanding tribute from the villages; he who had handed the captured weavers the wool of long-haired sheep and ordered them to weave it into the fine tunics he and his men now wore in place of the beaten felt they had brought from the steppes.

He, Nikhan, chief of the Shubhai, had personally rounded up the savage smiths and set them to work fashioning new treasures of gold and copper; he had been smart enough to see that old women held most of the power in the villages and had ordered his men to kill every female with gray hair. And while he hadn't actually invented slavery—the Hansi had taken women as slaves for generations—he had improved on it. He had realized that men could make good slaves too: men were stronger than women, and if you beat them regularly and didn't overfeed them they were as easy to control as a flock of sheep. Not one of the Motherpeople had the training or the balls to fight a Shubhai warrior hand to hand. They didn't even seem interested in revenge, the fools. What was life but revenge? It was the heart's blood of a warrior, sweeter than Shamban wine. Take his revenge against Zuhan, for instance: it wasn't complete yet, but someday it would be, and on that day, Nikhan thought, he would be a happy man.

He sat back balancing the full cup on his knee and let the spirit of the unnamed wine god fill him to the brim. Old Zuhan might be Great Chief of the Hansi, but the day the fort was completed Zuhan had forever lost the power to demand tribute from the Shubhai. Not that Zuhan knew that yet, but in time the old bastard would. Nikhan smiled at the thought of Zuhan's face when he heard that such a small, powerless tribe had rebelled. For generations the Twenty Tribes had humiliated the Shubhai and treated them with contempt, but the next time a Hansi raiding party showed up in Shambah, they were going to have a big surprise. He was going to fight them from behind the walls of this fort that he alone had had the genius to invent; he was going to order his warriors to slaughter the attackers at their leisure. The Hansi survivors—if there were any—would ride back to the steppes to report that a new, powerful chief now ruled the south, and Zuhan would be furious.

The thought of Zuhan's fury made Nikhan's smile broaden until the broken edges of his front teeth were visible. Lately he had been dreaming of a whole chain of forts stretching east and south. He would rule them all, and that would make him something entirely new; something the world had never seen before. As yet, he didn't have a name for a man who held land and power instead of cattle and horses, but he imagined it was something between a great chief and a god. The savages babbled of "priestess-queens" who governed the rich cities to the south, but those were women words and not to his liking.

Lifting the cup to his lips, he took a fresh sip of wine, rolled it around on his tongue, and drew it through his teeth with a hiss. He had reached the playful stage of drunkenness. Time for a bit of fun. For a woman, perhaps. Or two women. He liked to have them here in the main chamber, spread out on the pillows, tending to his pleasure in full view of the guards. Because he was short, there had always been rumors that he had a small penis. By the time he was twelve the other boys were all calling him "crow pizzle." Let those same boys, grown to men, see how wrong they had been. Let them see the fine spear of flesh Lord Han had given him.

He took another drink and looked around as if expecting women to appear out of nowhere without him even having to ask for them, but there was no one in sight but the ten-year-old slave girl, who was too young and too ugly for his tastes, and an awkward female creature who sat to his left with her legs crossed, playing some kind of outlandish stringed instrument, a bow-shaped thing covered with gaudily painted butterflies.

He had hardly been conscious of the music, but now he dimly recalled having requested it when he sat down to drink shortly after breakfast. What an ill-favored bitch, he thought, looking at the singer. As the woman played, tears formed in the corners of her eyes and ran down her cheeks, which might have been appealing if she had not had hair on her upper lip, and raw, reddish hands. Nikhan grunted with disgust and tried to remember if there were better-looking females in the slave pen.

The woman continued to play and cry. She was singing one of the songs traditionally sung during the Butterfly Festival, and each time she came to the name of the Goddess Chilana, she remembered the children who should have been dancing today, and she came close to breaking down and throwing her instrument to the ground. But Nikhan—who did not understand a word of Shamban—had no idea of this drama being acted out in his presence.

He yawned. The central room of the fort was warm and smoky thanks to the large fire pit in the center and the tiny hole in the ceiling—modeled on the smoke holes in the nomad tents only much farther up and not nearly so efficient. The husky contralto of the singer rose and fell like a slow wave. He tried to relax and enjoy it, but it was impossible to listen to such drivel. He wanted drums and excitement, music that made a man feel like he was having a good time. He took out his dagger and picked his teeth with the tip, wondering why the songs of the savages were always so dreary—even their love songs. Had he thought it over, he would have realized that his slaves were not likely to be in a good mood since he and his men had recently killed most of their relatives, but he was simply disappointed and annoyed.

After he had dislodged a stubborn string of meat from between his back teeth, he packed the dagger into its leather sheath, and stretched out a bony hand covered with gold rings that had been stripped off the priestesses of five nearby villages. "Enough," he said in a lazy, slurred voice that carried an edge of threat. The singer stopped immediately. Leaping to her feet like a startled goat, she bowed the way Nikhan had taught all his slaves to bow: deeply, without looking into his eyes. He appraised her for a moment and sighed. She really was a mess: swarthy with thick ankles and no breasts worth mentioning. He sighed and concluded that he wasn't drunk enough to touch her and the ones in the slave pens probably wouldn't be much better. His men had screwed most of the good-looking ones to death when they raided the villages. He would have to do something about this when he sent his warriors out to collect the summer tribute. Some of the village girls would be nine or ten by midsummer and it was time they were brought in to the fort and taught how to please a man. It was ridiculous to be drinking out of a gold cup and not have a woman in the whole camp worth screwing.

The singer, who was good at reading human faces, bit the insides of her cheeks and grasped her harp so tightly that her knuckles turned white. She knew the chief was thinking of having sex with her, and she was praying to Chilana as hard as she could that he would decide she wasn't pretty enough to take to bed. She slumped, screwed up her face, and tried to look as if she were about to pass gas. Make me ugly, she prayed. Make me disgusting. If he decides to grab me, he's going to get a nasty surprise.

She looked into his eyes and saw that he was thoroughly drunk, but when had that ever stopped a nomad? They weren't like normal men. She didn't much like to think how he would react if he actually saw her body. Kill her, no doubt; run her through immediately if she was lucky. But more likely he would do something worse, something slower.

Nikhan noticed the singer's fear and was mildly pleased. It was really beneath him to care what a slave thought, but he had spent much of his life feeling small and terrified, and it was always gratifying to remember that he was the one who now inspired terror.

"Get out," he ordered. As soon as she realized she was being dismissed, the singer picked up her harp and ran from the room as if wolves were at her heels. Nikhan chuckled. Sometimes scaring a woman was more fun than screwing her. For a moment he enjoyed the sensation, and then he dismissed the singer so completely from his mind that she would have wept with relief if she had known.

Taking another sip of wine, he relaxed. Two cups later, his head was hanging limply and he was drifting back through his childhood, his mouth slightly open, wine-colored saliva drying on his lips. In that twilight stage between sleep and waking, the wine brought back memories in long, brightly colored strings that snaked across his eyes like loose reins. He thought of red and yellow, of the smell of the steppes, of the horses' nostrils steaming in the cold. Gradually, the memories hardened and sharp edges began to appear, edges that cut sideways into his brain like blades. Without meaning to, he found himself remembering his father Brakhan. The old man had drunk too, and when the spirit of the *kersek* seized him, he turned mean. Nikhan remembered being beaten; he remembered how his father had stumbled into the tent reeking of sour milk and vomit; how he had hit anything that moved: children, women; once he'd even kicked a dog to death because it jumped up to welcome him.

He shook himself and stirred a little, and the blades of memory grew dull. Something cool blew through the room—perhaps one of the guards had opened the leather door curtain; he couldn't be bothered to look. But whatever the cause, he found himself thinking with absolute clarity, as if the wine had washed everything superfluous out of his brain. It had been his father's right to beat his family. A man owned his wives and children just as he owned his horses and cattle, and he could do anything he wanted with them, even kill them if he felt like it. Nikhan had never questioned that right, but it amused him to think that he could now beat anyone he wanted, warrior or slave. Not that he would, of course. A smart leader knew better than to humiliate his own men unnecessarily, but the point was: if he wanted to get up, go over to the guards, and knock their teeth out, he had the *power*. Even Zuhan, who had once threatened to cut off his balls if the Shubhai didn't stop scavenging after Hansi raids, even *he* would have to think twice before he insulted the new chief of the south.

He closed his eyes tighter, tilted back his head, and thought of how far he had come. Born the fifth of Brakhan's five sons, he had never been expected to live long enough to lead the Shubhai. When he was a child, his older brothers had delighted in persecuting him. They'd made fun of his bowed legs and skinny arms; his muddy complexion; his hair, which they'd claimed always looked like a badly groomed horse tail. He had been the runt, the ugly little weakling that only a mother could love. His only good feature had been his eyes: green, set beneath long, almost girlish lashes; but as he grew older he drank the whites yellow, so that by the time he was twenty, they had looked dissipated and greedy, like old grass stains on leather.

They were not entirely the eyes he deserved, for he did have a few admirable traits, if he did say so himself. Take the sequence of events that had made him chief, for example. One by one the men in his family had died, but he had had no part in killing them. First his older brothers had murdered their father, and then they had turned on one another. To be related to them was to run the risk of being thrown from a horse that had never thrown anyone before; to die suddenly of a strange stomach ailment; to be fed a poisonous mushroom by your own wife; to be found on the steppes with a Hansi arrow through your neck when there had been no Hansi sighted for months.

He'd been spared because he was too young to be worth killing, and too puny to cause trouble. Also, for some reason, he had a sense of honor his brothers lacked. No one knew why, not even he himself. It was something he'd been born with, like crooked teeth and green eyes. He was vain, ambitious, puffed up, and cruel, especially when he was drunk, but when he took an oath of loyalty, by Han, he kept it. As each of his older brothers in turn became chief, he promised to follow him faithfully, and to everyone's surprise, he never broke those promises. When the last two eliminated each other in a treacherous ambush, he had found himself chief of the Shubhai by default, oaths kept, hands unstained by the blood of his near relatives.

There were few nomad chiefs who could honestly claim not to have come to power on the back of a broken oath, and his reputation for keeping his word had won him the respect of the other warriors even though he was scrawny and not very chieflike. Of course, it helped that he had killed several enemies in battle and that he went half crazy every time someone challenged him to a fight. He had gouged out an eye or two, taken a few heads, and generally done what a man was expected to do, but his warriors knew he would kill only if he had a good reason. If you rode with little Nikhan, they told one another, you wouldn't end up with a dagger in your back—unless of course you were disloyal, in which case you would soon find yourself squirming on the end of a sharp stick.

The warriors were good judges of a man's character, especially when it concerned their own hides. Even though he was little, and ugly, and weak chinned, Nikhan had turned out to be a good chief: he made sure his men got fed; he saw that they had women whenever possible; and if there was any plunder to be shared, he never took more than his fair portion. So as he lay there, drunk and thinking over his accomplishments, the warriors who stood guard looked at him with admiration and something close to love.

The four of them had been on watch since early morning, waiting just outside the circle of firelight in case their chief needed them. All day they had stood without saying a word, barely moving except to swat at flies or lick their lips. Because of the heat, they were stripped to the waist, dressed only in boots and short wool tunics. If Nikhan had bothered to open his eyes, he could have seen the clan marks and tattoos on their arms and chests—the hawks and stars and wolves that would make them his men until the flesh fell from their bones or the skin was stripped from their bodies.

They were heavily armed—bristling with bows, spears, axes, and daggers—and if they had wanted to attack their little chief, he would not have had a chance, but since he was loyal to them, they were loyal to him. Besides, they were proud of him. Only a few months ago they had been skulking around, taking Hansi scraps. Now they were conquerors. Each of the four had a female slave to use as he wanted and two or three male slaves to order around. They were rich beyond their wildest dreams, eating meat every day, drinking Shamban wine, sleeping in dry beds, and living lives of unimaginable luxury.

Yes, by Han, their chief was a smart little bastard. Already the men were telling stories about him around the campfires: how the God of the Shining Sky had lain with his mother; how Nikhan was god made and god favored. Some said he'd just been lucky, but others insisted no arrow could strike him and no blade could pierce his flesh. Night by night, a hero story was being created with Nikhan at the center like the sun and his loyal men ranged around him like stars. In these stories, as in his own imagination, Nikhan was gradually getting taller.

The day turned warmer, the shadows lengthened, and the butterflies of Shambah floated over the ashes of the city, sucking nectar from flowers that knew nothing of war or invasions. The blue delphiniums danced in the breeze that blew off the Sweetwater Sea, and the honeysuckle opened and perfumed the air with a soft, voluptuous scent. For a time, everything was peaceful. Nikhan slept on his feather cushions, snoring softly, lost in drunken dreams of love, and power, and fine horses. His four guards relaxed, leaned their spears up against the wall, and began to eat their midday meal, putting thick slices of dried horsemeat between their lips and cutting off bits with their daggers. They chewed silently, like parents afraid of waking a restless child. On the wooden ledge that ringed the walls of the fort, the sentries stood yawning and blinking, keeping watch with the halfhearted attention of men who knew there was nothing to be seen. When they looked west over the ruins of the city, they saw only flowers and butterflies, and when they looked east toward the bar of sand that lay between the city and the sea, they saw only gulls, reeds, and sea foam blowing through the air like tufts of white wool.

Then suddenly something appeared on the horizon—something that sent the sentries crying out an alarm and putting arrows to their bows.

"Wake the chief!" they yelled.

"Ready the horses!"

"The Hansi have come back!"

"We're being attacked!"

Two had the presence of mind to run to the opening in the wooden wall and pile up logs so nothing could pass. The third ran to alert Nikhan. In an instant the chief was on his feet and ready to fight. Grabbing his spear and battle-ax, he began to yell orders. He had no need to think; no need to ask himself how a raiding party had managed to come so early in the season or why it had come at all. He had been expecting trouble the way an old dog expected a kick. Ambush was as much a part of his way of life as eating or sleeping, and as he ran toward the walls in his wine-stained tunic, he threw back his head and gave the Shubhai war cry, almost laughing as he did it, because he was finally going to meet his enemies and this time, by Han, he was going to win.

Scrambling up the braided ladder, he stood on the wooden ledge and looked out of one of the window holes while his warriors stood to one side, waiting for him to tell them what to do next. There was a long silence. Nikhan rubbed his tongue over the broken tips of his teeth and stared at five specks. They were moving in the direction of the fort, coming down the beach slowly like crabs. Horses, he thought, and the savages don't have horses, so what else can this be but the Hansi come back to claim the gold and slaves they stupidly left behind? But there's something wrong. He belched and tasted the sour flavor of wine. Five, he thought. An unlucky number. He squinted and counted the specks a third time, tolling them off on his fingers. There was no doubt about it. There were only five riders. Where were the rest? There should have been at least thirty warriors, armed to the teeth, and they should have been riding down on the fort like a pack of wolves. Were these scouts? Or did the Hansi hold him and his men in such contempt that they thought five of their warriors were worth twenty of his?

The specks grew larger and began to take on color and form. Nikhan watched the riders approach. He might be old, but his eyes were sharp and he could make out the details long before his sentries could see anything but outline. Soon he knew exactly what he was looking at. Giving a hiss of disgust and disappointment, he stepped back from the window and faced the sentries who had raised the alarm.

"You're idiots," he said, and then he began to laugh. His laugh was not pleasant even when he was truly amused, but now it had an ugly edge that made his warriors look down at their boots, swallow hard, and feel humiliated even though they did not yet understand why their chief was laughing.

They found out soon enough. Nikhan gave orders to remove the logs that had been piled across the opening in the wall. By the time that was done, the specks were no longer specks, and the shame-faced sentries could see that their so-called Hansi raiding party consisted of a man, a boy, and three women, two of whom were big-bellied and breeding.

As Marrah rode toward Shambah, the ruins of the city blossomed suddenly out of the forest like burned flowers strewn among the trunks of burned trees. The first solid thing she saw was the nomad war temple: a great, ugly box surrounded by a wall of upright wooden posts. The tops of the posts had been cut to sharp points, and brambles had been piled on them to discourage climbing. Just outside the wall, ten lopsided leather tents had been pitched in typical nomad fashion. Beyond the tents were corrals filled with goats and stolen cattle. Here and there, she could see half-wild Shubhai horses grazing on grass that had sprouted through the ashes.

She felt a peculiar sensation—not fear exactly, but a kind of intoxicating anxiety. For a moment she had the impression that she was standing still and the whole scene was floating toward them, swelling up like a bladder. She thought of all the signs of the Dark Goddess: vultures and crows and owls; the curl and hiss of poisonous snakes; white fogs and bones; and the ghostly sisters who came to call the living back to the Mother.

Now in the light of day, the advice Chilana had given them seemed simple to the point of idiocy. What if "relying on the truth" didn't work? What if her vision had not been a true vision but only a dream brought on by greasy stew and too much dancing? What if this Nikhan ordered his warriors to fill them full of arrows before they ever reached Shambah?

As they rode closer, she noticed a few miserable huts that had been built in a sad imitation of the old Shamban style. The huts were egg shaped, but neither Chilana nor any other Goddess seemed to have blessed them. No whitewashed walls shone in the afternoon sun, and no painted butterflies danced above the doors. The new huts were squalid and unadorned. Carelessly slapped together from mud and sticks, they were surrounded by fences of brambles, and even from a distance they didn't look fit to sty a pig. These must be the slave pens, she thought.

The wind began to blow, bringing a stench of excrement and sickness. Marrah breathed through her mouth, and tried to imagine what life must be like for the people who were forced to live in those huts. There was nothing she could do for the slaves—not yet. She looked at the war temple again, and then she looked at Stavan, Dalish, Hiknak, and Arang. How had they ever managed to convince themselves that they could carry off this crazy plan?

The wooden wall of the nomad fort had a narrow opening just wide enough to admit a horse. Stavan rode through boldly like a man who had nothing to fear, never once looking back. The yard was small and muddy, and from close up the war building looked poorly made, but there were armed Shubhai warriors everywhere. Marrah saw arrows pointing toward her head and spears pointing toward her heart, but she did not flinch. Stavan had warned that the slightest hint of cowardice would get them all killed.

When she and the others were inside, he sat for a moment looking at Nikhan's men as if they were bits of gristle and scraps of trash. His eyes were hard and he held his reins carelessly. Marrah had never seen him look so arrogant.

"I am Stavan, son of Zuhan," he announced. At the mention of Zuhan, the warriors looked impressed and a few lowered their spears. Others gazed insolently at Dalish, whose red tasseled hood proclaimed her a concubine. Hiknak was dressed as a concubine too, but since she had insisted on stuffing her robe so she looked more pregnant than Marrah, the two of them attracted only the indifference nomad warriors customarily displayed toward women who were breeding.

"All you all deaf?" Stavan snapped. "I say I am Stavan, son of the Great Chief of the Twenty Tribes, and I expect to be welcomed in this miserable camp. I've come to speak to your chief, Nikhan the Cowardly, and I've had a long ride and am not in the mood to explain my needs to fools. If you have no slaves, then lead these horses to water yourselves, make my wife and these women comfortable, and see that my nephew has something hot to eat. Or are the Shubhai so stupid that they do not know how to cook meat over a fire or pour out *kersek* for their betters?"

Marrah secretly made the sign of the Goddess for luck, and met the warriors' eyes with a courage she didn't feel. They were a seedy, mean-looking lot. Most bore ugly scars from past battles, and more than one had a broken nose or missing fingers or teeth filed to sharp points. They seemed more brutish and uglier than the Hansi. Their heads were partly shaved so what little hair they had stuck out like greasy horse tails, and instead of curving gracefully over their arms and chests, their tattoos were done in a peculiarly clumsy style, as if a pack of children had been let loose with hunks of charcoal. You could tell they were only a poor imitation of the Twenty Tribes, but you could also tell they were cruel and murderous. She hoped Stavan knew what he was doing.

He must have, because as he went on calling the warriors "trash" and "idiots" they became increasingly respectful. Those who had been smirking stopped smirking; and those who had looked as if they might put a spear through him, wavered. By the time he informed them in no uncertain terms that they were "bastard sons of slut

The
Horses
at
the
Gate

71

mothers," they became visibly hospitable. Finally one of the ugliest came forward and knelt on the muddy ground in front of his horse. The warrior had a great scar down one side of his face and a hawk with open talons tattooed on his forehead.

"May Lord Han bless the beast that brought you, son of Zuhan," he murmured. This must have been some sort of ritual greeting, because Stavan at once grew less abusive. Dismounting, he handed his reins to the kneeling warrior, and motioned to Marrah, Hiknak, Dalish, and Arang to dismount too. As his feet touched the ground, an amazing thing happened. All the Shubhai warriors knelt in the mud, and Marrah was treated to the sight of their shaved heads bowing respectfully.

Stavan stood with his hands on his hips, looking as if he would have kicked them had they been worth kicking. "Get up, you miserable hunks of horse shit," he said, "and take me to your cowardly chief."

The warriors got up, looking so humbled that Marrah would have laughed if she had not been worried half out of her mind, but her relief was short-lived. There was still something ugly lurking under the surface. As she stood beside Stavan and Dalish, she could smell violence in the air.

Inside the fort, Nikhan was in a dither. He tied on his sword and untied it; picked up a spear and put it close at hand, then heaved it sideways across the room with a groan of anguish. Finally he disarmed himself entirely except for one small dagger, which he concealed in his boot. He might have been brave enough to burn defenseless villages, seize slaves, and defy Zuhan (in his imagination), but the thought that he was about to face the Great Chief's son made him quiver to the tips of his boots.

Picking up a jar, he drank until the wine ran down his chin. If only this weren't happening. If only it were a mistake or this man were an impostor, but no one had to tell him one of Zuhan's sons had just ridden through the gate. Curse the long sight that let him read tattoos on a man as if they were signs of bad weather! No one but a legitimate son of Zuhan had the right to wear the Sacred Bolt of Han on his right shoulder. Only heirs of the Great Chief could display double suns on their arms or let the Horses of Heaven run across the pastures of their chests.

The little chief of the Shubhai sat down on the cushions, put his face in his hands, and moaned. There was only one reason the son of the Great Chief would ride up without bodyguards: a great Hansi war party was massed somewhere nearby, waiting to sweep down on the fort and burn it to the ground. He'd been a fool to think he could hold off the Twenty Tribes once Zuhan heard that the Shubhai were in rebellion. He remembered a story he'd heard once about how the Hansi treated traitors. He thought of his toes and fingers and how much he liked them, of his penis and how much pleasure it had given him over the years.

Self-pity swept over him and he began to sniffle and wipe his nose on the back of his hand. He didn't want to be chief of anything anymore, not even of the Shubhai. Only one thought gave him hope: this son of Zuhan had not come alone. He had a wife and two concubines with him. The wife and one of the concubines were visibly pregnant, and Nikhan had never heard of a Hansi war party that included breeding women.

For a while he sat there moaning and drinking. At last, he blew his nose on the sleeve of his tunic and straightened his belt. He thought about those big-bellied women who might, or might not, be his salvation, and prayed to the god of wine to save him, but the god of wine must have been drunk. Nikhan's prayer went unanswered. Soon he heard the clop of horses entering the fort, and a little while later he found himself kneeling in front of the son of Zuhan.

Zuhan's son looked down at him contemptuously. He was young and handsome: tall, blond, with a full beard and blue eyes so pale they looked like stones. In his ears he wore copper and gold rings marked with the signs of Han; a fine necklace of wolf teeth hung around his neck, and his upper body was covered with the old scars of some long-forgotten battle. His clothes were strangely shabby, as if he had lived in them for many months: a pair of badly stained leggings; a frayed tunic; a felt cloak that had seen better days. The three women and the boy stood behind him, but Nikhan hardly noticed them. His balls contracted with fear. He tried to say a few words of welcome and ended up gasping like a fish.

"H-honored," he sputtered.

"You should be," Zuhan's son said coldly. "I am Stavan, son of Zuhan, Great Chief of the Hansi, and now that Zuhan himself has gone to Paradise, I am his only legitimate heir, come to your miserable camp to claim hospitality on my way south."

Zuhan was dead? Did he say Zuhan was *dead?* Nikhan shook his head to clear it of wine fumes.

"Dead, *rahan?*" Roughly translated, *rahan* meant "breath of the wolf" or "son of Han," but if Zuhan's son was pleased by the title, he did not show it.

"Dead," Stavan repeated.

Nikhan had a moment of giddy delight that made his ears burn. If old Zuhan was eating dirt instead of killing his enemies and screwing their wives, then the Hansi would be fighting one another to see which subchief got to lead the Twenty Tribes. In that case, maybe there was no war party lurking in the woods. Could Zuhan's son have come south alone? He flipped his tongue against the back of his teeth and frowned. But why would a legitimate heir of the Great Chief run away from his own people?

He had the feeling that he knew something about this son of Zuhan's, something that might explain things, but he could not recall what it was. Then suddenly he remembered. Stavan! Of course! This was the crazy one—the one who they said slept with the horses, ate straw, and played with balls of wool like a child. He was god cursed and practically mindless!

Nikhan was so relieved he almost wet himself. He rose to his feet respectfully and smiled a broad, broken-toothed smile. "Welcome, *rahan*," he said. "You do honor to my humble camp. I have always been loyal to the Hansi. Everything I have is yours to command. Let me offer to shelter you, and," he smiled again, ". . . your warriors too, wherever they may be."

At that, the son of Zuhan proved himself a fool beyond all doubt, for he replied casually, as if the information had no importance, "I have no men riding with me except my nephew. He and the women and I have come south alone. I've decided to leave the life of a warrior and go to live among the Motherpeople."

Nikhan heard his guards hiss with surprise, but he kept his face a careful, smiling blank. The thought had just occurred to him that this might be a trap. Not even a crazy man would walk into a Shubhai camp and say what this man had just said. Perhaps Zuhan wasn't dead.

"And who now rules the Twenty Tribes in your place, *rahan?*" It was a touchy question, but Nikhan couldn't resist, and to his amazement the fool actually answered.

"Vlahan, my bastard brother, may the Goddess forgive him. He poisoned Zuhan and . . . " Stavan the Fool went on speaking like a man sharpening the point of the spear that would kill him. By the time he was finished, Nikhan was so thrilled by his own luck that it was all he could do to keep a straight face. He had a prize standing right in front of him that was worth more than all the plunder his men had ever taken. He would have to move cautiously, send out some scouts, make sure this wasn't a trap. If the scouts confirmed that there were no Hansi warriors lurking in the forest, he would seize Stavan, chop off his head, send it to Vlahan, and claim the reward.

The night was passing, and the wine jars were almost empty. In front of Stavan and Nikhan, the guards had spread a wooden gaming board strewn with small round stones. Arang sat beside Stavan with his eyes half closed, listening to the singer who was playing the old songs of Shambah one after another. Marrah, Hiknak, and Dalish sat in the shadows. No one spoke to them or acknowledged their presence. Dogs often got more attention around a nomad fire than women did. Tonight Marrah was happy to be invisible. She leaned her head on Dalish's shoulder and took Hiknak's hand, and the three women waited quietly.

"You play well, *rahan*," Nikhan said, smiling at Stavan.

Stavan looked at Nikhan with indifference. Picking up the gaming bones, he threw another winning combination. Nikhan gave a small sigh of despair as Stavan took three of his stones. After that, the two men played on in silence.

Around midnight, a Shubhai warrior drew aside the leather curtain, letting in a sudden rush of cold air. The warrior was dressed in a dark cloak, and his face and arms were smeared with mud. Four heavily armed guards accompanied him into the room. When Marrah saw the guards, she knew what was coming next.

Nikhan looked up from his gaming. "Speak," he commanded.

The scout bowed and said, "We have found no signs of a Hansi war party, my chief."

Nikhan toyed with one of the gaming stones, rubbed his tongue over his broken teeth, and looked thoughtful. "You're sure?"

"Yes. Sure."

Nikhan rose to his feet, and the rest of the stones clattered to the floor. "Then the game is over." He pointed to Stavan and Arang. "Seize them," he ordered.

The guards started forward, but before they could grab Arang and Stavan, Dalish stood up, pulled a dagger out from under her robe, and put it to Nikhan's throat. At the same moment, Marrah and Hiknak pulled out their daggers and pointed them at his back and crotch. Chilana had told them to rely on the truth, but She hadn't told them not to make other plans.

Nikhan started to shove them aside, but Dalish was too fast for him. She cut his throat a little—just enough to draw blood. He yelped with pain and drew back, astonished.

"Go ahead; fight us, you little bastard," Dalish said through clenched teeth. "Your people slaughtered my mother and my uncle, and my whole family, and I'd love an excuse to revenge them."

Nikhan looked so surprised that it was all Marrah could do not to laugh and spoil the effect. "On your knees!" he yelled. "What are you doing with weapons? You're women! Breeding women! Throw down those daggers and kneel, you sluts, or I'll have you all strangled."

The guards froze in midstep. Their mouths dropped open and they began to grin. The grins turned into chuckles. Sputtering and coughing, they clapped their hands over their mouths, but the more they tried not to laugh, the worse it got. The sight of their little chief held captive by pregnant women was hilarious. Nikhan turned white with humiliation. "Shut up!" he screamed, but the guards went on laughing.

"Nikhan of the Shubhai," Dalish said, "we have an offer to make you. Swear loyalty to Stavan, son of Zuhan, true Chief of the Twenty Tribes, and we'll let you live."

"Never!" Nikhan yelled. "Kill me now, you bitches! How could I live with the shame of this?" He began to moan. "I should have had you stripped and searched, you lousy sluts!" He turned on Stavan. "What kind of coward lets his women carry weapons?"

Stavan shrugged. "They aren't my women. They're their own women. Believe me, I don't control them."

Mary Mackey

"Be nice," Hiknak said, poking the tip of her dagger between Nikhan's legs. He let out another yell and tried to hop away, but he had nowhere to go except onto the points of Dalish and Marrah's daggers.

"Kill these bitches now," he screamed at the guards, "or I'll impale the lot of you!" But the guards were no longer obeying him. They looked at the big-bellied women and laughed until they were red-faced, and Nikhan knew he was lost.

"Swear loyalty to Stavan and no one ever has to know about this." Marrah pressed the tip of her dagger between his shoulder blades and thanked the Goddess her hand wasn't trembling. She knew she would never be able to kill him in cold blood, but she didn't want him to know that. "Swear, and Stavan will order your guards to keep silent."

"Never!"

"If you don't swear," Hiknak said, "perhaps we won't kill you after all." She smiled wickedly. "We're merciful. We'll just turn you out to pasture," she pricked him again, ". . . like an old gelding."

The word *gelding* decided it. Nikhan looked at the women and thought of his balls. They'd been good to him, his balls had, and now it was time to return the favor. "I'll swear!" he muttered sullenly.

And swear he did. Kneeling in front of Stavan, Nikhan, chief of the Shubhai, promised in the name of Han, Lord of the Shining Sky, to defend his new chief against all enemies; obey him in all things, and be loyal to him forever. Afterward, Stavan made the guards kneel and promise to keep their chief's secret, but Stavan might as well have saved his breath. The story was too delicious.

The Shamban singer had witnessed everything, and by the next afternoon she was singing a new ballad entitled "Nikhan and the Pregnant Warriors." It was obscene, insulting, and so funny that when Marrah first heard it, she almost laughed herself sick. In time the song became popular all up and down the coast of the Sweetwater Sea.

As soon as Nikhan informed his warriors that he had pledged himself to the son of Zuhan, Stavan became chief of the Shubhai in all but name.

"Lay down your arms," he commanded, and the Shubhai warriors laid down their arms.

"Free the slaves," he said, and they ran to open the gates of the pens.

The Shamban slaves were in bad shape. For months the nomads had thrown them scraps, beaten them, and used them cruelly. There were perhaps forty women and half as many men—all dirty and miserable and covered with lice. Many were sick and all had lost some friend or relative to the invaders, but no people were more forgiving than the Shambans or more capable of joy, and as they clustered around Marrah, laughing and weeping with relief, she knew they would somehow find the strength to rebuild their city

The Horses at the Gate

77

after the nomads left, so she laughed and wept with them and helped them build fires to warm themselves, and made sure they got the best food in the camp.

The next morning, several of the children wandered through the ruins of Shambah picking butterfly flowers. Weaving the purple and white blossoms into long chains, they twined them around their bodies, and as the adults looked on, they danced the butterfly dance. The festival had been delayed a long time, and there were no honey cakes or linen wings, but there were drums and a harp, and the adults stood around singing and clapping.

As Marrah watched the children, tears came to her eyes. Their faces were pinched, their arms were thin, and they were dressed in rags, yet they laughed and teased one another like children everywhere. With children like this, who could doubt that Shambah would rise from the ashes?

The next day, Stavan ordered the nomads to set their fort on fire, and everyone watched as it burned to the ground. The flames licked the pointed posts and consumed the brambles; they leapt through the window holes and toppled the ledges where the sentries had stood. They sighed through the room where Nikhan had drunk from the golden chalice of Chilana and turned the empty wine jars black. As the fire raged, two sheets of flame billowed out: one to the north and one to the south. Marrah stood shielding her face from the heat and watched the flames blow in the wind, thinking that they looked like the fiery wings of a giant butterfly.

When the fort was reduced to a pile of smoldering ashes, Stavan commanded Nikhan and his warriors to return to the steppes, camp along the border, and defend the Motherlands against raiders.

Mary Mackey

78

Nikhan obeyed without a word of protest. All afternoon his men rounded up their horses and packed their saddlebags. When they were finished, they slung their bows over their backs, strapped their quivers to their thighs, kicked dirt over their campfires, and rode away. By early evening, they were gone, and Shambah once more belonged to the Shambans.

BOOK TWO

The Motherlands

When I had given up hope
the Goddess gave me spring.
She put on a green shawl
and told me to dance

the buds are fat
and the twigs are red
the forest is a wall
against the wind

praise to the Goddess
who sends the gray geese flying
praise to Her
who sets the frogs to singing
praise to the Sweet Mother
who saved me from the nomads
and gave me back the laughter
I thought I had lost.

FROM "DALISH'S SONG"
BLACK SEA COAST
FIFTH MILLENNIUM B.C.

CHAPTER FIVE

The City of Shara, 4367 B.C.

On a warm morning in early summer, Marrah's grandmother, Lalah, stood barefoot on a ladder-tree outside the walls of Shara, painting one of the coils of the Great Snake of Time. The snake, which ran from house to house all along the south side of the city, was a representation of time the way the people of Shara experienced it: the past began at the tail, the present was in the middle, and the future was represented by the snake's triangular head and a red forked tongue flickering into the unknown. In the center of the city was another snake, made of blue and orange tiles, which ran all the way around the central plaza, catching its own tail in its mouth. The plaza snake was the Snake of Eternity; it represented time as it *really* was: an unbroken repetition of life after life, season after season. Every child knew that time was really circular, but every child also knew that human beings could not see it that way, so the Sharans kept both snakes to remind them.

Lalah slapped on more paint, gripped one of the branches of the ladder, and leaned back a little to admire the progress she was making. To her right, her eldest brother, Bindar, was painting away with great concentration, squinting as he applied a narrow band of yellow to the scale in front of him. The scale was not much larger than his hand, but he had been working on it for half the morning.

Lalah sighed and resisted the urge to tell him to hurry up. Bindar sat on the Council of Elders with her and had helped her govern the city for as long as she had been priestess-queen. There wasn't a man alive who had a better grasp of minute details than Bindar, but he was the slowest worker she'd ever met. He was a master potter, and his vases and libation cups were the pride of the city. There probably wasn't a better artist south of the River of Smoke, but he just wasn't the sort of person you should ask to help you repaint a wall. The Snake of Time was supposed to be finished before pilgrims started arriving for the festival of the summer moon, but at the rate Bindar was going it would be midwinter before his piece was done.

She dipped her rag in the small clay jar that hung from her belt and set to work at a furious rate, smearing green paint along the curve of the coil. She was wearing an old linen loincloth and not much else, and she liked the feeling of freedom that working half naked gave her. Her curly gray hair was tied back with a leather thong, but that had not saved it from the paint. At the moment she was sporting green spots on her breasts, her bare feet, and the tip of her nose—not to mention her hands, which looked as if she had dipped them directly into the jar.

She might have been messy, but she was accurate. The coil came to life as she progressed from top to bottom. Once she stopped to call for more paint, but for the most part she worked on with the energy of someone half her age. She was in remarkable shape for a woman entering her fifth decade: she had come into her cronedom eight years ago and had the dangling breasts of a woman who had nursed five children coupled with the sweet plumpness and round belly of a happy old age, but her arms were muscular and her toes were so strong that she easily could have clung to the branches of the ladder-tree without using her hands. As she tilted back her head to look at the wall, her dark eyes were as clear as the eyes of a child. She liked work—especially hard work. The people of Shara did not coddle their queens; they were expected to pitch in like everyone else when there was a communal task to be done.

There was always quite a bit of work to be parceled out among the seventy-two families. Shara had been a busy seaport and ceremonial center for generations. Built on the western shore of the

Sweetwater Sea, its dozen temples and hundred or so rectangular motherhouses lay between a river and a wall of granite cliffs. The city was sacred to Batal, the Snake Goddess, but Batal's snake had a tendency to fade, so this week each clan on the south side was repainting its own house, helped by those who lived in other neighborhoods. By the time they were finished, a glittering, mica-studded green and yellow serpent would run the whole length of the city, and traders who sailed up the coast would be able to see it from their boats.

As was usual on a workday, things were in a state of harmonious confusion. At the foot of the ladder-tree, Lalah's smallest grandchildren were running back and forth, bringing jars of brightly colored paint to the grown-ups and sloshing most of it on themselves in the process. To her left, her potbellied brother, Nazur, was hanging on with one hand, waving his rag, and arguing in a loud voice as Lalah's youngest daughter, Tarrah, pointed out spots that needed another going over. To Lalah's right, just beyond Bindar, cousin Inhala was working in an elegant linen shift that was going to be a complete loss by the time she finished. Inhala's lovers always spoke warmly of her, but she was rather vain and never went out of the house without dressing as if she were going to a festival. On the other hand, Inhala never cared what her lovers looked like as long as they were witty and had musical talent. Barrash, her main partner for many years, was a beetle-browed man with large, almost comic ears and the sweetest singing voice in the city. This morning he was dressed in an old deerskin loincloth that looked as if he had scrubbed out a pot with it, which, knowing Barrash, was all too likely.

The sight of Barrash made Lalah stop, paint rag in hand. A stream of green oozed down her bare arm, but she barely noticed. She liked Barrash a great deal, but lately every time she saw him, she was reminded of Arang and Marrah. That wasn't Barrash's fault, of course. She was just an old woman with too good a memory. For nearly twenty years she had thought of Barrash as Inhala's favorite partner, but since Marrah and Arang went north to Shambah, she had started to remember the days when he had been Marrah's mother's lover. Barrash and Sabalah had been inseparable in the months before Sabalah left for the west, and he had cried for weeks afterward until Inhala decided to comfort him. He was undoubtedly the man who had helped Sabalah start Marrah—not that that was a particularly important connection in Lalah's mind, but you could see a bit of Marrah in his face, especially in his eyes and the stubborn tilt of his chin.

No doubt Barrash had gotten over Sabalah long ago—or at least put her away in that part of his mind where the memories of youth are stored, but when Lalah saw him, she often thought of the daughter who had gone away and never come back, and then of the granddaughter and grandson who had done the same. Sabalah, Arang, and Marrah—three people she had loved—had left, leaving her behind to mourn. Were they dead or alive? She had no idea and no way of knowing. A dozen times over the past year, she had gone to the dreaming cave to beg the Goddess to tell her if Marrah and Arang had made it safely to Shambah, but she had always dreamed of other things: of temples that needed to be reroofed; fields that needed to be fertilized with sea grass; disputes that needed to be resolved. She wanted to dream the dreams of a mother and grandmother, but instead she dreamed the dreams of a queen.

For a moment she stood there letting paint drip down her arm as the old grief gnawed at her heart. There was no way she could have kept Sabalah in Shara. The Goddess Batal Herself had commanded Sabalah to go west. But Marrah and Arang were another matter. Lalah could have stopped them from leaving. It would have taken so little: only a word from her, only a firm "no." But she had not had the heart to say it. Marrah had been so determined. Messengers had come from Shambah to beg for help. They had said there was a terrible plague raging in the city. When Marrah heard them, she became convinced that she could cure the sickness. No doubt she had died of it instead, and Arang—who had run off to join her—had died too. By now the birds must have taken their flesh back to the Mother. Otherwise Marrah and Arang would have returned last fall as Marrah had promised.

Mary Mackey

Instead, disturbing rumors had come down from the north. For the most part they were too garbled or too ridiculous to be believed, but they fed Lalah's worst fears: Shambah had been destroyed—by a forest fire, an earthquake, or a volcano: you could take your pick. The plague had killed every living thing, even the birds. In the past two months, she had been told (by people who should have had more sense) that sea monsters had come out of the water to eat whole villages; that at night the eastern sky was full of mysterious glowing objects; that if you put your ear to the ground you could hear the Goddess Earth weeping.

Only a few weeks ago, a trader had arrived with a basket of rare herbs and dried mushrooms. He claimed he had just come from the holy city of Kataka, where the priestesses had looked into the pool of prophecy and seen the end of the world. According to him, the Katakans were burying their speaking-pottery in secret places so future generations would be able to reclaim the sacred knowledge that was about to be lost. It had come to the point where it was impossible to tell what was true and what wasn't, but there was definitely something terrible happening north of the River of Smoke.

Lalah went back to work, but her heart wasn't in painting anymore. The sun was getting hotter, and she suddenly felt all her fifty years piled up on her shoulders like stones. She bent forward, closed her eyes, and leaned her forehead against the trunk of the ladder-tree.

"Are you all right, sister?" Bindar asked.

She opened her eyes to find him staring at her, worried. There wasn't a spot of paint on him, and his linen loincloth was so white it was positively annoying.

"I'm fine," she snapped. She didn't feel like sharing her grief for Marrah and Arang or her fears about the future. Thanks to the rumors, everyone in the city was already on edge, but no one knew what to do—she least of all. There were times when even a queen had to keep her mouth shut.

Backing down the ladder-tree, she threw aside her rag, picked up one of the water jars, and took a long drink. Then she walked away from her house, removed a small section of the reed fence that separated the city from the fields, and stepped through. The fence had been built to keep animals from wandering the streets, which worked well enough for sheep and cows, but it was low and the goats were always jumping it and getting into mischief. Last week one had managed to eat most of a linen sheet and a whole basket of dried plums—basket and all—before anyone noticed. As she crossed from one side of the fence to the other, she thought for perhaps the hundredth time that she really ought to get together a work crew to make it higher.

For a moment she stood staring at the granite cliffs that lay south of the city. From here she could see the breastlike dome of the Temple of Children's Dreams, perched on a broad shelf beside the sacred hot springs where pilgrims came to bathe and be healed. Marrah had designed the temple after one she had seen on her travels, and Bindar had built it. There were a dozen temples in Shara and not one as beautiful. From here, you could just make out the snake head of Batal, but you couldn't see the designs the children had drawn in the wet clay or the prints of their little hands.

Lalah gave herself a shake. Everything was reminding her of Marrah today. Quit brooding, she ordered herself. She turned and looked back at the city. The Snake of Time was growing brighter by the moment. It had been a long while since they'd given it such a thorough refurbishing, and it was looking good, if she did say so herself.

It was never easy to get the snake into shape. There were some thirty motherhouses on the south side of the city, faced with white plaster and covered with paint and mica. Each house was a separate coil of the snake, and inside each coil a scene from the past had been painted. Anyone could work on the coils, but only artists like Bindar were allowed to touch up the murals.

The whole history of the world was there: the first coil showed the Frozen Times when ice lay over the land; the second depicted the Great Spring when the ice melted and the three Divine Sisters came to teach human beings how to plant and weave and raise animals; the third showed the city of Shara being hatched out of one of Batal's eggs. On the snake went, house by house, right down to the present. Lalah's mother and grandmother and great-grandmother and all their grandmothers before them were there: priestess-queens chosen to care for the spiritual and physical well-being of their people. They never stood alone, but always next to their brothers. The brothers had been painted to look like real people but the queens were abstract, big-hipped figures crowned by birds; their arms thrown around the necks of lions, flowers in their hair, and butter-flies in their hands. In one coil, the priestess-queens and their broth-ers danced with children; in another, they sat at the feet of their elders; here, they wove and made pots; there, they worked bare armed in the fields, gathering in the wheat. In some coils they made offerings to Batal or consulted with the Council of Elders, while in still others they knelt to knead bread or deliver babies. In Shara, a queen and her brother did not rule their people so much as serve them. They were expected to serve the Goddess Earth too and Her animals and to give their lives for them if it came to that.

Lalah stared at the tail of the snake and thought how many gen-erations it had been coiling over the houses of Shara; then she looked at the head and wondered—as she always wondered—where the snake and the city were going.

"Grandmother!" two shrill voices yelled. She looked up, mildly annoyed by the interruption, and saw ten-year-old Ranala and nine-year-old Kandar waving furiously to her from the roof of her house. The roof was flat, but they were jumping up and down much too close to the edge.

"Get down from there!" she yelled, but they were either too far away to hear or pretending to be out of earshot.

"Dogs!" Ranala was saying. She pointed to something on the other side of the house, and Kandar pointed with her.

Lalah strode toward the fence, determined to put an end to this nonsense before it ended in broken legs and necks. Dogs indeed! Probably mating. Why children always thought mating dogs were hilarious was beyond her. She pushed aside the reed fence and found complete chaos. No one—with the exception of Bindar—was still working on the snake. All along the south side of the city, people were scrambling up ladder-trees, headed for their roofs.

"Grandmother!" Kandar called again. He peered over the edge of the roof, his round little face flushed with excitement. "There's a pack of great big dogs coming up the beach and people are riding on some of them."

Lalah stopped short, and the reprimand died on her lips. "Did you say people riding on *dogs?*"

"Yes," several adults called down to her, "dogs!"

"No!" others insisted. "Look again. Those aren't dogs; they're too big. They have to be deer!" Dogs? Deer? Had everyone gone crazy at once? Lalah hurried to the nearest ladder-tree, scrambled up it, and pulled herself over the lip of the roof. She stood up and limped to the other side, thinking she was getting too old to chase hallucinations. Kandar, Ranala, Nazur, Tarrah, Barrash, and Inhala were standing in an excited clump, looking north. The grown-ups were yelling as loudly as the children.

"Look!" they cried, and they pushed her to the front so she could see better. Lalah squinted and put her hand up to shield her eyes from the glare. A big pack of animals really was moving toward the city, coming along the edge of the beach. The animals were strange: too large to be dogs and too stocky to be deer. They weren't cattle either—although that was her first thought—and there really were people riding on the backs of some of them.

The
Horses
at
the
Gate

Suddenly she knew what she was looking at. She dropped her hand and stood listening to the others jabbering excitedly, and a feeling of terror came over her. These had to be the beasts called "horses" that Marrah had told her about before she left for Shambah. The prophecies were coming true, and she was the only one who knew it because she was the only one who had ever seen a horse. It had not been a real horse, only a small copper pendant as thin as a fingernail, but the likeness was unmistakable. The beastmen had arrived.

Her first impulse was to turn and run for safety, but then she remembered who she was. A priestess-queen of Shara did not panic; she took care of her children no matter what. Lalah tried to gather her wits and assess the situation. There were at least a dozen horse-beasts but only a few riders. The beasts themselves didn't look dangerous. In fact, she'd bet they ate grass like cows.

She raised her hand, made a hole in her fist, and looked through it. The riders came into sharper focus. They were closer now: three women; two men. The sight of the women reassured her. She frowned and bit her lip. There was something familiar about one of those women—something about the way she held her head. One of the men looked familiar too.

The riders forded the river in the usual place, turned inland, and headed straight for the city, driving the extra beasts in front of them. The man who came first had strange yellow-white hair the color of an old bone; so did the smallest of the women. The other three looked more or less ordinary, except that one of the women was obviously pregnant. Lalah stared at the pregnant woman's belly and breathed a sigh of relief. Then she looked up at the woman's face and a thrill ran through her. It can't be, she thought. I'm making this up. That woman can't possibly be . . . Suddenly she gave a whoop of joy that startled everyone around her.

"Marrah!" she yelled. "Barrash, Tarrah, look! It's Marrah, and that has to be Arang riding behind her!" By now, other people had recognized the two and were taking up the cry, but Lalah did not stop to listen. She ran to the far side of the roof, heaved herself over the edge, and scrambled down the ladder-tree so fast that it was a miracle she didn't break her neck.

She never remembered later if she ran through the city or around it. She only knew that suddenly she was running across the pasture and the horse-beasts were running toward her. If she had had any sense she would have realized that she was in danger of being trampled, but she was too happy to care, and the Goddess and luck were with her. She heard the clop of the beasts' great feet as they passed by. Marrah and Arang were calling to her to be careful, but she went on running. The riders brought their beasts to halt, throwing up clods of mud. The creatures reared and pawed at the air with black hooves that looked as hard as stone. Without a moment's hesitation, Lalah ran beneath them and pressed her body against the huge, heaving side of Arang's animal. The smell of its sweat filled her nostrils. There was another odor too: strange and sweet and unfamiliar. She grabbed at Arang's legs and hugged them as if she intended never to let go. Then she ran to Marrah and hugged her legs too, and when she looked up she saw for certain that Marrah was huge with child and filled with the blessings of the Goddess.

"Grandmother," Marrah said, and she was laughing and there were tears streaming down her face. She climbed off her beast slowly, lowering herself to the ground with the clumsy grace of a woman carrying a child. Taking Lalah in her arms, she hugged her. Arang hugged her from the other side, and they all laughed together like fools.

Lalah pressed her body against Marrah's big, taut belly. She took Arang's face in her hands and kissed him and he kissed her back. By the time they were done, the three of them were smeared with green paint.

Lalah looked at the dabs of paint on Marrah's upper lip and the streaks on Arang's chin. Untying her belt, she slipped off the paint jar and held it out to them as if it were a libation cup. "Welcome home, my darlings," she said.

Sometimes as you are riding the Great Snake of Time, She twists Her divine body and you slip from one coil to another and return to your own past. For most people, these moments are over so quickly they seem like dreams, but as Marrah rode into Shara, she experienced something rare and wonderful: the world she had left behind was going on as it always had. The paths of white gravel were still lined with flowers; the roses of Batal's sacred city still climbed onto the roofs of the motherhouses, and the clan signs painted on the walls looked fresh and cheerful. In the central plaza, the Snake of Eternity whirled in its unbroken circle of peace, and as Marrah passed the modest, two-story temples, she could see the sacred bread ovens built like the bellies of pregnant women, the looms weighted with stones carved into the shapes of animals, and the piles of clay jars and figurines waiting their turn in the kilns just as they had waited on the day she left.

The city even smelled of peace. In Shambah, ashes had stung their eyes every time the wind blew, but here the breezes off the Sweetwater Sea carried the scent of salt and jasmine. She could smell bread baking and stews that had been left in the ashes to keep warm while families worked on repainting the south wall. From time to time a puff of sweet incense drifted out of one of the temple doors as if the only smoke the Sharans knew was the smoke of offerings to the Goddess Earth.

Here was a city built on the proposition that human beings were made to live in harmony with one another and with all the other living things around them. There was no fort beside the river, no refuge carved into the cliffs, no walls except a flimsy fence of reeds to keep out animals. When you came to Shara by land, it opened its arms to you like a mother, and when you came by sea it showed you its Great Snake to let you know that any stranger was welcome.

As Marrah looked from familiar face to familiar face, she saw nothing but innocent expectation. Since the Sharans had never seen mounted warriors, they did not run screaming as soon as they caught sight of people on horseback. They loved animals, and as they crowded around Marrah and Arang to welcome them home, they marveled at the strange and wonderful beasts who were kind enough to carry people on their backs. Children reached out fearlessly to pet Marrah's mare, and adults stroked her horse's short mane as if it were human hair.

The Sharans found Stavan and Hiknak fascinating too—having never seen blond hair and blue eyes before—and they gaped at the tattoos on Dalish's face as if they could not quite believe their eyes, but it was the horses that really caught their fancy. For some reason, the horses made people laugh. The Sharans stared at their big yellow teeth and inspected their hooves, and when they peered under the tails of the stallions they whistled with astonishment.

"What big balls they have!"

"How gentle they seem!"

"Don't your asses get sore?"

"I bet it feels good to have a beast like that between your legs!" This comment was accompanied by a raucous laugh. Marrah looked down and saw cousin Inhala grinning up at her. Inhala was dressed as elegantly as ever. At her side was Barrash, who looked as if he were wearing the same old sandals and clay-stained loincloth he'd had on a year ago.

"Not half as good as a man," Marrah called back.

The crowd roared with laughter.

"What did you do to this one to turn his hair white?" Inhala yelled, pointing at Stavan.

"She gave me a whole lifetime of love in a single night," Stavan called back. People were amazed to hear him speak Sharan. They stood in stunned silence for a moment and then laughed so hard that a few had to sit down to catch their breath.

"Blessings on all of you!" Dalish cried. She was almost beside herself with joy. "Blessings on this city and the Goddess Batal, who guards it!"

Marrah looked back at Hiknak. The little nomad, who understood barely a word of Sharan, was staring at the flowers and the motherhouses with wide, delighted eyes. Marrah remembered that this was the first city Hiknak had ever seen—unless you counted Shambah, which had not been much more than a pile of rubble. Hiknak seemed particularly taken by the women who crowded so boldly around the horses. Back in the steppes, they would have been forced to wait at a respectful distance until the men of the camp had greeted the visitors and determined if they were hostile. They would have worn shawls draped over their faces, lowered their eyes, and never dared speak out; but in this place women and men were obviously on an equal footing, and as Hiknak watched them jostling elbow to elbow for a better view, a smile of approval crept over her face. It was a triumphant smile, as if Hiknak was thinking that at last she had found a good place to be a woman.

The Sharans loved any excuse for a party. Marrah and Arang—whom they had given up for dead—had returned, which meant music had to be played, wine jars had to be unstopped, and a feast of gargantuan proportions had to be cooked and consumed. The repainting of the Snake of Time came to an abrupt halt, and people ran around busily pulling things out of storage jars, skewering meat onto spits, and chopping vegetables.

Cooking was considered a sacred skill, much loved by the Goddess Earth, and the cooks of the city were some of the best. All afternoon men and women worked side by side in the motherhouses, turning out one delicacy after another. They made pigeons in green sauce with honey, aromatic leaves, and vinegar; they cooked up wheat porridge with pork rind, garlic, olive oil, and ground herbs. Red mullet was smeared with lovage, rue, and crushed pine nuts and roasted over coals; whole fish were coated with salt and coriander, sealed in clay, and simmered until they made their own delicious sauce. Patties of chopped prawns and squid were fried in pork fat on stone griddles; steamed string beans and chickpeas were tossed together and flavored with oil, salt, and red wine. There were lentils with chestnuts; salads of boiled leeks; beets with mustard; piles of steamed greens.

And the sweets, ah the sweets! Marrah's mouth watered for weeks afterward at the thought of them: fried bread dipped in honey and covered with thick cream; rolls filled with sweet cheese; custards fortified with eggs; ropes of batter dipped in honey and chopped nuts; dried apples poached in red wine; and of course bowls of the curdled goat milk the Sharans loved, whipped with chopped cherries, sweetened with figs, and scented with rose water.

She ate and ate and then she ate some more, and as she ate, she laughed and talked and kissed old friends. She marveled at how much Ranala and Kandar had grown in the months she had been gone, and she let two of the old family dogs rest their heads on her belly while she scratched them behind the ears.

It was a perfect night, one that made her feel as if she had never left. Because the weather was mild, they sat in the central plaza on reed mats and cushions, seventy-two mother families packed elbow to elbow. As usual, everyone talked at the top of their lungs, stuffed their mouths with food, and carried on good-natured arguments while the children ran laughing and snatching up handfuls of fried sweets. No one asked Marrah where she had been or what had happened to her since she left for Shambah, so she was spared having to tell them anything that would have cast a pall over the party. It was not polite to interrogate people when they first arrived. There would be plenty of time for that tomorrow. For now, all she had to do was eat, rest, and receive congratulations on her pregnancy as one person after another came up to rub her belly for luck and wish her well. Seeing that Hiknak was pregnant too, they also tried to rub her belly, but Hiknak shrank back, frightened.

"What are they doing?" Hiknak asked Marrah.

Marrah ate some more fried bread and sighed with contentment. "Don't be afraid. They're just blessing you in the name of the

Goddess Earth. All pregnant women are sacred to the Goddess. My friends and relatives believe the two of us have brought the city good fortune and an easy harvest, and they want to thank us."

Hiknak smiled and relaxed. She took a drink of sweetened milk and wiped the white mustache off her upper lip with the back of her hand. "A pretty custom. Where I come from, no one honors pregnant women. They're expected to go on working until the day they give birth. As for strangers, they're usually treated more like enemies than guests. Tell them thank you."

Marrah translated, and the well-wishers smiled. One of the women reached out and touched Hiknak's hair. Her name was Jutima, and Marrah recalled that Jutima was a woman who loved women.

"So soft," Jutima said, stroking Hiknak's hair. "Like gold and fur intertwined. Does your friend have a permanent partner, or is she free to share joy with whomever she wants?"

"What did she say?" Hiknak demanded.

"She wants to know if you'd like to make love with her."

Hiknak turned bright red. She looked flattered and scandalized. "Tell her I belong to Arang and that he'd beat me if I slept with anyone else." She looked around apprehensively, but Arang was nowhere in sight.

"I won't tell her any such thing. In this city you belong to yourself, and Arang would never dream of hurting you if you wanted to share joy with Jutima. He might be upset because people sometimes do get jealous, and you'd certainly have to talk to him about it, but he'd never, *never* hurt you. The very idea is preposterous. If anyone so much as slaps a pregnant woman, they're cast out of the city."

It was sad to see how much trouble Hiknak had believing this.

"What did your sweet friend say?" Jutima asked.

Marrah took Hiknak's hand and patted it reassuringly. "I think you had better give her time to get used to our ways before you ask again," she told Jutima.

There was an awkward moment as Jutima apologized and Marrah tried to reassure her that no harm had been done, and then their conversation was interrupted by a sudden burst of drumming. The flutes took up the rhythm, the harps began to play, and all at once Arang appeared, dressed in a linen loincloth. His body was oiled, his long hair was plaited with feathers, and he wore a long green and yellow scarf wound snakelike around his head.

As the music swelled, people began to clap and sing. Arang stood uncertainly in the center of the plaza, looking from one face to another. He seemed to be overwhelmed, and for a moment it looked as if he had decided not to go on with the performance.

"Dance for us!" people cried. "Dance for us the way you used to, Arang!" They picked up their mats and pots, gathered together their children, moved back, and made room for him.

At last, Arang smiled, reached up, and uncoiled the scarf. Slowly, he began to move to the beat of the drums. He had not danced in a long time, and at first he seemed nervous, but soon he caught the rhythm and relaxed. His hips moved like a snake, his arms coiled and uncoiled, his feet flew. Twirling the scarf, he made it writhe around him like a living thing. The scarf became a circle and then an undulating line; it became a partner and a lover. Arang arched his back, stood on his hands, and did somersault after somersault; he leapt into the air and came down as lightly as a bit of thread.

He danced for a long time, and as he performed Marrah thought with pride that her brother was one of the best dancers she had ever seen. This was the man whom Vlahan had once beaten for dancing; the man whom the nomads had tried to turn into a vicious, coldhearted warrior.

That night Marrah slept in her grandmother's house, curled up under a soft linen sheet with her body pressed against Stavan's, and in the morning the baby kicked her awake, dancing like its uncle Arang.

The following afternoon, Arang and Marrah appeared before the Council of Elders to tell the story of their journey to Shambah. It was a moment they had both been dreading, so Stavan came along to give them courage and add his story to theirs.

The day was hot, so the council met outside under a blue linen canopy embroidered with snakes. From where she sat, comfortably installed on a pile of pillows, Marrah had a good view of the white sails of the *raspas*—those swift boats that brought trade goods to the city from as far away as the Sea of Blue Waves—and as she looked out across the water she thought how peaceful it all seemed, and she longed to keep her mouth shut.

The elders arrived in twos and threes, poured themselves cups of blackberry juice, and settled down to listen. There were nine: four men and five women, elected by lot every three years except for Lalah and Bindar, who were permanent. They ranged in age from forty-five to eighty, and Marrah knew all of them well. During the years she had spent in Shara, she had wiled away many afternoons sitting at their feet listening to them sing memory songs: Ulitsa was a composer of ballads and a fine harpist; Chemtar had taken her out in the woods and helped her learn the local herbs; Shantar had shown her how to read the sacred script; Uncle Bindar had taught her how to make passable ceramics; Walisha was head priestess of the Owl Temple; Yintesa still hunted in a small way—mostly snaring rabbits—even though she must be well over sixty; Blentsa spent much of her time caring for her grandchildren; and Dakar, the oldest, was Keeper of the Men's Rites. They were smart, compassionate, and stubborn; and it comforted her to think there was not one who was not equal to any emergency.

They usually met in a casual way at least two or three times a week to plan festivals, settle disputes, and do whatever else had to be done to govern the city, and the meetings were famously long, so in order not to waste time, they wove reed hats while they debated. When all nine had arrived, Lalah went from elder to elder passing out bundles of split reeds, and everyone set to work except Dakar and Blentsa, whose fingers were too stiff.

Over the years, the seriousness of a particular issue had come to be measured in how many hats were made before it was solved: goats wandering through the streets were a one-hat problem; allocation of the fields to the mother clans was always at least two hats; while something simple like who was responsible for picking up the trash after a big festival was half a hat at most.

This particular council meeting became famous in the memory songs as the Meeting of a Hundred Hats—not that a hundred hats were actually woven that afternoon, but because it was so traumatic for everyone involved. Right at the outset it nearly degenerated into chaos. Marrah began by telling the story of how she and Arang arrived at Shambah to find it in ruins, but she had barely started before the elders interrupted her with cries of horror.

"Shambah burned!"

"Its people slaughtered!"

"Its children murdered!"

Some dropped their reeds and rose to their feet, while others stared in disbelief.

"What kind of people are these?" Bindar demanded. "Are they cursed or crazy or both?" He pointed to Stavan. "Explain. Why do your people kill? Are they human, or are they the ghosts of rabid dogs? What is this disgusting thing they've brought into the world?"

Stavan flushed and bit his lips. He looked at Marrah, and she nodded for him to speak freely. "It's called 'war,'" he said, "and to my shame it's been the Hansi way of life ever since we tamed the horses."

"It's nothing but organized slaughter," Shantar snapped. He spat on the ground and made a sign to ward off evil. "This 'war' as you call it is murder dressed up with a fancy name."

"Your people are thieves!" Walisha yelled.

"They're vile!" cried Yintesa.

Stavan tried to speak, but they wouldn't let him.

"Anyone who lays violent hands on a child should be buried alive!" mild-mannered Blentsa hissed.

"May the snake-haired mother spirits torment your people while they live and the Goddess refuse to take their souls when they die," said Walisha, and she fingered the little bone goddess that hung from her neck as if she'd be only too happy to cast the spell.

"Not even a wolf pack kills *all* the deer," Yintesa said, turning on Stavan with the fury of a hunter who sees an animal taken without proper thanks. "You nomads must be completely insane."

Lalah put up her hand. "Silence," she commanded. "You're blaming him, and he isn't to blame. Stavan is our guest, and he's Marrah's lover. She's said she's going to make him the *aita* of her child, and I won't have you pile all the sins of his people on him. It isn't fair. As far as we know, he's done nothing wrong."

She turned to Marrah. "I think it would be better if *you* explained why the nomads burned Shambah. Surely they could have had all the gold in the city without killing anyone. The priestess would happily have handed over the temple adornments rather than see a single human life lost."

"The nomads didn't come just for gold," Marrah said. She took Stavan's hand and held it, defending him against the hostile stares. "They want to own the earth—and to own land, you have to take it away from the people who are already using it."

"Own Her?" several people cried. "The Goddess Earth can't be owned."

"That's what we believe, but the nomads believe their gods gave them the right to own Her and every living thing on Her, including the wild animals, cattle, horses, and their own women and children.

They own cattle they never eat, horses they never ride, goats they never milk. They're great believers in owning things."

Everyone was silent for a moment. The idea of owning things you never used just for the sake of owning them was hard to understand. In Shara people owned many small personal items, but everything important like fields and boats and temple adornments belonged to everyone.

Finally Lalah spoke. "You say the men believe they own the women? Then no wonder they invented this thing called 'war.' How can there be any peace between strangers when there is no peace at home? You'd think they'd have had enough sense to see that once men and women started fighting each other there would be no end to it." She paused and frowned. "How do you think this stupid idea of owning women came about?"

"I don't know," Marrah admitted. "Sometimes I think it's because they move around so much. When you're always on the move, pregnant women and small children slow you down. Perhaps the men came to think of their families as burdens rather than blessings—as property that had to be lugged around like a tent or a cooking pot. But there has to be more to it than that. When I lived with the Hansi, I often had the feeling that they had confused women with horses; everyone believed women had to be mastered and broken, even the women themselves, I'm sad to say. Horses aren't like people, you know. One stallion will run off all the other males and keep a whole herd of mares for himself. But I think there may be another reason, something darker we'll never quite understand, some grief that rests at the center of their souls. The Sea of Grass isn't an easy place to live. It's hot beyond belief in the summer and terribly cold in winter. There aren't any trees and not much water. I think maybe the nomads feel the Goddess Earth hates them. They feel She has abandoned them, so they act like little boys act who have been abandoned by their mothers: they treat women badly out of spite and a desire for revenge."

Lalah nodded. "That makes sense, but it still doesn't explain how the men came up with the idea of owning the women, much less why the women ever acquiesced to such a thing."

Marrah shrugged. "I wish I could tell you how it all started, but their memory songs don't even mention it."

Stavan nodded. "That's true," he said.

"All I know," Marrah continued, "is that nomad men and women hate and fear each other, and they teach that fear and hatred to their children." She spoke slowly, wanting to make it all make sense, but of course it didn't. "There's some connection between hating the Mother Earth and hating women; some connection between hating women and all the killing.

"The nomads say the earth is not a goddess and does not have a soul. The land under their feet is just dirt as far as they're concerned, a place of suffering, a platform to stand on. They believe everything sacred is in the sky. They say the stars are eternal, that the heavens never change, that change is a sign of corruption instead of a sign of growth. They say the gods are all men who live in the sky and that if you are brave and kill a lot of people, you get to join them in a place called Paradise after you die—unless, of course, you're a women. The sky Paradise is too good for women."

Everyone looked completely confused.

"What does the sky have to do with it?" Walisha asked. She pointed to the ground. "Everyone knows it's the Mother under your feet who counts."

"Mothers have no honor in that land." Marrah wondered how many times she would have to repeat this before they believed her.

Bindar frowned. "I know you said the nomad men hate women, but surely you aren't telling us they hate their own mothers? These men must have been children once, and their mothers must have nursed them and comforted them the way all mothers do."

"Stavan can tell you more about what it's like to be a nomad child than I can," Marrah said, "but you'll have to give him a chance to finish what he has to say before you all start yelling at him."

"Let him speak," Lalah said. She gave the council a stern look. "And this time I will see that he's not interrupted."

"Thank you." Stavan paused and looked at the elders. Marrah saw pride in his eyes and a little anger, but when he spoke his voice was low and reasonable. "My people do indeed love their mothers when they're young, but as they grow older they're taught not to respect women. In the Sea of Grass, men are ashamed to admit they love any woman—even the one who bore them. Love is considered a weak emotion, not worthy of a warrior who must learn to kill without flinching and slaughter his enemies without guilt or regret. The Hansi have a saying: 'Love is a madness that makes a strong man weak.'" He reached out and put his arm around Marrah. "I understand that saying because I used to be a Hansi warrior, and I too was once ashamed to feel anything but anger. But now I am proud to stand here in front of all of you and say how much I love Marrah and the child she is carrying."

Dakar had been sitting during this discussion. He had a disease of the joints that made it painful for him to stand. He was in his eighties, and as he slowly helped himself up with the aid of a stick, everyone fell silent. He cleared his throat and stood for a moment looking at Stavan and Marrah. His face was crisscrossed with wrinkles and his hands shook slightly, but he had great dignity. He was the oldest man in the city and, as Keeper of the Men's Rites, the most respected.

"My mother died fifty years ago," he said, "and every day for fifty years I have missed her. A mother is one of the greatest blessings a man has. I would give my right arm to hear my mother's voice again and the sight of my eyes just to feel her touch." His voice broke and he stopped, and the room was so quiet that Marrah could hear Stavan breathing beside her. "A man who doesn't love his mother and his *aita* can't love anyone." He looked at Stavan and shook his head. "If your people weren't so violent, I'd pity them. Bindar was right: they're both crazy *and* cursed, and in the name of the Goddess who heals all, I salute you for running away from them."

He turned and propped his stick up against one of the posts of the canopy. "We haven't been kind to you today or even polite," he continued. "In fact, I think we all have to admit that we've insulted you. On behalf of the Council of Elders, I want to apologize for those insults." He put his trembling hands together in the sign of the Goddess. "Welcome to our city, Stavan the nomad. May our families become your family; may the Mother of All become your mother; and may you live a long and happy life among us."

Dakar's blessing was not the end of the council meeting, but it set the tone for all that came after. By the time the moon rose over the Sweetwater Sea, the elders had heard Marrah's entire story and had more reason than ever to hate nomads, yet when they disbanded, every one of the nine came forward and kissed Stavan formally on both cheeks.

"Welcome to Shara," they said, and they embraced him as if he were one of their own.

It was a good thing Stavan felt welcome in the city, because over the next few days Marrah had very little time to help him settle in. Two nights after the council meeting, she went into an early labor, probably brought on—the midwives said—by riding so far on horseback. As soon as her waters broke, her grandmother and aunts led her to the temple where children came into the world.

Marrah had been to the birthing temple many times before to help other women have their babies, and she knew it well. It was a small, cheerful place: the walls and floor were plastered in smooth red clay and decorated with the zigzags and spirals of the Waters of Life, out of which all life came. On the ceiling, all the auspicious animals watched over the mother-to-be: frogs and hedgehogs; storks; herons; rabbits; fish; deer; dogs; and, of course, snakes, so that when she looked up, she saw an entire menagerie staring down at her, wishing her luck.

The temple had been designed with convenience in mind. There were shallow gutters around the sleeping platform so that everything could be kept clean, large jars of fresh water, a brazier that held a pot of warm broth and another pot of hot water for herbal teas, and even a screen in case Marrah wanted privacy. But the most important object in the room was the birthing stool. The stool had been used by the women of Shara for generations. When the time came for the baby to be born, Marrah would sit on it and lean back into the arms of her grandmother, spreading her thighs as wide apart as possible. One of the midwives would sit on a very low stool in front of her to receive the child. Marrah would push when they told her to push, and when the time was right, deliver her baby through the vulva-shaped opening in the seat. The Sharans called the stool the Gate of Life, but the real gate of life, the midwives assured Marrah, was the mother herself.

Since this was her first child, her labor was long and at times painful, but there was a certain ecstasy to it too. Most of the time, she just wanted to get the whole thing over as fast as possible, but at other moments she felt almost blissful. All night and well into the morning, the midwives bathed her forehead with warm water, rubbed her belly with scented oils, and encouraged her to try to relax as much as she could. Sometimes they broke into chants of praise to the Goddess, and sometimes they simply stood back and let Marrah do what her body was telling her to do. They were old hands at birthing, having ushered hundreds of children into the world, and they watched Marrah closely, making her walk up and down between contractions, and feeding her a special strengthening broth made from beef bones and herbs.

"We think you're going to have a surprise," they told her. And when she asked nervously if there was anything wrong, they laughed and told her to take heart, that she was as healthy a woman as had ever birthed a child and the Goddess had a special gift for her.

To Marrah's astonishment, the gift turned out to be an extra baby. Just before midday, the midwives led her to the birthing stool, and there in quick succession she gave birth to twins: a squalling baby girl with brown eyes and hair as dark as her own, and a quiet boy with hair the color of wheat and eyes like chestnuts.

The babies were small but vigorous and perfectly formed, and as she held them to her breasts, letting them suck for the first time, she saw that they were different from other children. Part of her was in them and part of Stavan too. They were born of the nomads and the Motherpeople, and as she kissed them, and took their tiny fingers in hers, and felt the softness of their bodies, she prayed that somehow there would be peace between the two.

It was not customary to name children until the first month of life had passed, but when the twins had spent four weeks sucking and growing fat and healthy, Marrah named the girl Luma after one of Stavan's sisters (actually, the sister's name had been Luminkak but that was too much of a mouthful). The boy she named Keru after one of her great-uncles, and as she had promised, she asked Stavan to be the *aita* of both children, even though it caused something of a scandal.

"Your brother Arang should be your children's *aita* as is our custom," several people informed Marrah indignantly, "and not some beast-riding, nomad stranger." But Marrah didn't see why it was anyone's business, and Lalah agreed.

"We have always believed a woman has the right to make any man she wants the *aita* of her child," Lalah said. "So as queen of this city, I'm ordering all of you to get your noses out of Marrah's affairs." She made this speech in public during the festival of the summer moon so that everyone in the city heard it. After that, if anyone thought Stavan shouldn't be an *aita* because he was a nomad, no one said so—at least not to Marrah's face.

As for Arang, he was perfectly happy that Marrah had asked Stavan to be responsible for Luma and Keru. Hiknak had promised to make him the *aita* of her child, and three babies would have been too much responsibility for a man who had been a man for less than a year.

The summer passed quickly, and the twins grew fat on Marrah's milk. Not long after the fall equinox, Hiknak gave birth to a little girl, whom she named Keshna. Like Luma and Keru, Keshna was a mix of north and south. Her hair was brown, but in the right light it had a reddish tint no one had ever seen before. Her skin was a soft tan color, and her eyes were as black as the sky on a moonless night. She was an exceptionally beautiful baby, but the most remarkable thing about her was her fearless disposition. Keshna seemed to have inherited Hiknak's wild streak, and as soon as she could crawl she had to be watched all the time so she didn't tumble down a flight of stairs or dump a pot of boiling soup over herself. She almost never cried like other children did when strangers took her in their arms, and even loud noises didn't frighten her.

Marrah thought privately that Keshna was born to be a warrior, but she said nothing to Hiknak. Instead she prayed that the Hansi would go on fighting among themselves, and that Nikhan would keep his promise and defend the Motherlands from raiders. She wanted Keshna, Luma, and Keru to grow up in a world where war did not exist and the word *warrior* made no more sense than the barking of dogs; but already in the steppes, forces were at work that would bring the nomads west again.

CHAPTER SIX

The Ukrainian Steppes, 4367 B.C.

Gather up bitter mushrooms and put them in your mouth. Gather up sacred mushrooms from shit and decay. You are Changar the great Hansi diviner, Changar who should be dead. You are Changar who survived the fall into Zuhan's grave; Changar whose back was broken, Changar whose legs were shattered; Changar who can walk only in dreams and visions; Changar who has the green eyes of a wolf; Changar whose eyes frighten Vlahan; Changar who hunts in the dream world.

Sometimes when you eat the sacred mushrooms, you can see skulls and bones. Sometimes you can see death. You can see the dust that will fill your mouth someday and the dust that will fill Vlahan's mouth and the mouths of all your enemies, but it isn't death you are looking for. You are looking for the witch who took your legs. You are looking for Marrah.

Your apprentices feed the mushrooms to you, chanting as they place them on your tongue. The mushrooms look like shriveled flesh, they look like dried balls, they look like the shit they sprang from. Your apprentices bring you a she-goat trussed with leather thongs; they bring you a woman—a slave girl of no account; they bring you fire and incense and fermented mare's milk.

All night long you lie with the woman. You grab her hair, pull back her head, and enter her mouth; you spread her legs and enter her body. She cries out, but you are deaf. Her face melts and twists into something not human. You see her mouth opening and closing like a black circle. Inside her is something you want and will have. It isn't the thing an ordinary man would want from a woman. It is not sex you're seeking, but power. You know the woman carries power in her womb, and you will take it. You will penetrate her; you will suck out that power, taste the sick-sweet flavor of woman things. You will soil yourself with it, ride it like a dirty path; and at the end of that path you will find Marrah, whom you hate more than any man has ever hated a woman. Marrah, the witch. Marrah, the one who took your legs.

The bitter mushrooms make you potent. Your penis rises up as hard as a spear. You take the slave woman again and again; you watch her twist under you like a snake.

"Now!" you cry.

The apprentices pick up the she-goat and carry it to where you lie. They lift it over the two of you and slit its throat with a bone-handled dagger. Goat blood drips down on you like rain. It covers you with a warm, red soup as if you were an unborn child. You roll in it and your naked body sticks to hers. The power of women is in blood, but you know how to take that power and make it your own.

You are Changar.

Before your eyes, the future unfolds in blood. This vision is for you alone. It comes from the Land of Things to Come, from the Forbidden World that only diviners are permitted to enter. If you tell Vlahan, your chief, what you have seen, he will have one of your own apprentices sacrifice you to Han. You feel the cord of sacrifice tightening around your throat; you see the ravens circling. If you want to live, you must hold these secrets deep inside you in a place as dark as the mouth of the woman who twists under you. But you ride the blood. You taste it. You know.

The slave woman tries to get away, but you pin her down and suck the breath from her mouth. You won't kill her. Once she has lain with you, she is more than a woman: she is a path.

As you breathe her breath mixed with the rank smell of goat blood, the gods give you one last vision. You see a man coming to Vlahan's camp, riding east through the tall grass. You give a cry of triumph and push the bloody woman off the bed. She lies curled up on the dirt with her hands around her knees, shaking and moaning, but you no longer see her.

The last of the goat blood drips down on your shoulders. The sacred mushrooms blossom in your head and the pupils of your eyes spread until they are as large as the tips of your little fingers. You know now that it doesn't matter whether Vlahan believes you. A warrior will come east with a message. Years will pass before he arrives, but when he does, you will be waiting for him. He's a greedy man, hungry for gold, a liar who's betrayed his chief, but you intend to make sure that Vlahan doesn't have him killed because this is the messenger who will lead you to Marrah.

For an instant you see a boy's face floating in the blackness behind your eyes. He is an infant with hair the color of dried grass and eyes as brown as acorn shells.

"You are going to be mine," you whisper, and you reach out with one bloody finger and put your invisible mark on his forehead.

One night three years later, when the high feathered grasses of the steppes were tossing in the wind and the stars were veiled by dust, Vlahan sat in the Great Chief's white tent eating toasted seeds and spitting the hulls into the fire. The tent, which was decorated with red and yellow sun signs, was the same tent old Zuhan had lived in for so many years, and it was pitched along the banks of Zuhan's favorite river, but ever since Zuhan died, the river had been shrinking. By now it was only a trickle, and when Vlahan stopped chewing he could hear the wind rushing over the stones, whipping up whirlwinds of dust. Every time the tent flap opened, he saw the wind blowing trash and bits of dry grass in all directions; it blew the women's shawls aside too, and spooked the horses. It was an evil wind: a wind that had brought four years of drought and rebellion, and Vlahan hated it from the bottom of his soul.

As he ate, Vlahan looked at Changar, who was sitting with his feet propped up on a cushion, drinking *kersek* and staring into the fire with half-closed eyes. They were not the eyes of an old man dozing in the warmth, although Changar's hair had turned the color of winter grass and the flesh on his face looked spotted and unhealthy. They were green, wolflike eyes, and there was something more; something in Changar's face that had not been there three years ago; something that burned. You had only to look at him to suspect that he had a secret, but if that was true he had not told it to Vlahan or anyone else for that matter, although Vlahan had asked often enough and even threatened once or twice to beat it out of him. Vlahan didn't like secrets unless he was the one keeping them. Secrets usually meant betrayal and a knife in the back.

Vlahan reached into the small woven basket by his elbow and picked out another handful of seeds. "Five tribes have already rebelled and five more are threatening," he said. He chose his words carefully, inspecting Changar's face to see if this statement pleased him in any way, but Changar was as unfathomable as ever.

"Uh," Changar grunted. The rebellions were news to no one and did not need to be commented on. Often, Vlahan talked to hear himself talk. Usually this made Changar impatient, but tonight he was willing to indulge him.

Vlahan frowned. "Are you listening to me?"

"I always listen to you, *rahan*."

"Well, listen with a little more enthusiasm. You're supposed to be my diviner. You're supposed to advise me, not sit there like a hunk of dried horse shit. As I was saying only yesterday: I need to kill Stavan, and I need to kidnap Arang before these rebellions get out of hand. Thanks to this cursed drought, the subchiefs are slaughtering one another right and left over water holes not fit for a goat to drink from. Someone has to make those stupid bastards see that their rebellion has a price, or I'm going to end up Chief of Twenty Tribes of nothing but rotting bones and rotting horseflesh."

Changar made a vague attempt to count the times he had heard Vlahan make this same speech since the day Marrah and the others escaped, but there were not enough fingers on a man's hands or enough stars in the sky to keep track.

Vlahan began to wax eloquent. His red, meaty face turned redder, and he waved his arms as if he were coming up with a brilliant new plan instead of one he had repeated dozens of times. "Once I get hold of Arang again, the subchiefs will obey him because Zuhan adopted him, even though the little black-haired son of a bitch is no more Zuhan's true grandson than you are." Vlahan spat a few hulls into the palm of his hand and tossed them aside. "Once I have Arang in my power, there will be no more talk of droughts and curses. I will step aside, and Arang will become the Great Chief, but when he opens his mouth, my words will come out, and when he gives orders they will be *my* orders."

Changar helped himself to more *kersek*. Vlahan was in rare form tonight, he thought. He put an expression of delighted interest on his face and settled back to listen. Every once in a while he nodded or made some sort of agreeable sound to keep Vlahan going. He never liked to rush things.

Finally he spoke. "But, as I've pointed out many times before, *rahan*, you can't kill a man if you can't find him, and you can't kidnap a boy if there's no boy around to be kidnapped. Stavan, Arang, Marrah the witch, and those two concubines of no worth—five people—and they disappeared into the snow like that." Changar snapped his fingers. "No one has seen them in four years, and no one has found their bones."

Vlahan frowned and narrowed his eyes until they were little, tight slits. He was a fleshy man, with a red beard, brown hair, and a cruel, sensual mouth. He and Stavan were half brothers, and there was something of Stavan in his face, but the appealing things about Stavan were debased and distorted in Vlahan: he had cunning instead of intelligence; arrogance instead of friendliness; lust instead of affection. He'd led a particularly evil life even for a nomad, and every bit of it showed.

"Do you think I'm a fool?" His voice was low and heavy like the edge of a dull spear.

Why yes, I do, Changar thought. "No, *rahan*," he said.

"Then why do you tell me what I already know?" Vlahan spat into the fire. "I'm tired of your drivel. You don't give me any advice, and you drink too much *kersek*. Shut up if you have nothing new to say, or I'll find myself a new diviner."

"But I do have something new to say, *rahan*." Changar smiled at Vlahan as if Vlahan had just paid him a compliment instead of insulting him. "Something you are going to find very interesting."

Vlahan snorted and tossed some hulls onto the fire. They burned with little snapping sounds. "Something new? I doubt it. Are you going to tell me that you took the sacred mushrooms and saw where the five of them went? So far your divining has been about as useful as a basket of piss. For all your magic you haven't been able to track them any better than Mukhan could. Sometimes I think I might as well sacrifice you to Han too and be done with it."

Changar ignored the threat, which—like everything else—he had heard many times before. "Suppose I *could* find them?"

"Suppose horses could fly."

"Suppose I could not only find them, but kill Stavan and bring Arang back to you? And suppose . . . "

There was something in Changar's voice that made Vlahan look up. "Suppose I had more news for you, *rahan*: news that would make you very happy. What would you give old Changar then?"

Vlahan looked at the diviner the way a man might look at an intelligent weasel. "That would depend," he said. "If you really did know where the five of them were hiding, then I'd give you as many men as you needed to go after them. And when you returned with Arang—if he was still alive and in passable shape—hadn't had his knees shattered or his nose cut off or anything of the sort, so I could show him to the subchiefs of the Twenty Tribes in one piece—why then I'd give you horses and gold enough to make you a rich man forever. But if you lied to me and took the men and horses I gave you and went off to join the rebels, why then, Changar, I'd have to track you down, cut off your balls, and hang them outside my tent where everyone could see them. And then . . . " Vlahan began to describe with great relish the way traitors were punished.

Changar waited patiently until he was finished. Finally there was silence. The fire burned low, and the two men sat facing each other. When Changar spoke again, his voice was soft and low.

"A man came today, *rahan*, a warrior from the west, a Shubhai."

Vlahan spat into the fire and watched the spit sizzle on the hot stones. "I hear rumors that Nikhan has rebelled too, but no one has taken the time to go to the Shubhai camps to see if it's true." He looked at Changar with grudging approval. "Still, I take your point. If this man is from the west, then maybe he knows something about the fugitives." He waved grandly to Changar. "You have my permission to torture him to see if you can get anything out of him."

"There's no need to torture him, *rahan*. He's not only willing to talk; he rode to our camp of his own free will to bring us a message. You remember I said there was more news?"

"So you did. Well, what is it? Out with it. It had better be good or you can try living without water for a week. That's a fair trade these days: good news for water. Otherwise you drink dust."

"I'd like the man himself to tell you, *rahan*."

Vlahan nodded, and Changar turned and clapped his hands, and an armed guard appeared. There was grease on the man's beard, which suggested he had been interrupted in the middle of his dinner.

"Bring me that Shubhai you've got trussed up somewhere," Vlahan growled. "And wipe your chin while you're at it."

The guard bowed and hurried out of the tent, pawing at his beard. A few moments later he and another guard returned dragging a stocky, battle-scarred Shubhai warrior between them. The man was probably in his midtwenties, but his tangled hair, broken nose, and chipped teeth made him look older. An angry red scar ran from the corner of his left eye to the corner of his mouth, and he had a hawk with open talons tattooed on his forehead. Like all Shubhai tattoos, the hawk was poorly drawn, but it made his face memorable. If Marrah had been present, she would have recognized him as the warrior who had knelt in front of Stavan's horse when they rode into the fort at Shambah.

The guards pushed the Shubhai down on his knees. His arms were tied behind his back, but that was only a precaution. He was a guest, not a prisoner—not yet at least. He stared at Vlahan open-mouthed. Vlahan was only wearing two or three gold necklaces, a small gold circle around his head, five or six rings in his ears, and a few bits of gold on his tunic, but he must have looked like a god to the Shubhai.

"Tell the Great Chief what you told me," Changar commanded.

The Shubhai swallowed several times before he could speak. "Four years ago," he stuttered, "a man who claimed to be Stavan, son of Zuhan, rode into our camp with a boy and three women. He said he was the Great Chief of the Hansi and he forced our chief, Nikhan, to swear loyalty to him, but I knew as soon as I saw him that he was no chief. He wore rags, and his horse was tired." The warrior described everything that had happened at Shambah including the burning of the fort, and Vlahan and Changar did not interrupt. The man had a thick western accent and several of his teeth were missing, so it was sometimes hard to understand him—especially when he started railing against Nikhan, who seemed to have offended him somehow over a matter involving a white mare—but in general what he had to say was clear enough: Stavan, Arang, Marrah, and the two concubines had crossed into the forest lands and were headed south toward some place called Shara.

Finally the Shubhai warrior finished talking, but Changar was not satisfied. He sat for a moment, remembering the vision he had had when he ate the sacred mushrooms. The future he had foreseen was unrolling in front of him as smoothly as a rug, and as he watched it spread and spread with each pattern in its proper place, he knew that everything he had been told would come to pass. He let the triumph of that knowledge burn through him, let it tingle through his shattered legs and run over his tongue. When he spoke, his voice was so soft that the Shubhai warrior had to strain to hear it.

"Go on," he ordered. "Tell the Great Chief the rest."

"But there's no more to tell."

"Tell him about the women."

"Oh, the women." The warrior grinned nervously. "Vicious little bitches, all three of them. They jumped Nikhan and held him at knife point, and Nikhan has been a laughingstock ever since. Imagine a chief being taken captive by breeding women."

Vlahan started. "Did you say the women were breeding?"

The Shubhai nodded. "The dark-haired one certainly was, and I think the little blonde was too, although some of hers was padding." He made a curving motion with his hand. "The dark-haired one had a belly out to here. Later, word came back to Nikhan that she had given birth to twins in that Shara place: a boy and a girl, they said."

Vlahan turned to Changar. "Marrah?"

Changar nodded.

"If Marrah gave birth to a boy, then I have a son!" Vlahan cried. "By Han, Changar, you old fox! After all these years, I have a son!"

The Shubhai warrior looked confused. "Stavan, son of Zuhan, said the woman was his wife, *rahan*, so wouldn't the boy be his—"

"Silence!" Vlahan yelled.

"Stavan lied," Changar said. "Marrah, witch though she may be, is Vlahan's wife, and any cubs she whelps are his."

"Don't waste your breath explaining it to him." Vlahan said. He turned to the warrior, who was staring at him in terror. Changar had often seen that look in the eyes of horses when the beasts realized they were going to be sacrificed. It was a white, rolled-back, glassy look. "I imagine that you expect to be well rewarded for telling me this story," Vlahan said. His voice was ominously calm, but evidently the Shubhai could not read the menace, because he relaxed a little and his eyes focused again.

"I heard you were offering gold and horses for news of them, *rahan*."

"Gold and horses too, and you shall have your share of both once you've led my warriors safely past your chief who stands between us and the forest lands." Vlahan paused and helped himself to some toasted seeds. He ate them thoughtfully without taking his eyes off the Shubhai. When he was finished he wiped his hand on his cloak and rose to his feet. "Of course we'll have to cut out your tongue, but—"

"Cut out my tongue!" the man screamed.

Vlahan turned to Changar. "Do it now," he said. "Do it before he talks to anyone else."

As always, Changar was happy to oblige.

Spring turned to summer. One warm evening about two weeks before the festival of animals, the moon rose over Shara revealing a city at peace with itself and its neighbors. In the fields, the cicadas called to one another in a steady, soothing hum. To the south, the Snake of Time lay in glittering, motionless coils, as if time itself had been suspended. Most people had spent the day working: some had weeded the communal vegetable patches; some had tended animals; some had sat telling stories to children; others had made pots, woven cloth, fished, repaired nets, hunted, mended fences, or cooked. Two women had given birth, a sick pilgrim had been bathed in the hot spring, and a *raspa* filled with rare herbs and baskets of jadeite had arrived from the south in the late afternoon, causing a small ripple of excitement. Now the streets were mostly empty. In the temples, the priestesses were tending the altar fires, kneading the next day's bread, and talking, but almost everyone else was in bed. Here and there, oil lamps burned, casting long flickering shadows on whitewashed walls. The shadows seemed to be alive. They moved back and forth, some slowly, some quickly. Rapid breathing, sighs, and sometimes soft laughter could be heard. Night in Shara was a time for lovers who spoke in whispers so as not to wake the children. The motherhouses had private sleeping compartments, but thin walls.

In Lalah's house, Hiknak and Arang had carried Keshna to the children's room, tucked her in, and gone back to their sleeping compartment. The compartment was small, only big enough for a water jug, a double mat, and three cushions, but it had a round window and a view of the Sweetwater Sea. Hiknak stood for a moment looking out the window. She had been born in a place with no hills, and she never stopped being amazed that a person could see so far from the second story of a house. Tonight the sea was washed in moonlight. Sometimes if she squinted her eyes, the white peaks of the waves looked like the feathered grasses of the steppes, but no grass had ever had so much power. The waves slapped against the rocks and pulled back with a murmuring sound that reminded her of the buzzing of innumerable bees. Someday, she thought, they would grind all the world to sand.

Arang came up behind her and put his arms around her waist. "Let me comb out your hair," he said. He took Hiknak's braids and untwisted them, winding them around his wrist, feeling their weight and softness. She smiled, sat down, and leaned back lazily against the feather cushions. She was no longer a skinny little nomad from the steppes with eyes like a frightened rabbit. She had put on weight since the birth of Keshna, and as Arang looked at the roundness of her arms and the fullness of her cheeks, he thought she looked as lovely as a fresh apple.

"Comb," she said. She laughed and pretended that she was his chief even though his people had no chiefs. She, Hiknak, was the best of chiefs, not cruel like Vlahan, but a Chief of the Bed, Chief of Love and Pleasure. She loved to command him and he loved to obey, and everything they did together they did for the joy of pleasing each other.

Slowly he began to comb out the tangles, pausing every once in a while to bury his face in her hair. Hiknak's hair smelled like rain and musk, and even after all these years of sharing joy with her, he found the color of it surprising. Sometimes when he was combing out her braids, he would think about the gold Zuhan had worn. He would remember the Great Chief's gold rings and earrings, his gold pendant shaped like the sun, the gold circles on his tunic, and the gold buckle of his belt. Zuhan had lived for gold and killed for gold, but as far as Arang could tell it had not brought him a moment of happiness. The only gold worth having was the gold of a woman's hair—or the gold of a man's hair if you loved men—or black hair, or brown hair, or white hair, or any color of hair for that matter. As he drew the comb down from the white line of Hiknak's part, he let his mind drift.

In another part of the house, Dalish was eating honey and fresh bread.

"Give me some," Jutima begged.

Dalish put a bit of honey on her lips and kissed Jutima, and they both laughed.

"What are you doing tomorrow?" Jutima asked.

"Finishing my mask for the festival of animals."

"What animal are you going to be?"

"I thought I'd wear a human face for once."

Jutima reached out and touched the tattoos on Dalish's face, tracing the blue vinelike patterns with the tip of one finger. "You shouldn't say that, Dalish. The pictures on your face are beautiful. Like honeysuckle vines."

"How I got them wasn't beautiful."

"Did it hurt a lot?"

Dalish nodded. "Irehan the Cowardly, my first lord and master, had two of his wives hold me down while the third cut my face with the tip of her dagger and rubbed some kind of yellow plant sap into the cuts. By the next day, the sap had turned blue."

Jutima took Dalish's hand, and they were silent for a moment. "Did you ever hear the story of the veiled Goddess?" Jutima asked. Dalish shook her head. "Before she put on her veil, the Goddess was so beautiful that when people caught sight of Her, they couldn't think of anything else. They couldn't work; they couldn't dance; they couldn't feed their animals; they couldn't even eat. When men and women saw Her, they became sick with love. So the Goddess took mercy on them. She put a veil over Her face, but it didn't work. Her soul was so bright that the beauty of it shone through anyway, and if you look up in the sky," Jutima pointed out the window, "you can still see Her, and Her beauty is still almost more than human beings can bear."

Dalish looked at the moon. "You're making all this up," she said. "You're telling me a false tale. This is Dalish you're talking to. I was trained to be a priestess once, remember? The moon was never a veiled Goddess."

Jutima looked sheepish. She cleared her throat and reached for the loaf of bread, but instead of tearing off a piece, she just sat there holding it. "You're right," she admitted. "I did make it up. But I only did it because I love you, and I wanted you to know that no matter what the nomads did to your face, it's still beautiful." She paused. "To tell the truth, I'd love you if you had a face like a cabbage."

Dalish laughed. "A face like a cabbage! Now that's devotion! Jutima, you're a sweet, hopeless, sentimental fool, and the worst liar I've ever met, but I have to admit that you're making me feel better."

"That's what lovers are for," Jutima said. She drew Dalish to her and kissed her for a long time. "Now," she said when the kiss was over, "tell me the truth. What kind of mask *are* you making for the festival of animals?"

"I'm going as a frog."

"Ribet, ribet, ribet," Jutima chuckled. "Somehow it fits."

Not everyone in Shara was making love that night: tired from working with the horses all day, Marrah and Stavan had fallen asleep in each other's arms like two children; Lalah was stretched out sideways, enjoying the sensation of having the sleeping mat to herself, and there were several people in the city who from birth to death never experienced desire. But if Batal had made the walls of the motherhouses transparent, there would have been many sleeping compartments with lighted lamps, and moving shadows, and whispering lovers. Sex was sacred to the Sharans. They believed it bound people together and helped them live in harmony. When Hiknak—newly arrived—asked them what they thought the greatest gifts of the Goddess were, the Sharans had told her: "children" and "sex." And then they had added "food" and "dancing" and "festivals"; and before they were finished they had listed a whole string of blessings including "the scent of flowers," "the songs of birds," and "the pleasures of good conversation." But of all of these, they said, love and sex were the most important.

Outside the city, the cicadas in the fields went on droning softly. As the moon rose higher, pale silver light fell through the branches of the great forest of oaks and arbutus that surrounded Shara to the north and west. The forest was usually a noisy place when the moon was full, but tonight one small part of it was unnaturally silent: just across the river, a little upstream from the ford, no owls hooted and no mice rustled through the underbrush.

A horse stamped and snorted. Something glittered in the moonlight. Pale faces smeared with mud seemed to float in the darkness like disembodied spirits. Something was watching the lamps of Shara with contempt; something that hid in the forest; something that thought love was for fools.

CHAPTER SEVEN

Morning. The motherhouses of Shara turned gray, then white, then light pink as the sun rose over the Sweetwater Sea. A bird twittered on Marrah's windowsill, and she opened her eyes. It was a sparrow with tiny black eyes like beads, and it stood there on two spindly legs, cocking its head and staring at her, before it began to peck at the grain she had spread for it last night.

Good morning, she thought.

Good morning, the bird seemed to reply.

Have you brought me a message?

No, Lady. But the day will be fair.

That's good because Hiknak is taking the children berry picking this morning.

The berries are ripe and black and fat and sweet as a lover's tongue.

What do you know of lovers' tongues?

Birds know everything.

Marrah laughed at herself for having a conversation with a bird, but since she was named after one—Marrah meant "seagull"—she was forever imagining them talking to her even though she knew the words they said were only in her mind. She yawned, stretched, and prepared to get out of bed.

The sparrow stopped pecking and stared at her, and she imagined that it was telling her to move quietly or she would wake Stavan, who was lying on his back, snoring softly with one arm thrown across his face.

Do I have a fine-looking man, bird?

You do, Lady.

And beautiful children?

Two of the most beautiful children in all Shara.

And am I a lucky woman?

You are.

With that the bird flew off, and Marrah got out of bed, slipped on her shift, and went down to the children's room to see if Luma and Keru were ready for their berry-picking expedition.

A circle of squirrels and children danced on the whitewashed walls of the children's room. Two storks and a pair of fat babies sailed kites around a large window that let in sea breezes and sunlight the color of butter. Already the yellow daisies were drooping in their pots and the ferns looked thirsty. Marrah stood in the doorway listening to the din of the children and thought it was going to be a hot day.

"Yes, you did," six-year-old Shutu cried.

"No, I didn't," Minha protested.

"I love honey," Keshna sang, dipping into the honey pot with one finger and dripping an amber-colored globe into her mouth. She licked the sticky sweetness from her upper lip and smiled at Marrah mischievously. At that moment Keru spotted his mother. Springing to his feet, he ran over to the nearest flowerpot and uprooted a yellow daisy.

"For you, Mama," he said, holding the flower out to her. "'Cause you're the prettiest mama in the world."

Marrah took the flower, and it seemed to grow in her hand. She turned it, and it shone in the sun. Each petal looked huge. Pollen flew up like dust, and she laughed at this gift of love from her little son. "Thank you, Keru," she said; and she knew she should ask him what he had done wrong because this flower was surely a gift to placate her, but he was right: he knew she would be too pleased to ask, and besides, she would find out soon enough. Keru was looking down at his little-boy feet, wiggling his bare toes on the red tiles. She bent over and kissed the top of his head. It was amazing how much his hair smelled like Stavan's. There was smoke in it and something musty and sweet, like the promise of rain on a dry day.

"You're a good boy," she told him, and Keru looked up at her with his big chestnut-colored eyes as if hoping that her saying it would make it true.

A moment later Nazur came puffing up with a baby tucked under each arm. His potbelly shook, and his face was red with exertion. He and Tarrah had been caring for the children all night and no doubt he would rather be eating his breakfast, but he had a message to deliver first. The babies wriggled and shrieked as if escaping from Nazur was some kind of wonderful game, but Nazur had grown children of his own and was an expert at baby juggling.

"I'm afraid I have some bad news for you," he said. And he proceeded to tell Marrah that Luma had thrown up twice last night because Keshna convinced her and Keru that it would be fun to have an apple-eating contest. "So the three of them went to the storeroom, opened a basket of dried apples, and stuffed themselves," he continued, pinning down the squirming babies with his massive arms. "Keshna won, of course. She has a stomach like a goat and so does Keru, but I think it's going to be a long time before Luma wants to eat dried apples again."

Marrah looked over at Keshna and Keru, who had suddenly developed an intense interest in their bowls of cracked wheat cereal. They huddled together like little conspirators, not once looking up.

"Keru, Keshna," she said, "that was a silly thing to do."

"Yes, Mama," Keru muttered, while Keshna dipped her head and licked her honey-covered finger.

"Now Luma can't go berry-picking with you."

"No, Mama."

"You won't ever do anything like that again, will you?"

"No, Mama."

Marrah looked down at the wilted daisy in her hand and decided she had reprimanded them enough. She would have felt better if Keshna had apologized too, but the girl was high-spirited and inclined to insist that she was innocent even when she was caught redhanded. Sometimes she thought the nomad blood ran very hot in Keshna.

She turned to leave and heard Keru calling after her, "I love you, Mama." He waved and blew her a kiss.

"I love you too," she called back. As she walked away, she was almost sure she heard Keshna's mischievous giggle.

She found Luma stretched out on her great-grandmother's sleeping mat, clutching the toy horse Stavan had carved for her. There were dark circles under her eyes, and her small face was pinched and pale. She was the perfect picture of misery and repentance. As soon as she saw her, Marrah knew she didn't have the heart to scold her for getting into the dried apples.

Lalah sat next to her, singing to her and feeding her sips of herb tea from a shell spoon. Every time the spoon approached her face, Luma opened her mouth like a baby bird, swallowed some of the tea, and made a face. Lalah's stomach remedies were famously bitter, but Luma was so fond of her great-grandmother that she probably would have eaten dirt if Lalah had offered it to her. When Luma saw Marrah she groaned, "Mama, I ated too much and my tummy hurts."

"My poor baby." Marrah scooped Luma up in her arms and began to rock her gently so as not to upset her stomach even more.

Lalah put down the tea, sat back, and kicked off her sandals. "Did you hear about the apple-eating contest?" Marrah nodded. "That Keshna is going to lead the other two off a cliff someday if we don't watch her," Lalah sighed.

Shortly after Marrah had left the children's room, Hiknak appeared to collect Keshna and Keru for the berry-picking expedition. Handing them two small baskets, she strapped her own on her back and led them down to the river.

The morning went by slowly as the sun moved along the walls of the motherhouses. As the shadows bent and shrank, the Snake of Time seemed to ripple, flaunting its glittering scales as if saying: Behold the most beautiful of all cities. In the wheat fields, the members of five motherhouses moved in long lines, singing songs in praise of the Goddess Earth as they uprooted weeds. Out on the tossing blue waves of the Sweetwater Sea, the Society of Men and Women Who Fished threw out their nets and waited. In the temples, the priests and priestesses dipped their hands in wet clay and made pots and braziers and ceremonial screens. Others knelt at the looms, tying on stone weights shaped like owls, while still others wove part of the linen canopy that would shade the pilgrims who came to watch the festival of animals.

Because the festival was so near, there was excitement in the air. People who had nothing more pressing to do were working on their costumes. All over the city, they sat in the shade in companionable groups, putting finishing touches on masks and headdresses. There were going to be quite a few birds this year if the piles of dyed feathers were any indication; not to mention pink bears, yellow deer, blue dogs, and all sorts of bizarre insects. But even with all this variety, Dalish's frog mask was causing a sensation. She had made it out of linen and wheat paste, with great bulging eyes and a huge comic mouth, but instead of painting it green, she had somehow managed to dye it bright purple.

"How did you produce that glorious color?" the weavers asked, but Dalish wasn't telling until after the festival.

"From the sea," she said, pointing to the waves as if salt water and foam were the secret. Even when Arang came along with an ax on his shoulders and stopped to admire her handiwork, she laughed and tried to send him on his way.

"Go chop down your oak," she said, "and leave mask making to an expert."

Arang leaned on his ax handle and looked longingly at the purple frog. "I'd love to have a scarf that color, Dalish. When I danced with it, it would look like sunset and purple smoke."

Dalish sighed. "Arang, you're too much of a poet to be resisted. This afternoon I'll dye you just such a scarf so I can have the pleasure of watching you dance with it."

"If it's dry, I'll dance with it tonight," he promised, and then he shouldered his double-headed ax and walked away to find Stavan.

Down by the river, Hiknak picked a berry and popped it into Keshna's mouth. Then she picked another and popped it into Keru's. The sun had climbed well into the sky, the berry picking had been a profitable endeavor, and already her basket was almost full. She helped herself to a big, sweet berry and looked at the children, whose hands were so stained with purple juice that they looked like the paws of bear cubs.

"Good job," she told them, even though most of the berries they had picked had gone into their stomachs instead of their baskets. The children grinned and stuck out stained tongues.

"Mmm," Keshna hummed.

"Mmmm," Keru hummed, joining her because he loved to do anything Keshna did.

Hiknak stuck out her own tongue, and they all laughed. When the laughing was over, she waded downstream a little and started in on a fresh patch of berries, and Keru and Keshna waded after her, kicking up silver sprays of water. Soon it would be time to feed them a meal and put them down for a nap—not that she expected them to eat much of the cheese and bread she had in her leather pocket or to sleep much either, for that matter. If there were two children in the world who chattered more than Keshna and Keru, she hadn't met them.

"Don't go too far away from the bank," she warned for perhaps the tenth time that morning. The two nodded innocently as if such a thought had never crossed their little minds, although Hiknak knew for a fact that they were both longing for a swim. They're fishes, she thought. And me sinking like a stone if I so much as try. Let them wait. Marrah can take them to the beach later and pull them out if the waves knock them under.

She shuddered a little at the thought of swimming, inspected the river, and decided she mistrusted it here as much as in the last place. They were picking close along the bank where the dark green tangle of brambles fringed the forest. The water was shallow and warm where they stood, but nearer the middle the current swirled quickly in long, oily coils.

For a while there was no sound but the chattering of the children and the soft plop of berries falling into her basket. Hiknak reached up for a particularly fat one and pricked her thumb on the brambles.

"Ouch!" she said. Muttering curses, she put it in her mouth and sucked until it stopped hurting. She was just about to make a second attempt to dislodge the berry when two shrill screams pierced the silence.

"Hiknak!"

"Help!"

She wheeled around and berries flew everywhere, raining into the river.

"Mama!"

"Hiknak!"

She saw the children first. They were trying to run toward her, but they were so little that the water came up to their knees, so they

flopped and struggled forward with their arms outstretched, screaming her name but not getting anywhere. Behind them, four armed
warriors were galloping through the shallows, running them down
like rabbits.

"Run!" she screamed. "Run!" She threw aside her basket and
started toward them, but the river sucked at her legs too, pulling
her back. For one long moment that seemed to go on forever, she
fought her way through the water, trapped in a nightmare from her
childhood. Keru and Keshna were screaming the same screams of
terror her younger brothers and sisters had screamed the day the
Hansi rode down on her father's camp and killed them all.

"Mama!"

"Hiknak!"

The water sucked and pulled and trapped her like honey. She
saw everything: the horses' short manes, their thick legs, the bare-
chested men, faces painted with wolves and skeletons and death
masks, spears and quivers and bows and filed teeth, but there was
no noise except her screaming and the screaming of the children
and the splash of hooves.

"Faster!" she begged them. "Run faster, for Han's sake!"

Keru tripped and went under and Keshna grabbed his wrist and
jerked him up again. He sputtered and gasped for breath. Then
Hiknak was with them, clutching Keshna around the waist and
throwing her out toward the center of the river because she knew
the nomads couldn't swim. "Swim away and hide yourself!" she
yelled to Keshna. "Swim for your life!"

Keshna's body left her hands and went into the swirling current,
under and down, and she didn't see her come up. I've drowned my
daughter, she thought; but there was no time to understand this because Keru had to be saved too. She threw herself at him and
scooped him up in her arms and started to throw him out where it
was deep, but before she could let go of his body, a hand appeared
above her and jerked him up and out of her arms.

Keru gave a shrill scream of terror that scalded the very air. She
leapt for him, trying to catch his legs and pull him back, but he was
already high above her, thrown over the neck of one of the warrior's
horses, wriggling there helplessly.

The warrior looked down at her with a cruel smile as if he enjoyed her desperation. He was ugly and battle scarred, with a broken nose, and a hawk with open talons tattooed on his forehead.
Where his tongue should have been was only a black stump. He

waved the stump at her and made a guttural sucking sound. Even though his clan signs were Shubhai, she knew that Vlahan had sent him.

Hlaluk! she yelled in Hansi, which meant "give him back!" and there was more in her throat, curses she would have yelled, but before she could yell them, the Shubhai warrior lifted his war club and hit her so hard that everything turned sideways with a sickening lurch. Something exploded in her head, white and hot like the sun. She experienced no pain, only surprise. The last thing she felt was the water closing in around her face. Even though she couldn't see, she knew the line between water and air was the line between life and death, and that if she didn't turn over she would drown, but her arms had gone limp, and when she tried to kick her legs, nothing happened.

In another part of the forest, Stavan and Arang had just felled an oak and were lopping off the limbs. It was hard work since their double-headed axes were made of stone, but both men liked physical labor. There was always something satisfying about the thunk of an ax against wood, so they hacked on in companionable silence, getting into the same rhythm until they were racing each other down the opposite sides of the trunk, branch by branch. Stavan was taller than Arang and the powerful muscles he had developed in the days when he was a warrior gave him an edge, but Arang was more accurate. He hit one stroke for Stavan's three, so they were pretty evenly matched, which made the whole race more enjoyable.

The tree was too large for two men to carry back to Shara by themselves, so they had brought the horses who were tethered nearby, chomping on leaves, swatting at flies, and looking at them with bland curiosity.

It had been a new idea to the Sharans—this thought that horses could be made to carry what people couldn't—and Stavan and Arang had caused a stir this morning when they rode out promising to bring back a single tree large enough to make a table as long as two men. The table was destined for the Council of Elders, and Sevar, the best woodworker in the city, had vowed he would carve it as marvelously as a table had ever been carved—with Goddess signs, and snakes, and other oaks so it wouldn't feel lonely separated from its kind—but first they had to get the huge trunk back without calling out the usual work crew.

Stavan paused for a moment and wiped his forehead, and Arang did the same. By now about half the branches were gone, tossed into piles on either side of the trunk. Before they left, they would plant six acorns around the stump so a new oak would grow up to replace the old one, but it was still a serious thing to cut down a great tree, even if you thanked it and blessed it before you took your ax to it.

"Do you think it's going to be too heavy for the horses to move?" Arang said, eyeing the trunk anxiously.

Stavan took a drink from his waterskin, rolled the water around in his mouth, and spat it out. His yellow hair was plastered to his head with sweat, and there was a big streak of dirt across the bridge of his nose. "Relax," he said. He smiled at Arang. "I've seen a pair of horses drag this much weight more times than I can count. My father's tent—when you figure in the poles and such—was probably at least as heavy. Of course we'll have to go slowly so the drag lines don't get caught on the bushes, but it isn't all that far, and once we get to the fields it should be fairly easy. In fact I have a route all worked out." He picked up a twig and began to draw in the soft earth. The oak had had such a thick brush of leaves that the ground underneath it was nearly bare except for moss and a few mushrooms.

"Now, imagine this wavy line is the river. We'll ford here in the usual place, but instead of heading straight for the city we'll let the horses drag the log along the bank like so. It's heavy, but it should float just fine. When we come to the pastures, we'll make them haul it around this bit of marshy land where the pigs like to wallow. From there it should be easy."

He looked up and saw Arang staring at him with total incomprehension. The Sharans were poor trackers by Hansi standards. Even the idea of a map was foreign to them. When they wanted to go from one place to another, they used songs. Arang had followed his mother's song all the way from the Sea of Gray Waves to Shara, traveling for the better part of two years without once getting lost, but he could no more understand the squiggles and lines Stavan was drawing in the mud than Stavan could understand the sacred script on the temple scrolls.

Stavan laughed and threw down his stick. "Never mind," he said. "Just remember that we're going to drag this tree through the pastures, not the wheat fields."

Arang grinned. "Good," he said, "because Grandmother is an impressive sight when she's angry. If we trampled the wheat, she'd give us a tongue lashing the likes of which you've never heard, and the clans in charge of this year's harvest would be furious."

They shared another pull at the waterskin, raised their axes, and were about to start lopping off the rest of the branches, when the horses suddenly started.

Stavan froze in midstroke and lowered his ax.

"What's wrong?" Arang asked.

"Shhh."

They listened for a moment, but there was no sound except the snorting of the horses and their own breathing.

"I don't hear anything."

"That's the problem," Stavan whispered. "It's too quiet. We've been making a lot of noise so it's not surprising the animals near us have taken cover; but we should be able to hear something in the distance: a bird, a squirrel—but every animal in the forest has suddenly gone silent. I think there's something out there—something that's in the wrong place." He turned around slowly and inspected the trees that surrounded them on all sides—oaks mostly, with bunches of mistletoe caught in their upper branches like birds' nests. Directly under the trees were mossy, bare spots, but between them, in the more open places, the underbrush was thick enough to hide almost anything.

Arang looked too, but all he could see were trunks and interlaced branches and brush, and beyond that, deeper in the woods, dark shadows that looked cool and rather inviting.

"What do you think it is?"

Stavan frowned and rubbed his tongue over his teeth the way he always did when something puzzled him. "I don't know. A big animal—maybe a lion."

Arang had once come very close to being eaten by a lion. He peered at the shadows and cleared his throat with a grating little sound that suddenly seemed very loud. "A lion, eh?" He laughed nervously. "What would a lion be doing so close to Shara? No one has seen one around here for years."

"That's true," Stavan whispered, "which is why I think it might be something else." He put his fingers to his lips. "Shhh. Listen. Did you hear that?"

Arang strained to listen, but again he heard only the horses and his own breathing. He smiled weakly. "Stavan, I have to hand it to you: your ears are like a hawk's eyes." He was just about to add that maybe this time Stavan was mistaken, when all at once the horses began to panic and suddenly the forest came alive—so swiftly and brutally that Arang was still looking for the lion when a band of warriors rode out of the underbrush howling like wolves.

There must have been half a dozen of them, tattooed and naked, with blackened teeth and hair stiffened into spikes with red mud. A warrior with yellow stripes on his face hurled a spear at Stavan, and it missed him and went into the trunk of the tree with a solid thunk. The feathers on the shaft caught in the twigs and exploded in a small puff. Arang heard the twang of singing bows and the hiss of arrows, and then the warriors closed in, and everything became screams, and spears, and painted faces, and horses kicking up clods of earth.

Leaping over the felled tree, Arang put his back to Stavan's and started to fight with him, swinging his ax and cursing in Hansi because there were no words in his own language for the rage he felt toward these cowards. When he had been a prisoner in Vlahan's camp, the nomads had trained him to fight like a warrior, but he forgot all that. He just slashed wildly at horses and legs and arms, at anything that came close, and as he did so a strange thing happened: the arrows stopped raining down and the warriors drew back a little and began to circle the tree, whooping and shaking their spears.

"Why aren't they killing us?" he yelled at Stavan.

"Because they want to take us alive."

"To torture us?"

"Yes."

"Then let's die now."

He spoke in Sharan but perhaps the warriors understood him, because the word *die* was no sooner out of his mouth than a man with yellow stars tattooed on his face rode closer, taunting and screaming, and as Arang and Stavan raised their axes to fight him off, another warrior rode up quickly and dealt Stavan a blow to the head that knocked him to the ground. As soon as Stavan fell away from Arang, one of the warriors threw a spear into him, pinning him to the earth. Stavan stopped screaming, his eyes rolled back, and blood came—just a little blood, like the petals of some terrible flower blooming across the sweat-stained side of his tunic. The warrior who had speared him prepared to leap from his horse to take his head, ignoring Arang.

For an instant Arang saw himself as the warrior must see him: a small man with a delicate body; a dancer and a coward who could be brushed aside like a child. With a cry of rage, he charged forward and struck at the warrior with his ax, but his aim was bad and he hit the man's horse instead, cutting it in the neck. The horse reared, and the warrior was forced to cling to it to keep from being thrown.

"Get away from Stavan!" Arang yelled. He straddled Stavan's body, screaming and chopping at air, and the warrior—who by now had his horse under control—cursed and backed off. The others drew their horses into a circle around Arang, but instead of filling him full of arrows, they just sat there, looking at him as if they were not sure what to do next.

Suddenly Arang understood what was going on. Someone had ordered them to take him not only alive but in one piece. Maybe they wanted to sacrifice him to Han or do something else with him, but whatever their reasons, they didn't dare shoot him or spear him or even club him. They were going to have to take him prisoner without drawing blood—something nomad warriors were never very good at. *I can lead them away from Stavan before they finish him off,* he thought. *I can run for it.*

All this came to him as fast as a shooting star falls across the sky. Before the thought was even complete, he had thrown down his ax and leapt forward through a space between the horses. He came so close he could have reached out and touched a man on either side and surely they would have caught him, except that he did something so strange that they were too startled to react: he did not move as a man should move. Instead he did a cartwheel, somersaulted twice, vaulted toward his horse, and flipped himself onto it, hands on rump, head over heels, then grabbed the reins, pulled them loose, and kicked the beast into motion.

It was a spectacular leap, the best, most perfect, and luckiest of his life. He did it without thinking, by instinct, as a great dancer will when mind and body come together in perfect grace. Before the warriors realized what had happened he was off, riding through the forest with a war cry of his own.

"Batal!" he yelled. As the name of the Goddess came out of his mouth, he had a moment of crazed ecstasy that was all riding, and trees, and ducking the low-hanging limbs. Leaves struck his face, twigs burned and whipped him. The forest itself seemed to revolve.

Behind him he heard the nomads riding in pursuit, crashing through the underbrush with war cries and curses as the limbs lashed them, but he didn't dare turn to see if they were overtaking him. He only prayed that all of them had come, that none had stayed behind to stick another spear into Stavan; and he prayed too, in that terrible riding, that he would be faster than they were, and for a time he was.

CHAPTER EIGHT

S tavan woke, opened his eyes, and tried to lift his head. For a moment he saw everything with unnatural clarity, and then the sky overhead began to spin, sucking in the trees. The blue-white clouds and green leaves whirled in slow circles like one of Arang's scarves. Nearby, a thin, strange-looking tree without leaves swayed back and forth in a wind he couldn't feel. He knew as soon as he saw the tree that there was something wrong with it because it had pheasant feathers at its crown instead of leaves.

Suddenly he realized that it wasn't a tree at all; it was the handle of a spear. He moved and the spear moved. He looked down and saw it was stuck in him, pinning him to the ground like a rabbit on a spit. The shaft was smeared with his blood and so were some of the oak leaves.

He felt giddy and sick but not afraid. There was a pain in his head, terrible and crushing as if someone had tried to push his eyes back into his skull, but hardly any pain at all in his side where the spear had struck him. He wondered dizzily if he should sing his death chant and summon the black horse that came to carry the brave to Paradise.

Then his mind cleared, and he remembered where he was and what had happened. He and Arang had been chopping down a tree and had been ambushed. The moment he knew that, he knew he wasn't dying, despite the spear; and putting his palms flat on the wet earth, he gave himself such a jerk that he pulled the flint tip out of the ground. The shaft toppled sideways, striking the trunk of the fallen oak, and he sat up cautiously, moaning and holding his head.

When he inspected the wound in his side, he saw that he had been lucky. The spear had gone through his tunic, between his ribs and arm, just grazing him, pinning him to the ground by cloth, not flesh. The blood was the dark blood of surface wounds, not the bright red of death. Already it had clotted.

He grabbed the spear, stuck it back in the ground, and used it to pull himself to his feet. The raiders must have left him for dead, but soon they would be back to take his head. I have to get out of here, he thought, but when he looked around, both horses were gone, and when he tried to take a step, such a black sickness came over him that had it not been for the spear, he would have fallen again. He stopped and waited until the nausea passed. Then slowly, step-by-step, he limped toward the underbrush.

Almost as soon as Stavan disappeared, the forest began to come alive around the fallen oak. Nothing human remained now except a few footprints and several arrows sticking out of the trunk like hedgehog spines. A spotted woodpecker with a red crown flew up, surveyed the scene, and deciding that there was nothing more to fear, began to hammer at a branch, searching for grubs. A pair of woodlarks called *tee-loo-ee* to each other from opposite sides of the clearing. A few flies buzzed lazily around the bloodstained oak leaves, and a small green toad hopped over a pile of twigs. Then suddenly the woodpecker gave a shrill *kee-kee-kee* and took flight. The larks fell silent, and the toad froze, blending in with the leaves. By the time the two nomad warriors walked into the clearing, only the flies were still circling.

The tall one with the shaved head and horses tattooed on his chest was the man who had speared Stavan. The warrior with the greasy mane of blond hair was the one who had clubbed him to the ground. Both had scratches on their faces where tree limbs had whipped them as they chased Arang, and their war paint was smeared and half sweated off their naked bodies.

They stood for a moment staring at the place where Stavan had lain. Then they frowned and began to scan the forest. When they spoke, they spoke in signs, moving their hands in the quick dialogue of Hansi scouts.

"Gone."

"Yes."

"He looked dead."

"Yes."

"But the dead don't walk."

"Maybe his people came and took away the body."

"You'd better hope they did."

The blond warrior knelt near the bloodstained oak leaves. He touched the blood with the tip of one finger to see if it was fresh, then lifted it to his lips and tasted it. Running his hand lightly over the wood chips, he felt for tiny variations in temperature that would indicate that a body had recently lain on them. He marked the shape of the hole that the spearhead had made when it passed through Stavan pinning him to the ground, and the other, rounder holes the butt of the spear had made when Stavan used it as a cane. The round holes led into the brush, accompanied by a single set of footprints.

"His people didn't come for him," he signed, and the other warrior looked worried.

"Did he walk?"

"Yes."

"Which way did he go?"

The blond warrior pointed west.

"He can't have gone far," the tall warrior signed.

"No."

The tall warrior made the sign for "Changar" and then drew one finger across his throat and made the sign for "two." The blond man winced and nodded. Changar had threatened to slit both their throats if they didn't bring back Stavan's head.

"Don't worry," he signed back. "We'll find him." And then he made the signs for "victory" and "death."

The trail was short, ending at a small creek.

"He went into the water," the blond warrior signed.

The tall warrior with the shaved head smiled triumphantly. "Then he'll have to come out."

They separated, one walking upstream and one walking down, looking for turned stones or leaves floating in the water for no reason. They did not expect to find a footprint in the mud or the mark of the spear butt, but such things were always possible when the man you were tracking was wounded. Still, it did not really matter if they found clear signs of their quarry. Vlahan had sent them on this raid because they were the two best trackers in the camp. The taller warrior liked to brag that they were even better than Mukhan, whom Vlahan had executed for letting the witch Marrah slip through his fingers. If Stavan came out of the water—and he would have to sooner or later—they would pick up his trail and finish the job of killing him.

The tall warrior walked for a long time, moving as silently as a shadow. He noted every ripple in the water, every bit of gravel, every tree limb low enough for a man to swing himself up and disappear. As he hunted, he grew impatient. The creek was beginning to narrow. No doubt it would end in some muddy marsh. Only a fool would run into a slough. He thought of Gukhan finding Stavan, taking his head, and getting all the glory. I never have any luck, he thought.

Soon he came to the source of the creek, a muddy pool full of reeds and scum. The water level had gone down recently, and the entire rim was wet clay of the sort that showed every mark. Carefully he circled the pool looking for human tracks, even though by now he was sure there was almost no chance that Stavan had come in this direction. All he found were the marks of deer hooves; the long, ribbonlike slither of a snake; the scrape of turtle claws; and bird tracks laced over one another by the dozens, which must have meant the fishing was good despite the murky water.

Disgusted, he sat down and stared for a while, hoping to see something of interest, but there was nothing to see but water, mud, reeds, and bird droppings. Finally he rose to his feet, spat into the water, and left, feeling very sorry for himself. No doubt by now Gukhan was back in the clearing stuffing Stavan's head into his saddlebag.

If Gukhan too had failed to pick up the trail, they were in serious trouble. The tall warrior had no intention of returning to camp empty-handed. He was too attached to his life to sacrifice it because some fool had wandered off to die where not even the best scout could find him.

He rubbed his shaved skull thoughtfully. Stavan had blond hair, he thought, and so did Gukhan. Gukhan and he had ridden all the way from the Sea of Grass together, sleeping side by side. He would get no pleasure in killing his friend and smashing in his face until it was unrecognizable, but one way or another he needed to bring to Changar a head.

After the scout left, the ripples on the pool ran to the sides, quivered, and stilled. Then all at once something rose out of the mud with a splash that sent waves slapping back against the clay banks. The thing was so wet and black and scum covered that if there had been people present to witness it, they might have imagined some mossy water-born monster was heaving itself up out of the muck. It spat out a long reed and gasped for air. Then it dipped down and washed off the mud and reemerged as a light-haired man. It was Stavan who had lain at the bottom of the pond, breathing through a reed, while the Hansi scout hunted him.

Stavan dragged himself up on the bank and lay for a while, panting. He had seen the black shadow of the scout loom over him and had thought that surely the man would see him too, but the gods had been merciful—or perhaps he should say the Goddess because it was certainly She who had hidden him in the dark mud of Her body. Praise Her, he thought.

He sat up and looked around to make sure he was safe. Then he waded back into the pool, retrieved the spear, and slid silently into the forest. Although his side still ached, the cold mud had sucked most of the pain out of the wound, and he was no longer dizzy.

He walked as quickly as he could, keeping to the brush and pausing every once in a while to listen for his pursuers. Soon he was back at the clearing. He crouched for a moment where he could see without being seen, planting his feet in the very hoofprints the horses of the raiders had left behind, and surveyed the area for signs of the enemy, but there was nothing to see but the fallen tree and a few flies buzzing over the spot where he had lain bleeding.

When he was sure he was alone, he rose to his feet and began to inspect the ground for tracks. It was badly churned, but he was able to make out the footprints of the scouts who had come looking for him. By the look of it, two of them had followed him as far as the creek and then had separated, one going upstream and one going down. On the other side of the creek, the tracks of the scout who had gone upstream appeared again, following the downstream route his companion had taken. With a little luck, the two of them were still wandering around down there, looking for overturned stones and broken twigs.

Stavan did his tracking very methodically, stopping often to make sure that he was reading the ground correctly. He saw every bent branch, every small scrape, every bit of displaced moss. When he was absolutely sure that the scouts were no longer on his trail, he went back to the clearing and began to follow another set of tracks as wide as a path. Here at least half a dozen horses had churned up the mud, all of them chasing a single horse that had veered through the forest at a furious pace, riding so close to trees and passing under such low limbs that only someone with great skill could have kept his seat.

As soon as Stavan saw this set of tracks, he knew Arang had somehow managed to escape, and he sucked in his breath in admiration. It must have taken a miracle for Arang to mount up in the middle of a battle. Why hadn't the warriors simply speared him as soon as he made a move toward his horse?

He stopped, knelt, and put his hand in the tracks of Arang's horse, measuring the depth of the prints. Since horses put more weight on their forelegs, the front hoofprints were always deeper than the rear, but these showed the signs of a full-out flight. He was almost certain Arang had been on that animal. Arang had made a run for it, and six warriors had gone after him without shooting a single arrow. Granted, it would have been hard to hit him the way he was zigzagging back and forth, but under ordinary circumstances that would not have stopped a band of raiders intent on killing: they would have shot until one of their arrows struck home. But they hadn't. There were no spent shafts on the ground, no gashes in the trees. Nothing.

He followed the hoofprints deeper into the forest, growing more and more puzzled. Why would six armed men—at considerable danger to themselves—chase one unarmed man without shooting at him? The only possible answer was that they wanted to take Arang alive—and not just alive but unharmed. Had torture been their aim? If so, they could easily have clubbed him off his horse without killing him, trussed him up, taken him back to their camp, and dealt with him at their leisure. But for some reason they had wanted him in perfect shape, which meant one of two things: either they intended to sacrifice him to Han, which was totally ridiculous since no warriors in their right minds would ride for months through unfamiliar lands just to capture a sacrificial victim, or someone had sent them to Shara to kidnap Arang—someone who had warned them that they would die if they so much as harmed a hair on his head.

Suddenly Stavan understood: Vlahan had sent the raiding party. By Han! Of course, it was Vlahan! But why? Vlahan loved revenge, but not enough to waste men on a fool's errand. No nomad warriors had ever gone south of Shambah. What would drive Vlahan to send a raiding party into the Motherlands? Stavan could think of only one thing: the tribes of the steppes must be in rebellion, and Vlahan must need Arang to legitimize his power. The Hansi had not accepted Vlahan as Great Chief because he was a bastard, so as an added precaution he had ordered his warriors to kill Stavan.

Stavan smiled grimly and brushed the mud off his hands. Only the fact that he was still in danger kept him from giving a shout of victory. He had been bracing himself for the sight of Arang's body hacked to pieces and headless, but if he was right about Vlahan, then Arang must still be alive.

He broke into a run and followed the tracks, no longer paying much attention to the particulars. Soon he came to a small, muddy clearing, and there—as he had expected—he found signs that the warriors had come up on either side of Arang, grabbed his horse by the bridle, and jerked it to a halt. He found other things too: marks of a scuffle; a few white linen threads from Arang's tunic caught on a branch; a string of leather; a pile of fresh dung, which meant the horses had stood for a while before going on.

The tracks that led away from the clearing confirmed his theory that Arang had been taken prisoner. The hoofprints were no longer deep. When they left, the warriors had been walking their mounts, not galloping in pursuit of something. The horse that had been out in front came third, walking very close to the horse in front of it as if it were being led. Presumably Arang had ridden on its back with his hands tied. The warriors were obviously making sure he didn't escape, because two had ridden in front of him, two behind, and one on either side.

Stavan stood for a moment, staring at the tracks and trying to decide what to do next. Should he head back to the city and sound the alarm, or should he go after Arang? If the nomads had taken Arang prisoner, then they would soon be taking their prize back to Vlahan. If he didn't go after them now, he might never catch them, but what chance did he have without a horse? A man on foot was no match for mounted warriors. They could move five times as fast as he could; they could ride him down, trample him, and kill him before he had a chance to raise his spear.

Realizing that he would be no good to Arang dead, he reluctantly decided to go to Shara, get a horse, and maybe even try to put together a band of the younger men and women before he went in pursuit of the raiders. A few of the Sharans could ride well enough, although none of them could really fight. The question was: would they be more trouble than they were worth? Inexperienced warriors had a way of getting themselves killed in short order. The Sharans were brave, but could he trust them not to panic?

He kicked at the ground impatiently, thinking that if Grandmother Lalah had listened to him and let him train a few warriors to defend the city he would not be faced with the prospect of taking a pack of inexperienced farmers in pursuit of Arang's kidnappers. But Lalah and the whole Council of Elders had been horrified at the thought of him teaching the young to kill. People had given him odd looks for weeks after he'd proposed the idea, and even Marrah, who had seen the nomads firsthand and should have known better, had treated him to a long lecture on the sacredness of human life in the lands of the Goddess. He could see her point: if the Sharans fought, they risked destroying the very values they were fighting to defend. But what did they intend to do? Sit around like sheep while the Hansi fed on them?

Defend yourself and lose yourself. What a muddle. His head ached from trying to work it all out. I'm a practical man, he thought. The Sharans are great talkers. Let them decide these things in their councils. Right now the only problem I'm interested in is how to get Arang back without ending up with my head on a spear. Who can help me? Who can I count on?

The only people he could think of were both women: Hiknak, who could ride and fight like a man, and Dalish, who hated the nomads so much that she'd jump at a chance for revenge. Marrah was another matter. She could ride like a demon but she wouldn't last long in a pitched fight, and he didn't relish the idea of telling Keru and Luma that he'd taken their mother out and gotten her killed. Still, for all her talk about the sacredness of life, it might be hard to persuade Marrah to stay behind once she learned Arang had been captured.

He walked on, making plans, yet always alert. On the outside nothing escaped him—not a bird track, not a turned stone or a breath of wind, but inside he was filled with foreboding. Arang, he thought, Arang, my friend, are you really alive or have I misread the signs? Whenever he thought about how Arang had been taken, he felt guilty. Somehow he should have been able to save him. Somehow he should have been able to fight off the nomads. Never mind that they had been outnumbered and taken by surprise.

Soon he came to the river, but instead of walking along in the open as he would normally have done, he kept to the brush. The scouts had probably given up by this time, but a man lived longer if he always assumed his enemies were after him.

He followed the bank until he came to a place where willows hung down to the water, making a screen of leaves. Holding the spear tightly in his right hand, he slipped so silently into the water that the turtles sunning themselves on a nearby rock did not even raise their heads. The current almost tore the spear out of his hand, but he was a strong swimmer and he made it to the opposite bank without once coming up for air.

He had no sooner pulled himself up out of the water and caught his breath than he heard a noise that made him leap to his feet. Directly in front of him the bushes were moving—not from the wind, because there was no wind blowing. He watched the branches sway ever so slightly and decided that one of the scouts had been tracking him after all. There couldn't be two, because in that case they would have already attacked.

He saw immediately that he had an advantage. The scout couldn't shoot at him without stepping out in the open because there wasn't room to draw a bow. He could throw a spear, of course, but if he had a spear, he would have thrown it by now.

Stavan approached the bushes carefully. They were so covered with blackberry vines and thorns that it was hard to believe a man could be in there, but he wasn't about to bet his life that an animal was causing the movement. Besides, there was always the off chance that a she-lion was waiting to pounce.

"Come out," he hissed in Hansi. The bushes stopped moving. "Come out, you cowardly bastard."

He took another step forward, and all at once the bushes parted and something sprang at him. Stavan was fast. Before he even knew what was attacking him, he had thrown his spear with all his might at the spot where a man's heart would have been, but the spear missed because the thing that attacked him wasn't a man. It was a ball of white flesh, which came screaming and biting and scratching, throwing itself at him like a bear cub.

"Keshna!" Stavan cried. He caught the little girl by the arms and tried to hold her, but she kept fighting him and yelling—not words, just high, incoherent screams like a trapped animal. Her eyes were wild with terror, and she kicked and bit like a mad thing.

"Keshna," he begged, "Keshna, stop. It's me, Uncle Stavan." But she wouldn't stop, and he had to pin both her arms and her legs before he could quiet her. Finally, she seemed to recognize him. With a wild cry, she hid her head in his shoulder and began to sob. He sat holding her, rocking her, trying to calm her, but she wouldn't stop crying. There was nothing childlike about her weeping; it was as deep as any adult grief and made her whole body shudder.

He felt sick. He had almost killed a child. A three-year-old. His own niece. "Keshna," he begged, "speak to me. Tell me what's wrong. Why are you by yourself? Where's Hiknak?" But Keshna wouldn't talk. She only made those odd, animal-like noises, like a rabbit caught in a snare, and when he rose to his feet with the child in his arms and parted the brush and saw what she had been guarding, he knew why.

Hiknak lay on the bank, half in the river and half out, as if she had decided to go to sleep with her feet in the water. There was no sign of anything wrong with her except for a small bruise on her forehead no bigger than a berry stain, but the instant Stavan saw it, he knew that the nomads had caught her by surprise and killed her.

For a moment he stood quietly with Keshna in his arms, looking at Hiknak. Keshna must have tried to pull her mother all the way out of the water because her muddy little footprints were everywhere. Hiknak's hands were neatly arranged over her breast; in them the child had placed a small, ragged bouquet of yellow and white flowers.

Stavan closed his eyes and said a Hansi prayer for the dead. It was the prayer for dead warriors, since there were no prayers for women, and it wished Hiknak safely into Paradise.

He put Keshna down and took her by the hand. She had stopped crying and gone ominously silent, her big, dark eyes wide with thoughts too painful for a child.

"Don't be afraid," he told her. His voice broke slightly and he was surprised because he had seen so much death, yet this one touched him more than any of the others. He realized that he had loved Hiknak—not the way Arang loved her, but as he might have loved a dear brother. That was what she had been to him. Not a sister, because his sisters—if he had ever had any—would never have fought beside him the way Hiknak had fought. She had been little and tough, and he had never known a woman with a tenth of her spirit, except Marrah.

He looked down at Keshna and saw Hiknak and Arang in her face. "Don't be afraid," he said softly. "I'm here now. I'm your uncle, and I'll take care of you."

If Keshna heard him, she made no sign. She pulled her hand out of his, sat down, wrapped her arms around her knees, and hid her face. He made a few more attempts to comfort her and then gave up. Let the child grieve in peace. She had reason enough.

He went over to Hiknak, knelt beside her, and placed his hand over her face. He had intended to close her eyes, but they were already closed. He was just thinking that Keshna had thought of everything, when suddenly he saw Hiknak's chest rise slightly. He gave a low whistle of surprise. Could she be alive? He put his ear to her chest, and to his amazement he heard her heart beating. She wasn't dead! By Han, she wasn't!

"Keshna!" he yelled. "Keshna, come here!" But when he turned to look for the child she was gone. Where in the name of a thousand demons had she got to? Well, there was no time to find out. He cursed the gods for trapping him between a lost child and a dying woman. Pulling Hiknak all the way out of the river, he turned her over, pumped on her back to rid her lungs of water, called her name, chaffed her wrists, threw cold water on her, even slapped her cheeks, but she wouldn't wake. And still Keshna didn't return.

"Keshna!" he yelled again. "Where are you? I could use some help!" He suddenly sensed the child standing beside him, but he was too busy with Hiknak to look up. Stripping off his tunic, he threw it toward her and said, "Fold that into a pillow so I can put it under her head."

Keshna made no move to pick up the tunic. With a sigh of frustration, Stavan reminded himself that she was only three.

"Here," he said gently. "I'll do it." As he turned to retrieve his tunic he saw Keshna holding something out to him. It was a dirty bracelet, smeared with mud, broken, and missing half its beads and shells. At the sight of it he knew that something more terrible had happened than he could possibly have imagined.

"Where did you get that?" he whispered.

Keshna said nothing. She just looked him straight in the eyes and dropped the bracelet in his hand. Stavan held it for a moment, fingering the little beads. There was a blue bead he had picked out himself and a small yellow one Marrah had chosen. The tiny white cylinders of spondylus shell had been a gift from Lalah, and Bindar had made the little red clay fish. There were only two bracelets like this in Shara. One, which was slightly different, was on Luma's wrist. This one belonged to Keru.

For a while he stared at the bracelet, trying to turn it into something else, but the torn leather and dirty beads spoke as clearly as if they had tongues. Since Hiknak could not talk and Keshna refused to, he had no idea whether Keru was dead or alive, but the thought that the boy might be dead put him beyond fear. The only thing he felt now was rage: rage against the cowards who had taken Arang and perhaps killed his son; and rage against himself for having been stupid enough to let down his guard.

Shoving the bracelet into his pouch, he heaved Hiknak over his shoulder, grabbed Keshna by the hand, and hurried toward Shara. The forest soon gave way to open fields, but he no longer worried about the scouts spotting him. Once they were clear of the woods, he ran, stumbling under the weight of Hiknak and dragging Keshna behind him. The green wheat bent under his feet and swayed like feathered fans. All the beauty of the Goddess was in it, but it was nothing to him.

As he approached the white motherhouses, he saw them as a nomad would see them: open to attack on all sides, surrounded by a flimsy goat fence, unguarded by so much as a sentry, and he thought bitterly that living here among Marrah's people had made him soft. He had begun to think as she did: that the world was a peaceful place. But there was evil in the world, evil that rode out of the woods. Evil that had taken his son from him. That the evil bore human faces made no difference: it was evil nevertheless; and as he came in sight of the mother clans working in the fields and heard their cries of alarm as they saw him, he promised himself he would never again be caught unprepared.

By the time he reached the city, he was surrounded by wailing Sharans. He had called out the news as briefly as possible: that nomad raiders had come out of the forest, kidnapping Arang, attacking Hiknak and leaving her senseless, and kidnapping or perhaps killing Keru. Around him the crowd grew, swirling like a whirlpool.

"A horse," he kept saying. "Bring me a horse." But people seemed bewildered. For some reason they didn't take Hiknak from him nor did they run to get the horses. They just followed him, crying and lamenting, making so much noise that he could barely hear himself think. When at last he came to the central plaza, handed Keshna over to old Blentsa, and laid Hiknak down under one of the linen canopies, he found out why: there were no horses. The whole herd—all fifteen of them—had been missing since midday.

Any child from the steppes would have known that this meant they had been stolen, but evidently this had never occurred to the Sharans. They had been looking for the horses in a casual way, as one might look for lost sheep or stray cows.

When Stavan heard that the whole herd was gone, he felt as if his legs had been cut out from under him. As far as he knew, there were no horses except those in all the Motherlands. In a moment, he thought, Marrah will come, and I will have to tell her that her brother has been kidnapped and that our son may be dead. And then I will have to tell her that we are going to have to go on foot after the bastards who did it.

CHAPTER NINE

From the moment Stavan appeared with the news that Arang and Keru had been taken by the nomads, Marrah's life changed forever. That very afternoon, she and Stavan and Dalish walked out of the city to track down the raiders and bring them back. They were armed with knives meant to skin animals and bows more fit for hunting deer than fighting men on horseback; the forest was vast; Keru might already be dead, and even if they did find him and Arang unharmed, they would probably be outnumbered five to one; but if the chances had been ten times as bad, they still would have gone.

"We'll wait until they let their guard down," they told one another. "Then we'll sneak into their camp and get Arang and Keru." They did not tell one another that they would rather die than sit back and do nothing. They did not dwell on the fact that the nomads had horses and they didn't. They had been through a lot together. Once, tied to posts on the brink of Zuhan's grave, they had almost died side by side. In some ways, each knew the others' thoughts as intimately as if they shared one heart. Dalish did not have to say Keru and Arang were as dear to her as the children she had never been able to have; Stavan did not have to explain the guilt and anger he felt because he had failed to protect them. Marrah did not have to cry that she wanted her boy back at any price.

They went straight to the clearing, picked up the nomads' trail beside the felled oak, and began to follow it in grim silence, moving as fast as they could. Besides weapons, they carried only flints, a little dried food, and an extra pair of sandals apiece. The hoofprints were clear, and they were able to see them all afternoon and as long as the summer dusk lasted, but when the shadows of the trees finally began to blend together and the first owls appeared, they were forced to stop. Crawling into the brush, they spread their cloaks and slept side by side, hidden like animals for safety's sake, although by then they already knew the nomads were far ahead of them and getting farther all the time.

That night Marrah had the first of the dreams of Keru that would haunt her in the days to come. She dreamed she saw him running toward her, holding a strange yellow flower in his hand. The flower was almost as large as his fist, and something bright and blood-colored burned at the center of it. Arang ran a little behind Keru, dancing joyfully and twirling a soft green scarf around his body like a trail of smoke.

When she saw the two of them alive and well, she felt a burst of joy. Blood rushed to her face and her fingers tingled and she felt as if she could rise in the air and fly like the bird she was named after. Yes! she thought. We've succeeded. Here they are. They're safe! But of course they are. This nonsense about a nomad raid was all a bad dream. How silly I was to get so upset.

"Keru, darling," she cried.

"Mama!" he said. He laughed his little-boy laugh and thrust the giant flower out to her, but when she reached to take it, the petals slipped through her fingers and she felt something sting her. She gave a cry of pain and bent down to sweep Keru up in her arms, but before she could touch him, he disappeared.

"Keru!" she called, "come back!" But there was nothing but a dead flower and a pair of small muddy footprints where he had stood, and when she turned to ask Arang where he was, Arang was gone too.

She woke in a cold sweat, grinding her teeth and sobbing. For less time than it took for her heart to beat, she had no idea where she was or why she was lying on the ground between Dalish and Stavan. Then grief and disappointment filled her stomach like a stone, weighing her down and taking all the joy out of the world. She wanted Arang back, safe and whole, but at least Arang was a man. He might escape on his own, but what chance did Keru have?

I hate the nomads, she thought. I thought I hated them before, when they killed the Shambans and took me and Arang prisoner. I thought I hated them when they murdered Akoah and strangled the slaves. But I didn't really know hatred until they took my son. She lay there, tasting the bitterness of her own rage. She wanted Keru back now, not tomorrow. She wanted to hold him in her arms and tell him he was safe; she wanted to feel his body curled into hers and smell the fresh scent of his hair. She never doubted for a moment that he was still alive. He was out there somewhere, afraid, missing her, and with the help of the Goddess, Mother of All Mothers, she was not only going to find him, she was going to make the men who had taken him regret it.

She reached for the small leather pouch that always hung at her waist, undid the drawstrings, and ran her fingers over the small clay balls of dried thunder that the priestess of Nar had given her so long ago. She knew that they would make a terrible noise if she threw them into a fire. Perhaps she could stampede the nomads' horses with them; perhaps . . .

She fell asleep dreaming of a dozen different ways to rescue Arang and Keru, but the next morning when she woke the trail was no longer fresh. The sides of the hoofprints were beginning to crumble; water had seeped into the hollows; a few leaves and sticks had drifted across them, and here and there a deer or a rabbit had layered its tracks over those of the raiders.

"They're moving a lot faster than we are," Dalish said. And indeed they were—about five times as fast.

Marrah knelt and touched the dried mud as if by touching it she could learn where Keru was, but the mud was mute and cold under her hands. The hatred burned more fiercely in her. Ever since she was a small child, she had been trained to think of human life as sacred. Now, for the first time, she felt as if she could enjoy fighting.

They walked most of the day, saying little, resting only when they were too exhausted to go on. Near evening a strong wind began to blow, and the sky turned the color of ashes.

"It looks like rain," Dalish murmured.

Marrah said nothing. She watched the sky growing darker and darker and felt the wet scent of the coming rain fill the air. "Don't let it storm," she prayed. "Don't let the tracks of the raiders be washed away." But perhaps the Goddess no longer listened to her. The rain came anyway, a series of quick showers that soaked them to the skin and left them shivering. That night they slept under a pile of brush again, listening to the water hit the deerskin cape Stavan had had the sense to stretch over their heads. Before they closed their eyes, he turned to Marrah.

"The hoofprints are deep," he said, "and there are a lot of them."

She went to sleep, clinging to that little bit of hope, but when she woke, rose to her feet, looked out at the forest, and saw what the rain had done, she yelled and shook her fist at the sky. "Han, you bastard of a sky god, you nomad son of a bitch, go back to the steppes!" she yelled, and then she sat down, put her hands over her face, and began to cry. It was the ugly kind of crying a person does only when everything is lost, the kind that leaves the crier red eyed and gasping for air. Up to that point, she had been sure they would rescue Keru, but now she saw that she had been a fool. Gradually, she realized Stavan was kneeling beside her.

"Don't touch me," she snarled, but he had the sense to know she didn't mean it. Putting his arms around her, he drew her to him, and she rested her cheek against his chest as if being close to him might help, only it didn't. There was no comfort in him or in anything else.

"Keru is still alive," he said.

"Don't lie to me."

"I am not lying to you." He took her by the chin and turned her face up to his. "Keru is alive and so is Arang."

She didn't know whether to believe him, but his words gave her hope. "How do you know they're alive?"

"They must be. Think, Marrah. You know what my people are like. You've seen a Hansi war party. If either Keru or Arang were dead, we would have found their bodies by now."

She pulled away and sat back, rigid as a bit of wood. "You mean all this time you've been looking for their . . . " She stopped. He nodded. Suddenly, she realized she had been looking too, looking in a terror so great that she had not been able to admit it even to herself. She rose to her feet, and he rose with her. For a moment they stood face to face. Finally he spoke.

"Marrah, I'm not very good with words. If I were a man of your own people, perhaps I'd know what to say to comfort you, but I don't. All I can do is promise you that we're going to pick up their

Mary
Mackey

146

trail again. It may not be easy, but I know how to do it. Mukhan himself trained me to scout when I was hardly more than a boy. As much as I hate the men who took our boy, I was born a nomad and I know how they think. I won't lie to you: they have a lot of advantages, not the least of which being that they have horses, but they're doing some stupid things—probably out of sheer arrogance.

"They're not going very fast, and they're not taking time to hide their tracks. We know they're heading north; we know they're sticking to the main trails; and we know they're driving fifteen of our horses, not counting the ones they're riding. A herd that size slows them down and leaves tracks a blind man could follow. It only rained in short bursts last night, which means that it didn't rain everywhere. There will be dry ground up ahead, and sooner or later we'll see hoofprints."

"And if we don't pick up their trail?"

"Then we go back to Shara, get on a *raspa*, sail up to Shambah, and walk north into the steppes until we either find some horses we can steal or find Nikhan and make him give us some. We know they're taking Keru and Arang straight to Vlahan. We just don't know the route they're traveling. Right now it's too soon to give up. I still think we have a chance to overtake them. They feel safe. They may grow careless and decide to pitch camp and rest for a day or two. You have to understand that warriors feel complete contempt for anyone who isn't riding a horse. I doubt that they can even imagine being tracked down by three people who have walked after them."

She wiped the tears off her face and stared at him for a long time. Finally, she spoke, "You really believe we have a chance?"

"I really do."

They stood for a moment confronting each other, and then she took a quick step forward and kissed him.

"Bless you," she said. They held each other until Dalish cleared her throat.

"Well, friends," she said, "what next?"

Stavan let go of Marrah, picked up Dalish's bag, and tossed it to her. "First," he said, "we eat because if we don't we're going to fall on our faces before midday. Then we start walking again."

The whole morning was hard going. The storm had left the ground muddy and swelled the creeks beyond their banks. More than once they had to wade in waist-deep water, but a little past midday, they picked up the nomads' trail again: a great swath of muddy hoofprints, made by the only horses south of Shambah. It led northwest, as wide and straight as the path and the trees would permit.

"They must be heading for Mahclah," Dalish said. Mahclah was only a tiny collection of mud and reed huts, but it lay on the banks of the River of Smoke at the first place the river could be forded by men on horseback. The two mother clans that lived in Mahclah ferried traders across in their fishing boats, but there never were many crossings even during the busiest part of the summer since most goods went by water.

Marrah looked at the muddy trail and thought of the great river rushing toward the sea, dividing the north from the south like a wall. The delta was an endless plain of reeds, hard enough to negotiate on foot but even harder to cross on horseback. She imagined the nomads lost, wandering in circles, their beasts floundering in the soft black mud. With luck, they might be delayed for several days before they reached the ford.

"The ground around Mahclah is only solid in a few places," she said.

Dalish rubbed her tongue over her teeth and thought this over. "They aren't likely to know which paths to follow."

"Do you think the River People will guide them?"

Dalish shrugged. "Who knows. By now all the mother clans along the river must have heard about the attack on Shambah, but put a spear to someone's back and there's no knowing what they'll do."

Stavan said nothing. He was kneeling beside the tracks, inspecting them with a thoughtful expression. He measured them with the palm of his hand, then rose and motioned for Marrah and Dalish to follow him as he walked along the trail, pointing out subtle differences that neither of them would have noticed without his help. The hoofprints were shallower and closer together than they had been, which meant the nomads were going slower. Perhaps they were finally getting tired, Stavan speculated, because if you looked carefully you could see that they had started to surround the stolen horses as if preparing to catch them and hobble them for the night.

"I think soon we'll come to the place where they camped," he said.

Dalish and Marrah said nothing. They had been walking for nearly two days, and only now were they reaching the place the warriors had spent the first night after the raid. By now they were so far behind that it might not matter if the nomads got lost in the delta reeds. We're like snails chasing a pack of wolves, Marrah thought. She looked down at her muddy sandals and remembered how quickly Eoru, her brown mare, had taken her to Shara. *Eoru* was the Hansi word for "purple iris," but there had been nothing delicate or irislike about her. She had been as sturdy as a boat and almost as fast. Marrah would have given anything to be riding Eoru now, but the nomads had stolen her along with the other horses.

At least the tracking was easy. The warriors continued to be careless, not making the slightest attempt to hide their trail. Marrah wondered if they had sat around their campfire that first night laughing at the thought of her anger and grief. She tried not to think about how frightened Keru must have been when it grew dark. Maybe Arang had comforted him. She hoped so. Keru had always loved Arang. She was just wondering if the nomads would let Arang and Keru sleep side by side, when Stavan, who was a little ahead of her, came to stop so suddenly that she nearly bumped into him.

"What's wrong?" she asked. He said nothing in reply; he just pointed. She followed his finger and saw that they were within a few steps of a good-sized clearing—one of the sort that was often formed when a large tree fell and took other smaller trees down with it. The trunks lay on the ground, covered with lichens and moss. Between them, partly buried in the brush, lay a dozen or more large, oddly shaped objects. At first she thought they were boulders. They were round and smooth: brown mostly or dun colored, but here and there lumps of black or white rose from the weeds like sleek, oversized mushrooms. Then she saw a hoof and a bit of mane, and suddenly she understood.

"The horses!" she gasped.

Dalish, who had come up beside her, gave a low cry of horror.

They walked into the clearing and saw dead horses lying everywhere. The "boulders" were their rumps; but now as she parted the brush, Marrah saw their necks and legs as well, and their large dark eyes glazed over with the film of death. All fifteen of the stolen horses were there. The nomads had hobbled them first and then killed them by slitting their throats. The poor animals lay on the earth with their forelegs still bound, and the sweet-sick smell of rotting horseflesh rose from their bodies and tainted the air.

Marrah gagged and turned away. Her eyes filled with tears, and she felt as if she might vomit. Leaning her forehead against a tree, she stood waiting for the nausea to pass. After a little while, the smell did not seem quite as bad. She returned to the clearing and began to walk slowly, passing from horse to horse. Every one was an old friend. Here lay Eoru; over there the gray gelding they had stolen from Mukhan's camp—the one Hiknak had become so fond of. The stallions had been killed on opposite sides of the clearing, probably because they got difficult to handle if you brought them too near one another. The nomads had not even spared the colts.

She knelt by Eoru and stroked her short mane. It was rough and familiar under her hand, but already the life force had left it. Stavan came and stood beside her. She looked up at him and her eyes filled with tears. She had loved that mare like a sister.

"Was it a sacrifice?"

He nodded. "Probably." He crouched down beside her. "I imagine they wanted to give thanks to Han for a successful raid, but they killed sloppily. I'd say from the looks of things they were in a hurry."

Marrah sat for a moment looking at her mare. "I'm going to cut off a bit of Eoru's mane."

"Why?"

"To make a bracelet to remember her by." She took out her knife and cut off a few strands of brown horsehair.

When she was finished, Stavan took her by the hand, drew her to her feet, and led her back into the woods. They stood together in the shade of a large oak. "I think we're going to find that the trail won't be as easy to follow from here on," he said. "I suspect when we look around, we're going to discover that they've split up into little groups. That's the Hansi way: make enough trails and your enemy won't know which one to follow. The extra horses would have just been in the way, so they gave them to Han."

Marrah expected him to say that now it was time for them to leave, but instead he just stood there as if at a loss for words.

"Dalish," he called.

Dalish, who had been standing by her own dead mare, turned and came slowly across the clearing, picking her way around the slain animals. When the three of them were together, Stavan took Marrah by one hand and Dalish by the other.

"We have to do something before we go on." He paused and pressed his lips together, and his eyes were grim. "We have to look for Keru."

Marrah jerked her hand out of his. "What are you talking about!"

"This looks like a sacrifice." His voice faltered, and he looked out at the horses, at the blood and the buzzing flies. "If it was, then the warriors might have offered more than horses to Han. A first-born son would be . . . "

"—The best of offerings!" Dalish cried.

Marrah did not wait to hear more. Turning around, she ran back to the clearing and began to search frantically among the dead horses. Dalish searched on one side of her and Stavan on the other. Sometimes they grabbed the animals by their short, bloody manes and lifted their necks to see if Keru lay under them, and sometimes all three of them pushed at one of the rumps, sweating and panting as they heaved the stiffened beast sideways. By the time they were finished they were covered with mud and horse blood, but Marrah didn't care. She was dizzy with relief. Keru's body wasn't anywhere to be found. There were dead horses aplenty but no little boy lying in the bloody dirt with his throat slit.

Dalish seized her by the hand again, and the two of them knelt and kissed the earth. "Great Mother of All Mothers," Marrah cried, "thank you. Thank you!"

They were just rising to their feet when Stavan came up to them with something in his hand. It was a dagger, finely made, with a sharp blade and a bone handle carved over with lightning bolts and clan signs. He said he had found it at the center of the clearing, stuck blade-first into the ground. All three of them knew that a dagger stuck into the ground was the Hansi sign for Lord Han and that its presence meant a sacrifice had indeed taken place; but Stavan had something more to tell them, something not even Dalish could have known.

"This is Changar's dagger," he announced. "I recognize the markings." He pointed at the bolts of lightning. "You realize what this means, don't you?"

"But Changar couldn't have been here: he's dead." Marrah turned to Dalish. "You saw him fall into Zuhan's grave; you heard his body hit the stones. He must have broken his neck. He might have been a diviner, but he was mortal. He couldn't have survived."

"He must have," Dalish said. "If he had died, they would have broken the blade of his dagger and buried it with him."

"Dalish is right." Stavan wiped the mud off the blade and stuck it in his belt. "A man's dagger never outlives him unless it's captured in battle or he offers it to Han. It isn't a good thing to lose a dagger. I think I'll keep Changar's until I have the pleasure of giving it back to him."

The Horses at the Gate

151

There was nothing to say after that. They simply picked up their food bags and walked around the edge of the clearing until they found the nomads' trail again. Even though there were only half as many horses the hoofprints were still easy to follow, and after a short while they came to the ashes of several campfires.

Stavan stirred the ashes with a stick. "Cold," he announced, "but not scattered." He turned to Marrah. "Don't be discouraged. The fact that they stopped to build fires means they aren't traveling like a war party. They're going slowly, and I think I know why." He patted Changar's dagger. "They've got Changar with them, and he's not a young man. No raw meat and cold beds for him. He's always liked his little comforts. Also they have Keru to consider. You can't make a four-year-old ride for days on end. You have to make sure he gets food and rest."

Marrah leapt at his words. "Then you think they're taking care of him?"

"Yes—in their way. He's a valuable bit of property."

The word *property* stung. She wanted to throw it back at him, to cry that Keru wasn't a pot or a sheep; but she knew Stavan was right. That was exactly the way the nomads would see him. Since they hadn't sacrificed Keru or killed him when they attacked Hiknak, they must believe he was the son of someone important—maybe Stavan but more likely Vlahan. Among the Hansi, men owned their wives and children the way they owned their horses. The raiders would take care of Keru the way they took care of a fine colt. She supposed she should find some comfort in that, but it was hard to think of her little boy being fed and put to bed at night by men who would have bashed out his brains without a second thought if circumstances had been different.

She helped Stavan and Dalish look around the campsite for more signs, but they found nothing of interest, only the usual trash: gnawed bones, guts and feathers from plucked birds, piles of dung, an old hobble, and a bit of hempen twine that might have been used to repair an arrow. They searched everywhere for Keru's footprints, but the ground was too churned up.

One tree did look like something—or someone—had been tied to it. In several places the bark was scarred with rope marks, and something had been scratched into the trunk with a sharp stone. At first Marrah thought the scratch might be a message from Arang, but when she looked more closely she saw that it was only the sort of scratch a warrior might make with the point of his dagger in an idle moment. Just as she was bending down to see if she could find anything else, Stavan came up behind her, clapped his hand over her mouth, and put his lips to her ear.

"Don't make a sound," he whispered. She stiffened in surprise and rose to see Dalish standing nearby. Dalish's tattooed cheeks were drawn tight, and she had wrinkled her forehead as if concentrating her entire being into her ears. *Listen,* Dalish mouthed.

Marrah listened. For a moment there was no sound except the rustle of the wind through the treetops and the chirping of a bird somewhere off in the distance. And then she heard the soft, unmistakable snuffle of a horse. Turning as one person, the three of them fled into the brush as quickly and silently as they could.

As she lay facedown on the ground between Dalish and Stavan, all Marrah could think of was the word *ambush.* The nomads always attacked without warning. What fools they had been to think that while they were hunting the Hansi, the Hansi weren't hunting them. In a moment, the warriors would ride out of the forest and kill them. She remembered what it had been like at Shambah on the day she and Arang were captured: how the warrior who had taken her prisoner had chased her, playing with her before he knocked her to the ground. He had been about to rape her when another warrior had stopped him, but there would be no one to save her this time. The warriors would kill Stavan outright, and then they would fall on her and Dalish.

She pulled her knife from her belt and waited as the sound of horses came still closer. She was determined to fight to the last, to force them to kill her. Stavan and Dalish must have been thinking the same thing, because Dalish had her knife out, and Stavan had risen into a crouch and was putting an arrow to his bow.

A crash of something large moving through the brush, the sound of a stick breaking, and then the nomad horses were upon them and they were discovered. Stavan leapt to his feet, raised his bow, drew back the string, yelled his war cry, and let it die in his throat. Marrah and Dalish lowered their knives. For a moment all three of them stared in amazement, and then they began to laugh the half-hysterical whoops people give when death has brushed them and passed by: a single horse stood looking at them placidly as it munched on a bunch of green leaves. It was not even a nomad horse; it was the sturdy black-and-white gelding Stavan had ridden the day he and Arang had gone out to cut down the oak.

"It's Morningstar!" Marrah cried.

"How did he get here?"

"Maybe he followed us."

"Maybe the nomads took him and he escaped."

"Look, he's still wearing his bridle."

"Come to give us a ride."

"What an ambush!"

"What a band of warriors!"

"I was so scared I nearly wet myself!" This from Dalish, who was leaning against a tree and gasping with laughter. "Great Goddess, Morningstar, my dear, what terror you inspired!"

Stavan put the arrow back in his quiver and slung his bow over his chest. "It's good he walked out of the bushes or I would have shot at him." He made the clicking sound the Hansi used to call their horses. "Say, old fellow, come here."

But Morningstar wasn't coming—or going either for that matter. He was simply standing serenely at the edge of the clearing, munching on his leaves, and looking at them with the great tolerance of a horse who understands that human beings are complicated creatures.

When they finally managed to stop laughing, Marrah went up to him and caught the trailing reins. Except for a few burrs in his coat, he seemed in good shape. His hooves were unsplit, he looked as if he had eaten his fill, and if he had been ridden hard there were no signs of it.

"This changes everything," Stavan said. He stroked Morningstar's nose and looked from Marrah to Dalish and back again. Marrah shifted the reins to her left hand and reached out to stroke the horse's flank. Dalish nodded. Once again, the three of them knew one another's minds without having to speak: now they had a chance to catch up with the nomads, but before they could mount the gelding and race north, they had a decision to make—there were three of them and only one horse. Only one person would be able to go on from here, and they all knew who that person had to be.

Marrah handed the reins to Stavan. "Here," she said. The word stuck in her throat. She wanted to climb on Morningstar and thunder after Keru, screaming her own war cry. She wanted to be the one who crept into the Hansi camp and untied Arang. She rested her hand on Stavan's and tried not to envy him. Perhaps he was riding to his death. Still, she would have given anything to be in his place. "You can track," she said, "and Dalish and I can't. You know how to fight, and we don't. You're the best rider, and when all is said and done, you're a warrior." She paused and pressed her lips together, swallowing the bitterness of her disappointment. "Dalish and I will walk back to Shara. It's not that far. We'll wait for you there."

Stavan took the reins and swung himself up onto Morningstar's back. He promised to bring back Arang and Keru or, failing that, to ride on to Nikhan's camp and send horses so she and Dalish could join him. He spoke as if they would be apart for only a few weeks, but his eyes said that he had no idea when he'd return.

"Give Luma my love," he said, and Marrah promised she would. They kissed, he bending down to reach her lips, she standing on her toes; and then he was gone, riding off into the forest with a kick of his heels, and she and Dalish were alone beside the nomads' abandoned campfires.

They started back toward Shara immediately, skirting the clearing where the slaughtered horses lay. Now there was no need to hurry, and as they made their way along the trail, Marrah felt a vast, blank emptiness open up in front of her. In the center of that emptiness was a small bit of hope: Stavan might rescue Keru and Arang; he really might be home in a week or ten days. All she could do now was wait. She had a vision of a new world where women spent most of their lives waiting, and she didn't like it at all.

Marrah spent the rest of the summer sitting in a dark room tending to Hiknak. There were some who said Marrah's heart had been broken when the nomads stole Keru and that she needed as much nursing as her friend, but that was hardly fair. Marrah knew who she was and what she was waiting for, even if the knowledge brought her pain; Hiknak, on the other hand, had no idea what had happened to her, particularly during the first few weeks when she hovered between life and death.

Hiknak had opened her eyes two days after Stavan carried her back to the city, but she no longer spoke a word of Sharan. Sometimes she would curse in Hansi and sometimes she would call for her mother in a babyish voice as if she were a small child, but most of the time she just lay passively on her sleeping mat, staring at Marrah in a puzzled way as if trying to figure out who Marrah was. The more Marrah tried to reassure her, the more confused Hiknak became, especially at night when she often grew restless and frightened. Before the raid, Hiknak had been right-handed, but now she reached for everything with her left hand. Sunlight—and even bright lamplight—gave her terrible headaches.

"Dark him!" she would moan in broken Hansi. "Bastard light teeth bite me spear tip him son of bitch!" Marrah could see her fighting to find the right words, but everything she said in those first few weeks came out garbled. Often Hiknak would end up crying and pounding the blankets in frustration while everyone stood by mystified.

When she finally understood that light made Hiknak's head hurt, Marrah fixed up her room so none could enter, draping the windows with sheets of black linen and covering the door with a heavy blanket. The room was the same one Hiknak had shared for many years with Arang, but she had lost so much of her memory that Arang no longer existed for her. As the days passed and her speech improved, it became clear that she believed she was still living in her father's tent. She would demand mare's milk and become annoyed when Marrah tried to explain that there were no mares; or she would beg to see her lover, Iriknak, who had been killed years ago in a Hansi raid.

Although many people came to help Marrah nurse Hiknak, only one stayed. For weeks Keshna sat by her mother, guarding her like a little dog. At first Lalah had forbidden Keshna to spend all her waking hours in the dark room. It was obvious to everyone that so small a child should be out in the sunshine playing with the other children, but Keshna threw such wild fits when they tried to take her away from Hiknak that it seemed better to let her do what she wanted. If she had been like the other children, Lalah would have insisted, because no child however young was allowed to defy her elders, but there was something wrong with Keshna that no one knew how to fix.

Before the raid, Keshna had been a talkative little girl who managed to get into an amazing amount of mischief for a three-year-old, but since that day at the river she had refused to speak. Marrah, Lalah, Dalish—everyone—begged her to tell them what had happened when the nomads attacked, but although Keshna clearly understood their questions, she acted like someone who had forgotten what language was for.

At first they thought the nomads were responsible, but except for a few scratches, Keshna seemed to have survived the raid without a mark, and she could make all sorts of noises: growls, grunts, howls, even—on very rare occasions—laughter. She was awake—all too awake, looking out at the world like an animal at bay, hard to control, given to sudden bursts of anger and wild crying fits that left her exhausted. Sometimes she attacked the other children without warning, but it was useless to punish her or try to reason with her when her own mother didn't recognize her.

Hiknak turned eighteen that summer, but for weeks she acted as if she were twelve. In Hiknak's mind her whole family was still alive; she had never stood by screaming in terror as Vlahan's warriors slaughtered them and then raped her; she had never been Vlahan's concubine or been beaten by him or been forced to sleep with the dogs. Perhaps that was a mercy, but there were good things missing as well. Those weeks she had spent in the snow cave making love with Arang no longer existed; she had never gotten pregnant, never helped defeat Nikhan, never lived in a place where women were respected, never been a mother. The first time Keshna tried to crawl up into her lap, Hiknak looked at the little girl as if she had never seen her before.

"Who be?" she asked.

"This is Keshna," Marrah said.

"Who?"

"Keshna, your daughter."

Hiknak laughed and then looked confused.

Keshna threw her arms around Hiknak's neck and tried to hug her, but Hiknak pushed her away.

"Sharanak?"

"This isn't Sharanak," Marrah explained patiently. "This is Keshna, your daughter."

A glimmer of recognition came into Hiknak's eyes, but before she could speak, it faded. She raised her weak right hand and passed it lightly over Keshna's face. "Yartanak?" She grew more confused. "Bretnak?" Perhaps she was listing her younger sisters or her nieces, or maybe the names had just come to her out of nowhere. "Utranak? Dremnak?" Tears seeped out of her eyes and began to flow down her cheeks. She pushed Keshna lightly on the chest. "Go way," she said.

After that Keshna was worse than ever. The priestesses who healed the sick finally decided she had the disease called *shohwar*. *Shohwar* was the same word the Sharans used when they spoke of empty spaces: cups with nothing in them, blank gray skies, unpainted walls, but it could also mean an empty space in the heart. The priestesses said Keshna was *shohwar* because she had given up on being human, and they ordered everyone to be especially kind to her, so she was allowed to sit with Marrah, crawling up into her lap and putting her head on her shoulder while Marrah rocked her and sang to her.

Sometimes Marrah sang lullabies, and sometimes she sang memory songs; once she even sang Sabalah's entire song map, running the route from the Sea of Gray Waves to Shara, but Keshna never seemed to care what she sang as long as she went on singing.

Luma often came in to listen, and Marrah would hold both of them, one girl under each arm like a mother bird settling down with her chicks. But Luma did not like the dark room and soon she would leave, and Marrah would hear her laughing and playing outside with the other children.

Sometimes when Marrah went out to take a breath of fresh air, she would see the children romping and giggling and falling over one another like a litter of puppies. She would watch Luma running across the fields with a kite string in one hand, her little bare feet pounding the earth; or she would watch her shrieking with laughter as she dumped a cup of cold water down Shutu's back or wrestled in the dust with Minha, and the sight of her daughter—well, healthy, and up to no good—would make her smile; and when she went back to the sickroom to feed Hiknak sips of broth or hold Keshna, she would take that smile with her to light up the darkness.

Such moments were rare. Waiting was the hardest work Marrah had ever done, and she often thought that if it weren't for Stavan she might have gone *shohwar* too. Twice he managed to send word to her. That wasn't nearly often enough, but it was enough to give her hope.

The first message came about two weeks after she and Dalish returned to Shara. One hot summer afternoon, a trader arrived from Mahclah with word that Stavan had forded the river and was heading north. He must not have caught up with the nomads, though, because just as the weather started to turn, a *raspa* sailed into the harbor bringing another message: Stavan had reached Shambah, stopped for a few days to rest, and then left for the steppes.

> *Tell Marrah I'm going to find Nikhan and see if I can put together a band of warriors. Tell her Vlahan brought the whole tribe right to the edge of the Motherlands and people say they saw a little boy and a young man handed over to*

him with great ceremony. Tell her not to come to Shambah until I send word, but that I'll send horses to her as soon as I can.

That night Marrah, Lalah, and Dalish went to the beach, sat down on the sand, and drank wine from a goatskin bag while the surf pounded and cold spray wet their faces. Keru and Arang were still alive, but Vlahan had them. Shall we laugh or shall we cry? they asked one another. Shall we celebrate or shall we mourn? They ended up doing both and making themselves sick in the process, but even so, it was the best night Marrah had had since the raid.

The priestesses who tended the sick tried everything they could think of to bring back Hiknak's memory. When she was still in danger of falling into the deadly stupor that often followed blows to the head, they came to her room every morning and sat with their hands on her, chanting special healing prayers. Afterward, they fed her rue mixed with vinegar and strong teas made from wormwood, hyssop, and vervain. When they saw that she was still wandering in the past, they made her drink a bitter potion made from sacred earth and the beans of a rare plant the traders sometimes brought from the east. The bean potion tasted terrible but it was supposed to be strong enough to wake the dead, and very slowly—so slowly that Marrah nearly gave up hope—it seemed to work. As the summer waned, Hiknak gradually began to remember things. At first they were all disconnected like the beads of a broken necklace: one day she would recall the Sharan word for "cup," and the next day she would forget it. But after a while the necklace began to restring itself again, the words became sentences, and sentences became loops of lost time.

One morning when Marrah was feeding her breakfast, Hiknak looked up at her and smiled.

"Is that you, Marrah?" she said in perfect Sharan. Marrah was so surprised that she nearly dumped the bowl of wheat mush into Hiknak's lap.

"Yes, Hiknak. It's me."

"Why am I in bed? Am I sick?"

Marrah set down the bowl and took Hiknak in her arms. Tears filled her eyes; she was so happy, she could barely speak.

"Welcome back," she said.

Hiknak looked puzzled. "Why are you crying?"

"You don't remember what happened?"

Hiknak shook her head.

Marrah wiped her eyes with the back of her hand and forced herself to speak calmly. "You've been gone for a long time, wandering in the past where none of us could reach you." She paused, wondering where she should begin. "Do you remember the day you took Keshna and Keru to the river to pick blackberries?"

Hiknak pressed her lips together and frowned. "I don't know. I don't think so."

"A nomad raiding party attacked you. One of them hit you on the head, and you fell facedown in the river. If Keshna hadn't pulled you out, you would have drowned. They took Arang and Keru." She stopped. Hiknak was staring at her blankly. "You remember who Arang is, don't you?"

"My brother?"

"No, Hiknak. Arang is my brother. He's your lover."

Hiknak blushed and twirled a bit of hair around her finger. "Is this Ar . . . " She groped for the name. "Is he handsome?"

"You always seemed to think so."

Hiknak frowned and looked around furtively. "Will V . . . " Once again she searched for a name and couldn't find it. "Will V . . . kill me when he finds out?"

"You mean Vlahan?"

Hiknak nodded.

Marrah sighed. Hiknak's mind was not like a necklace. It was more like a jar that had been dropped on a tile floor. None of the pieces quite fit together. "You aren't Vlahan's concubine anymore," she said. She took Hiknak's hands and held them for a moment. "What's the last thing you remember?"

"Gathering greens for old Zulike."

"How old are you, Hiknak?"

Hiknak frowned again and then her face brightened. "Fourteen?"

"No, you're eighteen. You're a mother. Four years have passed." Slowly, patiently, Marrah told Hiknak the story of her life, and slowly, like a child stumbling to take her first steps, Hiknak remembered and forgot, forgot and remembered.

It was hard to bring her back to the present, but Marrah was persistent. Every day, three or four times a day, she reminded Hiknak who she was, and every day Hiknak remembered a little more. Finally the time came when she knew her own child again, and calling Keshna to her, she covered her with kisses.

"My darling, my baby," Hiknak crooned, stroking Keshna's hair; but it was too late. Keshna wound her arms around Hiknak's neck and hung on so tightly that her fingers made small red marks on Hiknak's skin, but she refused to speak, and when Marrah begged her to say something to her mother, she made a little hissing noise like a baby snake.

The days grew shorter and the autumn wind swept off the sea with bone-chilling force, tossing the waves high onto the beach. Every morning before she went to Hiknak, Marrah climbed to the roof and looked north, hoping to see the horses Stavan had promised to send, and every day she saw only sand and trees, small herds of cattle, goats, and short-haired sheep. Then one morning, when she had given up all hope, four young Shambans arrived leading seven mares and a stallion tied together in a long line. The horses were a gift from Nikhan, and one of them was a brown mare so much like Eoru that when Marrah saw her, she knew Stavan had picked her out.

The Shambans brought another message from Stavan—a message so unbelievable that she made them repeat it three times.

Stavan son of Zuhan sends his love and says to Marrah daughter of Sabalah: don't come to Shambah. There's nothing you can do to help me get Arang and Keru back. Nikhan and some of the other rebel tribes have recognized me as Great Chief. In the spring, my warriors will attack Vlahan's camp, but I can't have a woman riding with me, not even you. If Nikhan and his men knew my wife could fight like a man, they would turn on me.

When Marrah heard that Stavan didn't want her, when she heard she was worse than useless and a danger to her own son and her own brother because she was a woman, she clenched her fist and struck out blindly, hitting a wall and splitting her knuckles.

That afternoon she went to the Council of Elders and asked permission to start fortifying the cliffs above the city. This time no one argued with her. It was as if they all had been waiting for her to speak.

Old Dakar rose to his feet and made a short speech. "Four years ago, you asked us to move Shara to the top of the cliffs, and we laughed at you. We told you this was holy ground and Batal would protect us no matter what happened. At that time, we knew nothing about war, but since then we have seen what happens when a vicious enemy attacks defenseless people. Hiknak, our dear adopted daughter, nearly died when the nomads raided us, and every morning we wake up knowing that Arang and Keru have been stolen, and we grieve over them, and our bread tastes bitter in our mouths. You are young, Marrah. In the past, the young listened to the old, but now the world is upside down. You know the nomads better than we do. You were their prisoner, and you lived among them. Tell us what we need to do to protect ourselves, and we will do it."

Marrah put her hands together and bowed respectfully to Dakar. Then she got down to business. "First," she said, "we have to post sentries. The nomads must never again take us by surprise."

The elders agreed, and Yintesa, who was head of the Society of Men and Women Who Hunt, promised to recruit sentries from the best hunters in the city.

"Next, we must store food in the Temple of Children's Dreams and build other shelters on the top of the cliffs so we can run to them if the nomads attack us. They won't be able to ride their horses up the path: it's too steep and too narrow. If they try to walk up, we can roll stones down on them." She paused. "Batal has been good to us. She's given us a safe place nearby, with plenty of water to drink and room for everyone. It won't be very comfortable up there, and we may have to sit by and watch the motherhouses down below burn, but in my opinion, if we wait long enough, the nomads will go away."

"We'll entertain ourselves by singing," Ulitsa said, and she strummed on her harp a bit by way of example. Everyone laughed uneasily and then fell silent.

"There's one more thing." Marrah paused and looked at the elders. "We must make a lot of arrows. We won't have a chance if we have to fight the nomads hand to hand, but our hunters have sharp eyes and a man is nearly as big as a deer."

For the next two months, Marrah supervised the fortification of the cliffs. For more than a week, a long line of men and women plodded up the path carrying baskets of grain, flour, dried fruit, jerked meat, salted fish, and oil to the Temple of Children's Dreams. The city had always had extra stores in case the crops failed, and now instead of being conveniently located in the temples, they were inconveniently located at the top of the cliffs.

Building extra shelters proved more difficult. There were few loose stones, no suitable clay, and only a few windblown trees on the wide ledge where the temple stood, and after a week of lugging rocks and baskets of mud up the steep trail, everyone was tired and discouraged. Then Dalish had a brilliant idea.

"Why don't we make some tents?" she suggested. "They're dry, warm, and light." She laughed. "Tents, horses, and long-haired sheep are the only good things the nomads have to offer. I say, when your enemy comes up with a good idea, steal it."

So they set to sewing tents, and by the time the first icy winter rains fell, they had enough to shelter all the children and old people in Shara.

When everything was finished, and the extra bows and arrows were stored in waterproof bundles, Lalah called Marrah to her. When she arrived, Marrah found her grandmother dressed in a long blue linen tunic embroidered with snakes and flowers. Lalah's curly gray hair was carefully parted and pulled into a chignon, and she wore a special ceremonial diadem made of snakeskin and white shells. Bindar sat beside her, dressed in a black tunic, red leggings, and the sacred headdress of the queen's brother: a simple crown woven of straw and dried flowers. As soon as Marrah saw the two of them, she knew this was no ordinary occasion.

"You have done a good job," Lalah said. Marrah thanked her and waited for her to continue, but instead she just sat there. Finally, she reached out and took Bindar's hand. "For a long time, Bindar and I have governed this city together as sister and brother in the old way. We have been . . . "

"The priestess and priest of peace," Bindar supplied.

"Yes." Lalah nodded. "That is a good way to put it. We have been the priestess and priest—the queen and king—of peace, and I think that on the whole we have done a good job. But now that the peace of so many generations has been broken, Bindar and I are no longer enough. Shara needs another brother and sister to lead us in wartime."

"A priestess-queen and priest-king of war?" Marrah said. "I don't like the sound of that."

Lalah snorted. She had been talking very formally, but now she returned to her everyday tone of voice. "I'm not asking you to like it. I'm telling you that it's necessary. How in the name of the Goddess do you expect two old people—who have never so much as seen a nomad warrior—to figure out what to do if we're attacked? Surely you're old enough by now to realize that your grandmother and uncle aren't all that different than you'll be at our age. We stumble along making mistakes like everyone else. There's no way to avoid this, so don't start looking for one: you're young and stubborn, but you've suffered a lot since Keru was taken and you have a lot more sense than you used to have. If the nomads attack, you'll have to be our war queen. You'll be queen anyway someday after I'm dead."

Marrah was horrified at the responsibility. "I'm not fit for such an honor," she protested.

"True," Bindar chuckled, "you aren't. I kept telling Lalah we should make Hiknak the war queen, but Lalah thinks—quite unreasonably in my opinion—that we have no business handing Shara over to a nomad woman, no matter how friendly she seems."

Lalah snorted again and reached up to adjust her diadem. "Hiknak's brains are still addled," she said. "As of now, you're the war queen, Marrah, and when we get Arang back, he can help you."

"And if I say no, that I'm not qualified, that you're making a mistake?"

"Then in all seriousness, our blood will be on your hands."

"Has the Council of Elders agreed to this?"

"Of course."

"You see," Bindar said, "you really don't have a choice."

Lalah gave Marrah a long, level look. "Well?"

"Well," Marrah said, but she still didn't say "yes."

"I know what you're thinking. You're thinking that this means you'll be stuck in Shara; that even if Stavan sends for you, you won't be able to go north to fight beside him and bring Arang and Keru back. Am I right?"

Marrah folded her arms across her chest and looked at her grandmother defiantly. "Yes," she said. "You're right. That's exactly what I was thinking. You can't tie me to the city, Grandmother, not now, not as long as those lumps of Hansi goat dung have my son."

Lalah laughed. "When you get angry, you're the perfect image of your mother, did you know that? Sabalah would have walked through boiling water to save her children, and you're just like her." She rose to her feet. "I'm not asking you to stay in Shara. On the contrary, I'm sending you north as soon as you can catch and bridle two of those horses Stavan sent. You were right when you said you weren't fit to be a war queen—or any other kind of queen for that matter. A queen needs to be a powerful priestess in her own right.

"I'm sending you to the city of Kataka for a full initiation into the powers of the Dark Goddess like my mother before me and her mother before her. And you're not going alone. Hiknak may have remembered who she is, but her right hand still doesn't work properly and she drags her foot when she walks, and Keshna gets more *shohwar* every day. You're going to take the two of them with you. You may have heard that the priestesses of Kataka can make the blind see and raise the dead. Well, that's nonsense. They can't. But with a little luck maybe Queen Glyntsa and her women can heal Hiknak's foot and persuade Keshna to do something besides snap at people like a sick puppy.

"Glyntsa will be happy to see you because you're going to bring her some very important information. She already knows the beastmen are coming. She had that vision years ago, about the same time your mother did, but I'm sure she has no idea how to defend her city. You're going to show her how to store food, and dig ditches, and do whatever else it takes to keep Kataka from falling to the nomads."

Marrah's heart leapt at the thought of going north. She put her hands together in the sign of the Goddess and bowed, first to Bindar and then to Lalah. "To hear is to obey," she said. "I will be the war queen of Shara and go to Kataka as you have ordered."

Lalah was amused. "To hear is to obey, is it? " She plucked off her diadem and scratched her head. "Don't ever try to sound humble, Marrah. It's just not convincing."

The Horses at the Gate

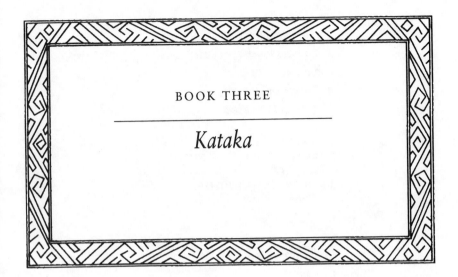

BOOK THREE

Kataka

When silver birds fly
and houses touch the clouds
and the lions are gone
and the frogs stop singing
Mother will come again

"PRAYER TO THE MUD"
INSCRIBED ON A CEREMONIAL SCREEN
KATAKAN COLLECTION, 4300 B.C.
MUSÉE NATIONAL D'HISTOIRE
BUCHAREST, RUMANIA

In the face of fear,
we dance.
In the face of death,
we make love.
We send our children
into the future
like doves
to sing Her holy names.
Here
there
everywhere:
Aba, Shallah, Nashah.

FROM "INITIATION SONG"
KATAKA, FIFTH MILLENNIUM B.C.

"What makes people violent?"
"Who invented war?"
"How can we defend ourselves against our enemies
without becoming like them?" [1]

FROM "THE SACRED BOOKS OF KATAKA"
NORTHERN RUMANIA
FIFTH MILLENNIUM B.C.

[1]*The answers have not been preserved.*

CHAPTER TEN

B elow Marrah and Hiknak, Kataka, the city of the Dark Mother, glittered in the black valley like a necklace of liquid silver. The city flickered and moved; it opened like a flower; its drums beat like a giant heart. At first sight, it seemed more than a city: it seemed a living thing: round like the circle of the seasons; round like the cycle of life and rebirth. Yet at the same time, it was built on a human scale. Ride down to it, Marrah thought, and you would find the Katakans eating the same kind of bread the Sharans ate; you'd find old dogs asleep by charcoal braziers and lovers quarreling over trifles. No doubt at this very moment, somewhere in that great circle of houses, some Katakan was stirring a pot of stew and some other was scrubbing a floor, but tonight the ordinary life of the city was hard to remember. From the cliff where she sat on her horse, staring in openmouthed wonder, Kataka looked like a basket of fiery stars. It was so bright that it was easy to imagine that only great priestesses lived there, floating on a spiral of fire.

"It's beautiful." Hiknak's voice was soft with awe. Marrah turned toward her and saw her there in the darkness, seated on Ylata, her mare. Hiknak was clutching Keshna with her good arm and peering out over the edge of the cliff toward the lights of the city. "How many tribes are camped together down there?"

"Only one," Marrah said, "and they aren't camped. The city never moves. Grandmother told me more people live in Kataka than have ever lived together anywhere on the body of the Goddess Earth."

These are all one tribe?"

"Yes."

Hiknak gave a low whistle. "How can they find enough grass for their animals? How can they grow enough wheat to feed themselves? Are those their campfires we're looking at?"

Marrah smiled. She had never heard Hiknak ask so many questions. "The Katakans are said to be the best farmers in the Motherlands. Even in bad years, they ship grain south and trade it for flint. As for all those lights down there, I doubt they're campfires. I think we must have stumbled on some kind of festival." She pointed. "See how the fires keep moving in a big circle? My best guess is that we're watching a torchlight procession."

"Hands," Hiknak murmured. "Hands and more hands. Too many hands to remember."

"Hiknak," Marrah said gently, "you aren't making any sense. Perhaps we should get down off these horses, gather some wood, and make a fire. Keshna is probably hungry, we can't reach the city tonight, and there's no use sitting here freezing our noses off."

Hiknak laughed. "You're worried about me, aren't you? Afraid I'll go back to being the Hiknak who thought she was fourteen and forgot she was a mother?" She bent forward and kissed Keshna on the top of the head. "My baby, my dear," she cooed, but Keshna said nothing. Hiknak turned back to Marrah. "'Hands' is the way my people count big things. 'Three hands of enemies are riding this way' our scouts used to say, and Vlahan would send six hands of warriors out to fight them."

"Fifteen?" Marrah said in Sharan. "Thirty?"

Hiknak nodded. "Exactly. Didn't you ever notice that in Hansi there aren't separate words for countings above ten? When things get beyond fingers, we measure them in hands. Even when we say the 'Twenty Tribes' we use two very old words that mean 'four' and 'hands.'" She paused and looked back at the circle of lights. "So how many hands of people live in this Kataka, do you think?"

Marrah frowned. She could count to 169 if she divided things up into groups of 13, but beyond that, the land of numbers was pretty much unexplored territory. "Less than the hairs on your head," she said, "but more than . . ." She tried to think of something that was many but not too many, but all she could think of were the moving lights and how beautiful they were.

Hiknak was made of more practical stuff. "But more than the hairs on your *shjetak*," she supplied.

Marrah laughed so hard that she started to cough. "I just hope Keshna doesn't understand what you just said," she gasped. "I just hope the word *shjetak* isn't in her vocabulary."

The next morning as they rode down into the valley they came to a small village where they were offered cups of hot milk laced with honey. Like Kataka, the village was built in a circle, and as they stood at the center of it talking to the villagers, Marrah learned that she had been right when she guessed that the lights of Kataka were part of a festival. The city was not often lit so splendidly, the villagers told them, but by chance they had caught sight of it on the last night of the Ceremony of the Returning Light, when, in honor of midwinter, all the mother clans marched through the streets carrying blazing torches.

"The Dark Mother must favor you," the villagers told Marrah and Hiknak. "She only opens her Eye of Fire once a year, and this year She opened it for you. You must be lucky women."

Marrah wondered if she should tell them how wrong they were, but this was no time to deliver the kind of message she was carrying. If they did not already know about the nomads, they would find out soon enough when the Katakans asked them to come to the city to help dig trenches and store up supplies.

"How much farther do we have to ride?" she asked politely.

"Not far, my dears," the village mother told her. "Not on those lovely beasts. Is there any chance you'd like to leave the big brown one with me? My old legs don't work as well as they used to, and it's a dear black-nosed pet of a thing with tail hair like a young girl's braids."

Marrah politely declined the invitation to hand over her mare, Nretsa, and the village mother sighed, pressed more hot milk on Keshna, and assured them they would get to Kataka by midday.

They rode on, fording the river and following it north. The weather had changed during the night, and a cold mist had crept into the valley. For most of the morning, they did not see much but fog, but near midday—just as the villagers had promised—the fog began to lift, and they discovered that they were approaching large strips of frost-covered pasture dotted with triangular haystacks. The Katakans had bound several saplings together to form a frame and draped the hay over the branches so it wouldn't rot—a smart thing to do in such a damp climate, Marrah thought.

They followed the edge of one of the pastures, and soon they came to dozens of grain bins made of fired clay. Each bin was in the shape of a large, pregnant Goddess with an open mouth and a big, round belly. The bins were so big that at first sight it looked as if a meeting of giants were taking place in the fields. Marrah was impressed. She had heard that the Katakans were skilled potters, but the grain bins, which were three times as large as she was, were as good as the finest jars Uncle Bindar had ever made. Each was painted with complicated, circular designs, and each had a human face and an individual personality. Some looked motherly, some looked sad, some looked playful, and some were licking their lips in a way that looked bawdy and hungry at the same time.

"I wonder if they're supposed to be the original clan mothers," she said, but Hiknak, as usual, was more practical.

"If you ask me, they double as scarecrows."

Soon the city of Kataka itself came into view. Just as Marrah had expected, it was unwalled, open on all sides to the forest and the fields and the sight of the river. The only thing that separated it from the surrounding countryside was a flimsy fence of rose bushes trained to grow on low wooden frames no higher than a man's chest. The great circle of bushes probably served two purposes: at this time of year it was leafless, but in the spring and summer it would band the city with a crown of sweet-smelling roses while its thorns would keep goats, cows, and sheep from wandering through the streets.

They rode up to the edge of the rose fence and followed it northeast past pigpens, goat stalls, and the blank, white-plastered backs of motherhouses. Children waved to them and people dropped what they were doing and turned to stare at the horses. The Katakans looked ordinary enough: short and a little stocky, with the brown hair, barrel chests, and broad foreheads of the north. Most of them were dressed in fur-lined capes because the weather was bitterly cold, but those who were chopping wood or doing other heavy work had stripped down to hempen shirts, leather leggings, and bulky sheepskin vests. From outside the rose fence, the city did not look all that different from Shara except that it was many times bigger.

Even though it did not have real walls, Kataka did have a gate of sorts, and they soon came to it. The gate was shaped like two horns or two crescent moons placed tip to tip, made of fine red clay glazed and painted with the same circular designs Marrah had seen on the grain bins. From a distance it looked like a human mouth or the womb-gate of a woman's body. Above it was an inscription in the sacred script—one of the few Marrah had ever seen outside a temple. There were only two signs: the one for "mother" and the one for "child."

Hiknak reined in her horse. People were already coming out of the city to greet them, but for the moment they were still alone. "What are those strange marks?" Hiknak asked, pointing to the inscription.

"That's writing. It talks."

Hiknak cupped her hand to her ear. "I don't hear anything."

Marrah did her best not to laugh. "Writing only talks to people who have been trained to hear it. Would you like to know what it's saying?"

Hiknak nodded eagerly.

Like most sacred inscriptions, the one over the gate could be interpreted in several ways, so Marrah obliged her with three translations: "It means: 'Kataka is a mother who loves the children she holds in her womb'; it means: 'When you enter this city, you must enter it as a child'—that is to say, with joy. And it also means, as near as I can make out: 'Welcome strangers; we make the best-looking babies in all the Motherlands.'"

The word *welcome* was no sooner out of her mouth than a whole crowd of people surrounded them, all talking at once in Katakan. It was a quick, musical language that sounded like the chattering of birds. A young man stroked the nose of Hiknak's horse and jumped back with a yelp when the mare snuffled and exposed her teeth. Several women began to pet Marrah's mare, Nretsa, as if she were a big dog, laughing and motioning for the others to join them. Suddenly, two little girls appeared out of nowhere carrying crowns of winter ivy. Tossing the crowns jauntily over the horses' ears, they ran away screaming in mock terror.

Marrah grinned at Hiknak. "I get the feeling they haven't seen horses before."

"You just better hope these animals don't bolt."

It was a reasonable fear. The crowd was growing larger now, and several dogs had appeared. The dogs were too afraid to attack the horses, but they stood in a circle barking their lungs out. Nretsa flared her nostrils at all the strange smells and laid her ears back against her head as if considering the possibility of kicking some of these high-strung, jabbering humans out of the way.

"Steady," Marrah pleaded. She stroked Nretsa's neck, and waved to the people to back off, but the Katakans had fallen in love with the horses and were practically climbing over one another to get a better view. Just when things were on the brink of getting out of hand, Hiknak's horse, Ylata, lifted her tail and let out a spray of urine that sent the Katakans who had been petting her rump dashing for safety. Then she calmly deposited a heap of dung on the path.

The Katakans drew back with exclamations of surprise and disapproval.

"What's all the excitement about?" Hiknak said. "Don't these people have cows? They act like they've never seen dung before."

"It's a mystery to me," Marrah said, "but Ylata gets an extra helping of hay tonight. If this pushing and shoving had gone on much longer, Nretsa would have bolted."

They were so busy trying to calm the mares that they did not notice that the crowd had fallen silent until someone called to them in a tongue Marrah immediately recognized as Old Language. Old Language was mostly spoken by priestesses, but it was also the language of trade, and in this particular case, the language of rebuke.

"Welcome to Kataka, pilgrims," a strong, deep voice cried. "What do you call these great animals you straddle, the ones that have just soiled the entrance to the sacred gate?"

Marrah looked down and saw a woman in her late thirties looking up at her with a mixture of amusement and annoyance. She was short and muscular, with a flat, wide nose, slate-gray eyes, and bushy black curls that fell from her part to her shoulders. Her tunic and leggings were black, and she wore a black hood with beaded fringe that came halfway down her forehead. Later Marrah learned that all the priestesses of the Dark Mother wore fringe across their foreheads, but at the time she was struck by the festive look of it as it blew back and forth in the wind like the feathered tail of a bird.

"We call our animals 'horses,'" she said politely. "I'm sorry if they've done something they shouldn't have, but I imagine your cows do the same, don't they?"

Mary Mackey

174

The woman shook her head, and the fringe fluttered like a fan. "No," she said. She pointed to the path, and Marrah noticed for the first time that it was paved with alternating stripes of black and white stones. "Our cows think those black lines are holes and those white ones are bars. They never cross for fear of getting their hooves stuck. We train them to it at an early age, to keep them out of the city, but these 'hornets' of yours—"

"Horses," Marrah corrected.

"These 'horses' of yours don't seem to know any better." The woman inspected the two mares and sighed. "Still, I've never seen more marvelous animals, so instead of making you get down and clean this mess up, I'm going to take you straight to Queen Glyntsa." She smiled, exposing a gap between her front teeth large enough to stick a small twig into. "I'm Redra, gatekeeper of Kataka for these twelve years. We get a lot of pilgrims, but in my memory none have made a more spectacular entrance. What did you say your names were?"

"Hiknak of the north and her daughter Keshna, and Marrah, daughter of Sabalah, granddaughter of Lalah of Shara."

Redra's face became grave at the mention of Lalah. "I've heard of Lalah of Shara. She took her initiation here with the old Imsha, but she never got to see Those Who Come After."

Marrah was amazed to hear that her grandmother had ever failed at anything. She wanted to ask who the "Imsha" was, but the gatekeeper did not give her a chance. She motioned for the crowd to step aside and waved Marrah and Hiknak through the gate.

From inside the rose fence, Kataka was just as impressive as it had been when Marrah saw it from the cliff, but in a different way. The streets were narrow spirals paved with river gravel, and the houses were simple rectangular structures of two or three rooms built of split planks daubed with clay and topped by steeply gabled roofs crowned with thick thatch. Only the temples had more than one story, but to say these things about the city was not to describe it.

What made Kataka spectacular were its ceramics. Huge pots and oversized flower vases were everywhere: sometimes they stood in pairs outside the motherhouses, decorated with snakes or twisting vines, and filled with neatly raked earth as if waiting for spring to bring forth flowers; there were gigantic water storage jars embellished with rain signs, circles, white dogs, and crescent moons; braziers shaped like women's hips, smoking lazily in the cold as the

Katakans grilled river fish or heated up pots of stew over the coals. Every domed bread oven was burnished and painted; every beehive was a masterwork of clay and color; every water cup looked like a ceremonial goblet.

The Katakans seemed incapable of making anything plain or ordinary. The simplest water ladle was a tangle of painted circles and crow's beaks, and when Marrah looked up at the eves of the houses she saw clay masks looking down at her. Some must have represented the faces of the people who lived there, since there were babies, and men and women of all shapes and sizes; but others were the face of the Dark Mother Herself, black and lovely, with braided hair and a crown of owl feathers. Although She was the lady of the winter earth and the dead, there was nothing frightening about Her, and She always greeted Marrah with an enigmatic smile.

The gatekeeper had said that many pilgrims came to Kataka. Now, as Marrah rode in a long, slow spiral toward the center of the city, she began to see some of them. Kataka was on the greatest pilgrimage route in the Motherlands, not because it was conveniently located—it was near the mountains many days away from the River of Smoke—but because its priestesses knew things no one else knew. The sick, the hopeful, and the curious arrived at its gate from places so distant that Marrah had never heard of them. Before she had gone halfway, she had seen a young man with a great deal of white linen wrapped around his head and an exotic red and blue bird perched on his shoulder; a tiny, dark woman dressed in the skins and fur boots of the northern Forest People; and a little girl with a long nose who reminded her of the islanders of Gira. The girl was cradling something that Marrah first took to be a baby, but as the horses approached, it sprung up with a shriek, and she saw that it was a fur-covered animal with a long tail and a pink-lipped, almost human face.

The central plaza was the largest circle Marrah had ever seen. Rimmed with statues and flowerpots, it offered a broad expanse of smooth ground paved with small bits of colored clay. The tiles had been ingeniously fitted together to form the principal signs of the Dark Mother. On the outer edges of the circle were the signs of death: the white dog, the raven, the snake, and the owl. Nearer the center came the signs of regeneration: brightly colored butterflies that reminded Marrah of Shambah, bees with golden wings, double-headed axes, and a great Tree of Life hung with fruit and birds that spread its branches everywhere in an exuberant tangle. At the exact center was the eye of the Mother Herself, half closed as if caught between sleeping and waking, and when Marrah got down off her horse to take a closer look, she saw that there were strange forms clustered together inside the pupil: tiny faces, imaginary animals, and other things that were beyond understanding.

Redra told them to hitch their horses to the red and black pillars of the speakers' platform and then warned the gathering crowd to keep a respectful distance from the beasts. A short while later, Marrah and Hiknak found themselves standing in the dimly lit room of a small temple facing a semicircle of silent women. There were thirteen, all dressed in black, with huge hips and tiny waists. Their heads seemed much too small for their bodies, and their faces were covered with the long black beaded fringe of the Dark Mother. Each sat—or rather half sat and half reclined—on a small clay chair, so gaudy with snake lines and energy coils that it made Marrah dizzy to look at them. Assuming this must be Queen Glyntsa and her Council of Elders, she waited for one of the women to speak, but the silence went on for some time, broken only by the sound of the gatekeeper's cough. Finally Marrah got up the courage to address them.

"Queen Glyntsa?" she said. More silence. This was certainly an odd way to greet pilgrims. Marrah wondered if her grandmother had done something truly unforgivable when she took her initiation at Kataka. She cleared her throat and tried again. "My name is Marrah, daughter of Sabalah, and I bring greetings from my grandmother Lalah and my great-uncle Bindar, priestess-queen and priest-king of Shara."

Suddenly Hiknak laughed. "Don't bother, Marrah. They aren't going to talk to you. They're nothing but clay dolls!"

Marrah took a few steps closer and saw that Hiknak was right. The women were dolls—or rather sacred statues—each as big as a real woman, each dressed in a real priestess's clothing. When Marrah took a good look under the fringe, she saw that their necks were many times longer than any human neck and their faces as small as the faces of squirrels.

She turned to the gatekeeper. "What's this?" she demanded.

"It's the custom. Pilgrims are always brought to the ladies first." Redra's face was impassive, but Marrah suspected that she was enjoying the trick she had played on them. On the other hand, she had probably done it so often that she no longer found it funny.

"And where," Marrah said with bright politeness, "is Queen Glyntsa?"

"This way," Redra said, ushering them out of the temple.

Queen Glyntsa proved to be an ordinary woman living in an ordinary house just off the central plaza. She was about ten years younger than Lalah, with a broad, practical face, copperish hair, and supple, calloused hands that suggested she might be a weaver. Like all queens, she worked alongside her friends and relatives, and the only benefit she got from her position was the chance to question the most interesting pilgrims before anyone else got to them. When Marrah, Hiknak, and Keshna were ushered into her presence, she was baking flatbread on a clay griddle.

"Welcome to Kataka," she said, grabbing them and kissing them on both cheeks as was the custom. She offered Keshna some warm bread dipped in honey, which Keshna seized and bolted down as if she hadn't eaten in weeks. If Glyntsa noticed that Keshna was a bit strange, she was too polite to comment on it. Placing a whole pile of fresh flatbread on the table, she invited them to help themselves. Then she sent the gatekeeper off in search of her brother.

There must have been more ceremony going on under the surface of things than met the eye, because all the time she waited for her brother, Glyntsa spoke to them as if they were neighbors who had dropped in for an afternoon chat. Not once did she ask them any of the questions Marrah would have asked strangers who had just shown up riding animals no one had ever seen before. She discussed the weather, commented on how tiring it was to travel in winter, and complained that last summer had been dry and the wheat crop rather poor.

But when her brother walked in, everything changed. He was much younger than his sister—somewhere in his twenties—short and dark like Arang only not quite as graceful; with slender shoulders, strong legs, glossy black hair, a large, handsome nose, and a quick, warm smile that exposed a set of the whitest teeth Marrah had ever seen. He stopped in front of her and Hiknak and folded his hands together in the sign of the Goddess.

"Welcome to Kataka, Marrah, granddaughter of Lalah, and Hiknak of the north," he said in flawless Sharan. He winked at them and laughed. "It's quite an honor to greet the brave women who pointed a dagger at Nikhan's balls and made him dance."

Marrah and Hiknak were so surprised that they nearly fell off their stools.

"How do you know all that?" Marrah cried. "We came north faster than any trader. We heard the priestesses of Kataka were powerful, but what kind of people can snatch news out of the air? Do they fly, these famous priestesses of yours?"

He chuckled. "Only in dreams and visions." He paused. "You don't remember me, do you?"

"How could we?" Hiknak snapped. "We've never seen you before in our lives." She sounded almost rude, but Marrah could sympathize.

"Oh, but we have met," he said. "Let me reintroduce myself: I'm Kal, Glyntsa's brother." He grinned at Glyntsa. "My sister probably already told you we're the *maytas* of Kataka, although the Council of Elders has the final say, of course." So far almost everything he had said—with the exception of his name—was gibberish as far as Marrah was concerned. Later she learned that the *maytas* of Kataka were its priestess-queen and priest-king, which meant Kal and Glyntsa governed jointly in the usual way; but at the time she had never heard the word, which only added to her confusion. "Remember that singer at Shambah?" Kal continued. "The one who made up the obscene song called 'Nikhan and the Pregnant Warriors'?"

"How could we forget her?" Hiknak tore off a bit of flatbread and chewed it thoughtfully. "I don't think there is anyone in Shara who doesn't know that song by heart. It gave Marrah and Dalish and me quite an undeserved reputation for bravery. That verse about Nikhan crying with fear when we told him to swear loyalty to Stavan was hilarious. He didn't really cry, of course, but it was a nice touch."

"I'm glad you liked it." Kal paused and stroked his chin for effect. "Because I wrote it."

"You? But the singer was a woman."

"That's what Nikhan thought, and a good thing too or he'd have had my balls on a stick." He smiled modestly. "I'm a harper; the city produces a lot of us and I'm hardly one of the best, but we all travel the trade routes singing the old memory songs and spreading the city's fame. About four years ago—before my mother died and Glyntsa and I became the *maytas* of Kataka—I was on my way to Shambah to sing at the Butterfly Festival.

"One afternoon I walked into a village where everything looked perfectly normal. Before I had time to sit down and take off my sandals, a band of naked madmen rode in on the first horses anyone had ever seen. Quicker than you can say 'nomad,' they set the motherhouses on fire, killed the men, and took me and about a dozen women prisoner.

"Luckily for me, Katakan harpers always wear women's clothing in honor of She Who Inspires All Music, and luckily the raiders were too preoccupied with murdering and looting to take a close look at the hair on my upper lip because we soon learned that they killed most men on sight. There's quite a bit more to this story, but the long and short of it is that I managed to hang on to my harp, and when the nomads discovered that I could sing, they dragged me into the presence of their little bandy-legged chief, and I was forced to spend most of my days wasting my talent on him while his ugly guards stood around picking their teeth with their daggers.

"I was sure that sooner or later one of them would realize I was a man, but fortunately I don't make a very attractive woman by nomad standards. The Shamban women pulled my beard hairs out with wooden pincers," he winced, "and I ate a lot of nasty herbs to keep my breath as rank as possible. Then too, Nikhan drank himself cross-eyed almost every day, and by the time you showed up, he was hardly noticing anything that didn't come in a wine jar."

"Amazing," Marrah said. "Why didn't you tell us who you were at the time?"

Kal looked embarrassed. "I would have except that being one of the nomads' slaves gives you a good close look at them, and the sight isn't one to inspire confidence. I never thought Nikhan would keep that promise he made to your nomad lover. I admired your courage, but I was sure you were all going to be slaughtered as soon as you turned your back on him, so as soon as I could, I slung my harp over my shoulder, and got out of Shambah as fast my legs could carry me. I heard later that you burned the fort."

"We did indeed," Marrah said, "and sent Nikhan back to the steppes, to boot. It's too bad you didn't wait around to enjoy the sight of all those horse rumps heading north."

Kal shrugged. "I'm a poet, not a fighter, but I intend to make it up to you. I brought a jar of our best wine." He produced it proudly. "I'm going to warm it up, and after you drink a cup or two and rest a little, you can tell Glyntsa and me what brings you to Kataka."

He unstopped the resin-scented wine, poured it into a clay jar, and set it on the brazier. Then, before Marrah or Hiknak could stop him, he walked over to Keshna. "Come here, you sweet little girl," he said, trying to pick Keshna up, but before he could touch her, Keshna leaned forward and bit him.

Kal yelled and jumped back. He sucked at his bloody finger and stared at Keshna in disbelief.

"What's wrong with that child?" Glyntsa said sharply. "Is she part dog?"

"She's protecting her mother," Marrah explained. "We're sorry she bit you, but we can't control her. We think she may be *shohwar*. She's one of the reasons we came to Kataka."

The conversation took a more serious turn after that. Glyntsa sat down and put her elbows on the table; Kal poured out the wine and sat down beside her, and the two of them asked Marrah and Hiknak to explain how such a little girl had come to be *shohwar*. Marrah and Hiknak told them, and as they spoke, the brother and sister nodded sympathetically.

The story was not nearly as long as it would have been without Kal's help, but thanks to him, they did not have to explain how dangerous the nomads were, or how Hiknak could have been taken by surprise and knocked into the river by the raiding party. Glyntsa was upset by the news that the beastmen had ridden so far south, but not nearly as surprised as Marrah had expected her to be. She listened without interrupting and patted Marrah on the shoulder in a motherly fashion when Marrah described how Keru and Arang had been stolen and how Stavan had gone after them.

When Marrah and Hiknak were finished, Kal and Glyntsa promised to arrange for two ceremonies: one to heal Hiknak's hand and leg, and another to heal Keshna. Marrah and Hiknak were surprised that things could be organized so quickly, but Glyntsa said the whole city of Kataka was dedicated to healing and such ceremonies went on all the time.

"What I want to know," Hiknak said later when she and Marrah and Keshna were alone together in one of the temple guest rooms, "is: will this work? I don't believe in the Dark Mother. I try to, but it's hard for me to shake the idea that all the gods are big, hairy, tattooed warriors who couldn't care less about my little girl." She sighed. "I'd gladly limp through the rest of my life if those priestesses could just get Keshna to talk."

Marrah reassured Hiknak that the ceremony would heal both her and Keshna, but she too had her doubts. Later she wondered if

Hiknak had unintentionally struck a bargain with the Dark Mother.

The healing ceremonies took place the next day, Hiknak's in the morning and Keshna's in the early afternoon. Of the two, Hiknak's was the most elaborate. Marrah and Hiknak had barely opened their eyes before five black-robed, black-fringed priestesses appeared, stripped Hiknak, and painted coiling snakes all over her. Producing a sharp flint knife, one of them gestured to Hiknak to stretch out on her sleeping mat, then carefully shaved every bit of hair off Hiknak's vulva and painted it bright red.

Hiknak was a little frightened at first, but when she realized the priestesses meant her no harm, she relaxed and began telling dirty jokes in Hansi that would have made a statue blush. Fortunately, the priestesses did not understand a word of it, and they went soberly about their business, painting Hiknak's weak hand and bad ankle red to match. When they were finished, they threw a warm cape over her and led her barefoot to the main temple, where they had her stretch out on a thin pallet in front of the clay ladies.

Marrah followed after them, carrying Keshna, who stared at everything and everyone with narrow, suspicious eyes as if deciding whom to bite next, but when they entered the temple and heard Kal playing his harp and Glyntsa and the other priestesses singing the healing songs, Keshna seemed to relax. The singing was beautiful, rising and dying on the morning air, and as Marrah sat there watching the priestesses light one candle after another until Hiknak was surrounded with rings and rings of light, a deep peace stole over her, and she was not surprised when she looked down and found Keshna asleep in her arms.

When all the candles were lit, Glyntsa and two other priestesses came forward with large shells of colored sand and cones made from rolls of bark lashed together with hempen threads. Pouring the sand into the cones color by color, they began to draw delicate designs all around Hiknak. Many of the designs were the same ones Marrah had seen on Katakan pots: white dogs, crescent moons, snakes, and swirls of energy. But there were other symbols she had never seen before: fantastic spotted animals with long necks; blue lions; egg-shaped nets the color of blood; and one very large, elaborate platter-shaped design that combined a many-branched tree with boats, birds, and sacred flowers. The priestesses finished by drawing a perfect hand and a perfect foot; then they rushed forward, scattered the sand in all directions, and called to Hiknak to rise from her pallet, healed.

It had been a beautiful ceremony, but unfortunately it did not work. Hiknak got up just as she had lain down: with a weak hand and a dragging foot, but if she was disappointed, she was too brave to show it. She asked Marrah to thank Glyntsa, Kal, and the priestesses for her, then wrapped the cloak around herself and limped back to the guesthouse to sluice off the paint.

"Tell her this kind of healing sometimes takes quite a while to work," Glyntsa said, and Marrah promised to pass the message along to Hiknak, but when she did, Hiknak said nothing. She only pressed her lips together and reached out for Keshna. The rest of the morning, Hiknak sat talking to herself in a low voice and braiding colored ribbons in Keshna's hair. It seemed an odd thing to do, but when Marrah listened more closely, she realized that Hiknak was praying in Hansi to some god she had never heard of.

Glyntsa came for Keshna shortly after midday. When she arrived, Marrah was surprised to see that there were no other priestesses with her and that she had changed out of her ritual garments.

"Dress the child in something warm, and put on your cloaks and mittens," Glyntsa said. "We're going to the healing spring. It's up in the foothills, and we won't get back before dark."

"Ask her if we can ride," Hiknak said.

When Marrah translated, Glyntsa shook her head. "No, we have to go on foot. Everything has to be as simple as possible. I might as well warn you, there won't be any ceremony. The Imsha won't permit so much as a candle around the spring."

"Who's this Imsha everyone keeps talking about?"

Glyntsa smiled a mysterious smile that seemed almost playful. "You'll see soon enough," she promised. She looked at Hiknak's foot. "Do you think you can walk that far?"

"If I bind my ankle." Hiknak sat down and wrapped several strips of soft leather around her ankle. "We'll have to go slowly."

They left the city, waving to Redra as they passed through the gate. At first the walking was easy. They simply followed a narrow dirt path that wound between the pastures and the fields. But when the path turned and began to climb into the hills, Keshna balked. Sitting down on the ground, she folded her little arms across her chest and refused to take another step, and when Marrah and Hiknak pleaded with her, she growled and spat at them.

"Pick her up and carry her," Glyntsa ordered.

Since Hiknak's hand was too weak to carry Keshna any distance, Marrah bent down and tucked Keshna under her arm. Keshna immediately began to kick and scream at the top of her lungs, but at least she didn't bite. It was like carrying a little bear cub, and several times Marrah was sure Keshna was going to plunge out of her arms and knock herself silly on the rocky path, but after a while Keshna either lost interest in screaming or ran out of breath, and by the time they came to the top of the first hill she was sullenly clinging to Marrah's back. She was a heavy little thing, but Marrah had once carried a trade basket on her shoulders for the better part of two years, so she plodded on, ignoring the low growls that Keshna gave every time she stopped to catch her breath.

They climbed several more hills, each a little steeper than the last. The hills were blue-gray in the winter light, rounded like the backs of fat hedgehogs and covered with the spines of bare trees. As they climbed, the sky clouded over and it grew colder, so that by the time Glyntsa pointed to a smaller path leading off from the main one, Marrah's nose was tingling and she was glad she'd worn her fur-lined mittens.

Finally they came to a steep rock wall. A small, partly frozen spring ran out of it, splashing into an ice-rimmed pool. On the other side of the pool, a heavily cloaked figure sat on a flat rock. Nothing showed, not so much as a fingertip. The thing could have been a man or a woman or a clay statue, but whoever or whatever it was, it was something important. Glyntsa stopped when she caught sight of the figure. Kneeling, she picked up a handful of earth and held it in both hands reverently. Kissing the earth, Glyntsa replaced it as tenderly as if it were a flower.

"The Imsha," she whispered to Marrah and Hiknak as she rose to her feet. She stood upright and raised her voice. "Dark One," she said in Old Language, "I bring you a child who is *shohwar*. What shall we do with her?"

The Imsha laughed a low, surprising laugh. It could have been the laugh of an old woman or a young man, and it was as warm and thick as honey. "Throw her in the spring," the Imsha said.

Marrah translated for Hiknak. "That thing over there, whoever it is, can't be serious!" Hiknak cried. "Why, it's cold enough to freeze the hairs inside your nose. I thought this healing spring was going to be warm. If you think I'm going to strip my daughter and toss in her in there," she pointed to the ice, "you're wrong."

But Glyntsa had no intention of stripping Keshna. Before Marrah could object or Hiknak could stop her, she simply picked Keshna up and threw her in the pool. As she hit the water, Keshna screamed as if she had been scalded. She went down once and came up sputtering and flailing her arms. She had not been in water since the day of the nomad raid, and she must have forgotten how to swim, because almost immediately she went under a second time.

"You're drowning my daughter!" Hiknak yelled, and she started toward the pool to pull Keshna out, but Glyntsa stopped her.

"Wait," she ordered. There was something in her voice as hard as stone, and Hiknak froze at the sound of it. On the other side of the pool the Imsha had risen to its feet.

Keshna came up again and began to swim furiously toward the side of the pool, but when she arrived, the Imsha was there before her. Putting a black-mittened hand on Keshna's head, the Imsha pushed her under again.

Keshna came up a third time. "Help!" she cried. "Mama, help!"

"She spoke!" Hiknak screamed.

Keshna was not only speaking, she was letting loose a stream of Hansi curses in such a perfect imitation of Hiknak that Marrah stood in openmouthed awe listening to her. Grabbing Keshna by the hair, the Imsha pulled her out of the water and set her on her feet. Keshna whirled around to face the Imsha. She looked like a small, angry, half-drowned rat. "You shit!" she yelled. "You mean black crow! You *shjetak!* That water is cold!"

Well, Marrah thought, that certainly proved that Keshna had been listening over the last few months. Her command of Hansi swear words was hair-raising. They should have been more careful not to curse in front of her, but when a child refused to talk, it was hard to remember that she could hear. The Imsha might not have understood what Keshna was saying, but there was no mistaking the sentiment. Laughing that low, warm laugh again, the figure in black returned to the rock and sat down.

By now Hiknak had Keshna in her arms and was crying over her, half crazy with joy. "You're talking," she kept saying, "you're talking. Why didn't you talk to me before, darling?"

Keshna leaned her head against her mother's breast, and her small face softened. "Because I forgot how," she said. And that was all the reason they ever got out of her.

After they returned to the city, Marrah took Hiknak aside and told her that she had had no idea what Glyntsa had planned to do to Keshna.

"No one in Shara would ever dream of throwing a little girl into a pool of icy water," she said. "It was a cruel thing to do to Keshna, and I apologize for getting you mixed up in it."

"What are you talking about?" Hiknak said. "It worked."

"But it was cruel."

Hiknak shook her head. "Marrah, I grew up in tribe where children Keshna's age were sacrificed on their father's graves. Tossing her in that pool wasn't cruelty; it was an act of mercy. Somehow the Imsha knew Keshna had to be thrown in the water so she could find her way back to the river where she left her tongue. Besides, it—or her or him or whatever it is—pulled Keshna out."

Marrah sat down on a clay stool and put her chin on her hands. The stool had the feet of a raven, and painted snakes trailed down its sides. Everywhere you went in Kataka the Dark Mother was present. Marrah looked at the white dogs on the charcoal brazier, the circles that swirled over the walls of the room. Bindar had told her that she would find wisdom here, and Lalah had said the priestesses might be able to help her get Arang and Keru back, but now doubts chewed at her like fleas.

"Grandmother Lalah has asked Glyntsa to give me a full initiation into the powers of the Dark Mother," she told Hiknak. "But after what I saw today, I'm not sure I can go through with it."

"Why not?"

"Frankly, I'm afraid. When the laughing priestess of Nar gave me the Tear of Compassion, and the dried thunder, and the powder of invisibility, I wasn't old enough to realize how dangerous it could be to possess such powers. Well, I'm not thirteen anymore. I've seen a hundred warriors driven mad and blind by a few pinches of powder. I like Glyntsa and Kal, but the ways of the Katakans are not our ways, and who knows what they'll ask me to do in the name of the Dark Mother."

"Don't be a fool," Hiknak said. "If they offer you this initiation, take it." She put her face close to Marrah's. "You were brave when the Hansi took you prisoner; you were brave when they tied you to that stake beside Zuhan's grave; you were brave when we tricked the scouts and stole their horses; and braver still when we made Nikhan dance on the tips of our daggers. You may not be able to throw a spear from a galloping horse, but you're going to be the war queen of Shara, and you have a chance to arm yourself with a weapon the nomads will never have. I don't know what to call it, but if Glyntsa offers it to you and you say 'no,' you'll regret it." She licked her thin, chapped lips, and her gray eyes narrowed. "You'll bring down the cold curse on all of us."

"What's the cold curse?"

"Cold heart, cold head, cold womb, cold bed."

Marrah shuddered. The Hansi words had an ugly sound that raised the hair on her arms. There was often something primitive and even a little crazy about the way Hiknak saw the world, but for once Marrah knew exactly what she meant.

The
Horses
at
the
Gate

CHAPTER ELEVEN

The Dark Mother gives three gifts
Aba, Shallah, Nashah,
One comes from the river
One comes from the earth
One comes from the land of dreams

FROM "THE RIDDLE SONG"
KATAKA, FIFTH MILLENNIUM B.C.

First Initiation: A Gift from the River

Kneel and take the bark cone in your hand. Pour in colored sand: pour in umber, yellow, and amethyst; pour in gold dust and powdered ocher; pour in the purple of late summer skies; the black of the Mother's body; the brown and green of the hills; the gray of duck down; the white of the egret; the blue of the heron; the black of the hawk; pour in the color of fawns' eyes; the tail of the fox; the ruff of the she-wolf; the back of the frog; pour in the rainbow; pour in the storm.

"Do you understand how the sand paintings are made?" Queen Glyntsa asked Marrah.

"I do," Marrah said.

"Come forward then, and draw."

Marrah came forward. She stood among the priestesses in the central temple of Kataka and began to draw with the colored sand, but her hand was unsteady. Green poured out of the bark cone and spilled into the cerulean; the red grains fell among the black, and everything smeared.

"How do I keep my hands steady?" she asked.

"By not thinking about them," Glyntsa told her.

Marrah tried not to think of her hands, but they were all she could think of. Again she came forward and drew, and again the lines bent and the sand spilled and her pictures were blotches. Around her the priestesses of Kataka drew quickly and surely, and not a grain of color fell in the wrong place.

"What are they doing that I'm not doing?"

"They're reciting the holy names of the Dark Mother: Aba, Shallah, Nashah."

Marrah refilled her bark cone with white sand and came forward again. Aba, Shallah, Nashah, she thought. Aba, Shallah, Nashah. She recited the names of the Dark Mother to herself over and over, and after a time her hand seemed to lift of its own accord.

Aba, Shallah, Nashah. She drew a small white dog.

Aba, Shallah, Nashah. She drew a delicate green vine.

Aba, Shallah, Nashah. She drew a blue flower filled with yellow pollen. A bee was poised on one of the petals, its veined wings stroking the air; the hairs on its legs were thinner than human hairs, but she drew them with a steady hand and hardly a grain was out of place.

Every day she came to the temple, recited the names of the Dark Mother, and let the sand go where it wished. After a while, her hands no longer seemed to belong to her.

"We don't draw the sacred paintings," Glyntsa said. "The Dark Mother draws through us."

"I understand."

A baby with an earache was brought to the temple. Marrah drew an ear; she drew a wooden flute; larks singing; leaves blowing in the wind; water purling over fine gravel. When she finished, she and the other priestesses ran forward and scattered the sand with their bare feet. They cried out the names of the Dark Mother, and the baby stopped crying.

"His ear has stopped hurting." Glyntsa picked up the little boy and placed him in Marrah's arms, and Marrah held him close and thought of Keru.

Second Initiation: A Gift from the Earth

Glyntsa led Marrah to her house and told her to sit down. She poured out a cup of fresh goat's milk and placed it on a low table at

Marrah's elbow. "Today you are going to learn to understand the language of animals," she announced.

Marrah bowed her head respectfully, thinking in her heart that this was, of course, impossible. She looked at the mask of the Dark Mother that hung above the door. The Goddess smiled down at her as if enjoying a good joke at her expense.

"Dogs are the easiest," Glyntsa continued. "Dogs want to talk to us so much that they try all the time. Spiders are the hardest: they're shy and don't much care for people, but they're very wise and they see everything. Have you ever heard an animal speak?"

"There was a sparrow that used to come to my window every morning. I used to imagine that it spoke to me."

"What did it say?"

"That I was a lucky woman."

"Was it right?"

"No, I was an unlucky woman—or about to be. It came for the last time on the morning my son Keru was stolen by the nomads, and if it came after that, I never noticed."

"Sparrows don't lie on purpose, but they're too innocent for their own good. Tell me, what animal do you love the best?"

Marrah fingered the horsehair bracelet on her wrist. "I loved a mare named Eoru once, but Changar, my enemy, sacrificed her."

Glyntsa pressed her lips together and looked grim. "An ugly business. Hiknak told me the nomads worship their gods by suffering. She said the Hansi sometimes kill fifty horses when one of their chiefs dies, and they sacrifice women and small children and lay them in the grave. The Dark Mother, who wants nothing but happiness for Her children, must weep to see such things, but this is no time to talk about such horrors. Let me ask you again: besides your dead mare, what animal have you loved best?"

Marrah thought for a long time. "In the village where I was born, there were two dogs. Their names were Zakur and Laino, and I loved them nearly as much as I loved my mother and brother."

"Then we'll start with dogs." She went away, leaving Marrah some hazelnuts to crack since no one in that house was ever idle. Soon she returned with a small, shaggy brown puppy and an old white dog that looked half wolf limping at her heels.

Marrah put the basket of nuts aside and took the puppy in her arms; it licked her face and tugged at her hair. She laughed and cradled it, but it wriggled so hard that she could barely hold it. The old dog stood by, looking on. Finally, it limped over, stretched out at Marrah's feet, and draped its nose over her boots.

Glyntsa brought a large pillow and tucked it behind Marrah's head. Then she took a small leather bag out of her pocket and emptied the contents into a clay dish. Marrah saw dried flower petals, powdered bark, and something that looked like crushed nuts. The mixture smelled sweet and sharp and earthy, like a riverbank.

"We call this *tamah*, which means 'animal tongues.'" Glyntsa picked up the cup of milk, added a pinch of the powder, and handed it to Marrah. "Drink this and listen to the dogs."

Marrah found the command funny, but she drank the milk as Glyntsa had ordered and settled back against the pillow to pet the puppy. It was a warm little thing, the pillow was soft, and soon a deep languor crept over her. Her arms felt boneless; her legs felt like warm mud; she could hear herself breathing, and when she tried to speak, her tongue was a bit of unbaked bread.

"That puppy is very ill-mannered," a deep voice said. Marrah woke with a start. "But then that's to be expected. They're all ill-mannered at that age. You'll be lucky if she doesn't wet you."

The voice was coming from the floor. Marrah looked down and saw the old, white dog looking up at her. "Your feet smell good," it said, but its lips didn't move.

Marrah was so stunned that all she could do was stare.

"Do you have any idea how many rabbits there are out beyond the rose fence?" the dog continued in a matter-of-fact tone. "In my youth, I used to catch quite of few, but these days I spend most of my time sleeping in front of the fire."

The puppy woke up with a yawn. "Play with me," it said. "Romp with me. Do you have a rag I can chew on? I love you so much, mother woman." It licked her hand. "You taste better than roast duck."

A spider in the corner of the room sent out a silver thread. "We were the first weavers," it said. "You humans learned weaving from us, sister woman."

A fly buzzed around Marrah's head and landed on the rim of the empty milk cup. "I see the world with a hundred eyes," it said. "Glyntsa and her lover are in the next room, lying in bed and eating honey cake."

In the eves of the house, the sparrows chattered that the weather was changing. "Wind from the north; snow by this evening at dusk; an owl hunts over the wheat fields; keep to your nests."

"Can you understand me?" Marrah asked the old dog.

"Yes," the dog said. "Do you howl at the moon?"

"No," Marrah said. The dog's question seemed sensible; she realized she was getting used to hearing it speak.

"You should try it sometime," the dog said. "There's nothing like a good howl on a moonlit night."

She started to answer, but suddenly her tongue felt heavy again and her eyes began to close of their own accord. The white dog became a white blur, and the puppy melted into her belly. She slept, and when she woke, the dogs were gone and Glyntsa was standing beside her.

"Did they speak to you?"

Marrah blinked and yawned. "I'm not sure. I thought they did, but perhaps I was only dreaming. A fly told me you were in the next room with your lover. Were you?"

Glyntsa laughed. "Indeed I was. That's why only initiated priestesses are allowed to take the *tamah*. Flies are terrible gossips, and if everyone could hear them speak, no one would have any privacy." She poured what was left of the powder back into the bag and tied the bag to her belt. "Tomorrow I'll take you to the temple where this powder is made. It's a long process, the herbs are rare and hard to find, and there's a curse on using them for idle purposes. When you put this powder in your mouth, you take on a sacred responsibility. You must promise never to listen to the animals except when a human life is at stake. Do you swear?"

"Yes, I swear."

"Good. Now that that is settled, I am going to allow you to use the powder one more time as part of your initiation. You have a horse-beast, brought out of the steppes. She's a lonely animal, far from her home, but you can't love her because you still love your dead mare, Eoru." She rolled a small pinch of the powder in a bit of flatbread, sealed the ends, and handed it to Marrah. "Wait five days. Then go to her, eat this, and listen."

Five days later, Marrah walked out to the pasture where the horses were tethered and found them cropping dry grass. Sitting down on a rock, she put the pellet of flatbread in her mouth and waited. For a long time nothing happened. Then, slowly, the languor crept over her again. She woke to find the horses standing nearby regarding her with curiosity.

"It's odd how they always sleep lying down," Ylata said. Her voice was soft. She rested her head on Nretsa's back and switched her tail.

Nretsa's nostrils flared slightly, and she studied Marrah with interest. "Do you think she's brought us apples?" Her voice was deep and a little husky.

Marrah stood up. For a moment, instead of the horses, she imagined that she saw two young women standing side by side with their arms wrapped around each other's waists. She reached out and stroked Nretsa's neck and felt the smooth glide of horsehair under her hand.

"Are you lonely?" she asked. The mare seemed to find nothing unusual in the question or the fact that Marrah had asked it.

"I miss the steppes," Nretsa said. "I miss the wide sky, the flat land, and the sweet smell of the tall grass crushed under my hooves when I gallop; but I don't miss the nomads who used to beat me." Nretsa put her soft nose in Marrah's hand and nuzzled it. "You never whip me. I love you, mother woman. I love it when you talk to me, but I love it most of all when we ride together and you sing to me."

"I'll sing to you more often," Marrah promised, and she threw her arm around Nretsa's neck and pressed her cheek against the mare's.

Third Initiation: A Gift from the Land of Dreams

A week after she spoke to Nretsa, Marrah sat by the spring where Keshna had been healed, watching it freeze over. The ice was slowly growing as milky as a blind eye. Not a bad comparison, she thought. She was staring at the healing spring and the spring was staring back at her without seeing her, just like the Imsha. Or maybe the Imsha did see her. Who could tell? Ever since she had arrived to begin the third stage of her initiation, the veiled figure had not so much as acknowledged her presence. It just sat on its rock with its arms clasped around its knees, presumably lost in thoughts too deep for ordinary mortals to share. So far they had not exchanged a single word. It was now late afternoon and a sharp wind was blowing down from the north, spitting snow and tossing dust and pine needles in their faces, but the Imsha seemed indifferent to the weather. Perhaps it lived outside all the time and paid no more attention to the cold than a beaver or a bear; or perhaps, Marrah thought, it had on more warm underclothes than she did.

She put her mitten over her nose and breathed a little warmth into it. She was just wondering wearily if they were going to sit there all day, when the Imsha suddenly turned to her in a sweep of black veils that reminded her of crows' wings.

"Cut off all your hair," it commanded. The words were in Old Language, but the accent was strange, as if each word were being rolled across its tongue like a small ball.

Although she didn't like the idea of cutting her hair in weather cold enough to freeze the paws off a rabbit, Marrah was relieved. Her patience had paid off: she had been accepted, and the third and final stage of her initiation had finally begun. She bowed obediently to the veiled figure, took her knife from its scabbard, and tried to figure out how to go about giving herself a haircut while wearing thick mittens. Finally she gave up, pulled off the mittens, and set about chopping off her hair as best she could.

It was an awkward process, and about halfway through it she realized that obeying the Imsha was going to be a lot harder than obeying Glyntsa. The flint blade was not particularly sharp, her fingers were stiff with cold, and she nicked her scalp more than once; but when you accepted an initiation, you did what you were told to do without asking questions, so she worked away doggedly, wondering if this was how Stavan felt when he scraped off his beard hairs. What would he have said if he could have seen her? He had always loved her hair. Black as a raven's wing, he used to say; curly as smoke; soft as new grass. He had combed it and braided it and even written a poem to it once a long time ago, before Keru and Luma were born, and now she was cutting it off with no more ceremony than if it were a patch of weeds.

Her hair fell into her lap and piled up at her feet—great hanks of it all tangled together like fine twine. She looked at it with growing regret, but she went on cutting. When she finished, she ran her hand over her nearly bare scalp. It felt cold and bristly, and she realized that she was going to have to wear a hat indoors as well as out—provided she ever got indoors again. She picked up her hair, untangled it as best she could, bound it with a bit of leather, and presented it to the Imsha with a bow.

To her surprise, the Imsha refused it. "Weave it into a snare."

A snare! Only fowlers could make a decent snare out of human hair, and they never worked outdoors in a stiff wind with a tangle of curls. Curly hair was fit for stuffing pillows maybe but not for weaving. Marrah reminded herself to be patient. This was undoubtedly a

The Horses at the Gate

test of her sincerity as an initiate, and if she had not been so cold, she might even have found it an interesting challenge.

Pulling off her mittens again, she blew some more warmth into her fingers and began to wind the longest strands of her hair together and tie them into one of those fine, knotted nets the fowlers used to catch small birds, but as she had feared, her hair was almost impossible to work with. She struggled for a long time, creating snarls and messes and knots. The light faded, but still she went on weaving. She hoped that the Imsha would tell her to stop, but the mysterious figure just sat there.

That night she slept behind a log, wrapped in her cloak, with her bare head tucked into her hood and the hair clutched to her chest so it would not blow away. When she woke the next morning, the Imsha was still sitting on the same rock, as if it had never moved. Marrah began to wonder if it was human. There was clearly to be no breakfast and no fire, but at least the sun was up and the wind had died down, so she went back to weaving her hair and by midday had a snare of sorts, irregular in places but strong enough to catch a sparrow. Spread between two bushes, the net would be invisible from a few paces, and if she was not careful she might forget and walk into it herself.

She rolled it up very carefully, making sure that none of the loose ends tangled. It took sure hands to make a snare of human hair, and she was proud of her work, but if the Imsha was pleased, it gave no sign. It held the snare for a moment and then returned it to her with no more ceremony than someone handing back an old basket.

"You'll use this to catch what you need," it said cryptically.

Marrah's heart sank. She tried to imagine herself spending an entire winter trapping birds with a snare the size of a child's tunic. She would much rather dig roots and crack nuts. Any bird small enough to get caught in that snare would hardly be worth the wood it would take to cook it. She was tempted to ask if she could go back to Kataka and get some fishhooks, but before she could get the words out, the veiled figure rose to its feet and motioned for her to follow. The two of them began to walk up a small path that led away from the pool, climbing the hillside through the bare trees.

With every step Marrah took, she grew more anxious. The trees looked strange in this part of the forest, bent and elderly with protruding roots that reminded her of birds' feet, and she could not help feeling that something unpleasant was about to happen. As the

Imsha walked, a cold white mist seemed to rise around her, and although it was broad daylight, Marrah heard the hoot of an owl. Somewhere in the distance a dog howled, and another dog joined it. As the wind blew small clouds over the sun, the shadows along the side of the trail seemed to take human shapes, and once she was sure she heard the call of a cuckoo—which would have been fine if it had been summer, but here in the midwinter forest, the bird's bubbling trill made the hair stand up on the back of her neck. She walked on, knowing it was too late to turn back, as a kind of slow terror crept over her.

The path crossed the ridge and then took a sharp turn to the left. They had gone downhill only a short distance when they came to a clearing. Suddenly the sun came out, a mild breeze sprang up, and Marrah's fears blew away like so many dry leaves. At the center of the clearing stood a small house, so beautiful and inviting that she wondered if the Imsha had conjured it out of the dream world. It was made of white clay and wheat-straw thatch like all the houses of Kataka, but it was shaped like the upper half of a large egg. The walls were covered with red spirals that swirled like smoke. Birds flew around the oval doorway; flowers of every color wreathed windows; strange animals marched at ground level or hung from the huge green vines that had been painted so that they seemed to climb into the smoke hole.

"Norhabi, lyrubu, wuburi," the Imsha said, pointing to the animals. "Mubumu, water reeds; patabi, the flowers of my land." Marrah did not understand any of the foreign words, but they had a melodious sound.

"Do you come from far away, honored one?" she asked, bowing respectfully to the Imsha. Under ordinary circumstances she would have said "honored mother" or "honored uncle," but the closer she got to the Imsha the less certain she became.

"I come from the south," the Imsha said, and it laughed that warm, ambiguous laugh that could have been a man's or a woman's. "Every third generation my people send a priestess north to Kataka, and the Katakans send us one in return. It's a long trip and I can recall getting quite seasick when the sailors took me across the Sea of Blue Waves, not to mention lonely, but it was my duty, so I did it. For time out of mind, my people and the Katakans have shared the wisdom of the Dark Mother, and now I'll share some of it with you if you prove worthy." The Imsha stepped forward, unhooked the leather curtain that covered the door of the house, and motioned for Marrah to enter. Before it stepped over the threshold, it paused as if inspecting Marrah from behind its black veils. The long black beads on its headdress swayed slightly. Approval? Marrah hoped so.

"You're a mother, aren't you?"

"Yes, honored one."

"I'd have rather had you when you were younger, but still motherhood is a great teacher. You'd be surprised how few initiates make it through the first night—even the young ones—but you're Lalah's granddaughter so I expected you to have the strength to do what you were ordered to do and the sense not to complain. There was never a more stubborn woman born than your grandmother. She came to me when her breasts were high, more years ago than I care to count, and if her hands had just been a little steadier," the Imsha held two gloved fingers together as if pinching salt, "I'd have given her the full initiation."

The inside of the house was as simple as the outside was elaborate: cool, whitewashed walls, a small clay bench that ran around one side, and a round fire pit filled with white sand and glowing charcoal that gave off welcome warmth. Marrah noticed a rough ladder that led to a small sleeping loft piled with sheepskins, a large Katakan water jar painted with the usual designs, a cup, a few pretty bowls, a grinding stone, and—best of all—baskets of nuts, grain, dried fruit, flour, and meat. Relieved that she was not going to have to live on sparrows all winter, she stood and waited for the Imsha to sit before she sat herself, but the Imsha had something more interesting in mind.

Standing with its back to Marrah, it began to unveil itself. It was wearing many layers, which explained why it had managed to survive the night outside in comfort, but as it dropped its cloak to the floor and turned around, Marrah gasped with surprise. The Imsha had the breasts of a woman, but its face was bearded.

"What are you?" Marrah cried, and was immediately embarrassed because what kind of question was that for an initiate to ask?

The Imsha laughed and went on taking off its outer wraps. It was as old a person as she had ever seen, old beyond all belief, thin as a bundle of twigs, with dark, bright eyes and not a tooth in its mouth as far as Marrah could tell, but it was its skin that was the most amazing thing about it. Marrah had seen many different kinds of people during the years she traveled with Stavan and Arang, but she had never before seen skin this shade. The Imsha was the color of the Goddess Earth Herself: not the reddish earth of the western forests or the pale dry earth of the cliffs, but the dark, fertile earth of a field that could grow wheat and lentils. If the Dark Mother ever appeared in a human body, Marrah thought, She would look like this. She felt a thrill of terror. What kind of power must lie in a being who united both sexes and was the color of the Mother?

The Imsha stripped to its inner tunic, sat down on the clay bench, and stretched out its legs to warm its feet by the fire. "Calm down," it said. "I'm not a divine being. I'm human, just like you. The only difference between us is that you were born woman and I was born both woman and man." It stroked its small, silky beard and closed its eyes as if remembering its strange southern land where animals hung from trees and water reeds flowered. "The priestesses who attended my birth told my mother that the Dark Mother had sent me to remind Her human children that All Is One. That well may be true." It grinned a slow, toothless grin. "But I think I was sent for a more pleasant reason. Do you remember the Sixth Commandment of the Divine Sisters?"

"The one that says we are to enjoy ourselves because our joy is pleasing to Her?"

The Imsha nodded. "Well, in my time I've had more joy than most people. I calculate that I'm somewhere near ninety years old, maybe more. For a good seventy of those years, I had the pleasure of a man and the pleasure of a woman both, much of it in this very room. If that sleeping mat up there could talk," the Imsha pointed to the loft, "it would sing like a chorus of nightingales."

"Which pleasure was better?" Marrah put her hand over her mouth and stared at the Imsha apologetically. She had not meant to ask such an intimate question, but it must have been all right because the Imsha leaned back and yawned, and its old face suddenly seemed younger.

"The pleasure of men is sharper, but the pleasure of women is longer," it said agreeably. "Often I pitied my lovers—although I must say they never complained about me. Most people look at the world as if they are staring at it through a little hole: they see a bit of elbow here and a bit of nose there, but never the whole." It paused. "But I always saw everything, and it is my job to show you as much of it as you can bear: man and woman; past and present; death and life; the great circle that goes and comes and comes and goes, and rolls on without ever stopping. But first . . . " The Imsha paused again and studied Marrah. "First, you must make me a perfect pot—or a perfect statue if you'd rather, although statues are harder."

For a moment, Marrah had the impression that she had not heard correctly. "A perfect pot?" she echoed. "A perfect statue?" This seemed too easy.

The Imsha nodded. It rose slowly to its feet, picked up its discarded clothing, and began to get dressed again. "You will find the picks you need to dig the clay, and the sieves, the soaking jars, and such things out in the little shed by the kiln. You will have to cut your own wood, but there's an ax. Glyntsa tells me you are already an accomplished potter, taught by Bindar himself. Did you know that your great-uncle came to me for initiation too? The trees around this house were little saplings in those days, and I still had my teeth." It sighed. "I turned Bindar into a master potter, but your grandmother, as I said before, was destined for other things. Unsteady hands; but a good queen, I hear; one of the best."

Marrah was relieved to discover that this third initiation was going to be so easy. The final powers of the Dark Mother were so shrouded in mystery that she had imagined she might be set to all sorts of terrifying, dangerous, even impossible tasks. But she was only being asked to make one perfect pot or statue, and she had made more pots and statues than she could count over the last six years. She might not be a master potter like her great-uncle, but she had steady hands.

"I'll bring the pot to you in three days," she said boldly.

The Imsha said nothing. It just turned and left.

At first, Marrah was afraid she had offended it by being immodest, but as she stood at the door she heard laughter coming from the retreating form. It was not the dignified laughter of an elder or the warm laughter of the Imsha. It was the wildly amused giggling of a young girl who has just heard a very funny story.

The Imsha had every reason to laugh. A perfect pot did not take three days to make or even three weeks. Marrah's hair had grown down to her ears, winter was over, and the frogs were singing in the healing spring before she made anything acceptable, and there were many days—especially at first—when she was half convinced that the final initiation of the Dark Goddess was nothing more than a bad joke foisted on unsuspecting strangers.

Had she been in Shara, making a pot would have involved rolling prepared clay into coils, smoothing them together, and firing the result in one of the temple kilns, but here she had to do everything as if no one had ever made a pot before. Some days she gathered and prepared the clay, prying large lumps of it out of the quarrying place with a deer-antler pick. Actually there were several quarrying places, and she visited them all in turn, sometimes coming home with baskets of red lumps, sometimes with white, sometimes with a pale yellow.

It was demanding work especially during the weeks when the ground was frozen, and every time she dug there were certain rituals to be observed, which she attended to scrupulously. Since clay was part of the body of the Goddess Earth, she would sprinkle holy water on it and pray to the damp mud before she took it from the ground. Then she would lug it back in a carrying basket, separate it into smaller lumps, and spread it out in front of the fire, turning it occasionally so it would dry evenly. When it crumbled in the palm of her hand, she would pick out the stones, soak it again, sieve it through an open-weave basket, and mix it with fine, volcanic binding sand in the usual way, spreading the wet mass out on the floor, tramping on it, and pulling up the edges as if she were kneading a giant loaf of bread. When the clay was mixed to the consistency of a heavy cake batter, she would spread it out to dry a bit more, and then divide it into equal-sized balls that she stored in a large basket wrapped in pieces of damp linen.

On other days, she would prepare slips and paints of various colors from the small baskets of pigmented earth that she found among her food stores: red mostly, but also yellow, buff, white, and gray. Or she would chop wood to feed the kilning fire. But most of the time she made pots and, later, statues. At first she made only a few, confident that they were as close to perfection as anyone could demand, but when she brought them to the Imsha, the Imsha would look at them for a moment and toss them over its shoulder.

"Not good enough," it would say. "Try again."

Marrah got used to the sound of breaking pottery that spring: first the dull crack and then the shards pattering down on the stones. Nothing she did was good enough, not the pretty, delicate statues of Batal, not the breast-shaped water jugs, not even the simple cups that every ten-year-old knew how to make.

"What do you want?" she cried one afternoon, completely frustrated.

"Bring them to me wet."

"You mean unkilned?"

"No, wet, and don't make one at a time; make several dozen."

So after that, Marrah brought undried pots by the score, and the Imsha stopped tossing them over its shoulder. Instead it took each one, balanced it in its hand, and inspected it. Then it would sit it down, cut it in half, and show Marrah what she had done wrong. Sometimes the sides of the pot were not of even thickness, sometimes the rim was just a little less than round, sometimes the flaw was something Marrah could not see no matter how hard she looked. Occasionally the Imsha would not even bother to cut a pot.

"This one will crack," it would declare, and sure enough, if Marrah fired that particular pot, it would come out of the kiln in pieces.

If anyone had asked Marrah what she was learning during those long, disappointing days, she would have said, "not much," but slowly she began to lose herself in pottery making, and for the first time in many months she spent long periods without mourning for Keru and Arang or worrying about Stavan. Grief and loneliness disappeared, her thoughts stayed in one place, and if she was not exactly happy, she was as close to happiness as she had been since the nomad raid.

She learned patience that spring, but she must have been learning other things too, things she didn't even know she was learning, because one rainy night in early summer she began to dream in an entirely new way. She never knew why her dreams changed. Perhaps all those weeks of struggling with the clay had changed the way she saw the world; perhaps the Imsha had thrown her into some kind of trance without her knowing it, or put something in her food; or perhaps the dreams were a gift from the Dark Mother. But wherever they came from, the dreams were as real as life.

The first dream came without warning: suddenly she found herself standing in a nomad tent inhaling the familiar scent of smoke, wet wool, and dogs. It was night, but a pale stream of moonlight was pouring through the smoke hole. She froze in terror, convinced for one terrible moment that she was still Vlahan's wife and prisoner. Then she saw Stavan lying on a pile of sheepskins, his face turned to the moonlight.

There was nothing in the scene to suggest that it was a dream. Everything was solid: the usual nomad cooking baskets were stacked by the fire pit; the felt rug was warm under her bare feet; and Stavan was as much there as he had been in all the years they'd been together.

She went over to him and knelt by his side. He looked thinner, and she saw a new, half-healed scar on his cheek. Bending down, she kissed him, feeling the warmth of his lips, breathing in the smell and taste of him. He started awake and clutched his dagger, but when he saw who was kissing him, he threw it aside.

"Marrah!" he cried. "How did you get here?"

"I don't know."

"What happened to your hair?"

"I cut it for my initiation."

"Come here, my darling; come here, my love." He took her in his arms and drew her down beside him, and they kissed each other, and she woke crying his name.

The next night she had the same dream, only this time it began with the kiss. Other things were different: Stavan's bed was on the opposite side of the tent, and there was an empty waterskin beside the fire pit.

"I've missed you," Stavan murmured.

"And I you."

"Are you real or only a dream?"

"I don't know."

They kissed again. He touched her breasts through her tunic and held her so close she could feel his heart beating. "Take off your things," he whispered.

She took off her clothes and crawled in beside him. Her feet were cold, and his were warm. For a long time they lay naked together under the sheepskins, holding each other, breast to breast, knee to knee, lip to lip, breathing as one person. Then he began to move down her body, kissing her neck and shoulders, her arms and the insides of her elbows. It took him a long time to reach her belly and longer still to reach her thighs, and when at last he buried his face between her legs, she arched her back and pulled him even closer, and they swayed together, and she floated up and out of herself, and cried out, and came in quick, fast, shuddering waves that left her breathless.

"Again?" he asked.

"Yes, again!"

They did it again. Afterward she slowly kissed him, lip to heel, until he pulled her on top of him with a moan of pleasure.

"Am I a good horse?" he asked, and his hair was like smoke in the moonlight.

"The best, my darling," she cried, and she rode him high and long.

For four nights in a row she dreamed of Stavan, and each night they made love. On the morning of the fifth day, she went in search of the Imsha. She found it sitting in its usual place beside the healing pool.

"How do you like the dream world?" it called out as it caught sight of her. "How do you like sharing joy again with your handsome nomad lover?"

Marrah stopped in her tracks. "How do you know what I've been dreaming?"

"It's my business to know. I could watch too, but I decided long ago not to. So tell me, has the lovemaking been enjoyable?"

"Yes, very." The idea that the Imsha could see her dreams was so disconcerting—not to mention embarrassing—that Marrah was speechless. Finally she found her tongue. "But are these dreams real?"

"Real?" The Imsha laughed.

"Am I really with Stavan? Does he know I'm there? Is he somewhere far away dreaming the same dreams, or am I alone in this? When Glyntsa taught me how to listen to the animals, I took a special powder; before I heard the voice of the Butterfly Goddess, Chilana, I ate a live caterpillar. But this time I've drunk nothing, eaten nothing—at least nothing that I know of—and still it keeps happening, so I need to know: what have you done to me? Please, honored one, help me understand. Have you put me in a trance without my realizing it? Am I really making love with Stavan, or is this just my longing for him speaking through my dreams?"

The Imsha stopped laughing. "I suggest you ask him those questions the next time you see him." It stretched out its hand. "Enough chatter. Give me your pots. You brought some, didn't you? Or have you been too busy dreaming love dreams to keep the kiln fire hot?"

Obviously it had no intention of telling her whether her dreams were real. Marrah felt more confused than ever. She fumbled in her carrying basket and took out the three small bowls she had packed as she hurried out the door. They were nothing much, just half globes of reddish brown clay painted with snake signs that had turned black in the kiln.

The Imsha took one of the bowls and balanced it on the palm of its hand. "Not bad," it said. It inspected another. "You're coming along nicely." It picked up the final bowl and was silent for a long time. Finally it handed the bowl back to Marrah. "Lovemaking must agree with you," it said. "This one is perfect."

Things moved quickly after that. As soon as it had pronounced the bowl perfect, the Imsha rose to its feet and ordered Marrah to go get her snare. Marrah obeyed, running so fast that briars tore at her tunic and twigs stung her legs. When she returned with the snare carefully rolled in a piece of linen, she stood panting, trying to catch her breath, but the Imsha gave her no time to recover.

"Hang it on that elderberry bush," it ordered. "And hang it low to the ground."

Marrah unrolled the snare and hung it on the elderberry bush with great care, knowing that if she dropped it, she would never be able to untangle the strands. The snare caught the wind and billowed. It was a delicate thing, a spiderweb of black hairs and every one from her own head.

The Imsha inspected it and gave a grunt of approval. "Do you remember when I told you that you'd catch what you needed in this?"

"Yes, honored one."

"Are you ready?"

Marrah had no idea what it meant by "ready," but she nodded, and as she did so, the Imsha suddenly grabbed her by the wrist. What happened next was so strange that it took away what little breath she had left. As soon as the Imsha's hand touched her arm, Marrah fell into a deep trance. For a moment everything was a confused jumble of color and light. Then suddenly the two of them began to shrink. Down and down they went, growing smaller and smaller until the boulders around the pool looked like mountains and the grass looked like trees. A butterfly flew over them, as huge as a ship, its blue and yellow wings glowing like fire, and a chorus of frogs roared in her ears like the rushing of a great river.

In front of them, the elderberry leaves became the size of sails, and the snare grew as large as a house. The Imsha led Marrah toward the great net woven of black ropes—each as thick as her arm—and as they approached, the snare suddenly stiffened and stopped billowing in the wind.

"Time has stopped," the Imsha announced, but Marrah barely heard. She was staring at a swallow that had frozen in the air above her, and she felt a rapture that was beyond terror.

"Look," the Imsha commanded.

Marrah looked and saw that every opening in the snare had become a window, each opening into a different world. In one window she saw herself on her coming-of-age day, leaping from a high cliff into the surf; in another she saw herself pulling Stavan from the sea; and in still another she saw Keru and Luma at the moment they were born. Shara was there and so were the steppes; here, she was Vlahan's wife and a prisoner, gathering dung in baskets and being beaten; there, she was Lalah's beloved granddaughter, nursing her babies on the roof as she chatted with Dalish. In some of the windows she was middle-aged, and in some she was an old woman sitting in the sun beside a young woman she didn't recognize. Frightened, she closed her eyes.

"I can't bear these visions!" she cried. "Take them away!"

The Imsha laughed and tightened its grip on Marrah's wrist.

"What are you afraid of?"

"I'm afraid I'll see my own death."

"You won't see your own death until you ask to see it. Open your eyes, Marrah, daughter of Sabalah. Be brave. Open your eyes and see the far, far-distant future."

Marrah opened her eyes and found that she and the Imsha were standing in front of one of the windows, looking into some kind of huge house, bigger than any motherhouse ever built. Blue-green light was coming from long, glowing lanterns, and people dressed in shining robes were walking slowly, looking at things in strange boxes. The sides of the boxes were clear like water, but they were solid. Marrah saw Hansi spears behind the solid water; arrows; daggers; and the bones of a man surrounded by a great quantity of weapons and gold.

"Come this way," the Imsha whispered, and it and Marrah seemed to float through the window into the house, drifting down endless dim corridors until they came to another room. There was only one person there, a middle-aged woman with gray-brown hair and boots with strange heels that looked like sticks. She was bending forward, examining something in one of the water boxes, and when Marrah looked closer she saw that it was the black and red bowl she had fired only yesterday.

"Now you see why the bowl had to be perfect," the Imsha said. It came up behind the woman and put its hand on her shoulder, but the woman seemed not to know the Imsha was there. She just went on looking at Marrah's bowl, frowning slightly like someone lost in thought.

"That bowl is speaking to her," the Imsha said. "She is hearing your voice over a gulf of years too great to count. She does not know that she is hearing it, but she is. In her time, the Goddess Earth has been forgotten, but your bowl is making her remember. You will make a great many bowls in your lifetime, but only this one will survive."

The Imsha let go of Marrah's wrist and suddenly the trance lifted and they were standing beside the healing pool again, and the snare was only a little net of human hairs not much bigger than Marrah's palm.

"How did you do that?" Marrah cried.

The Imsha did not answer. It bent forward and kissed Marrah on the forehead. "I did nothing," it said softly. "You did it all yourself. In the third initiation of the Dark Mother, she who is initiated must learn without knowing what it is she is learning. You are indeed blessed. The Dark Mother has granted you the powers of trance and prophecy that were withheld from your grandmother. Go home, dear child. There is nothing more I can teach you. You will be a great priestess and a great queen, but if a time ever comes when everything seems lost, hang up your snare and whisper the names of the Dark Mother."

"Tell me more!" Marrah begged. "What do you see? Will I get Keru back? Will Arang live to sit beside me in the Council of Elders? And Stavan? What of Stavan?" But the Imsha refused to speak another word, and turning, it disappeared into the forest.

That afternoon, Marrah packed her snare in a tight bundle, strapped on her sandals, and set out to walk back to Kataka. She was about halfway down the mountain when she saw Hiknak riding up the slope on Ylata and leading Nretsa behind her.

"Mount up!" Hiknak cried. "Queen Glyntsa sent me to get you; she wants you to come back to Kataka right away. Dalish rode in this morning with a message from your grandmother. One of Nikhan's warriors showed up in Shara. He claims Nikhan and Stavan fought Vlahan and lost!"

Marrah begged Hiknak to tell her more, but Hiknak knew nothing. She explained that she had started out to get Marrah almost the moment Dalish arrived in Kataka, sick with exhaustion.

"Dalish didn't want to tell me the rest of the message without you being there," Hiknak said. "I asked her about Arang, and Stavan, and Keru, but she just kept saying, 'Go get Marrah.' She was so tired that Kal had to lift her off her horse, and when Glyntsa brought her a cup of broth, she fell asleep with her head on her arms before she could drink it."

They looked at each other grimly, both thinking the same thought, but there was nothing more to be said. They rode in silence down the muddy trail, letting the horses pick their way around the stones. Marrah was tempted to urge Nretsa into a gallop, but she had learned long ago that you never raced downhill over loose gravel unless you were willing to risk your horse breaking its front legs. As she rode, she thought of a number of reasons why Dalish might be unwilling to tell Hiknak the rest of Lalah's message, and each was worse than the other.

Several times she closed her eyes and tried to see what news was waiting for her in Kataka, but all she saw were the backs of her eyelids. She might have been given the powers of trance and prophecy, but without hanging up her snare and whispering the names of the Dark Mother, she was no more capable of seeing into the future than she had been on the day the Imsha had first ordered her to cut her hair.

At last the ground leveled out, and they were able to kick the horses into a trot. Soon Kataka came into sight.

The wheat was already knee high, guarded by the same clay grain bins that had so impressed Marrah the first time she saw them, but the Kataka she came back to was not the same city she had left when she went up the mountain to receive the final initiation of the Dark Mother. While she had been trying to make a perfect pot for the Imsha, Glyntsa and Kal had been fortifying the city, supervised by Hiknak, who knew more about war than both of them put together. The rose fence still wrapped itself around the perimeter, leafed out now and blossoming, and as Marrah and Hiknak approached they could smell the sweet perfume of the roses; but outside the fence, there was a new gash in the land. The gash was a circle too, but no roses grew around it and no bees visited it; it was simply a muddy ditch, as deep as a man's height and some twenty paces across, lined with sharp sticks that pointed toward the sky. The dirt from the ditch had been piled up on the side farthest from the city, and the Katakans had already started to grow dense stands of blackberry bushes on the crest of the mound.

The stake-filled ditch and thorny mound were ingenious ways to keep out men on horseback, but Marrah frowned when she caught sight of them. Hiknak had done a good job, but there was something unsettling about the new circle that surrounded the motherhouses. In Shara, they had been able to carry most of what they needed up to the cliffs. Every time they turned to go back down the trail, they saw Shara as it had always been: open to the land and the sea. But the Katakans had no cliffs to run to in case the nomads attacked, and as a result their city would never look the same again. It was a fort now, like the wooden war temple Nikhan had built on the ashes of Shambah, only larger.

At the edge of the ditch they were obliged to dismount and tie their horses to the post that Hiknak had placed there for just such an occasion. Someone in Kataka must have made the post because it was a beautiful thing, carved over with roses, crescent moons, and dogs, and as Marrah looped the ends of Nretsa's reins around it, she thought that, as always, the Katakans were incapable of making anything ugly.

Walking down the side of the ditch, she and Hiknak threaded their way between the sharp stakes, which were far enough apart to drive a goat or a sheep through but much too narrow for a horse. A short set of narrow muddy stairs had been carved into the far wall just opposite the gate. They climbed them easily and entered the city through the gate, which had been fitted with a stout wooden door that stood wide open. The door would hardly keep out raiders since anyone with a good, sharp knife could break through the rose fence, but there were piles of logs lying about that suggested the Katakans intended to build a real wall. As Marrah passed through the gate, she noticed that Redra was nowhere in sight.

"She died this spring of a lung fever," Hiknak said, "and Glyntsa has yet to appoint a new gatekeeper."

Marrah had not known Redra very well, but what she had known of her, she had liked. Redra had died in a natural way that had nothing to do with the nomads, but Marrah could not help thinking how many years Redra had stood at the gate of Kataka greeting pilgrims. Her death was another sign that Kataka would never again be a city where all strangers were welcomed.

They found Dalish sitting in Glyntsa's kitchen at the same table where they had sat with Keshna the first morning they came to Kataka. A number of people were in the room including Glyntsa and Kal and most of the Council of Elders, but Marrah had eyes only for Dalish. One look at her face and Marrah knew that the news she brought was bad.

Dalish rose to her feet. Her cheeks were pale with fatigue and her dark hair was wind-tangled, but her eyes were as hard as they had been on that day so long ago when she told Marrah that Marrah must either marry Vlahan or die. Dalish was soft-hearted, so when she had to do something that might hurt someone, she drew a shield around herself and became abrupt and even rude.

"Hello, Marrah," she said curtly. "Your grandmother sends her greetings and says you are to return to Shara to become the war queen." She might have been a messenger instead of one of Marrah's closest friends; she did not even embrace her. She just stood there stiffly and spoke in a hoarse voice that sounded like wet wood. "The nomads are riding south and may attack at any time."

Tell me about Keru and Stavan and Arang! Marrah thought, but she was afraid to ask for fear of what she might hear.

"Why would the nomads bother to attack Shara?" Hiknak said. "There's nothing there they could possibly want. Stavan is gone, and Vlahan already has Keru and Arang, so why would they go to all the trouble of taking Shara when cities like Kataka are richer and closer?"

They were speaking in Sharan, but Kal understood. His eyes narrowed as Hiknak mentioned the riches of Kataka, but he said nothing. What Hiknak had said was true: Shara was a long way from the steppes, and if the nomads were after gold and cattle, there were much better pickings to the north. Changar might hate Marrah, but he was not fool enough to persuade Vlahan to cross the River of Smoke simply for the pleasure of bringing back her head.

"There is something Vlahan wants in Shara. Something—or rather someone—he wants very much." Dalish paused and looked from Hiknak to Marrah and back again. "Arang."

"Arang has escaped!" Hiknak cried.

"Yes. At this very moment he's in Shara. He begged to come to Kataka with me, but Lalah wouldn't let him. She said it would be an invitation to a nomad ambush. Arang came south with the messenger who brought the news of the battle. He says Stavan raided Vlahan's camp and set him free."

"You've spoken to him!" Hiknak clapped her hands and turned to Marrah. "Praise your gods and mine!" She turned back to Dalish. "How did he look? What did he say? Did he send me a message?"

Marrah was taken completely by surprise. She had been prepared to hear bad news, but Dalish had brought good instead.

"How is he?" Hiknak said. "Tell me everything, even if it's bad. Did they cut off his ears or balls or put out his eyes?" Marrah wished that for once Hiknak would be less blunt, but there was always something of the nomad in her. If Arang had been maimed, no one would grieve more, but still she would ask about the most terrible things as if they were commonplace.

Dalish shrugged. "When I left Shara, Arang had two eyes, two ears, two arms, two legs, and—to the best of my knowledge—two balls. He had been the Great Chief—in name only, of course, but Great Chief all the same—so Vlahan made sure he was well treated. Vlahan can't keep the Twenty Tribes together without him. I gather Arang spent most of his time sitting in the chief's tent, eating roast lamb and holding audiences with a dagger pressed to his back. He sends his love to both of you." She turned to Hiknak. "To you he says, 'Come back soon and bring Keshna so I can hold both of you in my arms again.'" She turned to Marrah. "And to you he says, 'Come back, dear sister, and help me defend Shara.'"

Marrah could not stand the suspense any longer. "And Keru? What about him? Did Stavan free him too? Is my boy in Shara?"

Dalish met Marrah's eyes and then looked away. "No," she said. "Arang says that Changar slept with Keru by his side, linked to his wrist with a rope of white wool. There were too many guards posted around Changar's tent when Stavan raided the camp. He couldn't even get close."

Marrah was stunned with disappointment. She felt Hiknak's hand on her arm, comforting her. "Stavan may have lost this battle, but he'll win the next one," Hiknak said. Her words were brave, but all Marrah could think of was Keru leashed to Changar like a dog.

Dalish coughed and reached for the clay pitcher that stood on the table. Pouring herself a cup of water, she drank it slowly.

"Marrah," she began. She stopped abruptly. "Marrah, there is something else I have to tell you." She suddenly took a few steps forward and seized Marrah by the shoulders as if she were going to shake her, but instead she drew her close. "Dear Marrah, dearest friend—" Her voice broke. "I didn't want to be the one to tell you this, but Lalah said I had to: Stavan can't free Keru. Stavan is dead."

BOOK FOUR

The Siege

In the days of Vlahan the Great, our warriors rode south to
bring the gods to a godless people.

INSCRIPTION ON THE HANDLE OF A HANSI DAGGER
WRITTEN IN THE SACRED SCRIPT OF OLD EUROPE—
POSSIBLY BY A SLAVE.
MUSEUM OF ART AND HISTORY
VARNA, BULGARIA
DATE UNKNOWN

No horse ever shot an arrow;
No horse ever burned a city.

When I sit on Nretsa's back
and feel her move under me
I know she is as innocent
as a swallow.

The evil is not in the horse.
The evil is in the rider.

FROM "THE SIEGE"
A MEMORY SONG OF THE SHARATANI PEOPLE
BLACK SEA COAST
FIFTH MILLENNIUM B.C.

CHAPTER TWELVE

T he drums grew louder, pulsing through darkness. Suddenly they fell silent, and a single drum took up the rhythm. In the warriors' camp, Vlahan's men sat around the chief's fire drinking *kersek* and listening to the man who had killed Stavan sing his bragging song. Puhan had sung the same brag every night for weeks, but the warriors never tired of it. Each night it grew more elaborate, and each night they nodded their tattooed faces in unison and beat out the rhythms on their thighs, shouting their approval every time Puhan got to the part where he had struck Stavan a mighty blow, knocking him off his horse.

> *I am Puhan,*
> *stronger than a stallion*
> *faster than a deer*
> *more cunning than a wolf:*
> *Puhan, son of Yerhan,*
> *Puhan brave and mighty.*
> *I alone killed Stavan,*
> *the cowardly rebel leader,*

Stavan the Hansi traitor,
Stavan the witch lover.
I struck a mighty blow,
and he fell beneath my club.

Puhan accompanied himself on the bragging drum as he sang, pounding it with doubled-up fists so it made a sound that all but drowned him out. The bragging drum was small as Hansi drums went, a circle of cowhide no more than two hands wide, stretched over a wooden frame and painted with suns and stars, but it had a loud voice. Puhan himself had a terrible voice—his singing was like the wailing of mice being trampled by horses—but no one minded. There was nothing more pleasurable than listening to a newly crowned hero boast, even if his crown was no more than a stiff strip of wolf pelt studded with shells instead of the golden circlet that Vlahan should have handed over to him for the evening. But with Arang gone for a second time, Vlahan's power was too shaky for him to trust anyone with the Great Chief's crown, so the gold stayed on Vlahan's head, and Puhan got the wolf.

Before Puhan killed Stavan, he had never done anything more remarkable than steal a few cattle. He was small and skinny, with a sharply pointed nose and slightly crossed eyes that had earned him the reputation of being the worst marksman in the tribe. Everyone said—or rather used to say—that when Puhan put an arrow to his bow, the men on both sides of him had better take cover; but now that he was a hero they had stopped making jokes at his expense—except for a few of Puhan's enemies who whispered enviously that his victory had been a piece of luck some better man deserved.

Puhan knew that his enemies were right: he was a coward by nature, but by an odd twist of circumstances, he had brought glory on himself and all his kin. In the heat of the raid, he had tried to run for safety and had, by accident, galloped straight toward the enemy. Suddenly he had found himself behind Stavan, son of Zuhan. Puhan, who knew Stavan on sight, had been so terrified that before he knew what he was doing, he lashed out wildly with his war club, landing a lucky blow and knocking Stavan off his horse.

At first he had been so stunned that he just sat there waiting for Stavan to get up and kill him, but when Stavan continued to lie motionless, he realized that Stavan was at the very least unconscious, and jumping off his horse, he went to see if by any chance he had killed him. To his joy, he discovered that he had. Giving a whoop of victory, he began to strip the body to prove that he had slain the man Vlahan most wanted dead. First he took Stavan's bracelet and jerked the gold earrings out of his ears; then he kicked him over onto his back and pulled the horse pendant from his neck and grabbed his dagger and belt with all the speed of a man used to looting on the run. But to Puhan's eternal chagrin, he had not managed to carry Stavan's head back to Vlahan because just as he was kneeling to take it, five enemy warriors had suddenly ridden down on him with bloodcurdling whoops that had sent him scrambling back to his horse.

Of course, the fact that he had galloped off in a panic was the reason why he was alive tonight to bang on the bragging drum, but naturally this version of the story did not appear in his song. In Puhan's brag, he had fought off a dozen Shubhai warriors single-handedly and killed five of them before a dozen more rode up to help. Forced at last to outrun them, he had hurled insults in their teeth and made them ashamed to be Shubhai.

> Sons of sluts, I am Puhan!
> Look on me and cry with fear!
> Puhan, the wolf, spits in your faces!
> Puhan pisses on you and your kin!

What he really had yelled was, "Help! Don't hurt me!" but that would not have made much of an impression had he admitted it. Although his bragging song was almost twice as long tonight as it had been last night, he was leaving out the parts of the story that reflected poorly on him and his family. For example, Vlahan's reaction to the news of Stavan's death appeared nowhere in Puhan's brag, and for good reason: Vlahan had been so mad when he learned that Puhan had failed to bring him Stavan's head that he had slashed a hole in the side of his own tent.

"You coward!" Vlahan had screamed. "You stupid little cross-eyed son of a bitch! You ran off and left the head of Stavan the traitor behind like it was an old boot!"

"I fought valiantly, *rahan*," Puhan had protested. "No man alive could have withstood such numbers. See, I bring you the bracelets and earrings of the traitor as proof of his death. Here is his dagger, red with his blood, and the belt I stripped off his lifeless corpse."

"I don't want this trash!" Vlahan had screamed. "I want his head!"

"I could not bring the traitor's head to you, *rahan*," Puhan had stuttered, "but many men saw me kill him." Which fortunately was true or else Puhan's own head might well have ended up decorating a stake outside Vlahan's tent. Several warriors had seen Puhan strike the fatal blow—men of great courage who never lied—but despite the fact that they all confirmed that Stavan was dead, Vlahan continued to rage and threaten until late that evening when the scouts galloped into camp to report that the Shubhai and their allies were in full flight. The next morning two spies appeared with the welcome news that little Nikhan had wailed and screamed like a madman when he learned of Stavan's death, slashing at his arms and face and cursing the gods until his own men had to restrain him.

As soon as the spies reported Nikhan's despair, Vlahan knew that Puhan really had killed Stavan. Grudgingly he had hailed Puhan as a hero, and grudgingly he had placed the sacred crown of shells and wolf fur on Puhan's brow with his own hands. But even though there was no longer any doubt that Stavan was dead, Vlahan remained in a dangerous temper at Puhan's failure to bring him Stavan's head.

Puhan drummed and bragged for a long time as the stars wheeled slowly across the sky, and the moon rose, slender as a stem of dead grass. When at last he finished, he proclaimed himself the bravest man who had ever lived, gave a final thump on the drum, and fell silent. There was a general mutter of approval, and everyone looked at Vlahan expectantly.

Vlahan sat for a long time staring at Puhan, his mouth twisted into a half smile that made Puhan's guts feel like water. Finally he spoke.

Mary
Mackey

218

"So this is the man who killed my half brother, the traitorous witch-lover Stavan—Stavan who stole Arang, grandson of Zuhan, true Great Chief of all the Hansi, and persuaded the miserable Shubhai and five other cowardly, shit-eating tribes to rebel?"

Puhan hoped this was not really a question. "Yes, *rahan*," he said meekly. His voice wavered, and he could not meet Vlahan's eyes. Everyone knew that Arang had not been "stolen" but had run to the Shubhai with open arms, just as everyone knew that Vlahan had kept Arang prisoner for months while he ruled the Twenty Tribes in his name, but no man who valued his life would dare show this by so much as a flicker of an eyelash.

Vlahan took a long pull of *kersek*, wiped his mouth on the back of his hand, and stared at Puhan until he squirmed. Vlahan had put on weight, and his red, meaty face had the sheen of heavy eating. This had been the best year in the last five, with the rains finally coming on time, thick forage for the herds, and the rebellion all but crushed. But even though Nikhan and his allies had run like frightened rabbits after Stavan was killed, it had been only a half victory since they had failed to recapture Arang. Without Arang, Vlahan knew that he could not expect to hold the tribes together for long. If Puhan had been anything but a sniveling coward, he would have brought back Stavan's head. Now there were rumors that Stavan's ghost walked and that he would come back from Paradise to avenge himself on the tribes that had failed to rally to him. Vlahan hated his half brother with the steady glow of a hot fire. Night after night he had lain awake imagining just how fine Stavan's head would look stuck on a spear outside his tent: eyes rotting, flesh peeling off, but thanks to Puhan there was nothing beside his fire ring but five sleeping dogs and a rack of smoked horsemeat.

"You're quite a hero, Puhan." Another long pause that made Puhan wish he were back in his own tent. Vlahan stared at him some more and something nasty flickered in the back of his eyes. I should have the coward strangled, Vlahan thought. But if he had Puhan strangled, it would be as good as admitting that Stavan's death had not been enough to make up for the loss of Arang. He would have to treat the little cross-eyed cattle stealer like a hero whether he wanted to or not. This realization did not improve Vlahan's mood.

"What reward do you think you deserve?"

Puhan opened his mouth and then closed it again, paralyzed by the look in Vlahan's eyes.

Vlahan leaned forward and smiled maliciously. He had just thought of the perfect way to reward Puhan and punish him at the same time. "Did you say you would like another wife? What a stallion you are, Puhan! What a hero indeed! With a beautiful wife like Shakshak whom no ordinary man could satisfy, you ask to take on another. But why one more wife? Why not several? A great hero like you should father many sons!"

Puhan turned the color of unwashed wool and made a gasping sound. His wife, Shakshak, was the most jealous woman in the whole camp, and if he brought another woman into their tent, she would claw his eyes out. Another man might have beaten Shakshak into submission, but he had never dared to strike her. She was nearly twice as big as he was, and she had once threatened to kill him in his sleep if he so much as looked at another woman.

"Ah," Vlahan persisted, "I can see you like the idea. Very well then, you stud, you bull, you man among men, I give you Utak, sister of Druhan; Erutak, daughter of Sdruhan; and Hwerkak, widow of Arawetahan, to be your second, third, and fourth wives."

Puhan wanted to beg Vlahan to stop, but he didn't dare. This was a nightmare. The widow Hwerkak had five children whom he would have to feed—five big, loud, nasty girls who ate their own weight at every meal. Puhan looked at Shakshak glaring at him from the edge of the crowd and knew that he would never again have a moment's peace.

"You do me too much honor, *rahan!*" he cried. "I am not worthy."

"Nonsense," Vlahan said. "You're a hero. In fact, the more I think about it, the more I think three women won't be enough for you, so I'm going to give you five of the Shubhai concubines we just captured in our great victory. They're all younger and even prettier than Shakshak."

Nine women in one tent! Puhan wondered if it would do any good to beg Vlahan to kill him and get it over with.

"Thank you, *rahan!*" he wailed. "Thank you, most generous of chiefs."

"Come forward," Vlahan said, "and sit up here beside me, and if you would like still more women, just say the word. You're our great hero, Puhan, and I'll deny you nothing."

Puhan slunk up next to Vlahan and sat beside him. His pointed nose seemed to droop, and the wolf-fur crown slipped down to his eyebrows. Never had a hero looked more dejected.

Vlahan rose to address his warriors. They all realized what he had done to Puhan, but not one smiled. "Now that the hero, Puhan, has finished his great brag and been rewarded, we must move on to other things. The traitor Stavan is dead and the rebellious tribes have been defeated, but our victory is not as sweet as it should have been. Our best scouts have hunted for signs of Arang for weeks with no luck, but this evening they came to me to say that the dung-eating cowards who stole him have carried him south to a cursed place called Shara, where trees grow side by side and women rule."

A murmur of surprise and anger rose from the warriors. Vlahan lifted his horse-headed scepter, tilted back his head, and addressed his next words to the sky. "Great Han, Lord of the Sun and Stars, hear me: tomorrow we will sacrifice four hands of horses to you to thank you for making our scouts' eyes sharp. When the earth has received their blood, we will break camp, ride on Shara, burn it to the ground, and bring back our Great Chief!"

A great howling rose around him as the warriors threw back their heads and gave the Hansi war cry. The drummers sent their hands flying across the drumheads, and once again the steppes vibrated until the stars themselves seemed to tremble overhead.

As Vlahan and his warriors rode south, Marrah, Hiknak, and Dalish galloped toward Shara. The women knew they were racing the nomads to the city, but they had no way of calculating how close the race would be. They stopped only long enough to eat cold meals, snatch a little sleep, and rest their horses, but even so, the threat of the coming invasion pursued them. Perhaps by now Vlahan's men had reached Shambah and burned it a second time; perhaps they had bypassed Shambah and even now were crossing the River of Smoke. Perhaps (oh let it not be true!) Shara already lay in ruins.

No one wanted to talk, but they rode side by side whenever they could, taking courage from the sight of one another. They knew they could be ambushed at any time, and at night they took turns standing watch. Hiknak never let Keshna out of her sight, and when one of them went to get a skin of water from a stream or an armload of firewood, the others went with her.

As the days passed with no sign of the nomads, they began to relax. The villagers along the way had heard nothing of a great band of men on horseback; the weather was mild with warm days and long, golden evenings. Sometimes they saw storks' nests; often deer. At sunset the great trees seemed to soften in the falling light, and when Marrah stood watch, the only sound she ever heard was the rustling of leaves or the occasional call of an owl.

She drew what comfort she could from the peacefulness of the land, but she started every time she heard a twig snap and her knife was rarely out of her hand even while she slept. Often she lay awake for hours staring at the night sky. The stars were particularly brilliant that summer, but she barely saw them. She saw the black spaces between them instead, and sometimes she felt as if she were falling upward into a place so lonely that no one would ever find her.

Several times when she found it impossible to get to sleep, she rose and went off a little distance from the others and hung her snare from a bush and whispered the names of the Dark Mother, but she was too upset to fall into a trance. There was no peace in her soul, no place that grief had not seared, so the snare went on being nothing more than a snare, and more than once when she finally gave up and went to retrieve it, she had to pick bits of leaves and stray twigs out of the threads. One night she even found a small white moth struggling to escape and took it for a bad sign.

She would have given anything to be able to see into the future, because now that Stavan was dead, most of her fears were concentrated on Luma and what might happen to her if Vlahan reached Shara before she did. Luma was only five, and if the nomads overran the city, she would not have a chance. If she had been a boy, some childless man might have given her to his wife to raise, but the best a little girl with dark hair and dark eyes could hope for was a mercifully quick death. The idea of losing Luma as well as Keru was so terrible that Marrah did her best not to dwell on it, but as she rode south, the horror of arriving too late to save her daughter was always with her, driving her forward with all possible speed. If only Stavan had been there, he might have been able to tell her how fast a nomad war party could travel, but he was gone, and no matter how much she longed to turn to him for help and comfort, she knew he would never be able to help her or comfort her again.

She missed him constantly. His death was the first thing she thought about when she woke up and the last thing she thought about when she lay down at night. They had been apart for many months before he died, but she had still sensed his presence. Now she felt the distance between them growing and growing like a dark valley that had no end. When she saw egrets, she remembered how much he had enjoyed watching the long-legged birds stalk through the reeds hunting for fish; and when she thought of Luma, she remembered how only Stavan had been able to sing the child to sleep when she was sick and restless. She remembered his voice and the touch of his hands, the smell of his hair, the pressure of his lips, the sound of his laugh. A dozen times a day she thought of something she wanted to tell him. There were jokes that only he would have understood, thoughts too intimate to confide to anyone else. Stavan had been her lover, the *aita* of her children, and her best friend, and she could bear the loss of him only because she had no choice. If she could have brought him back to life, she would have clawed rocks apart with her bare hands and walked barefoot over thorns; but she never dreamed of him anymore—she dreamed instead of great darkness and unbroken silence, and that more than anything else convinced her that he truly was dead.

Often she would find herself crying, and she would ride on without bothering to wipe away the tears. Dalish and Hiknak understood her grief and respected it, and she easily could have asked them for comfort, but she clung to her pain stubbornly and refused to discuss it. It was all she had left of Stavan, so she held it close, pressing it to her like a cape of thorns. The more she suffered, the less she spoke of her suffering, but Stavan's death was the greatest sorrow of her life, and with every day that passed, she missed him more.

A little less than two weeks after they left Kataka, they reached Shara to find it completely deserted. Not so much as a dog ran out to greet them, and as Marrah rode Nretsa through the empty streets, she felt a familiar terror creep over her, even though she could see that her friends and relatives were alive and well simply by looking up at the cliffs. The Temple of Children's Dreams no longer stood alone on the ledge. Tents cobbled together out of goat and sheepskins clustered around it, and small, dark shapes moved against the honey-colored granite. Here and there, smoke from cooking fires rose straight up in the calm air and drifted slowly out across the Sweetwater Sea.

They had beat the nomads to the city, but even though she knew she should rejoice, Marrah's throat tightened at the sight of so many empty houses. Shara reminded her of the abandoned villages she had seen north of Shambah. It was so quiet that she could hear the surf hitting the beach and the cicadas humming in the fields. In the central plaza the blue and orange Snake of Eternity still slid from tile to tile, but there were no children playing tag, no old people gossiping under the awnings, no mother clans sitting outside their houses scaling fish or curing hides. In the temples the looms had been hastily unstrung, and the owl-shaped weights lay scattered on the floors; the fires in the bread ovens—which had burned constantly for as long as Marrah could remember—had been allowed to go out, and fine potting clay had been tossed carelessly in baskets to crack and dry. Even the fishing boats were gone, and the white-sailed *raspas* that should have been anchored just off shore this time of year were nowhere in sight.

When they came to Lalah's house, it too was empty. Marrah wandered from room to room, thinking of Stavan and Keru and Luma and how happy they had been when they all lived under this roof. When she got to their sleeping compartment—bare as all the rest—she sat on the floor, put her face in her hands, and wept. When she finished crying, she dried her eyes on her sleeve, rose to her feet, and continued to explore the house. A few things had been left behind: a comb she recognized as cousin Inhala's; one of Barrash's old tunics; all of the larger pots and storage jars; but the sheepskin blankets were nowhere to be seen, and there was not so much as a string of dried apples hanging from the rafters.

"Lalah could have left us at least a few loaves of bread," Dalish grumbled. "She knew I was bringing the three of you right back."

Marrah went out to the vegetable gardens behind the goat fence, but everything had been picked or dug up. The dirt was newly turned—a few days old at most.

"Your people are smart," Hiknak said. "They're not leaving anything for the enemy to eat." She shaded her eyes and looked out at the fields, which were waist high with ripe wheat. "They've left the wheat though, which is a mistake. The Hansi aren't going to know how to harvest it, but when Vlahan catches sight of so much fodder, he'll pasture out his horses, and we'll never get rid of him."

Leaving the deserted city behind, they rode south through the wheat. As they approached the cliffs, Marrah tried to see them as the nomads might: from a distance the stone ridge looked like an irregular granite wall, fissured and cracked with loose gravel spilling down sheer sides. The trail to the temple snaked back and forth in half a dozen switchbacks until it reached the broad series of outcroppings where the Sharans had pitched their tents. In some places the trail was almost level, while in others it rose so steeply that ropes had been tied from rock to rock to help pilgrims pull themselves up. Most native-born Sharans could make the climb without help, but the drop-off was abrupt enough to make anyone born on flat land uneasy.

The lower portion of the trail was mostly dirt, wide enough for two people to pass each other comfortably; but about three-quarters of the way up, the dirt turned to stone and the path narrowed. Here each step of the upper trail had been cut out of the granite face of the cliff many generations ago when pilgrims first started coming to the sacred spring.

Above the camp itself, the cliffs continued in a smaller set, so bald that not even a lizard could find a toehold. Without the bald cliffs, the lower cliffs would have offered little protection since the nomads could simply have climbed to the summit from the other side. But the back side of the bald cliffs was so steep that no one had ever been able to climb it. Long cracks ran up the back slope as if someone had slashed the stone with a knife, and only a few hardy tufts of grass managed to hang on above the abyss. The bald cliffs were a little lower just to the left of the last switchback; but directly over the camp, where it counted most, they were high and slightly rounded. For generations, Sharan poets had compared the bald cliffs to the tight bellies of pregnant women, and as Marrah studied them, she felt reassured that her people had chosen the best possible refuge.

When they reached the trail, they dismounted and started up on foot, leading their horses. Marrah had taken only a few steps when suddenly a familiar voice called to her, and she looked up and saw Arang and two sentries standing on a boulder at the bend of the second switchback. Arang had his hands on his hips and was staring down at her, poised on the brink like a dancer about to make a leap.

"Get away from the edge," she yelled. "You might fall!"

"What a way to greet your brother!" Arang shouted, and he leapt down from rock to rock as lightly as a goat, and took her in his arms. "Marrah, sweet sister, you're the best sight I've seen in months!" He might have said more, only Hiknak and Keshna both threw themselves on him with screams of joy. When Arang finally emerged from their embrace and everyone wiped the tears from their eyes, Marrah asked after Luma.

"How is my girl? Is she well? When can I see her?" She was suddenly overcome with a desire to take Luma in her arms, hug her, and hear her laugh. A child of five might still laugh, even now. That was the glory of children: they lived in a world where joy was still possible. But there was to be no reunion with Luma, at least for the present.

"She's not here," Arang explained. "None of the small children are. We put them, the babies, and all the nursing mothers in the boats yesterday afternoon and sent them south to the island of Byana, where they'll be safe. I wish we could have sent everyone in the city, but with only eight boats . . . " He shrugged.

Marrah knew she should be relieved that Luma was out of danger, but she could not help feeling disappointed to have missed her, and by only a day. Hiknak must have been thinking along the same lines, because she looked at Arang with dismay.

"You sent away the children yesterday afternoon! But, Arang, what about Keshna? Couldn't you have waited until she got here?" Hiknak pulled Keshna to her and began to stroke her hair anxiously. "Why couldn't you at least have kept one boat back for her? She's been through too much; I want her out of here before she turns *shohwar* again."

"Climb up the trail a bit farther," he said, "and let me show you why we couldn't wait."

He picked up Keshna, put his arm around Hiknak, and led them higher. When they reached the second switchback, he motioned for everyone to turn around so they could look out over the river to the north. It was a familiar view: the fields and pastures; Shara; the forest; the long curve of the coast; the wide empty sea with its glittering waves. But there was something new on the horizon. It was not much—only a small dark blotch—but as soon as Marrah saw it, she knew it was smoke from a burning village.

"The sentries spotted the first smoke three days ago," Arang said, "and every day it's been coming closer."

Marrah felt the hairs rise on the back of her neck. So this was it: the invaders had really arrived. "Any refugees?" she asked quietly.

Arang nodded. "About a dozen so far. We've taken them in and done what we could for them, but they spend most of their time crying for their dead. They all tell the same story: a surprise attack by a nomad raiding party, most of the men killed, the women and children taken prisoner. Not many are getting away. We sent runners to warn the other villages, but what good is a warning when you can't imagine what's coming? Fortunately, the nomads didn't start raiding until they got close to Shara. Unfortunately, there are a lot of them riding this way—not just warriors but women and children. They're bringing their tents, their horses, and their cattle, which may mean that they plan to stay."

They stood side by side, looking at the smoke. Keshna leaned her cheek against Arang's. Her small face was pale, and she said nothing. Marrah wanted to comfort Keshna, but how did you comfort a little girl who had seen the nomads firsthand?

"How long before they get here?" Dalish asked.

"Two days, maybe less." Arang turned to Marrah. "I'm glad you've come home. I've done what I could to show the young men and women how to fight Hansi style so we won't be overrun like the villages, but it hasn't been easy. The Council of Elders has declared that we should defend ourselves at any price, but there are still a few fools who are convinced that if we just love the nomads enough, they'll go away. Some of the older priestesses told me in no uncertain terms that it was their sacred duty to go down and help any nomads we wounded. I told them exactly what would happen to them if they did, and I haven't heard another word out of them since; but you can see the kind of problems I've encountered. Uncle Bindar didn't want to leave the city. We almost had to drag him. As for Grandmother," he paused, "well, you'll see her for yourself soon, and you can judge."

"Is she sick?"

"Not exactly." He lowered his eyes the way he always did when he didn't want to talk, and Marrah knew she wasn't going to get another word out of him on the subject of Lalah. Turning to the horses, which were peacefully cropping bits of dry grass along the side of the trail, he put down Keshna, gathered up all three sets of reins, and held them slack in his hands.

"We'll have to take these horses back down, unbridle them, and drive them into the woods. We took all the cattle and most of the other animals upriver about five days ago. Two people from each clan are watching over them, but it's too late to herd these poor beasts to safety; and except for a few milk goats, we don't have room for animals up top."

"I can't do that," Marrah said. She took the reins from him and hung on to them stubbornly. "I promised these mares I'd never let the nomads get their hands on them again. Remember what Changar did to Eoru?"

"Marrah, I know you love these horses like cousins, but we have no choice. It's crowded up on the cliffs, and water could be a problem."

"Either the horses go up with us, or I stay down with them."

"But . . . "

"You're the war king, Arang, and I'm the war queen. We're supposed to work together, and when we disagree only the Council of Elders can decide between us. You were right to send the children away yesterday, and I'm right about this. When I tell the elders what a pile of sacrificed horses looks like, I think they'll agree with me."

Arang sighed. "Have it your way; but remember, there's not enough grass up there to feed three animals."

"There's enough hay in our pastures to feed a whole herd, and today we're going to start harvesting it along with whatever wheat we can salvage before we burn the fields."

"Burn the fields!"

Marrah realized she was going about this the wrong way. She was still treating Arang as if he were her little brother, when she should have been treating him like a grown man. He had just spent a year as Vlahan's prisoner, and he probably knew more about war than she ever would.

"I'm sorry," she said contritely. "I know I'm taking this all too fast, but, like you, I've had a lot of time to think, and the more I think, the more I worry about what's going to happen when the nomads arrive. You've already done a fine job preparing our defense, but I think there are some more things we need to do as quickly as possible. I didn't come back to issue commands like a Hansi chief. Disagree with me if you want, but hear me out before you make up your mind.

"Hiknak says we can't afford to leave fodder for Vlahan's beasts or he'll stay all winter. Tonight there's a full moon. I think we should go down and reap whatever we can by moonlight and carry it up to the cliffs. At dawn, we'll set fire to what's left. Then we'll seal off access to the trail by rolling a few big boulders down from the first switchback.

"That won't keep the nomads out because they can always climb over the boulders or heave them out of the way, but it will make their horses useless and slow them down long enough for our archers to take aim. I doubt that we can rout them, but after we pick off the first few, I think they'll realize that we're not just sheep waiting to be slaughtered. They're not a patient people. They're accustomed to swift victories, and if we hold them off long enough, they're sure to start quarreling among themselves. Vlahan may not be able to control the subchiefs, and sooner or later some of them are bound to leave, taking their warriors with them.

"Just to make sure they can't get to us, we'll cut the trail by digging out a section just before the path goes from dirt to stone. We'll have to rebuild it after they leave, but that's a small price to pay. Unless they can fly, they'll never be able to get from one switchback to another up the rock face, and as for the gap, we'll make it so wide that not even you could jump it."

Arang stood silently for a long time. Finally he said, "You've convinced me, Marrah. As your brother and war king of this city, I agree: we will cut the trail and burn the wheat." Picking up Keshna again, he led them up toward the camp without further objections.

It was a steep climb for the horses, but they were used to mountain trails so they ambled along docilely, even though they were aware that one misplaced hoof could send them plunging to the bottom. Hiknak, on the other hand, shied away from the edge as much as she could, and when they came to the place where the trail narrowed still further, she almost balked.

"I'm scared of heights," she said in a quavering voice. "I think it comes from growing up on the steppes. Until you brought me south, I never saw anything steeper than the back of a horse."

Marrah sat down with Hiknak while Hiknak caught her breath and got up the courage to continue. The thought occurred to Marrah that perhaps all nomads were afraid of heights, and when she asked Hiknak, Hiknak confirmed that it was possible. If so, the Sharans might have an advantage no one had thought of. It was reassuring to think of Vlahan's warriors trembling as they slunk up the trail, and if some of them got dizzy and fell, so much the better.

The color did not come back to Hiknak's cheeks until they reached the top and the trail broadened again. Soon they came to the first tents, pitched side by side with barely enough room to walk between the ropes. Baskets of food and bundles of household goods lay in piles, and the population of the whole city was milling about, talking, cooking over small fires, shaking out blankets, and waiting to get water from the spring. Goats bleated and dogs barked so loudly that people had to shout to make themselves heard. The air smelled of smoke, singed stew, and unwashed bodies. The Sharans were packed so closely that there was barely room to sit down.

As soon as they caught sight of Marrah, everyone rushed toward her and began to talk all at once: asking for news; offering their condolences; patting her shoulders; and kissing her cheeks. The hunters, who had been shooting at sacks of hay, displayed their bows proudly, and members of the newly formed Society for the Defense of Shara brandished their spears enthusiastically.

"Marrah's back from Kataka!"

"Marrah's back from taking the initiation of the Dark Mother!"

"She's a great priestess now."

"She's come home to be our war queen."

"Marrah, we're going to drive those nomads right back to the steppes!"

"Marrah, talk to the Goddess and ask Her to make these evil people go away."

"Marrah, we need more firewood."

"And more arrows."

"More tents."

"Shade from the sun."

When Arang had agreed to burn the wheat and let her bring the horses up to the top of the cliffs, Marrah had briefly enjoyed the sensation of power that being war queen brought with it, but by the time she had crossed half the camp, she was ready to go back to being an ordinary Sharan. How could she and Arang possibly be responsible for so many people? They were both too young and inexperienced. They had no idea what they were doing; they were more or less making up the defense of Shara as they went along; if it hadn't been for Hiknak, they wouldn't have known even to burn the wheat.

I'm not capable of being a queen, she thought, and she rushed to the Temple of Children's Dreams to find Lalah to tell her so. But any thought she might have had of turning power back to her grandmother vanished the moment Marrah saw her. Lalah looked terrible: her hair had turned completely gray; her once-plump arms were thin; her strong legs were so fragile they looked like sticks. Something was sucking all the life out of her, and Marrah did not have to try very hard to imagine what it was.

"I want to go down and fight the nomads, but Arang and Bindar won't let me," Lalah announced before Marrah had said more than three words. "I don't want to cower up here and leave the city to those murderers. The Great Snake needs me to defend Her." Lalah's eyes were still dark and fierce, but there was a new expression in them, one that made Marrah feel as if her grandmother barely saw her. Lalah seemed far away, like a person going out to sea in a small boat.

"Grandmother, that's not possible," Marrah said quietly, but Lalah didn't seem to hear.

"Bring me my bow. I've always been a good shot. Bring me some arrows, and make sure the tips are sharp." Lalah started to rise, but she must have thought better of it because she sat down again. She looked at Marrah and a puzzled frown crept over her face. "Why aren't you bringing me my bow, Marrah? Do you expect me to wait all day?"

"But, Grandmother ... "

"Hurry up. I'm a busy woman. And bring Sabalah here while you're about it. I need to tell her something. She can't go west after all. I want her to fight beside me."

When she heard her grandmother call for her mother, Marrah felt as if the earth had been knocked out from under her feet. She tried to explain that Sabalah had left Shara years ago, but Lalah either didn't understand or didn't want to. Rising to her feet, she hugged Marrah and, with tears in her eyes, pleaded with her to bring a bow and arrows so that she and Sabalah could go down and fight the nomads, and it was only by promising to do so that Marrah won permission to leave.

Shaken, she went in search of Arang, whom she found busily searching for the bone-blade scythes they always used to harvest wheat. In the confusion of taking refuge on the cliffs, people had dumped things wherever they could, and it was taking forever to sort them out.

"So you've seen Grandmother," he said. He put his arm around Marrah's shoulder and she put hers around his waist, and they stood side by side like two children lost in the woods.

"How long has she been like this?" Marrah asked.

"A few months. Cousin Inhala says she started acting a little strange not long after you left, but when she heard the nomads were coming to attack Shara, it got a lot worse."

"Why didn't anyone send for me?"

"The Council of Elders decided you were better off in Kataka. They wanted you to get the complete initiation."

"And Uncle Bindar?"

"He did a good job of governing the city until I showed up with the news that Stavan was dead and Vlahan and his warriors were on their way. In ordinary times, he would have had a lot of good advice to give us, but now ... " He shrugged.

"Then the defense of Shara is all up to us?"

"Yes, I'm afraid it is."

Marrah sighed wearily and let go of Arang. "Come on, brother," she said. "It's time for the war queen and the war king to announce that everyone under fifty has to go back down the trail and harvest wheat."

And so they went down and harvested what wheat they could by moonlight, and when the sun rose, they threw torches into the fields and sent their own column of smoke up to answer the smoke rising to the north. Then they climbed back up to the first switchback and, heaving and panting, pushed several large boulders down to block the trailhead. After the boulders had been tumbled into place, everyone retreated to the top of the cliffs and watched as several young men and women from the Society for the Defense of Shara dug out a section of the trail just below the ropes. As they worked, the diggers coughed and gasped for breath, wrapped in a pall of smoke that stung their eyes and turned the sun bloodred.

Quite a few people objected to the burning of the wheat, which they said was a terrible waste and a blasphemy against the gifts of Batal, but the Council of Elders supported Marrah and Arang, and so it was done, and just in time too. That very afternoon, before the fields even stopped smoldering, the first bands of nomads were sighted. More soon followed, like ants drawn to spilled honey. All day they poured out of the woods and crossed the river: half-naked, painted men; black-robed women; horses dragging sledges; packs of wolflike dogs; and boys driving flocks of goats, sheep, fine horses, and scrawny nomad cattle. By dusk, Shara was burning, and as they stood on the cliffs watching their city go up in flames, the Sharans moaned and cursed and begged Batal to put out the fire.

Lalah did a remarkable thing that evening. When Marrah came to tell her the city was on fire, she seemed to recollect who she was. Rising to her feet, she strode out of the temple and insisted that Arang lift her onto a boulder so she could see for herself. For a long time, she stood with her hands on her hips staring at the motherhouses going up in flames. She watched roofs crash in and walls fall, and the Great Snake of Time blister and crumble, and when it was all over, and the city was nothing but a line of ruins, she turned and spoke to her people.

"Listen to me!" she called, and everyone fell silent with astonishment. "Stop all this wailing. So what if our houses and temples are gone? We aren't our houses or our temples. We haven't lost Shara. We *are* Shara!"

Those were brave words, but the next morning when Marrah woke up and saw the nomads camped beside the ruined city, her courage failed, and going off where no one could see her, she buried her face in her hands and grieved for Stavan and Keru and Shara and everything they had lost.

But mourning was a luxury she could not afford. Soon she stopped crying, dried her eyes, and went to her tent to get her snare. As she started back toward the dreaming cave with it, she thought about the months she had spent in Kataka. She might not know everything she needed to know, but she was probably the only priestess south of the River of Smoke who had taken the full initiation of the Dark Mother, and the time had come for her to go to a place where she could finally use the powers she had been given.

The dreaming cave was actually three caves: two small and one large, reached by an entrance tunnel that twisted and turned until the silence was absolute. For uncounted generations, the priestess-queens of Shara had gone into the third cave to seek visions, and there was a tradition that long before Batal had founded the city, the first Sharan mother family had lived and worshipped there.

For a long time—longer than anyone alive could remember—the walls of the third cave had been painted red to symbolize the life-giving blood of the Mother, but other than that, it was undecorated except for a large stone platform covered with deerskins, where the dreamers lay, and one or two clay lamps that were always lit.

When Marrah got to the third cave, she stood quietly for a moment to let her eyes adjust to the light. Then she walked to the far wall and hung her snare between two small, snake-shaped lamp hooks. The snare billowed slightly, casting a lattice of shadows on the wall no bigger than the palm of her hand.

Sitting down on the dreaming platform, she crossed her legs and took a deep breath. "Aba," she said. "Shallah, Nashah." For a long time she sat there, reciting the names of the Dark Mother, but her mind refused to be still. The flame in the small oil lamp flickered hypnotically, but all she could think of was Stavan and Keru and the burning of Shara.

"Aba," she begged, "give me this gift; Shallah, make it happen; Nashah, let me see!" After a while she began to add the name Batal to her prayer, because the Dark Mother and the Mother Snake were really one Goddess called by different names. Her thoughts rose and swirled like a hive of bees, but no matter how hard she tried, she could not fall into a trance.

I'm like a broken bowl, she thought. Ever since Stavan died, I've been in pieces. I'm no good as a priestess and no good as a queen. If Stavan were alive, he might be able to tell me how to save my people without fighting, but I can't figure it out. Since he died, I've gone deaf to my own soul. More tears ran down her face, and she wiped them away impatiently and went on chanting, but still nothing happened.

Just when she was about to give up in despair, the Dark Mother suddenly granted her prayers. In the blink of an eyelash, all the grief and worry that had tormented her on the long ride back from Kataka vanished, and she felt something gentle reach down and embrace her, something so sweet and so filled with compassion that it was like resting in her mother's arms.

Suddenly time froze, the snare expanded, and she saw the windows. They came out of the darkness like giant eyes and were much larger than they had been in the forest, so large that each opening was like the entrance to a great valley, but there was no past or present or future in them, and no people either: there was only water. The water was grayish green, and it seemed to lap and dance against some invisible barrier. It looked so wet and so real that the first time it moved in Marrah's direction, she ducked, expecting to be drenched; but it couldn't touch her and she couldn't touch it.

When she looked more closely, she saw small waves in the top windows of the snare, and above them a thin band of blue sky. Below, at the very bottom, she saw a dim plain of pale sand littered with white shells. She knew the shells well because she had often made a savory stew from the little creatures that lived in them. As she watched, a school of minnows swam by, their silver bellies glittering in the shadows.

"What kind of riddle is this!" she cried. "Dear Mother, let me see the future! Tell me how to make the nomads leave . . . " She never got a chance to finish. The moment she spoke, time unfroze, the snare shrank, and the windows disappeared. For a long time she sat on the platform trying to catch her breath. When she finally rose to her feet, her legs trembled so badly that she could barely walk.

Placing the palms of her hands over her heart, she bowed in front of the snare and gave thanks to the Dark Mother. This had been a true vision, a holy gift, and she was grateful, but she was also confused. The Mother had let her see the inside of the ocean with the eyes of a fish; but why? What could such a thing possibly mean? Were they going to be rescued by a fleet of *raspas*? Was the Sweetwater Sea going to rise and drown the nomads? Was the whole world going to turn to water?

She sat down and tried again, and again the windows came, and again she saw that same puzzling sight: sea, sand, shells; shells, fish, sea. If the Imsha had been sitting beside her, perhaps it could have explained the riddle, but Marrah could not, and that afternoon when she called all the priestesses and priests of Shara together, they couldn't either.

When Arang and the Council of Elders also tried and failed to interpret her vision, Marrah stopped hoping for some miracle that would save them. The Dark Mother had spoken in a language no one could understand. Perhaps if they had had enough time they could have figured it out, but time was in short supply: soon the nomads would attack and—ready or not—the Sharans would be forced to fight.

The
Horses
at
the
Gate

CHAPTER THIRTEEN

We drank dust.
We ate stones.
We learned to fight.

FROM "THE SIEGE"
A MEMORY SONG OF THE SHARATANI PEOPLE
FIFTH MILLENNIUM B.C.

The nomads attacked the next day just after sunrise. From the cliffs, the Sharans watched the warriors ride out of their camp and gallop across the charred fields. They came in a cloud of dust and ashes, their bodies painted bloodred, their faces black. They had drawn skeletons on their chests and stiffened their hair with yellow mud so that it stood out around their heads like the rays of the sun. As they drew closer, those in front leapt to the backs of their horses and stood upright, balanced on the balls of their feet with a terrible grace that Marrah could not help admiring. The Hansi were the best horsemen on the steppes and the most deadly thing ever to come south of the River of Smoke. They pointed their spears at the Sharans and screamed insults like crazed acrobats dancing for a god of suffering and slaughter.

"Listen, you breast suckers!" they yelled.

"Listen, you cowards! Come down and we'll drink your blood!"

Some of the warriors pulled down their leather loincloths and urinated in the direction of the cliffs. "Here's the only water you'll get!"

"Send down your wives and daughters and let us show them what men are!"

The
Horses
at
the
Gate

237

The insults went on, each more obscene than the next, but since they were in Hansi, they were mostly lost on the Sharans. The children and old people stood side by side, clustered around the Temple of Children's Dreams. Some held hands and some put their arms around one another's waists and whispered a few words of comfort, but no one panicked. The younger men and women, armed with spears, clubs, and rocks, had positioned themselves along the edge of the cliffs and the top of the trail. Most of the hunters stood with them, but some of the most daring—including Arang and Dalish's lover, Jutima—had gone partway down the trail. These were in the most dangerous position, directly above the gap. As long as they crouched back and kept close to the cliff face, they would be out of range of the enemy arrows, but when the time came for them to lean forward and shoot, they would have nothing to hide behind. Since they would be the first to fight, Arang had made sure that they all had arrows tipped with razor-sharp obsidian.

As the Sharans watched the warriors charge toward the cliffs, their fear turned to outrage. Look at those painted maniacs, dancing on the backs of their horses! These were the men who had raided the villages and burned Shara! Look at them! Killers, proud that they killed; murderers flaunting their weapons!

A low murmur passed through the crowd. A woman spat, and a man lifted two fingers in a curse; those who had bows and spears brandished them. When Marrah saw this, she knew the time had come to take action. Lifting her hand, she gave a signal, and the priests and priestess of Shara broke into song. It was a new song, composed by a young weaver and tuned to the beat of her shuttle, and it was like no song the Sharans had ever sung before.

> Batal! Batal!
> Mother of Life,
> stand beside us and help us
> drive the nomads away!
>
> We are the Sharans!
> We are the Sharans!
> We love one another!
> We will never surrender!

Mary Mackey

238

Other voices joined in. Soon everyone was singing. Marrah sang with them, and as she sang, she felt the defiance pulsing through the crowd like a living thing. She was proud to be their queen. The Sharans were not going to run like terrified villagers or gape in paralyzed horror like those poor Shambans who had not known what war was until the Hansi warriors rode them down. The Sharans were going to stand their ground, win if they could, and if not, go down fighting. The words of the young weaver's song were true: they were all one people, bound together by love.

As the Sharans sang, the tide of battle had already started to turn in their favor. The nomads reached the base of the cliffs and—confronted by a wall of rock they could not scale and a path no horse could negotiate—they began to ride back and forth furiously, wheeling to the left and right like a school of fish trapped in an invisible net. Where was the swift victory Vlahan had promised? Where were the women, the gold, and the spineless Motherpeople who should have been so easy to conquer? According to Vlahan, the Sharans did not have warriors or horses or a spear worth spitting on, but there they were, just out of reach: too cowardly to fight and too smart to come down. The warriors wanted to take heads and win glory, but all they were doing was screaming, kicking up dust, and wearing out their horses while the Motherpeople stood there singing some crazy song like a pack of lunatics. If their enemies ever heard about this battle, the Hansi and their allies would be the laughingstock of the steppes.

Vlahan, who had led the charge, knew that if he did not do something soon he was going to get an arrow in his back. Lifting his hand, he brought the whole pack to a halt and sat glaring at them. Changar had promised him an easy victory, but instead he was trapped in the kind of position that got chiefs killed by their own men. Last night when his scouts confirmed that the Sharans had taken refuge on the cliffs, he had known they were in for trouble, but he had never imagined that not a single man would come down and fight. The men of these Motherpeople had no pride; they were vermin. He decided that when he finally overran them, he would impale the lot. Meanwhile he had to figure out how to placate several hundred of his own warriors before they turned on him.

"If the cowards won't come down," he yelled, "we'll go up and get them!" The warriors liked the sound of that. They cheered and waved their spears.

"Vlahan! Vlahan! Son of Han!"

Vlahan rode arrogantly to the trail, only to discover that a large boulder nearly as high as his head blocked the entrance as neatly as a stopper in a waterskin. He peered over it, ignoring the Sharans above him, and saw that there were several more boulders scattered on the lower part of the trail and large gouges where still other boulders had fallen and rolled off.

Vlahan turned to the subchiefs who sat at a respectful distance waiting for orders. "Get these stones out of my way," he hissed.

The subchiefs, who had no intention of dismounting in the middle of a battle, turned to their warriors. "Remove the stones," they commanded. For a moment it looked as if the warriors might rebel. Heavy work was something only women and slaves did, and no warrior could help but feel insulted at the prospect of working up a sweat rolling rocks off a trail.

The oldest of the subchiefs narrowed his eyes and looked from warrior to warrior. "A filly," he said, "to any man who'll volunteer." At that, half a dozen warriors from the poorest tribes trotted to the front and climbed off their horses. Ignoring the sneers of their comrades, they surrounded the first boulder and heaved and grunted until it rolled back far enough to permit a horse to pass. The rest of the boulders were moved in the same fashion, but even so the trail was considerably narrowed.

Vlahan was not pleased. Not having much experience with cliffs, he had imagined himself charging up to the top, but even he could see that a charge was out of the question. A man with more experience—or more sense—would have dismounted, but even the lowest Hansi warrior never got off his horse unless he had to, and the only chief in the history of the Twenty Tribes who had ever attacked an enemy on foot had earned himself the name Chochan the Stumbler.

Vlahan had no intention of becoming another Chochan. Kicking his stallion in the ribs, he urged him onto the trail. The stallion trotted forward obediently, skirting the first boulder and starting up the rise, but when he looked down and realized there was a sharp drop to the left, he balked. He was a high-spirited beast, but the Hansi had ridden south over low ground, and he had never seen anything higher than a hill.

Vlahan was enraged. Seizing his leather riding crop, he began to beat the stallion until blood stained its flanks. "Go forward, you miserable bag of bones!" he yelled. "Go or I'll feed you to the crows!" The stallion shuddered and started up the trail a second time, but as soon as he came to the drop-off, he reared up on his hind legs with a whinny of terror, lost his footing, and fell, throwing Vlahan into an ignominious pile.

Vlahan gave a scream of fury. Leaping to his feet, he pulled out his dagger and limped over to the stallion, who was still struggling to get up. Kicking the horse back down, he seized his forelock, pulled back his head, and slit his throat.

"Here's our first sacrifice to Han!" he yelled. The warriors, who admired any man who could harness such a rage, cheered. A white stallion was a precious possession. Sacrificing one was almost as good as sacrificing a man.

Up on the cliffs, the Sharans stopped singing. Marrah winced and turned away from the sight of the sacrifice, only to see Hiknak preparing to kill Vlahan. Hiknak's lamed right hand dangled at her side, but in her left she balanced the shaft of her spear, and she was bending forward, about to throw.

Marrah grabbed her arm. "Don't," she commanded. "Vlahan is too far away. You'll never be able to hit him at this distance."

Hiknak's face was pale with hatred, and her eyes were terrible to look at. Marrah knew she was thinking of Keshna and the blow to her own head that had crippled her. For a moment Hiknak looked as if she might throw the spear anyway, but instead she suddenly jammed it butt first into the dust.

"I'll get him," she hissed. Marrah had no doubt that she would. She was just about to remind Hiknak that spears were too precious to waste, when Vlahan turned from the dead stallion, stuck his fingers into his mouth, and gave a piercing whistle. At the sound, all the warriors charged up to the base of the cliffs and reined in their horses in a spray of dust and pebbles.

"Dismount!" Vlahan screamed. For a moment they milled around uncertainly. Then one by one they climbed off their horses. Vlahan stood staring them down with eyes so crazy that even the subchiefs shuddered. The Hansi had a word for that look: *vartak*. *Vartak* was the madness of the gods that overcame a man in battle.

Vlahan lifted his arm and pointed toward the trail. "Bring me heads!" he yelled. "Bring me the heads of these cowardly bastards!" At the sound of his voice, the craziness seemed to leap out of him and infect his warriors. In an instant they all were *vartak*. They waved their spears and screamed; blood filled their lips, and their eyes shone.

"Vlahan! Vlahan! Son of Han!"

The subchiefs charged up the trail and their men followed, pushing and shoving to be the first to reach the top. The trail was cut, but they could not see that from below, and even if they had, it might not have stopped them. Blinded by their own ecstasy, they rushed on, howling like wolves.

The sound of their howling made the hair stand up on Marrah's arms. She dug her fingernails into the palms of her hands, and for the first time since Shambah, she felt the full terror of a nomad raid. No one on the cliffs was singing now. The warriors were pouring up the trail at an unbelievable speed. They were stronger than she had ever imagined. Some left the path and climbed directly from switchback to switchback, pulling themselves up and over huge boulders without breaking stride, digging their toes into almost invisible crevices, and hanging on to handholds that even she couldn't see.

"Get ready to shoot!" she called to the hunters, but there was no need. The first warrior to come to the gap in the trail nearly fell in. Grabbing an outcropping, he stopped himself just in time.

"Back!" he screamed in guttural Hansi. He waved toward his comrades. "Stop!"

The war cry died on their lips. Some came forward and inspected the hole, and one spat over the side. As the news spread that the trail was cut, the warriors began to slow down. A few stopped entirely, braced their backs against rocks, and took aim at the Sharan hunters, but the hunters crouched back out of range, and most of the heavy-shafted, flint-tipped arrows of the nomads whistled through the air and fell back harmlessly.

When the Sharans saw that the hunters were safe, they began to cheer. Marrah considered giving the order to shoot, but she was reluctant to command the hunters to lean out over the edge of the trail where they would be more exposed. Before she could decide, one of the Hansi warriors decided for her. Uncoiling a rope, he flung it out over the gap and lassoed a scrawny tree. No one had noticed the tree before; no one had even thought about it, but it grew directly above the break in the trail, and as soon as Marrah saw that rope fly she knew with heart-stopping certainty what was about to happen.

Making sure the lasso was secure, the warrior ran back down the trail, paused for an instant, then raced forward and leapt into the gap. By the time Marrah yelled to the hunters to shoot, it was almost too late. The man was already in the air, on his way to the other side, and in a moment his feet would touch, he would push the rope back to his comrades, and more nomads would swing across.

At that moment, when the lives of everyone in Shara hung in balance, the hunters saved the city. Shouting "Batal!" they leaned over the edge, shot at the warrior, and sent him plunging into the gap. The nomad archers took aim at them, and someone would have surely been killed except that the rest of the Sharans fought too. The sky above the nomads opened. Spears and rocks poured down on Vlahan's men. The Sharans threw everything: old jars, boiling water, statues, loom weights, even firewood. The nomads tried to run for cover but there was no cover to be had.

"We're being defeated by women and cowards!" the subchiefs cried to their men. "Stand your ground! Any traitor who runs will be strangled!" But when the rocks kept falling and the arrows kept coming, even the white-robed subchiefs turned and scurried for safety, pushing past their own men and scrambling down the trail, to the eternal humiliation of their fathers, their families, and their tribes.

That night, the Sharans built bonfires on the top of the cliffs and celebrated their victory with dancing, singing, and prayers of thanksgiving. By what seemed a miracle, only five of their hunters had been wounded—probably because the nomad archers were accustomed to shooting straight at their enemies instead of aiming at an angle. Two of the injured hunters had received only superficial wounds, and the three who were more seriously hurt were expected to recover.

"We won!" Marrah told the Sharans, and calling the hunters to her, she passed out cups of wine—although wine was scarce—and everyone drank to their courage. Afterward, the Sharans sang the "Song of Defiance." They all knew they would have to fight again, but now they knew they could defend themselves. Hiknak put it best. Rising to her feet, she held up Keshna so that everyone could see her.

"Sharans!" she cried. "Today you fought bravely; today you gave this little girl a future!"

The Horses at the Gate

243

At about the same time Hiknak was congratulating the Sharans on their bravery, Changar was sitting in Vlahan's tent watching Vlahan work himself into a rage.

Vlahan stomped back and forth, lashing his leather crop against the tent poles. "You idiot!" he screamed. "You stupid whelp of a bitch mother!" Vlahan's eyes bulged and his red beard seemed to stand out from his chin like the skin around a frog's neck. "You call yourself a diviner?"

"Why yes, *rahan*," Changar said mildly. "I do." He looked up at Vlahan thoughtfully, wondering why Lord Han had saddled the Hansi with such a second-rate chief. When old Zuhan had lost a battle, Zuhan had blamed himself; but Vlahan always rushed to find someone else to blame.

Vlahan wheeled on Changar, and his voice was suddenly low and menacing. "Do you know what happened out there today, or have you been too busy eating your cursed mushrooms and drinking your own piss to notice?" He walked up to Changar, bent down, and stuck his face so close that their noses nearly touched. "You promised me an easy victory, you senile old fool, and instead we were *defeated*."

"Don't say 'defeated,' *rahan*; say 'delayed.'"

"Is that what you call it! Is that what you call forty hands of warriors routed by a pack of rock-throwing vermin? Is that what you say when they wound or kill ten of my best men?"

Changar nodded.

Vlahan reared back and spat in his face. "You're dead," he said. "I'm having you strangled."

Changer let the spittle run down his face as if it weren't there, but something wolflike flickered in the depths of his eyes. A smarter man than Vlahan would have seen that he was a dangerous man to humiliate. "As your diviner, I would advise against killing me, *rahan*."

Vlahan laughed nastily. "I bet you'd 'advise against it,' you old fake. Give me one reason why you shouldn't die."

"You can't win without me, *rahan*." Changar paused. "These Sharans are ruled by women, and you don't understand women at all."

"Ha!" Vlahan mocked. "I suppose you do; is that it? They say you have to have your women tied up to have them; they say you need to roll in the blood of a goat to get hard. They say your organ is the size of a mosquito's." He pushed his face so close to Changar's that Changar could smell the sour soup of his indigestion. "So what do *you* have to tell *me* about women?"

Changar suddenly seized both sides of Vlahan's head and drew him close. Putting his mouth to Vlahan's ear, he began to whisper.

As he spoke, something happened to Vlahan: his shoulders relaxed, his neck bowed, and the leather crop dropped unnoticed at his feet.

"Yes," Vlahan muttered. "Yes, that might work. Yes."

Changar went on whispering. There was one word he kept repeating. It was a name composed of two sounds, neither of them Hansi.

Not long after, Changar was back in his own tent. Keru was in his lap, and he was stroking the boy's cheeks as he gave him sips from a waterskin. The waterskin was filled with a thin honey-flavored fluid, and the little boy drank eagerly.

"Drink deep, little man," Changar cooed. "Drink deep, my little chief."

As he drank, Keru's face took on a sweet, lazy look. His lower lip became full and sensual, and his dark eyes fixed on Changar with open adoration. Keru had not liked Changar at all when he was a little baby of four, but now that he was older, he liked him a lot. Changar had green eyes that reminded Keru of the sea. He had rocked Keru and held him close and fed him sweets, and if Keru had not known that it was a terrible insult, he would have said that Changar had been like a mama to him.

When Keru finished drinking, Changar laid the empty skin aside and began to speak. His voice was low and quiet.

"Where are you, little chief?"

"In a pretty place."

"What does it look like?"

The boy did not answer. Changar waited patiently. Every day he gave the boy a little more of the love potion, and every day he drifted further and further away. The potion was made of honey and ground herbs, earth and blood, and a flower so poisonous that three pinches of it would kill a grown man; but Changar had been careful. He doled out the doses, giving the boy just enough and not a drop more. Two small Hansi girl children of no account had died before he had found exactly the right measure, but it had been well worth the trouble. As far as Changar could tell, the boy had no idea he was sitting in a tent pitched on the ruins of Shara. He never cried for his mother or pleaded to talk to his uncle Arang or begged to know when Stavan was coming to get him the way he had at first. He lived in a world of dreams and swirling lights, and he got upset only when Changar withheld the potion. Then he would toss and sweat and cry and beg, but once Changar put the skin to his lips and let him suck, he forgot everything.

Changar stroked the boy's hair softly. "Who do you belong to, little chief?"

Keru looked at him dreamily. "I belong to you, Uncle Changar."

"What are you supposed to do when you hear this sound?" Changar pursed his lips and made the rasping *tschack* of a white-throated warbler.

"I'm supposed to come to you."

"Will you always come to me, Keru?"

"Yes."

"And will you always do what I tell you?"

"Yes."

"Why will you always come, little chief? Why will you always do what I tell you to do?"

"Because I love you," Keru whispered, dreamily.

"Say it again."

"Because I love you, Uncle Changar."

The day after the first nomad attack, the sun rose through mist and the sky was soft with the promise of rain. All morning the Sharans stood on the edge of the cliffs waiting for the warriors to launch another assault, but the Hansi war drums were silent. Down in the nomad camp, life seemed to be going on as usual. There were no warriors in sight, but the Sharans could see dark-robed women squatting beside the milk mares. Others were gathering dung or cooking, while still others strolled through the ruins of Shara, leisurely sifting the ashes for whatever the fire had left behind. Nomad children played among the tents, shrieking in high voices that carried all the way across the valley. Sometimes a dog barked, but for the most part things were so quiet that if Marrah had not known the tents were full of armed men, she might have thought that the nomads were pilgrims, come to Shara to enjoy the hot springs.

About midday, a single warrior rode out of the camp. At the base of the cliffs, he reined in his horse and sat for a while, conferring with the nomad sentries. Then he dismounted and began to climb the trail with a slow, measured arrogance. He was a tall man with a fine white tunic that marked him as a subchief of some importance, and as he drew closer the Sharans could see that his face was painted with alternating stripes of black, red, and yellow.

Marrah turned to Hiknak, who was watching the man as he made his way from boulder to boulder. "What's he doing coming up alone?" she asked. "Should I tell the hunters to shoot at him, do you think?"

Hiknak said they should wait and see what the man did because the lines on his face meant that he was a messenger. Arang confirmed this, so they waited. The man went on climbing, stopping every once in a while to stare up at the faces peering down at him, but if he was afraid of being shot at, he did not show it. At last he reached the gap in the trail. The tree was gone, chopped out by night so no nomad could ever lasso it again, but if the messenger noticed, again he gave no sign. Putting his hands to his mouth, he leaned back and started to speak in a loud voice that echoed off the cliffs.

"Marrah of Shara, hear this. Marrah of Shara, witch of the south, are you there?"

Marrah leaned over the edge so that he could see her. "I'm here," she shouted in Hansi. "And I'm no witch but war queen of this city and a priestess of the Goddess Earth. What do you want?"

The messenger craned his neck and studied her impassively. "Vlahan the Great has sent me to say this: tell Marrah, the witch, that if she gives me Arang, grandson of Zuhan, whom she holds prisoner, I will give her her son, Keru, in exchange, and my warriors will go away and leave her people in peace."

Arang for Keru! What kind of fool did Vlahan take her for? Marrah knew that Vlahan would never give her son back, and if she were stupid enough to give him Arang, he would keep Keru and kill them all. This was not a real offer; it was an insult.

She turned to the hunters. "Vlahan wants an answer." She pointed to their bows. "Give him one, but don't hurt the messenger." Almost before the words were out of her mouth, the hunters shot. A cloud of arrows whizzed through the air, hissing like snakes. They came so close that one passed through the sleeve of the messenger's tunic and another appeared to part his hair. The spent shafts fell to earth with a clatter.

"There's your reply!" Marrah shouted. "Tell Vlahan that the people of Shara answer lies with arrows!"

The messenger turned and fled down the trail. It was a bitter triumph, because Vlahan still had Keru, but it was a triumph all the same. If Vlahan thought that he could torture her into surrendering because she was a mother, let him think again.

She was about to turn and congratulate the hunters, when she heard a familiar voice.

"Mama!"

There was a commotion behind her. "Look!" Arang yelled. "It's . . . " He must have said the name, but she didn't hear it because she was already looking, and what she saw made her feel as if her heart had stopped. While she had been watching the messenger, Changar had ridden to the base of the cliffs. He was mounted on a brown stallion, naked to the waist, his face painted gold, his hair stained with the bright red ocher the Hansi always sprinkled on the bodies of the dead. In his arms he held a small boy dressed all in white like a sacrifice.

"Mama!" Keru cried. He had grown, but his voice was the same, and as it rose up to her, Marrah almost forgot she was a queen.

It had been over a year since she had seen him; they had put tattoo marks on his cheeks and pierced his ears like a nomad, but he was her boy, her baby, her darling, and just seeing him whole and healthy made her almost sick with relief. Her first impulse was to run to him, and then with sickening clarity she saw that she couldn't.

"Marrah," Changar shouted. "Look at your son; see how healthy he is; see how well I've kept him for you. Give us Arang and you can have him." He suddenly lifted Keru over his head and shook him like a puppy.

"Mama!" Keru screamed. "Mama, help!"

She had twenty-seven children to protect; she was war queen of Shara; one word from her, one hint of weakness, and Vlahan would never leave. He would camp by the cliffs all winter until they ran out of food; he would attack again and again until their arrows were exhausted and they were forced to surrender. She knew how Vlahan thought. She had been his wife; she had seen him firsthand.

Changar shook Keru again. "We want Arang, grandson of Zuhan. Give him to us and you can have your boy."

Marrah stood with her arms folded across her chest and kept her face as blank as an empty sky as Changar went on shaking Keru, and with each cry her baby made she felt so much pain that she wanted to scream until she brought down the cliffs. She felt as if pieces of her body were being torn away, but always she remembered the people of Shara and those twenty-seven children.

Finally Keru stopped crying and went limp. Changar tossed the boy over the neck of his horse, and pranced around so that Marrah could get a good look. "You're a cold bitch," he shouted. He picked Keru up by the hair and dangled him like a dead rabbit. "He's still alive; but maybe soon we'll sacrifice him to Lord Han."

Marrah said nothing.

"Give us Arang and you can sing your little boy a lullaby tonight. I thought you Sharans were good mothers. What kind of mother are you? Give us Arang."

For a long time she stood and watched Changar ride back and forth, demanding her brother in exchange for her son. Keru lay across the neck of the horse, his small legs bobbing with each step the beast took. When Changar finally turned and took Keru away, her lips were bloody where she had bitten them to keep from saying "yes."

After Changar left, she walked away from the edge of the cliffs, and as she passed through the crowd, the Sharans stepped aside and silently made way for her. When she reached the Temple of Children's Dreams, she climbed onto the boulder where Lalah had stood and turned to face her people. Her face was pale, and there was a terrible light in her eyes. For a moment she looked at the crowd without speaking, and then she found her voice.

"Sharans!" she cried, "The nomads have attacked us once, and now that they see we won't bargain with them, they will attack us again. When that attack comes, we are going to be ready. We will chop up our looms and use the wood to make more arrows; we will strip the feathers from our ceremonial capes. The sticks we have used to stir our cooking pots will fly toward the enemy; and the handles of our scythes will pierce their hearts. We will pull stones from the sides of the cliffs and throw them; we will even take apart the temple if we need to. We will not buy peace! We will not negotiate with these murderers!"

The Horses at the Gate

The crowd cheered, and the hunters went away and came back with wood and feathers and distributed them. Some people mixed glue while others carved wooden tips. Those who knew how to make arrows taught those who didn't.

Marrah looked at the growing pile of arrows with grim satisfaction. Sitting down between Arang and Dalish, she pulled out her knife and set to work.

CHAPTER FOURTEEN

T ake the sacred mushrooms again, bitter on the tongue, and when the spirit of the gods comes upon you, throw open your tent flap and suck the hot night in like black milk. The stars of the Motherlands are the same as the stars of the steppes, dirtied by the mist that rises from this river too wide to cross. To the north you can see the War Club constellation and the Tent. Low on the western horizon, the bright Eye of Han Himself watches you with unblinking contempt.

You are Changar. You have failed again, and Vlahan is once again on the verge of having you strangled. Each day for seven days you have ridden to the base of the cliffs and forced the boy to plead with his mother, but she has not spoken, and as much as you hate to admit it, she is proving to be a worthy enemy.

But when a diviner eats the sacred mushrooms everything changes. The heavens become a black pool; down becomes up; up becomes down. New possibilities open; new worlds float out of the void like bubbles rising to the surface. By day, in the hot light of the sun, you are a man like other men, anchored to the earth by twisted legs that fold up under you when you try to stand. You walk with two sticks, poking your way forward like a maimed turtle. But tonight the sacred mushrooms will carry you to a world where legs don't matter. There you will take on a new body and a new name.

You motion to your apprentices to lift you to your feet and help you outside where you can look at the cliffs. Standing with your arms resting on their shoulders, you call for a finely woven basket shaped like a skull. The inside of the basket is sealed with pitch, and its sides are decorated with horses and stars and cryptic symbols only you can decipher. You give another command, and your words echo and re-echo inside your head, crossing one another like flocks of shrieking birds.

But your apprentices have understood. A boy with hair the color of dust kneels at your feet and holds the basket ready while another boy pulls aside your robe. You urinate in a long, strong stream, and when you are finished, they lift the foaming basket to your lips and you drink. You do this three times, and each time the brew becomes stronger, the bitterness more concentrated. As you wait to drink, the smoky stars drift across the sky and the contemptuous Eye of Han disappears below the horizon.

When the first stars of evening are gone, you begin to change: your eyeteeth grow long; your ears become huge and sensitive. Mouse face, you think. Fox face; fur body, gray and soft as dust. Clawed feet. Stick arms. Great leather wings with spreading veins.

Perhaps this new thing you have become is meant to fly, or perhaps not, because when the change is complete, you fall to the ground and begin to crawl on your belly. Your apprentices shrink in fear as you slide and twitter. They cannot see your new body, but you can.

The bitterness of the sacred mushrooms rises in your throat, and you rise with it. You flap your leather wings, dart into the sky, and fly straight toward the cliffs where the cowards sleep. Soon you see the Sharan tents, scattered like white and brown stones across the granite shelf. You see the barren summit of the bald cliffs rising above the camp; the loose gravel; the cracked wall of stone just to the left of the highest switchback; the breast temple with its snake head; the steam rising from the hot spring. Somewhere down there, Marrah the witch sleeps wrapped in terror because you own her son.

You would like to fly into her tent and sit at her ear whispering horrors, but there is not enough time for such pleasures. Your wings begin to fail, and you feel yourself being sucked back into your old,

Mary
Mackey

252

broken body. Down you go, back to the Hansi camp, back to the circle of terrified apprentices.

You are not reluctant to take on a human form again. You have seen enough. Now you know how the Sharans can be forced to surrender. The plan is so simple that you are annoyed that you didn't think of it sooner.

"Water wears rock," you whisper, and your apprentices, thinking you are asking for a drink, press a waterskin to your lips.

After he finished drinking, Changar slept heavily while his apprentices crouched around him, guarding him and feeding the fire. Sometime near dawn, they brought him a woman and he had her, but later he did not even remember her face.

In the morning he awoke feeling like a young man. The unpleasant taste in his mouth was gone, and he sang to himself as he ate a breakfast of skewered beef and soft cheese. There was always plenty of meat and milk, but fruit and other delicacies were in short supply since Vlahan had ordered the women to stay close to camp and the Sharans had burned whatever they did not take with them. Still, Changar always had the best of whatever was available. Lately he and the other warriors had been feasting on fish stews, but this morning he had a special treat: a small comb of honey to suck on. When they first attacked Shara, the nomads had kicked apart the clay hives, not knowing what they were. Now, after a number of nasty stings, they knew better.

Draining the sweetness from the honeycomb, he spat the wax on the ground, then called to his apprentices to bring him his horse. A man of less wit would have gone directly to Vlahan, but he was old and cunning. He knew Vlahan was a man of no imagination who believed only in things he could see and touch. Vlahan had never eaten the sacred mushrooms; he had no more sense of mystery than a sheep. If Changar went to Vlahan's tent and told Vlahan that he had transformed himself into a bat, flown to the cliffs, and seen a way to force the Sharans to surrender, Vlahan would set the dogs on him, or worse.

When his horse arrived, Changar hobbled out and fed the beast a small dried apple from the palm of his hand. It looked like a good day for a ride. The sky was clear, and a soft breeze blew off the water, cooling the air. Drawing his robes around him with majestic

The
Horses
at
the
Gate

253

arrogance, he ordered his apprentices to lift him onto the brown stallion and lash his legs securely so he would not fall. This morning he did not take Keru with him, and he did not ride toward the base of the cliffs. He rode up the river instead with three boys at his side, and when he was sure no Sharan could see him, he turned south and made his way slowly through the forest. Sometimes he stopped and sent one of his apprentices on ahead, but the boys always returned to report that the way was clear.

Soon they came to the back side of the cliffs. It was all scrub forest, full of stunted pines and low oaks that angled up the incline in small groves. Tethering his horse to a bush, Changar ordered his apprentices to carry him toward the summit, which they did, sweating and groaning, but never once daring to complain. Again, there was no sign of sentries. The Sharans obviously did not expect be attacked from behind, and for good reason: the bald cliffs were just as barren on this side. They rose from a jumble of giant boulders to form a wall of brownish white rock fissured by long, narrow crevices. Just getting to them would be difficult; climbing them appeared impossible.

This was just what Changar had expected. After that first, humiliating defeat, Vlahan had sent scouts to see if there was another way to storm the Sharan stronghold, and to a man they had reported that there was no way a band of warriors could get to the top of those cliffs. Vlahan had believed the scouts, but as far as Changar knew, he had never done what a good chief should do, which was go to see for himself.

When his apprentices could carry him no farther, Changar ordered them to put him down in the shade of a pine. He sat there for a long time, resting his back against the trunk and examining the terrain. Not a butterfly flapped by that he did not mark its route; not a hawk circled without him taking note. In short, he did all the things Vlahan should have done long ago. Vlahan really did have less imagination than a sheep, he thought. Old Zuhan would have been up here the first day.

The first thing Changar noticed was that here—as from the other side—the bald cliffs did not all look the same. Some were higher and rounder than others. For the most part, all the slopes were bare, but here and there, small tufts of grass grew from invisible cracks. He counted no fewer than ten ledges, all too inaccessible to be of any use, but interesting nevertheless. To the right, the cliffs dipped to a ridge with sides so steep and smooth that the sun shone off the rock as if it were water. The ridge was obviously the most vulnerable spot on the summit, but any band of warriors who managed by some miracle to climb to the top would find themselves looking straight down at a terrifying fall. The broad ledges of granite where the Sharans had pitched their tents were well to the left. No wonder the scouts had told Vlahan to forget attacking from the rear.

But the scouts had missed something, something Changar had seen last night when the spirit of the mushrooms gave him wings. It was something simple, something men terrified of heights would never notice. For as long as those cliffs had stood, it had rained. In the summer the rain had coursed down the steep slopes, wearing little grooves in the granite, and in the winter it had frozen, cracking the surface further. Year by year, the cracks had grown wider, until now the cliffs looked as if some angry gods long dead had slashed at the slopes with their daggers. As Changar looked at the handiwork of those dead gods, his eyes narrowed and he smiled a sharp, wolfish smile that would have made Marrah shudder if she had seen it.

There is no man among the Hansi smarter than I am, he thought. No diviner whose visions are more true. Those scouts have no eyes, and Vlahan is an idiot. They were right when they told him no man could climb the bald rock faces, but a man—a brave man, one not too terrified by the thought of falling—such a man could brace himself between the sides of one of the cuts and work his way up bit by bit until he reached the top. Of course, he would need a good cut, one that didn't end but went all the way to the summit. And is there such a cut? There is! Right there, on the ridge.

He looked at the cut triumphantly. From this distance it was a line no wider than a hair, but it was long and would be narrow enough for a man to touch both sides easily. He had known that such a cut must exist and that after he found it the rest would be easy. Still, he left nothing to chance. He licked his finger and estimated the strength of the wind; calculated when the sun would set; and imagined how the shadows would fall by moonlight. For a long time he could not figure out how the warriors could get down to the Sharan camp once they reached the top of the ridge, but then a strong wind blew, bending the pine, and he saw that the raiders could fix a rope to a boulder and swing a little until they were directly over one of the switchbacks. It would take brave men to make the drop, but only brave men would be chosen for such a raiding party in the first place.

Once the warriors were actually on the trail, the danger would be even greater. Because the path was so narrow, they would have to sneak up one by one and regroup at the top. At this point, the element of surprise would be crucial; if the Sharan sentries spotted them before they were all in place, they would be trapped between a sheer rock wall and a sheer drop. Still, they had only a little way to go to win eternal glory. If they failed, they would die serving their chief, which was how all men—except diviners—should die.

The wind shifted, and he smelled the smoke of the Sharans' fires. They were cooking on the other side of the bald cliffs. He imagined them turning the spits and gathering the drippings, gazing anxiously out at the nomad camp but never thinking to look over their shoulders. The odor of roasting meat made his mouth water. Summoning his apprentices, he had them unpack his midday meal and lay it out on a clean cloth. Like breakfast, it was a delicate affair: fresh cheese; two plump, roasted dormice rolled in seeds and honey; a small jar of wine looted from some nameless village. Changar ate with relish, wondering how the Sharans would feel if they knew the smell of their cooking had given him such an appetite.

By late afternoon, he was back in camp explaining his plan to Vlahan, but Vlahan was in a stubborn, arrogant mood—even more stubborn and arrogant than usual—and more times than Changar cared to count, he quoted the scouts who had reported that a raiding party could only make it to the top of the ridge if they grew wings.

Changar listened patiently to this nonsense, repeating simply that the scouts had been wrong and that a climb was possible. Finally, he picked up a stick, drew a picture of the ridge, and traced the cut from base to summit. Then he called one of his apprentices over and had the boy spread his arms and legs and pantomime the ascent. As the boy pushed against the imaginary sides of the imaginary walls, Vlahan finally saw what Changar was getting at.

"You say we'll need a long rope?" Vlahan looked at Changar with hard eyes like a man sizing up a horse. He was in the process of having his head shaved by two concubines who fluttered timidly around him, afraid they might cut him by accident. His skull was covered with some kind of foaming grease that made the shaving easier. It had begun to melt and drip into his red beard, giving him a gluttonous look that Changar thought was completely appropriate. Vlahan would have been happy to eat the Sharans alive without salt if the opportunity presented itself, and now Changar was giving him that opportunity, but Changar expected no gratitude and Vlahan offered none.

"Only for the climb down, *rahan*. Not for the climb up. On the way up, one of the men can wear the rope coiled around his waist. Once he reaches the top he—"

"You don't have to tell me again," Vlahan snapped. "I'm not stupid." As soon as Vlahan said that, Changar knew that he had won. Vlahan tugged at his greasy beard and narrowed his eyes. "Are you sure one rope will do the job? Why not four or even ten? If my warriors go down one at a time, it will take half the night."

Changar pretended to take this idiotic question seriously. "You are wise, as always, *rahan*; ten ropes would indeed be better. I foolishly thought . . . " He paused and waited for Vlahan to take the bait.

"Thought what?"

"That if we used more than one rope, they might tangle when the men swing over to the switchback." Vlahan, who had not considered this possibility, was furious.

"And where do you propose we get the hemp to plait a rope long enough to carry out this plan of yours?" he yelled. "The bogs of this cursed land are full of brittle reeds that break every time our women try to weave them into baskets!"

"We should make the rope out of leather, *rahan*."

"Leather shrinks in wet weather, you idiot!" Vlahan gestured toward the sky as if a great storm were coming. There was not a cloud in sight, but Changar knew it was vital to look impressed.

"You are right as always, *rahan*. Leather ropes do shrink, but they also slide smoothly across a rough rock face, so, as you have so wisely pointed out, we will have to pick a fair night; with a little luck, we will need to use the rope only once."

With a bellow of rage, Vlahan rose to his feet dripping grease and foam. Seizing a shaving knife from one of the frightened concubines, he hurled it at Changar. The knife whizzed by Changar's ear, taking off a tiny piece of it. The attack had not been meant to kill, just to terrify, but it failed. Changar sat quietly staring at Vlahan in a way that made Vlahan's skin crawl. The apprentices had reported that Changar had spent a whole night writhing on the ground and twittering like a bat. Then in the morning he had gone riding off to inspect the back side of the cliffs. Vlahan didn't mind the bat part—the old man could fart like a dog or croak like a frog for all he cared—but he didn't like the idea that Changar had ridden out to scout the enemy. He was furious that Changar had come up with such a good plan. It might work, and if it did, Changar would have far too much power.

"I suppose Lord Han told you that I should order my women to cut up my tent and dedicate the leather to our victory," Vlahan snarled.

"That will not be necessary, *rahan*." Changar bowed humbly, but there was a triumphant note in his voice. "There is plenty of leather lying about, and the tents of lesser men if it comes to that."

Vlahan strode over to his tent, grabbed a skin of *kersek*, pulled out the stopper, and took a long drink. He ran his hand over his shaved head, and looked at Changar with contempt mixed with fear. As far as he knew, no diviner had ever become a chief, but any man who was as smart as Changar was a threat. "Lesser men," Vlahan murmured. He took another drink of *kersek*. "Yes," he repeated, "lesser men."

The next morning Changar woke to the sound of women's voices. When he limped out of his tent, he saw Vlahan's wife, Timak, knife in hand. Four concubines stood beside her, all similarly armed.

"Good morning, you pack of miserable bitches," he said. "Has Vlahan sent you to kill me?"

Timak laughed, exposing yellowed eyeteeth filed to points. "No, old man. He's sent us to make a rope from your tent." And before he could call to his apprentices to stop them, the women had pulled up the stakes, spread his tent on the ground, and were cutting it into long, thin strips.

The weather was fair for the next three days. On the night of the new moon, the Sharan sentries noticed nothing out of the ordinary. The nomad camp was quiet. A few fires burned—perhaps fewer than usual. One sentry yawned and sat down on the edge to stare sleepily at distant lights. He noticed that for some reason all the fires were burning near the front of the nomad camp tonight, but it did not occur to him to mention this to anyone. Now that the nomads had destroyed the city he loved, what did it matter where they built their fires?

Beyond the firelight, something was moving in the shadows, something thick and muffled that made almost no sound. The young sentry could not see it, but the nomad dogs did, and they cowered as it passed. It was not really one thing but many, and it crept quietly toward the river, one piece at a time. Sometimes it looked like gray mist; sometimes like a mounted warrior; sometimes like nothing at all. Dark shapes crossed the black, starlit water and disappeared into the forest, and each time one entered the ford, there was a soft splash. Soon the scorched fields were empty again, and by the time Arang came to take his turn standing watch, there was nothing to be seen but the stars.

It was a night filled with secrets and stealth. On the opposite side of the cliffs, a band of Hansi warriors began to climb the ridge by pressing their arms and legs against the sides of the cut. The warriors had smeared black soot over their bodies and covered their hair with mud. They wore no boots so that they could grip the rock with their toes, and as they panted their way up the incline, they were almost invisible except for the whites of their eyes.

When the first man reached the top, he fell on his belly and crawled toward the far edge. He looked at the Sharan camp for a long time, taking in the tents, the temple, the spring, and the fires. He made particular note of the positioning of the sentries and then crawled back to his comrades. As always, when circumstances made it necessary, he spoke in sign language, holding his hands up to the sky to take advantage of the starlight. His name was Chirkhan and he was the same tall warrior who had once tracked Stavan to the pond and failed to find him. Why Vlahan had not had Chirkhan executed when he found out that Stavan was still alive was anyone's guess, but the fact that he was the best scout the Hansi had ever produced probably had something to do with it.

"The wind is blowing our way," Chirkhan signed. The warriors nodded, knowing this meant that the Sharan dogs would not smell them and sound the alarm. "The sentries are looking toward the city. Their fires are burning low. Everyone else is asleep." So far all the news was good, but now Chirkhan told them something they had expected but that nevertheless sent a silent ripple of disappointment through the raiders. "Changar was right. We won't be coming

down in the enemy camp itself, but to the right of the camp."
Chirkhan made a swinging motion with his right hand.

So instead of throwing the rope over the edge and descending
directly on the unsuspecting Sharans, they were going to have to
swing back and forth, drop onto the trail, and sneak up one by one.
Several of the warriors frowned and made signs to ward off evil.
Climbing up that crack had been bad enough, but this made a man
long to go back to the flatness of the steppes.

"Gap?" their leader signed. If they were coming down below the
gap in the trail, they might as well not bother. They did not need a
rope to get there. They could walk up from the bottom.

"Just above the gap," Chirkhan reassured him. This was not the
best of news since it meant they would have to climb down much
farther than they had hoped. Still, things might have been worse:
the men on the rope would be easy targets for Sharan arrows. At
least if they came down two full switchbacks below the ledges, no
sentry was likely to spot them.

"Is the rope long enough?"

"Long plus two," Chirkhan signed back impatiently, meaning
that the rope was in his estimation a full two man-lengths longer
than necessary.

That was all the warrior who had carried the rope to the top
needed to hear. Falling on his belly as Chirkhan had done, he
crawled forward and secured one end to a boulder. Then he crawled
back, and two men pulled with all their might to make sure it
would hold. The rope had to be retied, but finally it was in place.
Slipping their bows over their backs, the warriors put their daggers
between their teeth and checked the quivers that hung at their belts.
When they were ready, the leader gave the signal, and Chirkhan
tossed the free end over the edge. Hemp would have caught on
thorns and snarled on tree limbs, but, as Changar had foreseen, the
braided leather slid swiftly down the face of the rock.

Below, Arang was standing beside Dalish's lover, Jutima, looking out
over the valley. The nomad fires were still burning, but that was not
the cause of their concern. Not long ago, a small band of warriors
had ridden out of the camp. The nomads favored surprise attacks,
but although these had galloped toward the cliffs in complete silence, they had made no attempt to hide themselves from the Sharan
sentries. Arang had been on the verge of sounding the alarm, when

the whole band turned and galloped back toward the river. A few moments later they wheeled and rode in the direction of the sea.

"Seems like an odd time to exercise the horses," Arang murmured. Jutima agreed that it was indeed. All the sentries came to the edge and stood there watching the nomads ride back and forth. Suddenly Jutima stiffened and grabbed Arang's shoulder.

"Listen!" she whispered. Arang and the sentries fell silent and listened, but no one heard anything. "That's just the point." Jutima picked up her bow and reached for an arrow. "The crickets have stopped singing!"

She was right. In the camp itself they could hear the ordinary sounds of burning fires and restless sleepers, but above it the great monotonous chorus of crickets that always sang through the night had fallen unaccountably silent. There were many reasons why crickets stopped: a passing owl or a fox hunting on the ridge could interrupt their song. Even a strong gust of wind could quiet them for a time, and when it grew cool, they seemed to go to sleep just like people; but there was only a very mild breeze coming in off the sea, and the night was balmy.

Arang did not like the sudden silence, especially when combined with the strange antics of the warriors down below. "Spread out," he told the sentries. "Check the whole camp and if you see or hear anything strange, cry a warning." His first thought was that a raiding party might be sneaking up the trail, but when he leaned over and saw it dimly winding past the dark humps of boulders, it appeared empty, though it was hard to be certain. In any event, the gap was still unbridged. Jutima had already turned and was walking toward the temple, peering into the shadows and freezing every once in a while like a lion stalking a deer. Arang caught up with her.

"I'm going down the trail a little way to see if I can hear anything," he whispered. She nodded and went on. Arang drew his hunting knife and, feeling slightly ridiculous, walked down the trail until he came to the gap. When he reached the edge, he sat for a while, dangling his legs and listening, but the only thing he heard was the hoot of an owl. So an owl had stopped the crickets' singing. Relieved, he started up the trail again.

He was just rounding the first switchback when he saw something that made him catch his breath and freeze in his tracks. A dark shape was moving silently down the side of the ridge, swinging as it descended. For a moment he thought he was seeing a ghost, and then he understood.

"Nomads!" he cried. "Help! Nomads!" As soon as the words left his mouth, the raider let go of the rope and fell on Arang like a hawk falling on a sparrow. Arang grabbed for the man and the man grabbed for Arang, and for a moment they gouged and struck and grappled with each other on the narrow trail. Arang saw a dark face, white teeth, the bone blade of a dagger. Rearing back, he butted the warrior in the stomach as hard as he could, and they both lost their footing and plunged over the edge. Before Arang had time to understand what had happened, the ground flew up and hit him, knocking the wind out of his lungs. He lay on his back, stunned and gasping for breath. By some stroke of luck, they had tumbled onto a switchback instead of falling to the base of the cliffs.

The warrior, who had landed on top, rose to his feet and gave the Hansi war cry. Seizing Arang by the hair, he bent back his neck and prepared to slit his throat and take his head. Then suddenly he stopped and lowered his arm.

"Ha!" he cried. Grabbing Arang by either side of the head, he pulled him close like a lover about to bestow a kiss. "Ha!" he cried again.

Up above in the Sharan camp, torches were flaring and the sentries were raising the alarm. As the man turned Arang's face up to catch the light, Arang saw the gap in the trail and realized that they were now below it. He caught a quick glimpse of another armed warrior sliding down the rope, and heard the twang of a bow—a Sharan bow, he prayed—and the hiss of arrows, and then the man who had captured him jerked his head back down and shook him until his teeth rattled.

"Arang, grandson of Zuhan!" the warrior cried. "By Han, it's the little Great Chief himself!"

"Chirkhan!" Arang gasped.

Mary Mackey

The scout smiled triumphantly and pulled Arang to his feet. On the cliffs overhead a fierce battle was being waged, but Chirkhan no longer cared much about the outcome. He had a prize worth far more than anything he could have looted out of the Sharan camp. Tying Arang's hands behind his back, he put the point of his dagger to his throat and marched him down the trail to claim his reward.

At the top, the Sharans were fighting for their lives. Now it was their arrows that pointed up and the nomads' that pointed down.

As Jutima and the other sentries stood in the torchlight trying to shoot the next warrior off the rope, the warriors on the ridge let loose a deadly hail of arrows that hissed through the air and clattered to the ground, piling up at the top of the trail like kindling.

If the raiders had not been forced once again to take aim at an angle, every Sharan sentry would have been killed. Still, the losses were terrible. Four sentries were wounded and two died in that first attack, and as the Sharans saw their companions falling around them, some threw down their weapons and ran to pull the injured and dying to safety.

"They're trying to drive us back!" Jutima yelled. "Keep shooting!" Rallied by her voice, the remaining sentries stood their ground and shot until they hit the warrior on the rope and sent him plunging. As soon as he fell, another took his place, and when he was low enough, they shot him too. By now two more sentries had been wounded, but the rest kept on fighting with a stubborn courage that surprised the nomads, who had expected the Sharans to run in panic as soon as one of their own was killed.

After the sentries knocked two more men off the rope, the nomads pulled it up, and arrows rained down from the ridge with redoubled fury. The nomads had planned to take the Sharans by surprise, but they had also come armed with enough arrows to hammer them into submission if necessary. By now they had realized that Jutima was the leader, and on both sides of her people were hit: a young woman took an arrow in the leg, a man in the arm. Behind her more arrows ripped through the nearest tents as the children inside screamed. Dogs barked and people ran for their weapons, and still the arrows kept coming.

"Take cover!" Jutima shouted over the din. "There's no use shooting at them anymore. They're too high; we can't hit them!" But now the Sharans were full of the madness of battle. Standing side by side, they kept on shooting, until enemy arrows took down three of them at once. When that happened, the rest finally came to their senses, grabbed the wounded, and scrambled out of range.

Again the nomads threw the rope over the edge, and again Jutima and the others ran forward through that rain of death and shot back, and another enemy warrior lost his hold and fell. That night Dalish and Hiknak fought shoulder to shoulder with Yintesa, who was well over sixty, and a brave boy named Surmech, who was barely twelve. Marrah fought too. She had not shot a bow in a long time, so instead of trying to hit anything, she ran out into the line of

The
Horses
at
the
Gate

263

fire to gather up arrows when the Sharan supply was exhausted. The Hansi arrows were superior, flint tipped and razor sharp, and she felt a crazy thrill as they clattered around her.

"Give us more!" she screamed. Like the hunters and the sentries, she was *vartak*, and as long as she was fighting, she felt immortal.

As the battle raged, Lalah lay in the Temple of Children's Dreams tossing in a fitful sleep. Earlier in the evening, the priestesses who had been tending to her had given her a cup of catnip tea mixed with valerian and poppy juice. She had been especially restless lately, often waking in the middle of the night to call for friends long dead, and the priestesses had been worried that constant fatigue was adding to her confusion.

When they heard the first shouts of alarm, the priestesses had run to see what was happening, confident that Lalah would not wake. They had not expected to be gone for long, but they had stayed to help care for the wounded, and now the effects of the tea were starting to wear off.

Outside, the noise of the battle grew louder. Suddenly Lalah woke and sat upright, listening. If the priestesses could have seen her, they would have given her more sleeping tea because there was a wild look in her eyes. At first she appeared merely afraid and disoriented. Then slowly the ominous light of delusion began to fill her face. Her dark eyes glittered, and she gazed around her with the quick, sharp stare of a lioness. In some ways it was the look of the old Lalah, but in others, it was the look of a sick woman who was a stranger even to herself.

She stood up too suddenly, and for a moment the world spun around her. Steadying herself, she reached out, grabbed her long blue tunic from the stool beside her sleeping platform, put it in her mouth, and bit a hole in the linen. With one quick motion, she ripped a wide strip off the bottom, so when she slipped the tunic over her head it hung just below her knees.

Without pausing to admire her handiwork, she bent down and picked up her walking stick. Balancing the staff of polished cherry-wood in the palm of her hand, she gazed with satisfaction at the handle, which was carved in the shape of a small coiled snake. She did not see a stick but a spear tipped with flint. It was a good spear, the best she had ever owned. But whose hand was this? Whose wrinkled skin and skinny fingers?

Confusion descended on her again like a black cloud. She blinked, and then all at once she laughed. What could she have been thinking? The hand that held the spear was the hand of a twenty-year-old woman, a woman who had the strength to hurl it five times the length of a man. She was young and her fingers were brown and strong, and the power of the Goddess was in them.

On the other side of the camp the Sharans were barely managing to hold their own against the nomad onslaught. "Shoot!" Jutima yelled, and again the Sharan archers shot and the nomads shot back, and everything was noise and confusion. A tent was burning because the former inhabitants had upset a lamp as they fled. The smoke was acrid; it burned in the sentries' throats and made their eyes sting, but it gave them a little cover too, and so they were grateful for it.

"Aim at . . . " The command died in Jutima's throat as Lalah, queen of Shara, unexpectedly charged out of the smoke waving a stick and yelling that she had come to defend the Great Snake. The queen was an impressive sight: her gray hair was unbound, flying in all directions, and her face was full of a wild light. She moved with the speed of a much younger woman, and the sentries instinctively gave way to her before they realized that she was unarmed and rushing straight toward the most exposed part of the trailhead.

"Stop her!" Jutima yelled, but Lalah was too fast and all the hands that caught at her missed.

"Batal!" Lalah cried defiantly, brandishing the stick as if it were a spear. "Batal and victory!"

"Grandmother!" Marrah screamed. "Stop! Turn back!" But her warning was lost in the cry of alarm that came from the throats of the sentries when they saw their old queen rushing unprotected into the open.

Before anyone could run to her and drag her to safety, an arrow struck her in the arm. When their queen was hit, the Sharans all cried out in a single voice as if they had been hit too, but Lalah just stopped running and stood there, looking at the shaft with childlike bewilderment as if she did not quite know where she was or what had happened. Standing still, she became a perfect target. Another arrow struck her, slamming into her chest. She reeled back a few steps and dropped the stick, and the light went out of her face.

"Sabalah!" she cried in a surprisingly loud voice. "Sabalah, my daughter, come get me! I'm hurt!" Tears sprang to her eyes. She looked back at the horrified Sharans, knelt, and crumpled to the ground very slowly. For a long time, the arrows went on raining down around her, and by the time Marrah and the others were able to get to her, she was dead.

Marrah never knew how long the battle lasted after her grandmother died. She knew only that she ran into the line of fire to gather arrows and pull the wounded to safety until the tears dried on her cheeks and her breath burned in her throat. At last the nomads on the ridge stopped shooting. Perhaps they decided there was no use continuing the raid without the element of surprise, or perhaps they were frustrated because they could only shoot into a small part of the camp. They might have tired of dying on the rope, or they might finally have run out of arrows.

The Sharans waited until dawn, but no more warriors tried to swing down from the top. When the sun rose, the ridge appeared deserted, but no one was naive enough to think the enemy had left for good. The cliffs were no longer safe. From now on, the Sharan sentries would have to watch the ridge night and day. Part of the camp—that part closest to the top of the trail and in range of enemy arrows—would have to be abandoned. As for the trail itself, the nomads now controlled both the upper and lower halves.

The Sharans had killed at least seven nomads, but they had lost over a dozen of their own, including old Yintesa and Jutima's youngest sister, Trimata. Arang was missing and presumed dead. Ten of the best archers in the camp had been wounded or killed, and Jutima, who fought so courageously, had taken an arrow in the shoulder and might never pull a bow again.

But the loss that most stunned everyone was the loss of Lalah. It was always sad when a queen died, but no queen in the history of Shara had ever died so violently or so needlessly.

The morning after the battle was hot and overcast. As Marrah sat beside the sacred spring numbly watching the priestesses and priests tend to the wounded, she could hear people moaning and lamenting as they washed the bodies of the dead and combed out their hair. She should have been with them, cradling her grandmother's head in her arms and sobbing along with her aunts and uncles and cousins. She should have been proclaiming Lalah's goodness along with them, describing the great events in her grandmother's life in a loud voice so everyone would hear and remember.

This is what a dutiful granddaughter did in normal times. This is what all grandsons and granddaughters had done from generation to generation before the nomads came. But this morning, with the whole weight of Shara resting on her shoulders, Marrah had no time to mourn anyone, not even the grandmother she had loved. She had to think of a way to preserve her people, because she was no longer just the war queen: she was the only queen the Sharans had.

The voices behind her rose and fell in a mournful chorus:

"Yintesa, daughter of the priestess Bunara . . . "

". . . taken from us, alas!"

"Trimata, cut down in the flower of her youth . . . "

"Krendar, a good man, killed by the nomads . . . "

"Lalah who ruled with a mother's kindness . . . "

Marrah thought of thorns and stones. She thought of the black edge of thunder, the blank moment between sleep and waking, the mystery of death, the certainty of loss. Last night they had won. They had kept the nomads from overrunning the camp, but it had been a hollow victory, purchased at a terrible price. Now that Vlahan and his warriors controlled the ridge, they could force the Sharans to fight anytime they pleased. Sooner or later, Marrah thought, all the hunters would be killed or wounded. When that happened, there would be no one left to shoot the raiders off the rope. Lalah, her beloved grandmother, and Arang, her dear brother, were already dead, and last night she too could easily have been killed. Unless she cowered in her tent, it was only a matter of time before she went back to the Mother. When she was gone, who would be queen of Shara? Bindar had no idea how to defend the cliffs; Dalish would probably be dead by that time and so would Hiknak.

She sat in despair and grief, listening to the funeral dirges and tasting the full bitterness of Vlahan's inevitable triumph. There was always a slim possibility that once Vlahan realized that Arang was dead, he would leave; but why should he? He had the Sharans in the palm of his hand. All he and his warriors had to do was fight—and they loved fighting.

"Dear Goddess, tell me what to do," she prayed. "Give me the strength to bear Lalah and Arang's deaths and the deaths of so many of my people; give me the will to go on; give me some sign I can understand." But no sign came, and when she rose to her feet and went to the edge of the cliff to look toward the nomad camp, she saw that Vlahan and his warriors were celebrating.

All morning the nomads sat beating their drums and drinking *kersek*. Sometimes a dozen or more warriors would rise to their feet and dance fiercely while their dark-robed women circled around them; and twice the Sharans saw horses being sacrificed. When the second sacrifice was over and the women had finished butchering the horses, the drumming stopped, and for a time nothing happened.

The Sharans waited and watched. In the early afternoon, a cool breeze began to blow off the Sweetwater Sea, whipping up the dust and ashes so the ruins of Shara seemed to burn all over again. The ashes of Shara rose into the sky like a grimy veil, staining the horizon, and as Marrah stood waiting to see what the nomads would do next, that reminder of her people's defeat stung her eyes and filled her lungs.

In the late afternoon the wind stopped, and the sun came out. When the shadows of the nomads' tents grew long enough to touch one another, a band of warriors rode out of the camp and headed toward the cliffs. It was an odd group, so small it could not possibly be another raiding party, yet too large to be a mere changing of the guard. Five of the fifteen riders wore white, which meant they were men of some importance; one was a woman; and one was clearly a child.

Marrah stood beside Hiknak and Dalish and watched them approach, and as they drew closer her puzzlement turned to surprise, then elation, then horror. The leader of the band was Vlahan; Changar rode to his left beside Keru, who was mounted on a pony; but it was the man who rode to Vlahan's right who made Marrah feel like crying with relief and cursing the cruel joke the nomads were playing on them.

Hiknak's face was so pale it looked like ice. She grabbed Marrah's wrist, digging her nails into Marrah's flesh. "Look," she whispered. One of the men in white was Arang, unmistakably Arang, alive and riding beside Vlahan, wearing the gold crown of the Great Chief and holding the horse-headed scepter of the Hansi as if he had gone over to the enemy. There was no one near him—no warrior pressing a dagger to his throat or a spear to his back—so he seemed to come of his own free will, but as soon as Marrah recognized him, her first thought was, He's alive! and her second thought was, They've forced him!

The riders continued to the base of the cliffs and reined in their horses. Vlahan was the first to speak.

"Marrah, you witch," he called, "are you there?"

She stepped out so he could see her. "I'm here," she said.

"You're a whore," he yelled. "A whore and a slut and instead of marrying you, I should have had you strangled." He sat there cursing her, each curse more obscene than the next, but she said nothing because he had Keru and Arang. Finally he ran out of curses, and Changar took over.

"Arang, grandson of Zuhan and Great Chief of the Twenty Tribes, wants to talk to you," Changar yelled.

"Then let him talk."

"He wants to come up the trail."

"Let him come."

"I'm coming up with him."

That was another matter. Marrah could not think of anything she would like better than to have Changar in range of Sharan arrows. "Come up, then," she said.

"I'm bringing your son with me," Changar shouted. "And if one arrow flies in my direction, I'll throw him over the edge." There was no doubt that he meant it. Marrah looked at Keru and felt sick with anger and frustration. No matter what Changar said, she would have to listen. Now she knew for certain why Arang had agreed to dress up like the Great Chief.

Changar gave a bird call that Marrah recognized as the *tschack* of a white-throated warbler. At the sound, Keru instantly slid off his horse and came running to Changar like an obedient puppy, staggering a little as if he were dizzy or sick. Soon they were all headed up the trail. Changar came first, carried on the back of one of his apprentices. The old diviner rode the apprentice like a horse, kicking him in the ribs and shouting directions, and every time he looked up at Marrah, a cruel, wolfish smile crossed his face. Arang walked slowly behind Changar, his face blank and unreadable. Behind Arang came Keru, also carried by an apprentice. The little boy lay passively in the man's arms, staring at the cliffs with a vague, sweet expression.

Several armed warriors followed the man who carried Keru. Last of all came the woman, dressed in a long shapeless brown tunic. She was bareheaded, and this and the garish tattoos on her face proclaimed she was a slave. As the woman drew closer, Marrah could see she had the dark skin and black hair of the south.

"She's not a nomad," Dalish said.

Marrah agreed, and they watched in silence as the woman climbed stolidly up the trail, looking neither to the left or right. There was no need to wonder why Changar had brought her along. Whenever the Hansi needed a translator, they always used some slave or concubine they had captured from the Motherlands.

When Changar reached the gap, he motioned for his apprentice to set him down. Leaning comfortably back against a boulder, he stared up at Marrah and yawned. It was not a real yawn; it was a formal insult, but Changar made it look real, and for a moment he seemed infinitely bored, as if Marrah and all the Sharans looking down at him were only so many birds perched on a ledge. Yawning a second time, he motioned for the man who carried Keru to step up to the edge of the trail and hold the little boy over the gap. Then he summoned the translator.

Marrah stood very still, barely daring to breathe.

"Did you enjoy the visit we paid you last night?" Changar asked in a conversational tone. The woman translated so that every Sharan on the cliffs could understand, and a murmur of anger rolled through the crowd, but no one spoke because they could all see Keru.

"You killed a few of our men," Changar continued, "but they died bravely as men should and we have many more warriors eager to fight." He shrugged. "I don't think you do; I think you're already running out of people who know how to pull a bow." He gave some sort of signal, and the man who was holding Keru suddenly took the little boy by the wrists and swung him out over the gap. Keru looked surprised, and then, to Marrah's horror, he laughed. The apprentice swung him again.

Marrah gritted her teeth and forced herself not to beg. When he realized she wasn't going to speak, Changar stopped pretending to be bored. "Surrender!" he yelled. "The Great Whore you worship has abandoned you. Surrender and pull down that abomination of a temple; smash the statues of your slut Mother Goddess." He pointed to the sun. "Han, Lord of the Shining Sky, has given us back our Great Chief. Han, the All Powerful, has made us victorious. We're His wolves, and we were born to rule the earth and all its people. Surrender, Sharans, and we'll let you live as our slaves and concubines."

As the slave translated this, Marrah looked at Dalish and Hiknak and the faces of her relatives; then she looked at Arang and Keru. There was no choice.

"What's your answer?" Changar screamed. "Will you live or die?"

"We'll live," Marrah said, and Changar gave a yell of triumph. "But we won't surrender!" Changar's yell turned to one of rage, but now it was her turn. Words she had never imagined she'd speak came from her mouth: "We know what you do to the prisoners you take; we know how you treat your slaves and concubines. Your Han isn't a god; he's a murdering lunatic you have made in your own image, and there isn't a man or woman on this cliff who wouldn't rather fight to the death than worship him! And I swear by the Sweet Goddess Herself that if that man drops my son over the edge, our archers will fill you so full of arrows not even the crows will want to eat you!"

Suddenly Arang, who had stood by silently all this time, was yelling too, adding his voice to hers. "Marrah!" he cried in Sharan. "Don't surrender! We can still win!" The nomads didn't know what he was saying, but they could guess. As Marrah looked on helplessly, two warriors rushed forward and began to beat him across the face with the shafts of their spears. "I finally understood your vision! It's not the water! It's the shellfish!"

His words hit Marrah like a revelation. The great windows of the snare bloomed in her mind, and again she saw the gray-green water, the minnows, the white sand, and the shells. Suddenly she understood what the Dark Mother had been trying to tell her; what she'd been trying to tell herself; what she'd known all along without knowing she knew. The shells—of course! How could she have been so blind! Every child in Shara knew that the shellfish were poison at this season! Another blow to the face, another to the mouth, and Arang fell senseless to the ground.

Changar turned to the translator, who was staring in white-faced terror at the bloodied man at her feet. "What did he say?" Changar demanded.

The slave looked up at Marrah and the Sharans, and then she looked back at the man who had the power of life and death over her. She seemed ready to faint with fright, but when she spoke it was in a clear voice that carried all the way to the top of the cliffs.

"He said that they should surrender; he said they were fools to fight on," she said in Hansi, and then she repeated herself in Sharan so everyone on the cliffs would understand that she had lied.

Changar—who did not speak a word of Sharan—gave a snort of disgust. "If I had known he was urging her to surrender, I would have let him go on talking." Losing interest in the translator, he turned back to Marrah. "Did you hear the Great Chief tell you to surrender?" he shouted.

"I heard." She looked at the translator and wondered what the nomads had done to her family to make her take such a risk. Thank you, she thought. Bless you. Because of you, Changar has no idea what Arang really said, which is a good thing because he is almost smart enough to figure it out.

"Do you still refuse?" Changar yelled.

"No." Her answer was so unexpected that Changar was taken off guard. He motioned to his apprentices to lift him to his feet, and he stood with his hands on their shoulders, staring up at her as if she were something impossible and altogether unknown. All around her, she felt the Sharans registering the same sense of disbelief.

"Give us five days to burn our dead and send them back to the Mother," she cried. "On the afternoon of the fifth day, we'll come down and give ourselves up to you." If the Sharans had not heard the translator lie, she would have stopped being the war queen as soon as those words left her lips. She had no right to make such a decision without consulting with the Council of Elders and the oldest man and woman in every mother clan. But they had heard, and although they did not understand what was going on, they had faith in Marrah, so no one cried out against her.

Changar finally found his tongue. "I don't think I heard you right, witch. Did you say you would surrender in five days?"

"Yes."

He looked at her cunningly. "I think you're lying. I think you're trying to stall for time. Why should you have such a sudden change of heart?"

She tried to think of a lie he might believe, and then she realized it was before her, and only a half lie at that. She pointed to Keru, and when she did so, she made sure her finger shook and her voice trembled.

"I can't stand to see my boy in danger. Stop dangling him over the edge of the cliff, I beg you. You win. I'll do anything to save him."

Changar studied her without speaking. Finally he gestured for the apprentice to pull up Keru and carry him away from the gap. A warrior was sent back down the trail to confer with Vlahan, and Marrah could see Vlahan nod with satisfaction when he learned of her capitulation. When the messenger returned, Changar spoke again. "The great Vlahan, whose boots you are not fit to lick, has agreed to give you five days," he shouted. "But he says that if you don't surrender, the boy dies and all of you die with him."

He might have left it at that, but he was a Hansi diviner with a position to uphold, and it was time to call down the wrath of Han, to strut and posture and impress on Vlahan and his warriors that only he, Changar, could terrorize the Sharans and break their will to fight, so for some time he stood on the trail, making more threats. It was a dreary list, and once Marrah was sure that Keru and Arang were safe, she stopped listening. By the time the nomads left, she had the beginnings of a plan.

The first thing she did was go straight to Hiknak and ask her what tribe the translator belonged to. Hiknak, who could read tattoos as well as a priestess could read sacred script, replied that the woman had to be a Zaxtusi slave.

"Those two blue lines on her lips mean she doesn't have an owner—if she did, she'd have five lines. The red bow on her left cheek means any warrior can have sex with her. They're all Zaxtusi markings, so the Zaxtusi must have been the tribe that originally captured her, and since the tattoos are so bright, I'd say she was taken pretty recently, perhaps as recently as this summer."

Marrah was encouraged by this. "Where do the Zaxtusi camp?" she asked, and once again Hiknak could tell her.

"They're a tribe of the second order, which means they camp to the northwest of the Hansi." She gave Marrah an appraising look. "Why do you care where they camp?"

"Do the Zaxtusi pen their slaves like Nikhan did?"

"No, they don't have to pen them. They keep them in tents, guard them well, and kill any who try to escape. The Zaxtusi are very efficient. Vlahan often uses them as executioners because they're one of the few tribes who use the garrote in battle. They like to come in close for the kill." She paused. "You aren't going to tell me why you're asking all these questions, are you?"

"Not yet," Marrah said, and she went off to call a meeting of the Council of Elders.

CHAPTER FIFTEEN

Once again a rope was thrown down the cliff face. This time it was not made of leather, but of linen strips, twisted together and dyed black so the nomad sentries at the bottom could not see it. The rope fell from the Sharan camp to the trail below the gap where, not long before, Changar had stood; and when the Batal who sat on top of the Temple of Children's Dreams saw it, She smiled and gave it Her blessing. Then She laughed and the stars overhead clashed together like tiny copper bells, and the owls who were hunting in the woods across the river heard the music and the divine laughter of the Goddess, and they danced to it, swooping and diving in the cool night air.

Marrah's feet touched the trail, and she let go of the rope, stepped back, and gave it a sharp tug. Hiknak climbed down next, followed by Dalish. When all three were safely on solid ground, they stood for a moment listening. Then they began to make their way down the trail, keeping close to the cliff wall.

They were a strange sight, so unlike their usual selves that if the sentries had spotted them, they might have thought ghosts were abroad. Marrah carried a second, shorter rope looped over her shoulder, which gave her a hunched silhouette. Instead of wearing embroidered linen tunics and Sharan sandals, she and the others were once again dressed as Hansi concubines—or as much like Hansi concubines as the combined resources of Shara could muster. The costumers who had made their disguises had had no woolen cloth to work with since only the long-haired nomad sheep had fleece suitable for spinning, but squirrel fur dyed with chestnut juice, smashed flat, and secured with an invisible net of linen threads looked remarkably like beaten felt, especially at night. Once the problem of wool had been solved, it had been fairly easy to produce three pairs of baggy leggings, three shapeless tunics, and three mud-brown shawls. The nomad boots had taken a bit longer, especially since the cobbler had insisted on making them with padded soles so that the women could walk without making a sound; but the red tasseled headbands had been the work of a moment, and the necklaces of shell and copper already existed.

That left only the tattoos. Dalish, of course, was already tattooed like a concubine, and Hiknak too had a few small clan marks on her face, but Marrah's cheeks were as unscarred as the day she was born, so the other two had rounded up some blue dye and fixed that. Vines now trailed down Marrah's cheeks, her eyes were rimmed with black paint, and her lips were smeared with red grease. As she led the way down the trail, she was glad for the paint and tattoos. They hid her face, breaking up the outline of her nose and mouth; combined with the bulky, colorless robes, they made her almost invisible.

She moved on the balls of her feet, hardly daring to breathe. At the bend of the second switchback from the bottom, she stopped, uncoiled the short rope, and tied it to a boulder, and again the three women slipped silently down the cliff face. This time, when their feet touched ground they were at the bottom, far to the right of the sentries but close enough to smell the smoke of their fires.

From there it was an easy walk to the nomad camp. The moon was still down, and the stars gave off a milky light that hid as much as it revealed. As long as they were walking on the burned fields, they made swift progress, but when they came to the outskirts of Shara, they found themselves stumbling over stones that had once been houses and charred logs that had been roof beams. They did not have time to brood about what it meant to walk through the ashes of the city they had loved, because the nomads had pitched their camp close to the ruins, and before they had gone much farther, they were challenged by the first sentry.

"Who's there?" the sentry called, and he might have raised a general alarm except that Hiknak said quickly, "Only women," and they pulled their shawls over their faces and stepped out where he could see them.

The sentry peered at them, decided they were indeed women, and lowered his spear. "What in the name of Han are you doing wandering around the camp in the middle of the night?" he demanded.

"We've been serving the men who guard the cliff," Dalish said. The word *serving* meant more than food, and when the warrior heard it, he relaxed. It was reasonable for someone to send three concubines out to entertain the guards; only he wished that someone had told him beforehand because he had very nearly put his spear through the short one.

"Who owns you?"

They were prepared for this question and had a ready answer. "Vlahan," Hiknak said with a perfectly straight face. Vlahan, of course, would have the most concubines—so many that it was unlikely any sentry would know them all on sight.

The sentry looked impressed. No man who valued his head would harm concubines who belonged to Vlahan. "Get on with you," he said, "and next time you go out of camp to serve the guards, stop and tell someone first."

Hiknak assured him in the most humble terms possible that they would, and he waved them on. Having successfully passed the first test of their disguises, they made their way around the edge of the camp, keeping as far from Vlahan's tent as possible. His tent, which stood at the exact center, was easy to see, being white and larger than the others. Marrah could not help wondering if Keru and Arang were sleeping inside, but she was not tempted to go closer to try to catch sight of them. There was no place she was more likely to be recognized.

It was late and few people were about, but whenever they met anyone, they pulled their shawls more firmly around their faces and lowered their eyes as good concubines should, and since there were many tribes camped together, no one realized they were intruders. This was much more dangerous than the time they had ridden into Shambah disguised as Stavan's women, but Marrah was still impressed by how easily they could move unremarked through an armed camp. If they had been men, they would have been dead by now, but no one paid any attention to them except one old warrior who called out to them to bring him water, which Hiknak did, carrying him the waterskin that hung from the pole of his tent and presenting it to him with the usual pretense of not looking into his face.

After that—which they considered a very close call—they moved swiftly through the campsites of four or five tribes, each a little less elaborate than the last, and in the far northwest corner, just as Hiknak had promised, they found the Zaxtusi. At the very edge of the Zaxtusi camp was a pitiful collection of shabby, lopsided tents all pitched together in a jumble around a small fire. Hiknak mouthed the word *slaves,* and they stopped in the shadows to look things over.

The translator was nowhere in sight, but there were three women sitting around the fire, all bareheaded. Their faces were tattooed but unpainted, and they wore no jewelry. In a nomad camp any bareheaded, unpainted woman was a slave. Marrah was relieved to see that they were all dark-skinned and dark-haired, which meant that they had been captured from the Motherpeople. Even though they were thin and underfed, you could tell they had had other lives. Perhaps they had been priestesses or carpenters, potters or fishers; they might have delivered babies, or tilled the fields, or hunted deer side by side with their brothers and lovers. They did not look proud or rebellious—no slave who valued her life could afford the luxury of looking anything but subservient—but there was a solidity to them that nomad slaves never had. They still sat on the Goddess Earth as if they drew strength from Her, and when they spoke, their voices had the soft, musical accents of the south.

These were the women they were depending on, and as Marrah watched them sitting wearily by their meager fire, she prayed to the Goddess to make them sympathetic because the fate of the Sharans was in their hands. As if in answer to her prayer, the fire flared up a little, and the translator came out of one of the tents and sat down with the others. She was taller than she had looked from the cliffs, and the tattoos on her face were so fresh that some of the scars were still unhealed.

"Where were you all day, Vrimyta?" one of the women asked.

The translator smiled bitterly. Picking up a stick, she poked at the fire, sending up a thin stream of sparks. "Lying to Changar again," she said. "Not that it does any good. Step in shit and all you end up with is shit on your sandals."

That was all Marrah needed to hear. Looking around to make sure there were no nomads nearby, she stepped out of the shadows, followed by Hiknak and Dalish.

"Hello, sisters," she said. "We have come to tell you how you can stop being slaves."

The four women rose to their feet and looked at the three of them with a mixture of terror and confusion that would have been comic had there not been hundreds of armed warriors within shouting distance. Realizing that the slaves had quite reasonably mistaken them for *real* Hansi concubines, Marrah snatched the shawl off her head, and Hiknak and Dalish followed suit.

"I'm no nomad," she said. "I'm Marrah, priestess-queen of Shara." But the translator, who had recognized her, was already running forward with outstretched arms. The woman caught Marrah up in a wild hug, smiling and crying and pounding Marrah on the back as if Marrah were her older sister, but she already had been a slave too long to make any sound that might alert the guards. When the first wave of her enthusiasm receded a little, she wiped the tears from her eyes and turned to the others, who were staring at her as if she had lost her mind.

"Do you remember the ballad 'Nikhan and the Pregnant Warriors'?" she asked, and when they nodded, she pointed to Marrah, Hiknak, and Dalish. "These are the ones; these are the women who rode into that Shubhai fort and freed the slaves of Shambah!"

As soon as the other slaves understood that Marrah and her friends had come from the stronghold on top of the cliffs, they sprang into action. Seizing them by the hands, they led them quickly into one of the tents. Not all the slaves in the Zaxtusi camp were sympathetic to the Sharan cause, and it would have been extremely awkward if they had been forced to explain why three well-dressed Hansi concubines were paying a call on them in the middle of the night. When they were all inside, one of the women secured the tent flap, plunging them into darkness. From then on, Marrah never saw their faces, and when they talked, their voices were as soft as sand falling on sand.

Right from the start, there was no question that the slaves were eager to regain their freedom, which was fortunate because Marrah had bet her life and the lives of Dalish and Hiknak that they would be; but what they were willing to do for that freedom was another matter. As Marrah sat in the stuffy tent laying out her plan piece by piece, and repeating it until they understood, she could feel their fear growing until it filled up what little space was left.

First she told them that she planned to poison the nomads, seed confusion in their ranks, and drive them away from Shara and perhaps out of the Motherlands altogether. They understood that easily enough and greeted the idea with some enthusiasm. But when she went on to explain that the poison was to be found in the shellfish that lay strewn on the bottom of the Sweetwater Sea or buried under the sand along the beach, and that she needed their help to harvest the shellfish, and that they would have to recruit more slaves to help them, and that these slaves—not the Sharans—would be responsible for sneaking the shellfish into the nomads' cooking pots, they fell silent.

All around her, she felt the women going rigid with terror, and before she was half finished, they barely seemed to be breathing. Knowing she was losing them, she tried to point out how unlikely it was that the nomads would suspect anything until it was too late. They came from the steppes; they ate only freshwater shellfish; they had no sense of the seasons of the sea; but everything she said seemed only to make things worse. She could hardly blame the women for being terrified at the prospect of poisoning their masters, because if the nomads caught them, Vlahan would make sure that they died a death so horrible that the very thought of it made Marrah's stomach turn over. But she had risked that same death herself and so had Hiknak and Dalish; and to risk it for nothing, to have the power to win and not be able to use it, to be so close to victory and have it snatched from her hands, was as harsh a disappointment as she had ever experienced.

She urged; she begged; she pleaded with them not to waste the power the Dark Mother had put in their hands. Finally, when she had run out of ideas, she stopped talking and waited for them to respond, but they just sat there like the clay statues of Kataka.

I've lost them, she thought, and she imagined what it would be like to go back to the Council of Elders and tell them she had failed. Without the slaves, the gift of the Dark Mother was useless; the siege would go on all winter, and the nomads would never leave until the last Sharan was dead.

In the darkness someone coughed, and someone else—or it might have been the same woman—rose to her feet, fumbled around, opened the tent flap, and went out. Another followed. That left two. She waited for them to leave also, but time stretched on and neither did.

"So," a voice said, "so you say we have to recruit other slaves to help us gather the shellfish. What do these shellfish look like, and how many baskets of them do you think we need to poison the bastards?" The word *bastard* was spoken in Hansi, of course, since there was no such word in Sharan or in any other of the languages of the Motherpeople, and as soon as Marrah heard it, she knew she had won at least one supporter.

Before she could reply, the translator spoke up. "Don't worry, Shacta. Just follow me and I'll show you enough shellfish to fill a hundred baskets. I come from a little village on the edge of the Sweetwater Sea, bless its poor memory, and I've dug for shellfish all my life—in season, of course. They're deadly poison this time of year and no one with any sense would eat them, but the warriors adore fish soup; they've been slurping it up like pigs ever since we pitched camp here, and I guarantee that if we toss a few more tasty bits into the broth, they'll thank us. Like Marrah said, they come from a place where there's no salt water, so how are they to know until it's too late? I say, freedom is worth any risk. Better to die fighting than live penned up here forever to be raped at their pleasure."

Marrah could not have put it better herself, and she felt like kissing the women, but now that she had won them over, she had something more to say, and she knew she had to say it quickly before they thought of it themselves. It was a terrible thing, so terrible that the Council of Elders had almost forbidden her to come to the nomad camp when she had explained it to them, but in this new world of war and death, there were painful choices to be made. This particular choice violated every custom of the Motherpeople and the laws of the Goddess Earth Herself, but no one in Shara had been able to think of a way of avoiding it. Still, Marrah had hope, so when she spoke, she posed what she had to say as a question.

"When you put the shellfish in the fish soup, is there any way you can make sure that only the warriors eat it?"

There was a long silence as the implications of this sunk in. If the soup could not be kept for the warriors, then women and children would eat it too, and they too would die.

"No," the translator said at last. It was only a word, but so cold and so simple that it seemed to freeze in the darkness. "We're only slaves. We can gather the shellfish and make the soups, but we can't

The Horses at the Gate

281

say who eats and who doesn't. The warriors are always served first, and fish soup is a treat, so they may finish most of it before the women and children get a taste, but . . ." She let her voice trail off, and they sat in silence again.

After a time, Marrah spoke. "As you know, I have a son in this camp."

"One you love with your heart and soul." Again the translator.

"One I love with my heart and soul."

"And yet you have come to us and asked us to do this?"

"I have." She had no need to tell them that it was the most agonizing decision she had ever made, no need to explain how she felt. Hands came out of the darkness and clasped hers. The women patted her and touched her and pulled her close, and when they felt the tears on her cheeks, they began to cry with her. "We understand," they whispered. "You're a mother; we once were mothers. We had daughters; we had sons before the nomads killed them. We understand, little queen. We understand."

While Marrah and the slaves sat in that dark tent, crying over their children, Vlahan was making plans that would have chilled the women into silence. He began by calling Changar to his tent. The hour was late and he was quite drunk when Changar arrived, but when he spoke his tongue was clean and his words came out clearly, without a hint of the thickness that usually settled over him after a skin or two of *kersek*.

"I've been thinking," Vlahan began.

Changar tried to look pleased. When Vlahan "thought" it was usually a bad sign.

"About this surrender . . . "

Changar waited, but Vlahan just sat there tugging at his beard and staring at one of the tent poles as if he expected it to sprout branches. Outside, a dog barked and someone—probably one of the guards—coughed. Finally Changar lost his patience.

"You've been thinking," he prompted.

"Yes." The word had a strange quality. It fell out of Vlahan's mouth in a long roll like bones rattling in a bag. "We're going to sacrifice them."

Changar was not sure he understood. "Sacrifice whom? The Sharans?"

"Who else?" Vlahan looked at Changar thoughtfully. "After they surrender, I mean to offer all of them to Han except Arang, whom I need to control the subchiefs, and Keru, who is most certainly Zuhan's grandson whether I begat him or my dead brother did. Besides, I've grown fond of the boy." Changar was amazed to hear that Vlahan was fond of anyone, but then Vlahan was always full of surprises.

"This will be the biggest sacrifice any chief has ever made. For generations our people will sing of Vlahan the Great who gave a whole city to Han. We will offer the children first; then the women; then the men." He spoke quite simply, as though he were describing the distribution of food. They would take no slaves or concubines; the sacrifice would be conducted just before sunset with all the proper ceremonies. "We will need a lot of wooden stakes, so you will have to send the old men and boys to the forest to cut them and set them up where the Sharans won't see them. I'm putting you in charge of the sacrifice itself. We will offer horses too, of course."

Vlahan spoke for a long time, laying out all the details. For once, Changar was impressed.

Four days came and went. On the morning of the fifth day, while the warriors shaved their heads, painted their bodies, and readied themselves for the Sharan surrender, small groups of women passed quietly through the nomad camp, heading for the beach. They were slaves of the lowest sort, and they went in twos and threes so as not to attract attention to themselves. If Vlahan and his warriors had not been so busy adorning themselves, they might have remarked on how unusual it was to see so many slaves from so many different tribes all going in the same direction.

Some of the women carried baskets, and others carried digging sticks. A few carried fish lines and nets, and one or two bore poles that on closer inspection would have proven to be crude rakes. When they arrived at the edge of the sea, they hiked up their robes, took off their leggings, and went to work. Some waded into the surf with the makeshift rakes while others began to probe the sand with the digging sticks. Often they found what they were searching for, and when they did, they threw it into one of the baskets that sat ranged along the water's edge. Little by little the baskets began to fill, and when they saw this, the women worked even harder.

Those with nets cast them into the waves and pulled out fish in wiggling clumps. Dumping the fish on the sand, they cast again, and more fish came to wriggle and gasp beside the first catch. Each time a net was dumped, barefoot women waded into the wriggling school, selected some, and threw others back. Most of these women had lived on the shores of the Sweetwater Sea before the nomads captured them, and they knew how to pick the fish that tasted best.

When they had filled a second set of baskets, the women sat down to clean the fish. Soon the others joined them. The fishers spread their nets out on the sand to dry, while those who had been raking put up their rakes, and those who had been digging stuffed their sticks into their belts. The slaves worked quickly: scaling, slitting, dumping the fish entrails in a pile for the gulls, and shucking the shellfish out of their shells. Before the first warrior rode out of camp, the women had finished, and when they left—again in small groups—each carried the makings for a hearty fish soup.

Shortly after midday, the nomads rode to the cliffs to accept the Sharan surrender. Vlahan, who led them all, was resplendent. He galloped out of camp on a great white stallion, twice as fine as the one he had sacrificed, and he wore so much gold that when Marrah first saw him racing across the charred fields, she was amazed that he could sit upright: gold crown; gold necklaces; gold earrings; gold breastplate; gold horse scepter; gold bracelets; gold lacings in his boots; gold threaded through his cloak; gold powder on his face and upper body so that he glittered; gold paste in his hair so that it stood out from his head like the rays of the sun. She hadn't known there was so much gold in all the world.

Behind him and on either side of him, the subchiefs rode in lesser splendor, copper imitations of his glory, but fierce-looking nevertheless. They were naked except for loincloths, their faces painted bloodred, their hair as stiff as his, if not as glorious. Such a clacking of spears, such a whinnying of spirited beasts, such war cries and howling, and dust and confusion had never been seen in the Motherlands before. This was no mere raiding party; it was every warrior who had followed Vlahan south, every boy old enough to pull a bow.

There was not a Sharan on the cliffs that afternoon who did not remember when such a sight would have terrified them. Marrah remembered Shambah; Hiknak remembered the night the Hansi massacred her whole tribe; Dalish remembered the day she was taken from her mother. The hunters remembered what it had been like the first time the nomads attacked, and the sentries remembered how the sight of warriors slipping down the cliff face had made their hearts rise to their throats.

What great actors the nomads were, the Sharans told one another as they watched the horsemen approach. They knew how to inspire terror without so much as lifting a spear. They specialized in taking their victims by surprise and cowing them with spectacle. But this afternoon, the nomads' favorite trick was not going to work.

"You can always learn from your enemies," Marrah had said when she had called them together five days ago to tell them the second part of her plan. And the Sharans had learned. They still feared the sharpness of the nomads' spears and the range of their arrows, but all the war paint and the howling no longer intimidated them. They had been very busy since Marrah returned with the news that the slaves were willing to gather the shellfish, and today they had a surprise of their own in store for Vlahan's warriors. Part of the surprise burned in the small fires they had lit along the rim of the cliffs; part of it was in their pockets; part of it was tied to linen strings; part of it crouched out of sight.

"We have to help the slaves," Marrah had explained. "We can't rely on them to poison all the nomads. We can hope for Vlahan and Changar, for most of the subchiefs, for some of the principal warriors, but we can't count on it. So we have to be prepared; we have to sew confusion; we have to make the nomads afraid."

As the warriors thundered arrogantly toward the cliffs, kicking up a cloud of ashes, the sound of their horses' hooves echoed across the valley. Come swiftly, the Sharans thought. We have something special waiting for you; we have terror.

This time there was no question of Keru or Arang being held hostage while Changar negotiated. Vlahan reined in his stallion at the foot of the cliffs and sat there like a glittering statue until the subchiefs and their warriors caught up with him. The Sharans were not surprised to see a packhorse loaded with ropes and poles long enough to bridge the gap in the trail. Before this could happen, the Sharans would have to give the nomads somewhere to tie their ropes, but Vlahan obviously had expected that they would.

"Marrah of Shara," Vlahan yelled. His voice was so loud that it startled a flock of seagulls on the third switchback. The gulls rose all at once and darted over the nomads' heads, screeching as they flew. As the cries of the gulls died away, Marrah stepped out where Vlahan could see her. She was an amazing sight—fully as amazing as he was: on her head she wore a great crown of black crow feathers that trailed off both sides of her shoulders to form double streamers. From neck to ankle she was draped in a tunic covered with small disks of brightly polished copper so that every time she moved, she seemed to sparkle. Her arms and legs were painted bright blue, but her face was the strangest of all. She wore a mask—not one of the cheerful masks of Sharan festivals, but a great, frightful concoction of linen and wheat paste that made her look like a cross between a snake and a bird. The mask—which was at least three times as large as her face—had the lidless eyes of a serpent and the beak of a vulture, but there were teeth in that beak, as white and sharp as all the skill of the Sharan maskmakers could produce.

"Who calls the queen of Shara?" she cried in Hansi, and due to a special feature of the mask, her voice was amplified into a low-pitched, ominous growl.

Vlahan was so surprised that he started, and his horse danced backward a few paces. The warriors assembled behind him were staring at Marrah in consternation, which was just the effect she had wanted. She silently thanked the costumers for their skill, and Hiknak and Dalish for their advice.

"Are you beast or human?" Vlahan yelled, and Marrah heard with satisfaction that there was fear in his voice.

"I am the Goddess Earth," she cried, feeling slightly ridiculous, "come to curse you!" She lifted her arms and the copper mirrors on her breast sparkled so brightly that she seemed made of pure light. "Vlahan, son of no one, bastard and tyrant, I curse you for bringing war to the south. Vlahan the cowardly, I curse you for murdering your father, Zuhan, and your half brother, Stavan. Vlahan who has no right to lead the Hansi, I curse you for killing innocent children, for burning villages, for laying waste to a peaceful land. . . . "

Changar was suddenly beside Vlahan. "Pay no attention to her ravings!" he screamed. "It's just that bitch Marrah got up in a costume." He turned to the subchiefs. "I'm a diviner. I know these tricks. That thing up there is no goddess. It's a woman, you idiots!"

"Every warrior who rides with you will die; every man who follows you will have his guts turned to water."

"Shut up!" Changar screamed.

"His penis will fall off; his eyes will rot in his head; he will squirm on the ground in torment and beg for death; worms will eat his flesh and . . . "

Changar turned to Vlahan, who was staring at the snake-bird spirit in horror. "Say something, *rahan!* Don't let her get away with this!" He grabbed Vlahan by the shoulder and shook him. "Speak to your men! Tell them that she's a harmless fake!"

"That thing up there isn't dangerous?" Vlahan asked weakly.

"No, *rahan.* It's just Marrah, your slut of a wife, dressed up in feathers like a concubine."

Vlahan took heart at this. He cleared his throat and clutched at the reins of his horse. When he spoke, his voice carried authority. "Enough!" he yelled. He turned to his men. "That's no goddess!" He turned back to Marrah. "Surrender, you poor, pathetic slut, or we'll exterminate you and your people like so many lice!" When the warriors heard their chief yelling back at the thing on the cliff, they were encouraged. A few began to cheer; soon more joined in.

"Come down and surrender!"

"You don't scare us!"

"You're no goddess—you're just a slut in feathers!"

When Marrah saw that they were no longer afraid of her, she knew it was time to take the next step. Lifting her arms, she gave a great cry—half caw, half hiss—and as she did so, the Sharans behind her sprang into action. Drums rolled and flutes screamed like a flock of eagles. Children concealed behind the boulders threw powdered minerals and herbs on the charcoal fires, and a great pillar of colored smoke suddenly billowed up behind Marrah. The smoke was red and green and blue; gold and deep violet. The Sharans had used it for generations at the midwinter festival, but the nomads had never seen colored smoke before, and they gasped in awe as it drifted across the top of the cliffs.

"Look!" a warrior cried. "That thing up there has conjured up a rainbow!"

As the colored smoke enveloped her, Marrah began to turn. Every time she made one complete revolution, something new and even more terrifying happened. First, a long line of masked Sharans stuck their heads over the edge of the cliff and began to moan like a chorus of evil spirits. Once again the maskmakers had outdone themselves. The nomads were treated to the sight of giant frogs with pigs' snouts; lions with the eyes of fish; half-human things that looked as if they had slithered their way out of a nightmare.

Marrah turned again, and the Sharans flung dozens of kites into the air. Like the masks, each kite had been constructed to look like a monster of some kind: there were deformed birds and leering rabbits; predatory fish and snarling bears; even wolves. The nomads had never seen kites before, and from the bottom of the cliffs the linen strings were invisible.

"Demons!" cried the subchief nearest to Changar, and the subchief's warriors moaned and some covered their eyes.

"It's a fake! It's all a fake!" Changar rode back and forth frantically, begging the men to understand what the Sharans were trying to do. "Those things up there in the sky aren't demons!"

"Then what are they?" Vlahan demanded.

Changar did not have an answer for that, and when Marrah turned for the last time, something rose behind her that made even him give a cry of astonishment. The creature—which was as long as four men—was a snake; not the benevolent Snake of Time or the sweet Snake of Eternity, but a snake as the nomads saw snakes: evil, fanged, and horrible, with black and white scales and a belly the color of rotten flesh. The snake writhed, coiled, lifted its head, and began to rise. Up and up it went, climbing far over Marrah's head as the boys and girls inside climbed on one another's shoulders.

The snake alone might have routed the nomads, because by that time even the bravest warriors were making signs to ward off evil, but the Sharans had one more surprise in store for Vlahan and his men. When the snake was as tall as the boys and girls could manage, the drums stopped, and Marrah stopped with them. Again she lifted her arms.

"I, the Goddess Earth, curse you for all eternity!" she yelled. "Warriors, look on the sun for the last time! Before it rises again, you will all die!" Having finished uttering this alarming prediction, she opened her hand and threw six small clay balls onto the charcoal brazier that lay concealed at her feet. When the priestess of Nar had given the balls to her, they had called them "dried thunder" for good reason. If what was inside those balls had not gone bad, the nomads were in for a nasty shock.

Marrah stepped back hurriedly and waited. For a long, agonizing moment, nothing happened. Then the first ball exploded with a terrific boom. Resisting an urge to reach under her mask and stick her fingers in her ears, Marrah stood her ground. There was another boom and another, each so loud it sounded as if lightning had struck the earth. Even though she knew what to expect, the violence of the explosions took her breath away.

The Sharans, who had been warned beforehand, gasped and clutched at one another, and if the children who held up the snake had not been so brave, they would have fallen. But the nomads had not been warned, and by the time the third clay ball exploded, they were in a panic. They screamed and wept and begged Changar to save them, but Changar was helpless. He had seen many things in his life, most of them quite terrible, but he had never seen a human being bring thunder out of a clear sky.

"What shall we do!" Vlahan cried.

Changar opened his mouth, but no sound came out. He shook and sweated, and every time another explosion boomed out over the valley, he cringed.

When Vlahan saw Changar's terror, he went crazy with fear. "Come away!" he yelled to his subchiefs, but by now many of the horses were panicking and no orderly retreat was possible. The warriors fought for control as their terrified beasts reared and kicked. When a subchief from one of the lesser tribes was thrown by his own stallion, his men turned and fled toward the forest, crying that the curse of the Snake-Bird Goddess was already on them. Others soon followed, and by the time the sixth ball exploded, the Sharans were treated to the sight of the entire nomad force galloping away in a disorderly rout.

The Sharan victory celebration lasted until the last jar of wine was empty. When it was finally over and the masks and kites and snake had been safely stored away, the waiting began. For the rest of the afternoon, the Sharans watched anxiously as small bands of mounted warriors drifted back to the nomad camp. By dusk, it looked as if the whole force might have reassembled. Campfires were lit as usual, and if there were warriors sitting around those fires shaking with terror because they had been cursed, or plotting to mutiny against Vlahan, there was no sign.

Were the slaves serving the nomad men fish soup? Were the warriors eating it? Were the women? The children? The western sky went from red to dull gray, and the brown tents of the nomads became part of the general brown of the burned fields. Soon all the Sharans could see were the fires, and after a time even they disappeared. Dark clouds blew in off the Sweetwater Sea, and it began to rain steadily and hard. By midnight, the floor of Marrah's tent had become a shallow pool, and when she stood beside the sentries and looked up toward the top of the bald cliffs, she could see dozens of small waterfalls cascading down from the summit.

"At least if they attack us again, it won't be tonight," Jutima said, "not in this weather." But Marrah was not ready to rely on the storm for protection. If Vlahan and his warriors had discovered the plot to poison them, they would be wild for revenge, and what better time to attack than in the middle of a storm when your enemies would least expect it?

"Keep the torches lit," she told Jutima, "and keep close watch." But she might as well have ordered Jutima to grow gills and breathe water. The rain came down in great, cold sheets, dousing the torches almost as soon as they were kindled.

The sentries were so busy watching the ridge that none of them noticed when Hiknak slipped quietly out of her tent and made her way through the camp. She was muffled from head to ankles in a hooded leather cape, which made perfect sense in the driving rain, and the bag she carried could have had anything in it; she had her spear with her, but that too seemed reasonable under the circumstances, so the people she encountered simply nodded and hurried on toward somewhere warmer and drier.

When Hiknak reached the edge of the cliffs, she looked around to make sure no one was watching. Satisfied that she was unobserved, she opened the bag, pulled out a linen rope, tied it to a rock, and tossed the free end over the side so it dropped through the gap to the trail below. Throwing off her cape, she slung her spear over her back using a piece of leather she had tied to the shaft in the privacy of her own tent. In less time than it took to take a breath, she had slid over the edge and was kicking her way down toward the trail, holding on with her good hand and bracing her feet against the sheer cliff face.

If it had not been raining so hard, the Sharan sentries might have spotted her and filled her full of arrows on the mistaken assumption that she was a nomad warrior. She was dressed in the same mud-brown leggings and tunic she had worn when she and Marrah and

Dalish went to persuade the slaves to gather the shellfish, but this time she wore no paint and carried no shawl to cover her face. She had no intention of disguising herself as a concubine, and a shawl would only get in the way when she went for her dagger.

Hiknak was not missed. The Sharans spent a wet, cold night huddled in their tents, at the mercy of the weather, their enemies, and their own fears. Near dawn, the rain finally stopped, but by that time the linen rope was long gone. Hiknak had pulled it down so that Marrah would not see it hanging and go after her, and her footprints had been erased by the storm.

As soon as it grew light, the Sharans hurried to the edge of the cliffs to look down at the nomad camp. The granite under their feet was washed clean, and the air had the tang of salt and crushed mint. To the north, a mist hung low over the valley, rising from the wet fields and concealing everything.

Up on top of the Temple of Children's Dreams, Batal laughed and cast the sun over the horizon like a golden kite. The mist began to lift, and the seagulls swirled up toward sky to dry their wings. Small waves broke peacefully along the beach, and the river ran clear and green past the edge of the forest. In all the history of Shara there had never been such a dawn-drenched beautiful morning.

The nomads were gone! Behind the ruins of Shara, there was nothing left but a sea of mud where they had pitched their camp. Only a few tents remained, lopsided and mashed into the mire as if they had been trampled, but as far as the Sharans could see, the great troop of men, women, children, and horses had disappeared overnight. And they had not even taken their cattle! Not even the cattle they so often fought, and died, and killed one another for!

Dalish gave a cry of triumph and pounded Marrah on the back so hard that she almost knocked her over. "We've won!" Dalish shouted. "They ran! All my life I've waited for this day! Ever since they killed my mother and grandmother and . . . " She began to cry and then she began to laugh, and then she began to cry again, but it did not matter, because everyone else including Marrah was laughing and crying too.

Placing their hands on one another's shoulders, the children who had formed the snake began to dance around, singing the "Song of Defiance," and soon everyone joined in. There was no wine left, not much firewood, no food worth feasting on, but they

The
Horses
at
the
Gate

did not need wine, or warmth, or honey cakes: they were drunk with relief.

> *We are the Sharans!*
> *We are the Sharans!*
> *We love one another!*
> *We will never surrender!*

"This day will be a festival for all time!" Marrah cried over the din.

"Festival of what?" they called to her. "Name it, Marrah! Name it!"

"Festival of Deliverance."

"Too somber! Too stuffy!"

"Festival of Thanks."

"Too pious! Too dull!"

"How about Festival of the Thundering Shellfish," she cried in exasperation. Everyone laughed, but the name stuck, and from that time on the Sharans celebrated the day of their greatest victory with a title that never failed to puzzle pilgrims.

When the dancing was over, things took a more somber turn. Marrah called for Hiknak, Dalish, and six of the hunters to descend to the base of the cliffs and inspect the nomad campsite, but Hiknak was nowhere to be found. She was not in her tent or in the dreaming cave or in the temple or in anyone else's tent. Had the nomads somehow managed to steal her in the middle of the night? Was she lying dead at the bottom of the cliffs with an arrow through her heart?

Keshna finally provided the answer. "Mama's gone to kill Vlahan," she said. "She told me not to tell anyone until it was light enough to see color, but I waited even longer because I knew you would try to stop her if you could."

When Marrah heard this, she was so angry with Keshna that for a moment she was speechless. She knew that Hiknak's crazy one-woman raid on the nomad camp was not the child's fault; but to have waited so long!—to have waited until nothing could be done! She thought of Keru and Arang, and of the nomad women and children who might have eaten the poison soup, and then of Hiknak, who had gone to join them—Hiknak, the reckless, stubborn, brave little nomad who was going to get revenge on Vlahan if it killed her.

When she looked at Keshna, she saw the mother's stubbornness in the daughter's eyes. "Go find someone to give you your breakfast," she snapped. "What you have done is nothing to be proud of."

Keshna began to cry, but Marrah was in no mood to comfort her. Turning her back on the child, she hurried to where Dalish and the hunters were waiting. As soon as they heard the news, they threw their ropes over the edge and went down as fast as they could. They did not walk toward the nomad camp; they ran: but the Dark Mother, who takes all things back to Herself, had been there before them.

CHAPTER SIXTEEN

T he previous evening, just after it began to rain, Turthan, chief of the Zaxtusi, had returned to his tent and found a slave waiting to attend him. Marrah would have recognized the slave as the translator, Vrimyta, but Turthan saw only a bareheaded woman of no particular importance shaking out his bedcovers and throwing dried dung on the fire. When she had finished these routine tasks, the slave knelt in front of him and offered a bowl of soup fragrant with thyme and chopped mint. Steam rose from the broth and curled seductively toward Turthan's nose.

"What's this?" Turthan demanded sharply. He was accustomed to eating roasted meat in the evenings and, although he liked soup, he believed that things should come in their proper order. Besides, he was in a foul mood: cold, wet, and furious with his men, who had run like cowards when that witch on the cliffs had brought down the thunder. All afternoon he had been combing the forest, dragging them back one by one, threatening them with the loss of their cattle, their women, and their lives if they did not return and fight like men.

"There is no curse!" he had yelled at them. "It was all faked, you idiots. Didn't you hear Changar say it was faked?" Several times he had grabbed the most reluctant and put his knife to their throats. He did not believe in curses or in the gods either, for that matter. Turthan was a deeply cynical man who believed in only one thing: force.

"Come back or die," he had threatened; and the warriors had always come, shame-faced and looking around nervously, as if they were rabbits who expected the Sharan snake to strike from every tree and bush. It was disgusting, completely disgusting: armed men, hardened veterans of dozens of battles, so scared they pissed in their loincloths. And what had terrified them? What had sent them running like a herd of sheep to disgrace their own names and the whole Zaxtusi tribe? A *woman!*

The slave mumbled something about the soup being made of fish, and he realized she was still kneeling in front of him holding the bowl. "Get out of here!" he yelled. She put down the bowl and scurried out of the tent. Turthan immediately forgot about her. He had more important things on his mind: how to persuade his men to hold the Sharan threat in contempt; how to galvanize them into a fighting force again; how to deal with Vlahan's cowardice. Vlahan was to blame for their defeat. Turthan ground his teeth at the thought of Vlahan's headlong flight for safety. How could you expect warriors to stand and fight when their leader ran?

He took off his wet cape and threw it to the ground. He stripped off his boots and sat down beside the fire to warm his feet. Vlahan was through, finished. The Twenty Tribes were not even twenty tribes anymore; there were five tribes in rebellion, and now this unspeakable humiliation! There was someone much more fit to lead the tribes, and Turthan knew just who it was.

He smiled grimly and picked up the bowl of soup the slave had left beside the fire. He drank the broth first and found it surprisingly good. With a grunt of satisfaction, he reached into the bowl and began to eat the bits of fish. When he was finished he licked his fingers and sat back, contented. This is a rich land, Turthan thought. A

land worth fighting for. Vlahan's head would look nice on a stake. He was so absorbed in thinking of the best way to go about putting it there that a little while later, when Vlahan himself suddenly walked into the tent unannounced, Turthan gave a cry of surprise and clapped his hand to his dagger.

"Greetings, *rahan*," he muttered guiltily. He rose to his feet, wondering why in the name of all the demons in the Underworld his guards had not warned him that Vlahan was about to pay him a visit. "Welcome to my humble tent."

Vlahan sat on one of the padded saddlebags Turthan's people used for cushions and looked at Turthan wearily. He was getting tired of his own subchiefs turning the color of curdled milk when they caught sight of him.

"Will you do me the honor of taking *kersek* with me, *rahan*?"

Vlahan said that nothing would give him more pleasure, but he had serious business to conduct, so as soon as they had both had the ritual drinks from the *kersek* skin that custom demanded, he got right to the reason for his visit. "I have come to reassure you that there is no curse on you or me or any of us," Vlahan said. "Changar was right. That spectacle we witnessed this afternoon was a fake."

But you ran anyway, didn't you, you miserable coward, Turthan thought; but he said, "I never believed that we were cursed, *rahan*."

Vlahan brightened at this. "You didn't?"

"Not for a moment." Turthan said this with great conviction because it had the advantage of being true. "But how do you suppose your witch of a wife worked that thunder?" He lingered on the word *wife*, which was as close as he dared come to insulting Vlahan, but if Vlahan noticed, he gave no sign; he just shrugged and took another pull on the *kersek* skin.

"I haven't the slightest idea, but it doesn't matter. As soon as I got back to camp, I came to my senses and realized that we had been deceived." He lowered his voice and leaned confidentially toward Turthan. "This was a black day for us, Turthan. Our honor is stained."

Yours most of all, Turthan thought.

"I have already been to half the campsites. Many of the subchiefs are not as brave as you, and many of our warriors are still too frightened to fight." When Turthan heard that Vlahan had been walking around the camp to encourage the other subchiefs, he felt a grudging respect for him. It took real courage to face your men when you'd run like a sick rabbit. Vlahan had to be aware that his life hung by a thread, and yet he had gone out to try to reassure his warriors and give them courage. This was how a Great Chief should act, how old Zuhan would have acted. For the first time that Turthan could recall, Vlahan was behaving like his father's son.

"Some of the subchiefs were afraid to receive me," Vlahan continued. "They sent word that they were feeling unwell."

Now that he thought about it, Turthan wasn't feeling all that well himself. He had a tingling sensation in his head, and his stomach was turning sour. He reached for the *kersek*, took a drink, and belched with the discretion a subchief should show in the presence of the man who was Great Chief in all but name.

"What I want to know," Vlahan said, "is this: are you and your warriors with me?"

"To the end," Turthan said, not bothering to mention that he meant Vlahan's end and not his own.

Vlahan smiled wryly. "Ah," he said. He rose to his feet and looked at Turthan for a long time. "Then the Zaxtusi will fight beside the Hansi tomorrow?"

"Are we going to raid the Sharan camp?"

"Raid and exterminate."

"Over the top of the cliffs?"

"Over the top."

"Then we're with you."

"You're sure you understand about the curse?"

"Why do you ask a second time, *rahan*? I tell you, the curse means nothing to me." Turthan snapped his fingers to show how little it meant, but Vlahan still looked unconvinced.

"You look green, Turthan. Is it fear?"

Turthan was so insulted by this that he had a notion to do away with Vlahan then and there, but there was no knowing how many Hansi guards lurked outside the tent.

"I fear no man," he said, adding silently: Not even you—especially not you—you piece of shit.

"And no woman, either?"

The two men laughed at this, but their laughter had the sick greenness of Turthan's face. When they were through laughing, Vlahan left to go to the next campsite, and Turthan went outside to relieve himself. The tingling in his head was much worse, and he had an unpleasant pain in the lower part of his back.

When he returned to his tent, he called for his wife and told her to bring him more food and his two-year-old daughter, Tarknak. He was fond of the child, although he would have preferred that she had been a boy, and he spent a while holding her on his knee and listening to her prattle. Tarknak complained that the slaves had not let her have any of the fish soup, and she demanded some of his, but the bowl was empty so he fed her raisins, which she ate greedily. Soon his wife came in and took the child, saying it was long past her bedtime. Turthan was glad to see Tarknak leave, because he had begun to feel horribly nauseated. When his wife came back for the third time, to bring him a bowl of milk and several skewers of roasted meat, she found him curled up on his bed moaning. He had vomited onto the sheepskins, and the air around him smelled foul.

"The curse of the Snake-Bird!" she cried, dropping the skewers, but Turthan was not so sick that he had to lie still and hear such nonsense spew from the mouth of his own wife.

"Be silent!" he yelled. "There is no curse!" But later when he began to gasp for breath and claw at the ground and beg for something to quench the fire burning in his belly, he changed his mind.

Confusion in the nomad camp. Tents thrown to the ground, saddlebags hastily stuffed, horses rounded up in the middle of the night. The rain comes down in cold sheets, wetting the faces of the terrified women as they drag their sick men to the sledges. Some of the men jerk uncontrollably and scream as if they are fighting off demons; others retch and gasp for breath. Nine of the fifteen subchiefs die; a hundred warriors, perhaps more. A few women, but not many. Perhaps no children. The slaves had watched the children; they had pulled them away when they came close to the cooking pots, knocked bowls of fish soup out of their hands, bumped into them and been beaten for their clumsiness. Now most of the slaves have run off, and the guards who should have been watching them are too sick to care.

The rain falls harder and harder, turning the earth under the women's boots into a mucky swamp. Everything is splattered with mud, even the faces of the dead. Moaning and screaming, the panicked women drag the bodies of their husbands and masters to the sledges and tie them in place with the thought of burying them later as men should be buried; but that night as they flee north, more die. By morning, the women's fear of the curse of the Snake-Bird has become so great that they begin to cut the dead loose, dump them in the bushes, and ride off without them. No one ever knows how many perish, but for years Sharan hunters stumble on the moss-covered skeletons of Vlahan's men.

Fifteen large tribes become thirty smaller ones; the thirty quickly disintegrate into dozens of tiny bands as each warrior well enough to ride flees for his life. Sometimes he takes his family with him; sometimes he does not. The women who are left behind often end up with new men and the children with new fathers. All the old Hansi blood lines are mixed and broken, and when the many pieces are finally rejoined into several dozen tribes, there is no more talk of a Great Chief.

"Vlahan the Great died at Shara," the nomad poets sing. "Cursed by the Snake-Bird." The siege quickly becomes a legend. In the story the nomads tell around their campfires, Vlahan, the bastard son of Zuhan, battles a giant female serpent named Marrah and is finally eaten by her. But the stories are wrong, and the truth is even more interesting than the legend.

When the storm was at its height, Hiknak walked down the trail toward the bottom of the cliffs, keeping close to the cliff wall so she would not slip in the mud and tumble over the edge. Just before she rounded the last switchback, she stopped, fell to her knees, and crawled far enough to see if there were any nomad sentries at the bottom of the trail (there weren't). This was not only a good sign, it made her descent much easier. Leaving the rope behind, she hurried the rest of the way down without bothering to stay out of sight. At the bottom, she unslung her spear and pulled her dagger partway out of its sheath. As she strode across the wet fields, the mud sucked at her boots and the rain stung her face, but she barely noticed. She was drunk with the desire for revenge. For six years, ever since Vlahan and his men had ridden into her father's camp and massacred her people, she had been waiting to get even.

Hiknak was willing to die for the satisfaction of personally fighting Vlahan and killing him, but she was not willing to die for no reason, so she kept a sharp watch all the way to the ruins of Shara, but there was no sign of the sentries who should have ringed the nomad camp. When she saw this, she knew the slaves had done what they had promised to do, and she silently thanked them.

By the time she reached the first ring of tents, she could hear cries of panic. Between the city and the river was a broad, flat expanse that had once been pasture land and wheat fields. Now, as the nomad camp broke up, it was a scene out of a nightmare. Women were running in all directions, taking down tents, harnessing horses, dragging sick and dying—and dead—men to the sledges. Babies shrieked; terrified children yelled for their mothers; warriors screamed for something to stop the pain. Hiknak knew that the sound of so much terror would have made Marrah sick, but Hiknak was a nomad and made of sterner stuff. She did not exactly enjoy their suffering, but she felt satisfied by it. These were her enemies, and after what they had done, she was not about to waste sympathy on them.

She stood for a while watching one family after another flee. They nearly trampled one another in their haste, and they left a lot behind: saddlebags, rugs, all of the clay pots they had taken from the ruins of Shara. Sometimes they even left their dogs, but they never left their tent poles or their weapons or their horses, so they were nomads to the end despite everything.

The panic in the camp grew with each passing moment as the poison struck down one warrior after another. When Hiknak was sure that everyone was too sick or too terrified to notice, she simply walked into the milling throng and made her way to the center where the Hansi had pitched their tents. No one so much as looked at her—rather, they looked at her but did not see her because they were too busy seeing their own fear. What was one more skinny, blond nomad woman among so many screaming, terrified wives and concubines? Even if she was bareheaded. Even if she was carrying a spear.

It was almost too easy. She had been prepared to fight, but when she reached the Hansi campsite, most of them had already left, and Vlahan's great white tent was still standing undisturbed. She walked right up to it without being stopped or questioned. There were no guards posted outside, no guards anywhere in sight for that matter. Perhaps they had run; perhaps they were dead. In any event, they were gone. As for Vlahan's wife, Timak, she too was conspicuously absent. Maybe old Timak dined on fish soup tonight, Hiknak thought; and as she remembered how mercilessly Timak had beaten her, she was once again satisfied by the justice of such an end.

Putting her hand on the tent flap, she gave a push. The flap was not even battened down from inside. "Let the bastard be in here, and let him still be alive," she prayed, although she could not have said to what god, because by now she no longer had faith in Han and the Goddess of the Sharans was too merciful for such work. The spear was too long to be useful inside the tent, so she left it behind, drew out her dagger, and entered.

A low fire burned in a small pit under the smoke hole, and by its light she could see at once that she had been cheated of her revenge.

Vlahan lay facedown on the sheepskins, sprawled in a pool of his own vomit. Disappointed to find him already dead, she stood with her dagger in her hand, wondering if she should take his head—but what would be the point? The Sharans would find such a trophy disgusting, and after living among them for so many years, she had to admit she felt the same. Let Vlahan keep his head, for all the good it would do him.

She turned to leave, but as soon as she was outside taking gulps of fresh air, she remembered she had once heard her father tell one of her uncles that a good warrior always made sure his enemies were dead. Braving the smell for a second time, she went back into the tent. This was a fortunate decision, because as she approached Vlahan's body, she saw him move and realized he was not dead after all. When she bent down for a closer look, she realized he probably had not even been poisoned. He was in a condition familiar to her since she had seen it almost nightly when she was his concubine: he was drunk.

She could have slit his throat and taken her revenge with no danger to herself, but she was a Tcvali chief's daughter and that had never been the way of the Tcvali. Rising to her feet, she kicked him hard in the ribs. "Wake up, you bastard!" she yelled. "Wake up and fight!"

Vlahan moaned and opened his eyes; realizing that he had been asleep in a pool of his own vomit, he gave a snort of disgust and sat up. Earlier in the evening he had visited all fifteen subchiefs, which meant he had drunk *kersek* on fifteen different occasions. When he returned to his tent, Timak had offered him some fish soup, but he had been too drunk to eat it—a bit of luck he was not aware of, because when the poison began to do its deadly work, no one had dared wake him. He had slept as his own guards fled from him in terror, crying that he was cursed; slept as his wife died; slept as his warriors screamed in agony. Unaware of the panic swirling through the camp, he stared at Hiknak groggily and saw not a deadly enemy but a bareheaded slave.

"Bring me some water," he commanded.

Hiknak's laughter rang through the tent like copper striking copper. "Stand up and fight," she yelled at him. "I'm going to kill you."

"Guards!"

"You don't have any guards. They've all died or run away. Everyone has died or run away. They're all afraid of the Snake-Bird curse. No one wants to get near you except me, and that's only be-

Mary
Mackey

302

cause I want the pleasure of slitting you from throat to gut." She was so disgusted with him that she did something very foolish: she grabbed him by the tunic and tried to heave him to his feet; but she had only one good arm, she was more than a head shorter than he was, and she only weighed half as much. "Stand up!" she yelled.

For a moment his body was as limp as a sack of wet meal. Then, without warning, he lunged and butted her in the stomach with his head. She reeled back, gasping, and would have fallen if she had not collided with a tent pole. It was a good thing she kept her balance, because in an instant he was on his feet and coming toward her. The veins stood out on his neck, and his face was twisted with rage.

"You little bitch!" He tried to hit her, but she dodged, and he missed and struck the tent pole instead. By the time he was ready to hit her again, she was crouched with her dagger ready.

"Fight me," she hissed. "Take your dagger out and fight me."

He looked at her with contempt. "I don't fight women, you stupid slut, but I'll be more than happy to break your neck."

"Do you know who I am yet, or has the *kersek* blinded you? I'm Hiknak, who was once your concubine. You killed my dear lover Iriknak; you massacred my people; you raped me and made me sleep with your dogs. You stole Arang, my husband; made my baby girl, Keshna, *shohwar*; you took my right hand. And now I've come to kill you."

Vlahan laughed until his face turned the color of raw meat. "Do you know what you look like?" he mocked. "You look like an angry little mouse. Fight you? Why, I could break you with one finger. Put down that Sharan knife. It's not long enough. Come here, and I'll be happy to kill you, but I want to have you first. You never were much good for anything but sex. As for your 'husband,' I've had him sacrificed, and the boy Keru with him."

When she heard him say that Arang and Keru were dead at his orders, something broke inside her, and suddenly she was as *vartak* as any warrior. "You're lying!" she screamed. Vlahan saw the battle madness come over her, and he was ready when she jumped at him. He hit her hard on the side of the head, knocking her to the ground. Falling on top of her, he ripped the dagger out of her hand and threw it aside.

"Fight you? Fight *you*, you stupid little bitch!" He grabbed her neck and shook her until her teeth rattled. Then he reached for her leggings and began to pull them down. But Hiknak was not a twelve-year-old concubine anymore. As Vlahan prepared to rape her, she went for his dagger. Her right hand was almost useless, but her left hand was so strong she could use it to climb down a rope. Seizing the bone handle of his knife, she drew it from its sheath. He easily could have broken her wrist, but he was too drunk and too full of lust to notice.

"How do you want it?" he taunted.

"Like this!" she yelled as she buried the blade in his back.

CHAPTER SEVENTEEN

E ight months later, pilgrims coming to Shara for the Festival of Flowers found a new city built on the ashes of the old. Once again the white motherhouses and temples gleamed in the spring sunshine, embraced by the Great Snake of Time. In the fields, a fine crop of wheat had sprouted from the scorched earth, and the pastures were lush with buttercups, violets, lilies, and corn-flowers. Out on the Sweetwater Sea, the fishers cast their nets in graceful swirls, and white-sailed *raspas* from the south once again glided into the port bearing jars of oil and wine from Omu, copper from Shifaz, flint from Gira, and rare feathered capes from the land of the Shore People.

The Horses at the Gate

Now that the nomads were gone, boats also came down from the north, and the news the traders brought was reassuring: Kataka had not been attacked; the glazed temples of Takash still stood along the banks of the River of Smoke; and even Shambah had been spared. The nomads had fled back to the steppes by a different route, leaving Shambah's flower gardens untouched, and once again Chilana—the Divine Butterfly, Most Gentle Mother, She Who Over-comes Death—was being worshipped with the old dances.

When the Goddess Batal looked down from the Temple of Children's Dreams and saw Her city, She was pleased. The Sharans had won the fight to preserve their way of life. But Batal, who saw everything, also saw that the coils of the future were not the same as the coils of the past, and that as much as the new Shara looked like the old, it would always be different.

After the nomads had fled in panic, the Sharans had to spend several days repairing the trail before they could come down from the cliffs; but when they finally returned to the valley and began to sift through the ruins of their beloved city, they had found something unexpected. The motherhouses had burned, the temples had burned, and the original Great Snake of Time had crumbled and fallen, but when they went to the place where the central plaza had once been and brushed the ashes off the Great Snake of Eternity, its blue and orange tiles were as bright as they had been before the nomads set fire to the city. "I endure forever," the Snake Goddess had said to the survivors, and catching Her tail in Her mouth, She had laughed and coiled around them, giving them hope.

As they wandered through the rubble trying to figure out where their motherhouses and temples had been, this miracle was repeated, and they began to cry out with joy and drop to their knees—not to pray but to brush and blow aside ashes. Like the Snake of Eternity, the floors of their homes and places of worship had been made of colored tiles, and these too had survived, tempered by the great fire as the Sharans themselves had been tempered.

"We can rebuild Shara just as it was!" the people cried when they saw the floors of their homes shining beneath the ashes, but Marrah—remembering the rose fence of Kataka—went before the Council of Elders and argued that they should make one important change. It was true that the motherhouses should be rebuilt over their own floors, she argued, but each should also be extended until it touched the house next to it, so that the city would close in on itself and never again be vulnerable to attack.

"But Shara has never been closed!" the members of the council objected. "It has always been coiled between the forest and the sea like a running snake."

"You're forgetting the slaves and the nomad concubines who have taken refuge with us," Marrah reminded them. "We are going to have to build new motherhouses for them." Which was true, and seeing the wisdom of her proposal and the great advantage of having the city walled, the council approved the plan, stipulating that the roofs of all the motherhouses should connect so people could walk from one to another and visit during peacetime.

The new shape of Shara—coiled and curled in on itself—was the most obvious change, but when Batal looked down from Her temple, She saw other differences—more subtle yet in many ways more enduring. In the temples, many of the sacred looms were strung with wool spun from the fleeces of the long-haired sheep the nomads had left behind when they fled in panic. These same nomad sheep now grazed in the pasture nearest the river, separated from the Sharan flock so they would not mate with them and lose their special quality. Wool could be made into a warm, soft cloth, lighter than fur and stronger than linen, but until the Sharan priestesses laid it on their looms, it had never been woven. The nomads had beaten it into clumsy felt leggings and thick blankets, but now the Sharan shuttles sang with it, and it came off in wide strips as light as clouds, to be loaded on the *raspas* and traded south to amaze everyone who saw it.

The nomad cattle had been another matter altogether—skinny, ill-tempered, and skittish. Fearing that the fierce, half-wild bulls would breed with their placid cows, the Sharans—who had no desire to own large herds—had driven most of them into the forest and set them free. But the horses—ah, the horses—the Sharans adored them! They knew that if the nomads had never tamed horses, they never could have ridden south to bring war to the Motherlands, but they also were wise enough to appreciate that the horses were not to blame. Like slaves and concubines, these beautiful beasts had been forced to serve cruel masters, but now they would be loved and well kept: tamed, but never broken by force. So as Batal looked out over the pastures toward the river, She saw the three mares Marrah had saved during the siege of Shara, the four mares the Sharan herders had hidden, and the fine stallion who had been hidden too. These horses had spent the winter feasting on hay and chestnuts; and although it was too early for colts to be born, the mares had flirted and pranced so seductively and the stallion had been so attentive that no one had any doubt that by this time next year the herd of eight easily could be a herd of fifteen.

These colts-to-be were the topic of much discussion one sunny spring afternoon as three Sharans sat together in the children's room of a new motherhouse. Two of the Sharans were short and high voiced, and one—their mother—was priestess-queen of the city. The queen, who was of course Marrah, sat on a big brown pillow with her bare heels resting on the cool tiles. In front of her lay a basket of small, sweet strawberries. Every time she put a berry in her mouth, she also put one in each of the little mouths to her left and right. Whenever she did this, the children wiggled their noses and laughed. For some time they had been playing a silly game called "bunny," but this did not prevent them from talking about more serious things like colts.

"When the baby horses are born," Keru said, "I want one."

Marrah laughed, popped another strawberry into his mouth, and tucked him under her arm. Under the other arm she held her daughter, Luma. Directly in front of them was a small clay jar planted with ferns and yellow daisies, and beyond the jar, a large window. Through the window of this motherhouse, which she had built with her own hands, Marrah could see nothing but peace in all directions: fertile fields and green pastures and a sea without waves, and if there was any happiness greater than the simple pleasure of being reunited with her children, she could not imagine it.

"I want a colt too," Luma insisted, and she moved closer to Marrah, saying with her body: Do you love me as much as Keru? and Marrah hugged her, popped a strawberry into her mouth, and said back with her own body: Yes, Luma. Always and forever. Both you and Keru are the same in my heart.

But with her lips she said, "You'll both have horses someday and ride along the beach with the wind blowing in your hair. When that day is over, I'll call to you: 'Luma, Keru, come back!' And when you come, I'll be waiting with a basket full of honey cakes for you and apples for your horses, and I hope you'll dismount from your glorious beasts and give your old mother a kiss."

"You'll never be old!" Luma objected.

"No," Keru agreed. "Never."

"But I will be," Marrah teased, distributing more berries. "By the time you two are old enough to ride off by yourselves, I'll have gray hair and wrinkles of wisdom all over my face."

Luma wound Marrah's dark, curly hair around her hand and looked at it thoughtfully. "When you are all wrinkled, will you tell stories like Great-grandmother used to—about the time Grandmother Sabalah left to walk to the West Beyond the West, and the old city of Shara, and how things were before the nomads came?"

"Yes," Marrah agreed. "When I look like a dried apple, I'll tell all the stories of the old days, just like your great-grandmother Lalah used to."

"Tell us a story now," Keru begged.

"Which one?"

"The one where we come back to you."

Marrah sighed, pulled them closer, and fed each another berry. Keru always asked for the same story, which worried her sometimes, because he had been present and should have remembered what had happened, but perhaps it was a blessing that he recalled so little. She looked down at his face, scarred with Hansi clan marks, and then at Luma, whose brown eyes were as clear as honey.

"Shall I tell that story again?" she asked Luma.

"Yes," Luma nodded, "but be sure to put me in at the end."

"I'll always put you in," Marrah promised, and she balanced the two children on each arm, thinking that they were already very different people. The boy, who had been through so much, seemed to gallop through life on an invisible horse, never looking back except to recall the moment when he and his mother had been reunited. If he ever brooded about the time he had spent as a nomad prisoner, he gave no sign. Every once in a while he would slip and say a word or two in Hansi, and then he would look embarrassed. Perhaps she should have encouraged him to talk more about the past. Now it was too late. The gates of his memory were so securely fastened that sometimes she wondered if he would suffer for it later.

Luma was just the opposite. She had been spared the nomad raid and all the horrors of the siege, yet she seemed able to imagine everything as clearly as if she had been there. She worried far too much for a nearly six-year-old, and sometimes Marrah wondered guiltily if she had neglected her daughter. After Keru and Arang were taken, she had not time or energy to think about anything except getting them back, and Luma had been too young to understand. The girl had what the Sharans called "clear sight": nothing passed her unnoticed. Someday Luma might put this talent in service of the Goddess and become a great priestess, but right now she was too sensitive for her own good.

"A story, a story!" the children chanted. Marrah blinked, came out of her reverie, and picked three juicy strawberries out of the basket.

"Long ago," she began. "Very, very long ago, which is to say last summer when you were only five . . . " The children, who would not be six for another month yet, laughed. "Long ago, I came down from the cliffs with Dalish and the hunters and walked toward the ruins of Shara, which the nomads had burned to ashes." She did not mention the terror she had felt; the bodies she had feared to find; her relief when there were none. "And when I walked into the muddy field where the nomads had pitched their tents, guess what I saw?"

"Uncle Arang!" they cried in unison.

"Yes, Uncle Arang. And do you know what Uncle Arang said to me?"

"'Come to the forest, Marrah'!"

"Yes, that's just what he said: 'Come to the forest, Marrah. I have something to show you.' So I ran to the forest and I found . . . "

"Me!" Keru cried.

"You!" Marrah laughed and kissed him on the nose. "I found you asleep in Hiknak's arms." She did not say that when she saw him she thought he was dead, and when she realized he was only drugged, she had wept and hugged him and vowed to kill Changar for doing such a thing to her baby, only it was too late because Changar had disappeared without a trace.

"Hiknak handed you to me, Keru, and I hugged you and kissed you." (And Hiknak said, "Vlahan is dead. I stabbed the bastard in the back, and here is your son back," but this was a story for children.) "And I said to her, 'Where did you find him?' and Uncle Arang said, 'The nomads ran away and left both of us behind because they were . . . "

"Afraid of the Snake-Bird curse!" Luma and Keru giggled. They knew there was no such curse, and it amused them that grown-ups could have ever believed in such a silly thing.

Mary Mackey

310

Marrah drew them closer and thought of all the things they were not old enough to know. She thought of the warriors who had eaten the poison shellfish; the panicked women; and the skeletons grinning from half the blackberry patches between Shara and the River of Smoke. But most of all she thought of the place Arang and Hiknak had shown her. It was a part of the forest, close to the river, cleared of all underbrush: a wide space and every bit of it filled with fresh-cut stakes.

("Vlahan was going to sacrifice every one of us," Hiknak had said, and she had begun to pull up the stakes, throwing them to the ground. Marrah and Arang had joined in, and soon the women who had been slaves and concubines came too, and they all worked together until they were exhausted and their hands bled. By noon not a single stake was still standing. Later they burned them and gagged on the green-wood smoke, but this too was no story for children.)

"About two weeks later," she continued, "the boats began to come back from the island of Byana, bringing the nursing mothers and babies and children who had been sent there to keep them safe. One afternoon, I was standing on the beach looking out to sea and I saw . . ."

"Me!" Luma yelled. "You saw me! And you ran into the water right up to your waist and grabbed me out of the boat and kissed me and said . . ."

"'Now I have my girl back!'"

"'Now I have my girl back!' And you cried."

"I cried with happiness," Marrah said. "Because now both my darlings were safe. And that," she said, kissing Luma on the nose and Keru on the forehead, "that, my dear little rabbits, is the end of the story."

But she was wrong: it was not the end of the story. The real end came a month later.

Marrah was in the kitchen of her motherhouse stirring a pot of lentils when one of her nieces rushed in to tell her that a band of nomads on horseback was riding toward the city. In an instant, Marrah saw the whole future of Shara fall apart like a vase slammed against a wall. Throwing down her stirring stick, she ran to the plaza. There, she found everything in confusion: children were screaming; dogs were barking; people were snatching up hoes, digging sticks, anything that might serve as a weapon. In front of the speakers' platform, the drummers were frantically beating the alarm drums, but it was too late to bring the workers in from the fields. People on the roofs were pointing to the north and shouting that the nomads had already crossed the river.

"Close the gate!" Marrah yelled, but the gate was already being closed by a crowd of desperate Sharans who had thrown their bodies against it. Marrah heard the big wooden door creak and saw the shadow of it pass over their faces. The bar came down, carved from the heart of an oak, as thick as the arms of four men, but like the gate it was made of wood, and as she ran past it on her way to the roofs, she imagined Shara burning for a second time, and herself, her children, her friends, and all her relatives burning with it.

Hiknak met her on the roof and thrust a bow into her hand. All around her the hunters were kneeling to take aim, and when Marrah looked over their heads and out toward the river, she saw the nomads. To her surprise, there were only five and they were riding slowly, picking their way among the cows and sheep as if they were trying to be careful not to startle them. She motioned to the hunters to wait until she gave them the signal to shoot.

"Do you think they're going to attack?" she yelled at Hiknak.

"Not unless there are a lot more of them hidden in the woods."

They stared at the forest, trying to see men and horses, but the only thing they could see were leaves rippling in the breeze. If there was a great band of nomads waiting to ride down on the city, they were so well hidden that not even the wild animals had noticed them. Flocks of ducks fed carelessly along the far bank of the river, small birds pecked at the blackberry bushes, and in the sky a hawk made slow circles.

The riders came on, and as they drew closer, the hunters began to murmur that one was a child—a girl of no more than seven or eight. She was a little blond-haired thing, dressed in a long white gown that came to the tops of her tiny white boots. Her head was partially covered with a white shawl, nomad style, and her body seemed to glitter.

"The four men aren't painted for war," Hiknak said, "and they're carrying rabbit tails." She pointed to a long pole one of the warriors held. Several small bits of what Marrah had taken to be white cloth fluttered from the tip.

"What does that mean?"

Hiknak smiled grimly. "It means they come in peace, but I wouldn't count on it. I've seen the Hansi bring out the rabbit tails, ride into a camp, and start killing."

"Are these Hansi warriors?"

Hiknak examined the riders and shook her head. "No. They're too poorly dressed, and even though I can't read their clan marks from here, I can see that their tattoos are crudely done." She paused and waited as the nomads rode closer. By now Marrah could make out their faces: one was heavyset with a broken nose; one a young man with a face so tattooed it looked like a piece of clumsily embroidered cloth. The young man was riding beside the girl, and Marrah could see him talking to her.

Hiknak suddenly grabbed Marrah's shoulder. "I know who these warriors are!" she cried. "I know which tribe they belong to, and so do you! We've both seen them before. They're Nikhan's men!"

"Nikhan's men? Are you telling me these are the same nomads who fought with Stavan against Vlahan?"

"They not only fought with Stavan, they must have come to bring us a message from Nikhan. The snow only melted off the steppes a month or two ago. They must have ridden hard to get here this early. Why would they do such a thing unless—"

"Unless Stavan were alive!"

Hiknak grabbed Marrah by the shoulders. "Marrah, don't even hope. Stavan died a year ago. He's not coming back, not ever. Maybe he's riding with the Lord of the Shining Sky in Paradise, or maybe he's sleeping in the womb of your Goddess Earth, but wherever he is, he'll never . . ."

She was right, of course, but Marrah didn't care. She didn't want to hear good advice; she wanted to hope. Pulling away from Hiknak, she ran to the rooftop nearest the gate, gripped the rail, and leaned over as far as she dared.

"Hail, strangers. The city of Shara greets you and bids you welcome!" she cried. Somehow she managed to speak with power and dignity, knowing that the nomads always saw excitement as a sign of weakness, but inside she was so filled with hope and dread that she felt as if a swarm of bees were buzzing inside her skull. She looked down at her hands and saw that they were trembling. Be calm, she told herself; be measured, be queenly in the presence of these men.

The warriors kicked their horses into a trot and rode up to the colored tiles that marked the entrance to the city. Reining in their mounts, they stared up at her. The one carrying the rabbit tails waved them in her direction, but the old one did all the talking.

"We come in peace."

"Welcome," Marrah repeated. "What news do you bring from the north?" The men stared at her in surprise, and she remembered too late that when the other messengers had arrived from the steppes, they had waited until they were offered something to drink before they spoke. It would never do for a queen to apologize or give the least sign that she knew she had been rude, so she went on without missing a beat. "Is there dust in your throats?" she asked in carefully formal Hansi.

"There is dust," the old warrior said gravely. He cast an approving glance at her and then looked at his comrades as if to say: You see, she knows the right way to greet messengers even if she is a woman.

Marrah was not about to invite armed warriors into Shara no matter how many rabbit tails they carried, but the refreshment could be arranged. She turned and found her aunt Tarrah standing next to her. "Get me some wine, aunt," she said, "and please hurry." Tarrah—who spoke no Hansi—gave her a puzzled look, but she ran away and soon reappeared carrying a wine jar. Marrah studied the jar, trying to think of some way to get it down to the warriors. If she threw it, it might break or, worse, hit one of them.

"May I borrow your belt?" she asked her aunt. Tarrah nodded and untied her belt, and Marrah untied her own and knotted the two belts together. Attaching the handle of the wine jar to one end, she lowered it toward the older warrior, who caught it neatly, and pulled out the wooden stopper with his teeth, which Marrah could not help noticing had been filed to points. The man drank, then passed the jar to the others. Each nomad drank in turn, wiping his mouth on the back of his hand and staring glumly at Marrah. Drinking was a sacred rite among them, and even though there was a good chance none of them had ever tasted wine before, they did not indicate this by so much as a flicker of an eyelash. Marrah noticed that the girl got nothing, which was a good thing because she was far too young for unwatered wine.

When they were finished, Marrah spoke again. "What tribe do you belong to, brave warriors?" she asked. Once again, it was a purely formal question since she already knew the answer.

"Shubhai, *rahan*." Marrah was surprised to hear herself referred to as *rahan*—which meant "son of Han"—but as far as she knew, the nomads had no word for a powerful woman so *rahan* she must be.

"Who is the brave chief who leads you?"

"Nikhan, *rahan*."

Well, that was out of the way. Now on to the only question that mattered: "And what news do you bring, warriors of Nikhan?" Great Goddess, she thought, don't just sit there like statues! Tell me! But she kept her face a careful blank.

"Our message is for Marrah, chief of the Sharans."

Marrah decided that this was no time to explain that the Motherpeople did not have chiefs. "I am Marrah. Speak."

The warrior cleared his throat. "Stavan, son of Zuhan, sends his love and greetings and says—"

"He *is* alive!" she cried. "By the ears, eyes, nose, and sweet thighs of the Goddess, I knew he couldn't be dead!" She realized at once that she had made a mistake. She was so relieved that she wanted to fall down and kiss the ground and thank the Goddess Earth for this miracle, but she was a queen with a queen's duties to perform, so she bit her lips and clenched her hands into fists, quelling her excitement. "Continue," she ordered sternly, and she stood straight, as a queen should stand.

The warrior looked at her uncertainly. Nomad messages were not designed to be interrupted. He began again. "Stavan, son of Zuhan, sends his love and greetings to Marrah of Shara and says thus: *Good news. The Twenty Tribes no longer exist, the power of the Hansi is broken, and the nomads fight among themselves. The Motherlands are safe; our children are safe; rejoice.*"

Marrah wanted to do more than rejoice. She wanted to dance, and laugh and cry with relief, but this time she managed to hold her tongue. She knew that if she interrupted the warrior again, he would recite the message from the beginning.

"Stavan, son of Zuhan, says to Marrah of Shara: *My love, I would have fought with you against Vlahan, but until a few months ago I was a prisoner of Rikhan, chief of the Xarkarbai, who found me in a swoon on the field of battle and who—thinking I was dead—carried off my body to strip it of belt and boots.*"

The warrior paused for breath. There was a short silence while he refreshed himself with a pull on the wine jar. Marrah gripped the rail harder and pressed her lips together to keep herself from urging him to get on with it.

"Stavan, son of Zuhan, says to Marrah of Shara: *Rikhan the Toad kept me in his tent, tied hand and foot. When I overheard his warriors say that Vlahan the Bastard had ridden into the Motherlands to recapture Arang and fight a tribe he called the 'Snara,' my despair knew no bounds, and I was desperate to get away and warn you, but the leather thongs were tight, the guards were many, and Rikhan had plans to ransom me for cattle and gold.*"

The warrior paused to take another drink of wine. When he had wet his throat, he stared at Marrah impassively and continued in the same monotonous drone, as if this story of near death, imprisonment, and miraculous resurrection were quite ordinary.

"Stavan, son of Zuhan, says to Marrah of Shara: *While I lay bound in Rikhan's tent, his daughter Driknak fed me. Driknak, daughter of Rikhan, looked kindly on me, and Rikhan said that if I*

would marry her he would give me my freedom. So I did, and as soon as the snow melted, I left the camp of the Xarkarbai with my wife and . . . "

What had he just said? Had he said that Stavan was married? That he had a nomad wife? The bees in Marrah's head buzzed more loudly, and the relief she had felt on learning that Stavan was alive was replaced by confusion and a gnawing anxiety about his welfare. She knew that he loved her, she had no doubt of that, but he had always insisted that he would never take another woman into his bed. She could easily understand him changing his mind—he had been away a long time, and they had never actually exchanged permanent vows of partnership—but what kind of intrigues must he have been drawn into to take a wife in the manner of the nomads? Ever since he'd learned the ways of the Motherpeople, Stavan had hated the idea that a man could own a woman as he would a horse or a dog, and that was what nomad marriage always came down to: the owner and the owned.

She looked up to find that the messenger had stopped speaking and was staring at her uncertainly. "Continue," she ordered, and once again she did her best to listen without interrupting.

"Stavan, son of Zuhan, sends his love and greetings to Marrah of Shara and says thus," the messenger said. *"Good news. The Twenty Tribes . . . "*

Marrah realized that he was starting over again from the beginning. This was too much. She had waited patiently, waited with dignity, and now she would wait no longer. She had had enough of these ridiculous formalities. Nikhan's warriors were not in the steppes anymore, and it was time they learned the ways of the Motherpeople.

She held up her hand. "Stop!" she commanded.

Her voice rang out sharply, and the old warrior closed his mouth faster than a turtle could pull its head inside its shell, and gave a humble half bow as if to say that he would do whatever she wished. Marrah was gratified to see that she had the power to make him act like a sensible human being.

"Just talk to me," she ordered. "Forget the message you have memorized. Just tell me in your own words: has Stavan really taken this Driknak as a wife in the nomad way?"

"He has, *rahan.*"

"Where is he then? And why hasn't he himself come to tell me of this marriage? Is he in good health?" She wanted to ask if the nomad chief who had captured him had tortured him, but the thought was so grim that she hesitated to put it into words.

"Bad leg," the old warrior muttered uneasily.

"You mean he has been injured?"

"Yes, *rahan*."

"How badly?"

"Broken, mending. Not now. Later."

Marrah was relieved. She unclenched her fists and prayed to Batal for patience. "Are you saying that Stavan's leg is healing and that he will come to Shara later this summer?"

The warrior nodded nervously.

"Ah," Marrah said. "Thank you. And his new wife? Will he bring her with him?"

"Stavan, son of Zuhan, sends his love and greetings to Marrah of Shara, and says thus: . . . " She started to order him to stop, but he held up his hand and plunged ahead, and as he spoke she realized that this time he was not starting at the beginning. "*I will come to you when the days grow shorter. My wife also must come to Shara where it is safe, and I know when you meet her you will love her . . . *"

Love her, Marrah thought. That might not be easy but she would do her best. She realized that she was jealous and was immediately ashamed. She would welcome this wife of Stavan's to Shara and help her get used to the ways of the Motherpeople. Would the nomad woman be strong spirited or meek? Clear faced or tattooed like Dalish? And . . .

"*As a daughter,*" the warrior concluded.

Marrah started. Daughter? Had he just said *daughter*?

"And that, *rahan,* is the end the message. And here she is!" With that, the warrior motioned to the little girl, who kicked her horse in the sides and rode forward. The child's white dress was so embroidered with shells and bits of copper that it jangled with every step her horse took, but above all that finery, her face was as pale as bread dough. She looked up at Marrah with big, terrified eyes.

"Greetings, great wife," she stuttered. "I'm Driknak, second wife of . . . " And then she began to cry.

Suddenly Marrah understood. "A child!" she cried. "They forced Stavan to marry a *child!*" There was no longer any need to act the part of a nomad chief. She ran to the other side of the roof where the Sharans were still waiting with their bows strung and their spears in their hands. "Put down your weapons and open the gates!" she cried. "There's nothing to be afraid of!" And she told them everything, translating in a loud voice that was so full of joy that the whole city didn't seem large enough to contain it.

A few moments later the gate was open and she was holding little Driknak in her arms and petting the girl's silky hair as the child cried and trembled.

"Hush, hush," she murmured. "You're a strange gift, my dear, but a very precious one." When Driknak stopped crying, Marrah lifted her over her head so everyone could see her. "From this day on," she cried, "I, Marrah, daughter of Sabalah, am the mother of this child, and Stavan, the nomad, is her *aita*. Driknak will live in my motherhouse with my daughter, Luma, and my son, Keru, and all my kin will love her as much as if she had been born from my womb."

"I don't understand," Driknak wailed. "What are you saying, great wife? I can't speak your language."

Marrah lowered the child and set her firmly on the earth. "You'll soon learn," she promised, and taking her new daughter in her arms, she kissed and blessed her.

EPILOGUE

J ust before the wheat was harvested, Stavan returned to Shara. When Marrah saw him riding
toward the city, she ran out through the fields to
meet him. He was thinner and older than he had
been when he left, but his kisses were still as sweet. Seizing her by
the hand, he helped her mount up behind him, and the two rode off
into the forest together.

They spent a long time talking before they returned to the city.
Marrah laughed and cried, and Stavan held her close and told her
how much he loved her and how very much he had missed her, but
he could not say everything that was in his heart because he was no
poet; he was only a man who loved his family and who had been
given a second chance to live with them in a dangerous world where
the north still lay under the shadow of war and the south moved toward an uncertain destiny.

That evening as they rode back to Shara through the fields of
heavy-headed wheat, Marrah heard the rasping *tschack* of a white-
throated warbler. She flinched at the sound, and tightened her grip
around Stavan's waist. The warbler's call filled her with foreboding,
and she glanced over her shoulder, sure she would see storm clouds

The
Horses
at
the
Gate

massing on the horizon, but the sun was setting in a blaze of orange and the sky was clear.

The warbler broke into a sweet, melodious song, and she relaxed and rested her cheek against Stavan's back. Up ahead, Luma, Keru, and Driknak were waiting, and her whole life stretched out before her like a path through the wheat. It would be a good life, she thought; a peaceful life with Stavan and the children.

Tschack! the warbler warned in the tongue of birds.

And Marrah rode on.

ACKNOWLEDGMENTS

Once again, I owe a special debt of gratitude to novelist Sheldon Greene, who read every version of this novel in manuscript. His suggestions and criticisms were invaluable, and working with him for the last fifteen years has been a rare privilege. I also want to extend special thanks to Joan Marler, who traveled through Rumania and Bulgaria with me and who generously made her research on the life and work of Marija Gimbutas available to me. Her photographs of Old European artifacts were a precious resource and her conversation a never-failing inspiration.

Thanks also to William Calvin, Miriam Davis, Judith Goldsmith, Flash Gordon, Heather Hafleigh, Jane Hirshfield, Barbara Moulton, Vicki Noble, Angus Wright, and the WELL Writers Conference; to Rumanian archaeologist Dragomir Popovici, who shared his research on the Cernovoda site with us one long afternoon in Bucharest, and to M. George Trohani, Directeur Adjoint of the Musée National d'Histoire, who permitted us to take photographs of Cucuteni ceramics, discussed the cultures of Old Europe with us, and then hospitably put us up in the museum's guest room. Finally, I would like to thank the people of Bulgaria and Rumania for the many kindnesses they extended to us as we traveled through those lands where priestesses like Marrah may have lived so many centuries ago.

Like its predecessor, *The Year the Horses Came*, this novel was inspired by archaeologist Marija Gimbutas's two ground-breaking studies of Old Europe: *The Language of the Goddess* and *The Civilization of the Goddess*.

321